Grizzly Killer
Hell Hath No Fury
(Grizzly Killer IV)

Lane R Warenski

WOLFPACK
PUBLISHING
— EST 2013 —

Print Edition
© Copyright 2017 Lane R Warenski

Wolfpack Publishing
6032 Wheat Penny Avenue
Las Vegas, NV 89122

Cover Art: Public Domain Painting by Charles M. Russell (Dakota Chief, circa; 1897)

ISBN 978-1-64119-075-6

Dedicated to my wife Cathy for all of the encouragement and support,
For all of the long hours of editing and all the years of making me a better person

Chapter 1

Hard Winter Gone

IT WAS A COLD, blustery early spring day in the year of our Lord 1829 and the cold north wind would not let up. The snow flurries that it brought sent chills right through a man. It had been a long hard winter and the cold that gripped this land did not want to let go. The snow had been so thick they had not been able to hunt, and even if they could have, the game had left in early winter to escape the deep snow. Zach knew he had to make meat no matter how far he had to go to find it, for his family depended on him.

This was the first winter in the six years he had lived in the Rocky Mountains that they had been completely snowed in. The heavy snowfall had started in November or as his wives called it the *Ezhe'i-mea,* the Moon of Winter Coming and it had continued throughout the winter. They had plenty of dried meat and pemmican stored for a typical winter, but this one was the worst any of them had ever seen and had lasted longer for they had not taken any fresh meat in over three months. Last year at Rendezvous they couldn't get enough flour, cornmeal, and other supplies that they usually depended on. The meat they had dried had lasted until just a few days ago and they were now rationing the little pemmican that was left. Shining Star and Raven Wing were nursing their babies that had been born last year, so they were getting by far bigger rations than the rest of them.

Ol' Red, his trusted mule, along with their horses had lost so much weight Zach wondered if he would have the strength to carry him to find the game he so desperately needed. He had brought two pack horses with him, the two that his friend, partner, and brother in law, Running Wolf thought was in the best shape of their small herd. Even his beloved dog Jimbo had lost a lot of his nearly two-hundred-pound weight. He often stopped to rest the weakened stock so even though he had been out for two days he wasn't more than fifty miles from their home and he had seen no sign of any game.

The ice had broken up on the river now, but the snow was still covering much of the ground. He could feel the weakened muscles of Ol' Red under him strain as he pushed through even the smallest snow drifts. He waited in a stand of cottonwoods along the river using the trees and brush as protection against the cold wind for Jimbo to return. He had sent Jimbo to scout the area ahead while he let Ol' Red and the two horses rest out of the cold wind.

While he waited, he stripped the bark off the cottonwoods and fed it to the hungry animals. He knew it wasn't enough, but it was the best he could do for now. He scanned the area carefully and smiled as he seen some blue sky up over the towering peaks of the Uintah Mountains to the south. He knew if the clouds would part then the warming spring sun would make them all feel better.

As he patiently stripped the bark, he thought of his wives Sun Flower and Shining Star and his little girl Star. Star wasn't quite a year old but had become the joy of his life. He worried about Shining Star having enough milk for the rapidly growing child and Raven Wing, Running Wolf's wife and Sun Flower's sister for she too was nursing their little boy Gray Wolf.

Star and Gray Wolf had been born last spring only about a week apart at their home on Black's Fork. It was where Zach and his Pa had first decided they would spend the winter after they came to the mountains with William Ashley bringing supplies for the very first Rendezvous. It was where Zach had spent that first winter alone after a grizzly had killed his Pa. It was his home now, and he loved it there. This was the first winter he had not been able to hunt at all, and he feared now for the wellbeing of them all.

He was as hungry as his animals were for he hadn't had anything to eat for the last two days. He didn't want to take any food away from his family for he didn't know how long he would be gone. He longed to find a buffalo and the thought of hump ribs roasting over his fire was making his mouth water. He tried not to think about food but as hungry as he was that was just about all that was on his mind. He knew Running Wolf would butcher one of their horses if necessary to keep the family fed but he still worried, wondering just how much longer before the long cold winter would give up and let spring take over the Rockies.

They had a successful fall trapping season with nearly two hundred plews bundled and cached waiting to trade at the summer Rendezvous as the spring trapping season was just getting started. Rendezvous was to be held this year on the Popo Agie which was the home range of the Shoshone village of Chief Charging Bull, the village where Sun Flower and Raven Wing were from. Running Wolf and his sister Shining Star were Ute from the village of Two Feathers which was over the mountains on the south slope of the towering Uintah's.

Zach thought about these things as he continually stripped bark from the broadleaf cottonwoods that grew along the river and waited for Jimbo to return. He looked around after he had fed the last handful of the green bark strips just as Jimbo came trotting through the brush right toward him. As soon as Jimbo entered the trees, Zach smiled in relief at the cottontail rabbit he had in his mouth.

He wasted no time in stripping the hide off the small thin rabbit and then built a fire. As the rabbit roasted over the flickering flames, he rubbed Jimbo's ears and talked to him about where they should look for bigger game. Most of the Indians of the mountains believed the Great Medicine Dog and Grizzly Killer could speak with one another, those being the Indian's names for Jimbo and Zach. When the rabbit was roasted Zach offered half of it to Jimbo, but he stepped away leaving it all for Zach. As Zach bit into a hind quarter of the small rabbit and the juices filled his mouth, he smiled at Jimbo again, swallowed the mouth full and said, "Well feller, it ain't hump ribs, but it tastes mighty good just the same." Zach felt the energy from the first food in two days almost immediately and rubbed Jimbo's ears again to thank him for the meal.

They started out again, and Zach saw a flock of geese land on the river several hundred yards ahead of them. Not knowing when they might find the next meal he decided to sneak up onto the river bank and try for one of the geese. As he rode out away from the river, he thought if the geese were returning from wherever they go to the south then the winter must be about over, and he smiled hoping he was right.

He was about a quarter mile away from the river bend where the geese had landed when he stopped and got off Ol' Red. He just dropped Red's reins but tied off the two horses to the sage then got down on his hands and knees and started crawling toward the river. He had tried sneaking up on these wary birds many times before but with their excellent eyesight and wary disposition he had failed just as many times as he had succeeded. Jimbo was right by his side as they approached the river and as Zach dropped to his belly so did Jimbo. The geese hadn't moved from where they had landed, but several of them were up on the opposite bank. Zach knew from experience if any of them saw movement or heard a sound they would fly. He was concealed in sage where he was, but if he tried to get any closer, he would never get a shot. He moved ever so slowly, bringing up his .50 Caliber Hawken, and for just a second, wished he had his Pa's old .36 caliber squirrel gun. But he had given it to Sun Flower.

He couldn't see the geese that were still in the river, so he knew he had to take the nearly seventy-yard shot from where he was. With intense concentration and a steady aim, he slowly squeezed off the shot. With the familiar feel of the recoil kicking back against his shoulder, he knew the shot was true even before he seen the explosion of feathers on the far bank. With the gunshot still ringing in the air, nearly two dozen geese immediately took flight. Jimbo sprang into action at the same instance and jumped after one goose just as it was leaving the water. He landed in the icy water and went under coming up just a moment later with only a mouth full of tail feathers.

Zach watched the geese fly away and wished he could see the world from up there. He might be able to find the game he was looking for a whole lot faster. Jimbo crossed the river and retrieved the plump goose while Zach headed back to Ol' Red and the horses.

The blue sky over the mountains was growing, and the wind had shifted now coming from the south. He could feel a definite temperature change as the warmer south wind started to blow. The warmer air felt mighty good, but he worried, he knew that the warmer south wind usually preceded a storm. Jimbo reached him with the goose just as he got to Ol' Red. He quickly gutted the goose pulling out the heart, liver, and gizzard and gave them to Jimbo along with a gentle pat on the head. After putting the goose in one of the panniers, he mounted up and continued downstream.

The south wind continued to increase throughout the day, and by late afternoon they were out on the flatlands well away from the protection of any trees to block the fierce wind gusts. He had to find a place to spend the night, someplace that had some feed for Ol' Red and the tired, hungry horses.

Another mile ahead he could see a small rolling hill on the other side of the river that was free of snow and from where he sat in his saddle it looked like it was covered with the dry stiff prairie grass common to this area. He knew his animals wouldn't like it, but it was better than nothing, so he headed there. This land had always been so kind to him and the game so plentiful he wondered why this winter had been so different. The deep snow by their teepees had kept them inside for most of the winter. Even with their willow and rawhide snowshoes moving through the snow was extremely hard. Shoveling areas of the big meadow after each storm so their horses could get to the dry grass to eat took every bit a strength he and Running Wolf had throughout the winter.

As the sun dropped closer to the western horizon, the temperature fell as well, and Zach shuttered at the thought of spending the night with no protection from the wind. Even with the long shaggy winter hair on Ol' Red and the two horses he knew they too would spend a long miserable night.

As the river flowed out around the south-facing hill, it spread out some, and he crossed in water that was only a foot deep and was relieved to see a small group of willows on the river bank. They weren't much protection, but they would help cut the wind a little.

After stripping the saddles and packs off his stock and turning them loose on the dry grass, he moved his hand in a full circle over his head signaling Jimbo to scout the area for danger. He then walked the barren hill looking for buffalo chips for a fire. He found several, but most were still moist from the melting snow. He knew they would dry out if he could get a fire started but with what he had to work with and the wind, a fire would be no easy task.

He found a few dead dry willow shoots that he pulled out of the willows along the river and pulled up a large clump of the grass. He always carried a little tinder from a squirrel's nest or whatever else he could find in his fire starter kit along with some charred patch cloth to catch a spark. Once he was satisfied, he had enough material to not only start a fire but keep it burning he scraped out a pit and lined it with rocks from along the river. Once the rocks were heated, he could use them to keep himself warm through the night.

The first strike of his fire steel on the flint sent a good spark right into the waiting charred cloth but as he gently set the kindling on it a gust of wind blew the small glowing ember out. He tried, again and again, trying to block the wind with his body, but each time he got the same result. Jimbo came back wagging his tail, so Zach knew he was safe enough for now, but he needed a fire. Zach had always been patient, he had learned patience very young hunting the woods near his parents homestead back in Kentucky, but this wind was testing him to his limit. Just as he was ready to give up his latest little spark caught on the soft dry tinder and by blowing ever so gently on it a flame slowly grew until he had a small fire going. He set the moist buffalo chips around the edges and before long he could see the moisture steaming out of them.

It was dark by the time he had the goose on a willow branch roasting over the flames and he knew it would take a couple of hours to cook the plump bird. He rolled out his bedroll, which was a Hudson Bay wool blanket inside a buffalo hide robe, between the fire and willows. While he waited, he fed the now dry buffalo chips into the fire, keeping the heat up and watched the sky continue to clear.

The fat dripping into the fire and the smell of the roasting goose had him slicing off a piece of the breast to try before it was quite ready. Jimbo wasn't at all concerned whether it was cooked through, he ate the piece Zach threw to him without hesitation and set right up wanting more.

By the time the goose was cooked enough for Zach, the wind was starting to die down and the clouds had moved entirely, leaving the stars lighting the night sky, but the clear sky brought a bitter cold with it. The cold air seemed to make the stars stand out even more than usual and he marveled at how they looked close enough to reach out and touch.

Before he crawled into his bedroll for the night, he rolled some of the rocks from around the fire into his buffalo robe knowing they would help keep him warm for at least part of the night. He then placed the remaining buffalo chips over the dying embers of the fire hoping they would smoke all night and he could easily restart the fire in the morning. Jimbo curled up next to him, and they both raised their heads slightly as a wolf howled way off in the distance.

When he woke the next morning, he was cold and uncomfortable. The warm stones from around the fire had lost all their heat. He thought about the soft, warm bodies of his beautiful wives Sun Flower and Shining Star and the warmth of their teepee and wished he was there. The stars were nearly faded as the gray of dawn spread across the full, clear sky. Jimbo had left on his usual morning hunt, and Zach hoped he would find something to bring back.

He reached out and moved some of the buffalo chips that were covering the coals from the fire of the night before and by blowing on them had a warm fire burning in no time at all. Leaving the blanket wrapped around his shoulders, he walked up past Ol' Red and the horses to the top of the hill where he could see the prairie around him for miles in all directions. To his disappointment, all he could see was barren prairie.

Walking back to the fire, he stopped and talked to Ol' Red, rubbing his neck while he did so. The big red mule responded by nuzzling his hand. Zach had been riding Ol' Red for years now, the two of them had developed as close a bond as he and Jimbo had. Ol' Red and his sister Jenny had been just a year old when he and his Pa left their Kentucky homestead to see the Rocky Mountains. Jenny had been gone for years now, stolen by Shoshones that first winter while he was alone. Ol' Red had been taken too but he had broken free and returned to Zach, and he had been riding the big mule ever since.

Jimbo came running through the sage from the north, and just as he got back to the fire, Zach knew Jimbo had found something for the dog was excited and barked to get him to follow. If there was danger, he knew Jimbo would tell him with his deep rumbling growl from way down in his throat.

It was a cold, blustery early spring day in the year of our lord 1829 and the cold north wind would not let up. The snow flurries that it brought sent chills right through a man. It had been a long hard winter and the cold that gripped this land did not want to let go. The snow had been so deep they had not been able to hunt and even if they could have, the game had left in early winter to escape the deep snow. Zach knew he had to make meat no matter how far he had to go to find it, for his family depended on him.

This was the first winter in the six years he had lived in the Rocky Mountains that they had been completely snowed in. The heavy snowfall had started in November or as his wives called it the *Ezhe'i-mea,* the Moon of Winter Coming and it had continued throughout the winter. They had plenty of dried meat and pemmican stored for a normal winter but this one was the worst any of them had ever seen and had lasted longer for they had not taken any fresh meat in over three months. Last year at Rendezvous they weren't able tocouldn't get enough flour, cornmeal and other supplies that they normally depended on. The meat they had dried had lasted until just a few days ago and they were now rationing the little pemmican that was left. Shining Star and Raven Wing were nursing their babies that had been born last year so they were getting by far bigger rations than the rest of them.

Ol' Red, his trusted mule, along with their horses had lost so much weight Zach wondered if he would have the strength to carry him to find the game he so desperately needed. He had brought two pack horses with him, the two that his friend, partner, and brother in law, Running Wolf thought was in the best shape of their small herd. Even his beloved dog Jimbo had lost a lot of his nearly two- hundred- pound weight. He stopped often to rest the weakened stock so even though he had been out for two days he wasn't more than fifty miles from their home and he had seen no sign of any game.

The ice had broken up on the river now but snow was still covering much of the ground. He could feel the weakened muscles of Ol' Red under him strain as he pushed through even the smallest snow drifts. He waited in a stand of cottonwoods along the river using the trees and brush as protection against the cold wind for Jimbo to return. He had sent Jimbo to scout the area ahead while he let Ol' Red and the two horses rest out of the cold wind.

While he waited he stripped bark off the cottonwoods and fed it to the hungry animals. He knew it wasn't enough but it was the best he could do for now. He scanned the area carefully and smiled as he seen some blue sky up over the towering peaks of the Uintah Mountains to the south. He knew if the clouds would part the warming spring sun would make them all feel better.

As he patiently stripped the bark he thought of his wives Sun Flower and Shining Star and his little girl Star. Star wasn't quite a year old but had become the joy of his life. He worried about Shining Star having enough milk for the rapidly growing child and Raven Wing, Running Wolf's wife and Sun Flower's sister for she too was nursing their little boy Gray Wolf.

Star and Gray Wolf had been born last spring only about a week apart at their home on Black's Fork. It was where Zach and his Pa had first decided they would spend the winter after they came to the mountains with William Ashley bringing supplies for the very first Rendezvous. It was where Zach had spent that first winter alone after a grizzly had killed his Pa. It was his home now and he loved it there. This was the first winter he had not been able to hunt at all and he feared now for the wellbeing of them all.

He was as hungry as his animals were for he hadn't had anything to eat for the last two days. He didn't want to take any food away from his family for he didn't know how long he would be gone. He longed to find a buffalo and the thought of hump ribs roasting over his fire was making his mouth water. He tried not to think about food but as hungry as he was that was just about all that was on his mind. He knew Running Wolf would butcher one of their horses if necessary to keep the family fed but he still worried, wondering just how much longer before the long cold winter would give up and let spring take over the Rockies.

They had a successful fall trapping season with nearly two hundred plews bundled and cached waiting to trade at the summer Rendezvous as the spring trapping season was just getting started. Rendezvous was to be held this year on the Popo Agie which was the home range of the Shoshone village of Chief Charging Bull, the village where Sun Flower and Raven Wing were from. Running Wolf and his sister Shining Star were Ute from the village of Two Feathers which was over the mountains on the south slope of the towering Uintah's.

Zach thought about all of thesethese things as he continually stripped bark from the broad leaf cottonwoods that grew along the river and waited for Jimbo to return. He looked around after he had fed the last handful of the green bark strips just as Jimbo came trotting through the brush right toward him. As soon as Jimbo entered the trees Zach smiled in relief at the cottontail rabbit he had in his mouth.

He wasted no time in stripping the hide off the small thin rabbit and then built a fire. As the rabbit roasted over the flickering flames he rubbed Jimbo's ears and talked to him about where they should look for bigger game. Most of the Indians of the mountains believed the Great Medicine Dog and Grizzly Killer could talk to one another, those being the Indian's names for Jimbo and Zach. When the rabbit was roasted Zach offered half of it to Jimbo but he stepped away leaving it all for Zach. As

Zach bit into a hind quarter of the small rabbit and the juices filled his mouth he smiled at Jimbo again, swallowed the mouth full and said, "Well feller, it ain't hump ribs but it tastes mighty good just the same." Zach felt the energy from the first food in two days almost immediately and rubbed Jimbo's ears again to thank him for the meal.

They started out again and Zach saw a flock of geese land on the river several hundred yards ahead of them. Not knowing when they might find the next meal he decided to sneak up onto the river bank and try for one of the geese. As he rode out away from the river he thought if the geese were returning from wherever they go to the south then the winter must be about over and he smiled hoping he was right.

He was about a quarter mile away from the river bend where the geese had landed when he stopped and got off Ol' Red. He just dropped Red's reins but tied off the two horses to the sage then got down on his hands and knees and started crawling toward the river. He had tried sneaking up on these wary birds many times before but with their excellent eye sight and wary disposition he had failed just as many times as he had succeeded. Jimbo was right by his side as they approached the river and as Zach dropped to his belly so did Jimbo. The geese hadn't moved from where they had landed but several of them were up on the opposite bank. Zach knew from past experienceexperience if any of them saw movement or heard a sound they would fly. He was concealed in sage where he was but if he tried to get any closer he knew he would never get a shot. He moved ever so slowly bringing up his .50 Caliber Hawken and for just a second wished he had his Pa's old .36 caliber squirrel gun but he had given that to Sun Flower.

He couldn't see the geese that were still in the river that were actually closer to him so he knew he had to take the nearly seventy yard shot from where he was. With intense concentration and a steady aimaim, he slowly squeezed off the shot. With the familiar feel of the recoil kicking back against his shoulder he knew the shot was true even before he seen the explosion of feathers on the far bank. With the gun shot still ringing in the air nearly two dozen geese immediately took flight. Jimbo sprang into action at the same instance and jumped after one goose just as it was leaving the water. He landed in the icy water and went under coming up just a moment later with only a mouth full of tail feathers.

Zach watched the geese fly away and wished he could see the world from up there. He might be able find the game he was looking for a whole lot faster. Jimbo crossed the river and retrieved the plump goose while Zach headed back to Ol' Red and the horses.

The blue sky over the mountains was growing larger and the wind had shifted now coming from the south. He could feel a definite temperature change as the warmer south wind started to blow. The warmer air felt mighty good but he worried, he knew that the warmer south wind usually preceded a storm. Jimbo reached him with the goose just as he got to Ol' Red. He quickly gutted the goose pulling out the heart, liver, and gizzard and gave them to Jimbo along with a gentle pat on the head. After putting the goose in one of the panniers he mounted up and continued downstream.

The south wind continued to increase throughout the day and by late afternoon they were out on the flatlands well away of the protection of any trees to block the fierce wind gusts. He had to find a place to spend the night, someplace that had some feed for Ol' Red and the tired hungry horses.

Another mile ahead he could see a small rolling hill on the other side of the river that was free of snow and from where he sat in his saddle it looked like it was covered with the dry stiff prairie grass common to this area. He knew his animals wouldn't like it, but it was better than nothing so he headed there. This land had always been so good to him and the game so plentiful he wondered why this winter had been so different. The deep snow byat their teepee'steepees had kept them inside for most of the winter. Even with their willow and rawhide snow shoes moving through the deep snow was extremely hard. Shoveling areas of the big meadow after each storm so their horses could get to the dry grass to eat took every bit a strength he and Running Wolf had throughout the winter.

As the sun dropped closer to the western horizon the temperature fell as well and Zach shuttered at the thought of spending the night with no protection from the wind. Even with the long shaggy winter hair on Ol' Red and the two horses he knew they too would spend a long miserable night.

As the river flowed out around the south facing hill it spread out some and he crossed in water that was only a foot deep and was relieved to see a small group of willows on the river bank. They weren't much protection but they would help cut the wind a little.

After stripping the saddles and packs off ofoff his stock and turning them loose on the dry grass, he moved his hand in a full circle over his head signaling Jimbo to scout the area for danger. He then walked the barren hill looking for buffalo chips for a fire. He found several but most were still moist from the melting snow. He knew they would dry out if he could get a fire started but with what he had to work with and the wind, a fire would be no easy task.

He found a few dead dry willow shoots that he pulled out of the willows along the river and pulled up a large clump of the grass. He always carried a little tinder from a squirrel's nest or whatever else he could find in his fire starter kit along with some charred patch cloth to catch a spark. Once he was satisfied he had enough material to not only start a fire but keep it burning he scraped out a pit and lined it with rocks from along the river. Once the rocks were heated he could use them to keep himself warm through the night.

The first strike of his fire steel on the flint sent a good spark right into the waiting charred cloth but as he gently set the kindling on it a gust of wind blew the small glowing ember out. He tried again and again trying to block the wind with his body but each time he got the same result. Jimbo came back wagging his tail so Zach knew he was safe enough for now but he needed a fire. Zach had always been patient, he had learned patience very young hunting the woods near his parents homestead back in Kentucky, but this wind was testing him to his limit. Just as he was ready to give up his latest little spark caught on the soft dry tinder and by blowing ever so gently on it a flame slowly grew until he had a small fire going. He set the moist buffalo chips around the edges and before long he could see the moisture steaming out of them.

It was dark by the time he had the goose on a willow branch roasting over the flames and he knew it would take a couple of hours to cook the plump bird. He rolled out his bed roll, which was a Hudson Bay wool blanket inside a buffalo hide robe, between the fire and willows. While he waited he fed the now dry buffalo chips into the fire keeping the heat up and watched the sky continue to clear.

The fat dripping into the fire and the smell of the roasting goose had him slicing off a piece of the breast to try before it was quite ready. Jimbo wasn't at all concerned whether it was cooked through, he ate the piece Zach threw to him without hesitation and set right up wanting more.

By the time the goose was cooked enough for Zach, the wind was starting to die down and the clouds had completely moved off leaving the stars lighting the night sky, but the clear sky brought a bitter cold with it. The cold air seemed to make the stars stand out even more than usual and he marveled at how they looked close enough to reach out and touch.

Before he crawled into his bed roll for the night he rolled some of the rocks from around the fire into his buffalo robe knowing they would help keep him warm for at least part of the night. He then placed the remaining buffalo chips over the dying embers of the fire hoping they would smolder all night and he could easily restart the fire in the morning. Jimbo curled up next to him and they both raised their heads slightly as a wolf howled way off in the distance.

When he woke the next morningmorning, he was cold and uncomfortable. The warm stones from around the fire had lost all ofall their heat. He thought about the soft warm bodies of his beautiful wives Sun Flower and

Shining Star and the warmth of their teepee and wished he was there. The stars were nearly faded as the gray of dawn spread across the wide clear sky. Jimbo had left on his usual morning hunt and Zach hoped he would find something to bring back.

He reached out and moved some of the buffalo chips that were covering the coals from the fire of the night before and by blowing on them had a warm fire burning in no time at all. Leaving the blanket wrapped around his shoulders he walked up past Ol' Red and the horses to the top of the hill where he could see the prairie around him for miles in all directions. To his disappointment all he could see was barren prairie.

Walking back to the fire he stopped and talked to Ol' Red, rubbing his neck while he did so and the big red mule responded by nuzzling his hand. Zach had been riding Ol' Red for years now, the two of them had developed as close a bond as he and Jimbo had. Ol' Red and his sister Jenny had been just a year old when he and his Pa left their Kentucky homestead to see the Rocky Mountains. Jenny had been gone for years now, stolen by Shoshones that first winter while he was alone. Ol' Red had been taken too but he had broken free and returned to Zach and he had been riding the big mule ever since.

Jimbo came running through the sage from the north and just as he got back to the fire Zach knew immediately Jimbo had found something for the dog was excited and barked to get him to follow. If there was danger he knew Jimbo would tell him with his deep rumbling growl from way down in his throat.

Chapter 2

Finding Buffalo

ZACH KICKED OUT the fire and saddled Ol' Red and the horses without wasting any time at all then headed out through the sage to the north following his big dog. The sun was coming up over the eastern horizon as he urged Ol' Red into a lope to keep up with Jimbo as the dog led him nearly straight north. In good shape, a gentle slope of a few miles wouldn't bother either Ol' Red or the horses, but he knew the horses were tiring mighty fast as they started pulling back on their lead rope. He could even feel Ol' Red straining to keep up with the long-legged dog. He eased back to just a walk, and a few minutes later Jimbo came running back to see what the delay was, then he too slowed his pace staying within a couple of hundred yards of Zach.

After they had covered five or six miles, they started up a gentle slope, and from the shadows cast by the early morning sun, he could tell the rise they were riding upended only another quarter mile ahead. Jimbo stopped and dropped down to his belly, and Zach knew then to stop and approach the crest of the rise with care. He dropped Ol' Red's reins and tied off the horses to a sage then hurried up to where Jimbo waited. They crawled the rest of the way to the top until he could see the broad, shallow basin that spread out in front of them.

He figured the basin was four or five miles across and there was only patchy snow across its bottom. There were warm springs out in the middle for he could see steam coming off a couple of ponds and the creek that ran between them. The creek then ran out disappearing into the prairie grass but what caught his attention most was the several dozen buffalo. Some of the buffalo were laying in the grass around the ponds, but most were up grazing. He then noticed three separate herds of antelope way off to the west.

Zach studied the area carefully. He had to figure out a way to get within range of one of the big shaggy beasts without spooking them and in this open basin that wasn't going to be easy. He wished Running Wolf was with him just for the next hour or two, so they could approach from different sides, that way if he spooked the buffalo they might run right to Running Wolf so they would get the meat either way, but it was just him and Jimbo and he knew it.

He could see no gulley, ditch, or any other depression for him to hide in. Even the sage stopped once he got off the rim, then there was just grass and he knew that wasn't enough to protect him. He watched as three antelope walked right out toward the far pond and right past several buffalo and they didn't bother one another at all. He wondered if horses could do the same thing.

They backed off the rim far enough to be out of sight then gave Jimbo the signal to go get Ol' Red and the dog took off on a dead run back through the sage to where the mule and horses were. He pulled on the lead rope untying it from the sage and with the rope in his mouth he led the horses with Ol' Red following right back to Zach.

Zach stripped the saddles and packs off them all and, holding the lead rope of the first horse and Ol' Red's reign, he stepped between the two and started right toward the ponds. The second horse just followed along. Once they got to the floor of the basin, he figured it was close to a mile to the closest pond with the first buffalo just a little closer. As they got about a quarter mile away, he could see most of the buffalo looking right at them, but none of them were moving. By the time they were nearly in rifle range most of the big animals had gone back to grazing.

He walked right past several of them getting to the edge of the pond and as the horse and Ol' Red put their heads down to drink Zach slowly raised his rifle up over Ol' Red's back, took aim on a large cow about forty yards away and fired. She took two steps to the side and fell. At hearing the shot, Jimbo left the rim and ran straight out to his master. All the buffalo raised their heads and watched but to Zach's surprise they didn't run. He reloaded just as fast as he could and wished he had a way to carry more meat for he figured it would be easy enough to take another one. He knew the two horses wouldn't be able to carry all the meat from just this one. If he could take the time to dry it they could carry a lot more but he couldn't, he had to get this meat back to his family, and that was still at least a two-day journey.

As he stepped out from between his horse and mule the other buffalo near him trotted away, but there was no stampede. They just moved off about a half mile and started milling around again. He smiled thinking that had been a lot easier than he expected.

He got right to work gutting and skinning the large cow, and he was amazed she was as fat as she was after coming through this hard of a winter. As he worked on her, he thought these warm springs must have kept the ground clear around them for these animals to stay on the thick tall grass.

Once he had the hide off her, he jumped up on Ol' Red bareback and rode back to where he had left the saddles and packs letting the horses graze. This was the best grass they had been on for many months, and he knew even a couple of hours good grazing would help the weakened animals. Once he had Ol' Red saddled, he carried the pack saddles and panniers behind his saddle and headed back to the kill.

Ol' Red went right over by the horses to graze as Zach started cutting the best cuts of meat off the bones and stacking it all on the flesh side of the hide. When he had one front shoulder nearly stripped of the best cuts, he finished cutting it off and gave it to Jimbo. The big dog started right in on it, and as Zach watched him eat for a minute, his belly began to growl. He cut several thin strips off the liver and ate them raw.

When he had as much meat cut off the carcass as he figured the two horses could carry, he walked over to the pond and washed in the tepid water. He let his stock graze for another half hour then put the pack saddles and panniers on the horses and started loading the meat keeping the loads as balanced as he could.

He was nearly done loading the second horse when Jimbo jumped up and started the low growl as he watched and stared off to the east. As Zach looked up, he could see the buffalo in that direction start to run right toward him. Then just behind the buffalo, there were a half-dozen or more riders on a dead run heading right for him.

Knowing he couldn't outrun them with his heavy loaded animals and not willing to leave them and the much-needed meat behind, he took a chance and shot another buffalo as they ran by. He was thinking if these Indians were hostile maybe giving them a buffalo would keep things peaceful. As the Indians approached they spread out and then surrounded him and he could see, then these were young Cheyenne warriors. They weren't painted for war, so he figured they were here hunting just as he was. This was a long way from the Cheyenne's normal range so he figured the winter must have been mighty hard on them as well.

Zach was wearing his grizzly claw necklace and as Jimbo sat down by his side the grizzly claws on his collar stood out plain as well. The reputation of Grizzly Killer and the Great Medicine Dog had spread all through the mountains and across the plains. Zach saw the expression change on the face of the young warrior that was the apparent leader, and he knew he had been recognized.

All seven of these young men had either arrows drawn or lances ready, and Zach knew well if trouble started this could be his end. He slowly laid his rifle and pistol down then made the sign for friend, but the warrior right in front of him yelled something to the others, and he knew then he was in real trouble. Although he didn't speak

Cheyenne, he could read the tone and gestures well enough to know these Cheyenne thought they had just taken a prize much more significant than a buffalo.

In sign, the leader of this hunting party pointed at Zach making the sign for Grizzly Killer, then big medicine only after big medicine he made the sign for small and all the Cheyenne laughed. Zach could see this wasn't going well and with nothing more than a slight movement of his hand sent Jimbo away. The dog responded without hesitation, and the speed of the dog's departure caught the Cheyenne off guard. Two of them shot arrows at him as he bolted away but both arrows hit the ground well behind the fast running dog.

The Cheyenne leader signed he was Three Eagles, and his medicine was stronger than Grizzly Killer's, and he would show all the people he was stronger than Grizzly Killer. Zach knew they would respect bravery and despise fear, so he responded with his own sign, "Three Eagles is only strong when he is backed by six other armed warriors, while I laid my weapons down and offered peace."

Three Eagles turned red at that insult and rode over next to Zach and kicked him in the face knocking him to the ground. Two of the others then came and bound his hands with rawhide. After they got him back to his feet, Three Eagles put a rawhide lead rope around his neck, told the others to bring the horses, mule, and meat then led Zach off heading toward the eastern side of the basin.

To show Zach he was in complete control, Three Eagles would jerk on the lead rope regularly causing him to stumble forward then laugh and do it again. Zach had fought Indians many times in the past, the Arapaho, Blackfeet, Snake, Crow and even a Ute but this was the first time he had ever been taken prisoner. He knew Three Eagles was afraid of the great Grizzly Killer. He could see it in his eyes. That was why he wouldn't take any chances by fighting him alone.

As they started the climb up the eastern side of the basin, Zach glanced back and saw the others were over a hundred yards behind. He thought this might be his best chance to try an escape. He tightened his neck muscles just as much as he could then reached for the lead rope and jumped back. The sudden jerk threw Three Eagles off balance, and he tumbled off the back of his horse. Zach ran forward and kicked him just as hard as he could as he ran toward the horse. Three Eagles doubled over holding his broken ribs and could do nothing about Zach reaching for the mane of his beautiful pinto.

Zach could hear horses right behind him as he kicked the pinto into a dead run. An arrow flew past his head missing by less than an inch, and he leaned forward as he urged the pinto faster trying to make a smaller target. He had made it up over the rim of the basin and was now on a full out run through the short sage and sparse grass prairie when he saw Jimbo a quarter mile in front running toward him.

He veered the pinto slightly toward his dog and then glanced back to see three of the Cheyenne still behind him nearly in range with their deadly arrows. Jimbo crouched down in the sage as Zach approached and waited for him to pass but as the first Cheyenne warrior approached, Jimbo attacked. When the nearly two-hundred-pound dog jumped he bit down on the warrior's leg and his horse went berserk trying to get away from the attacking dog. Jimbo released the Indian but the horse stumbled and fell right in front of one of the others and that horse and rider went down as well. Zach again glanced back to find there was one of the Cheyenne still in pursuit.

He wished he still had his guns or his old Cherokee Tomahawk but the Cheyenne had taken that as well as his belt knife. He still had the small boot knife tucked into the outside of his moccasin, but he didn't think that was enough to go up against the well-armed Cheyenne.

He could feel the strength fading fast now in this beautiful pinto mare. He glanced back again to see the two horses that had fallen no longer in pursuit. They were without riders but still on a dead run heading east. Zach wondered what had happened as he pulled the pinto back into a gentle lope and slowly brought her to a stop. He watched behind while the horse got back its wind and he patted her on the side of her neck thanking her for his escape.

It was only a couple of minutes later when he saw Jimbo's head and neck above the sage running back to him. The blood on his face told Zach what had happened to the last Cheyenne that was chasing him.

He figured he was now two, or maybe three miles from where he had started and the Cheyenne had his guns, tomahawk, and knife, his two horses, Ol' Red, and all of the buffalo meat. His hands were still bound with the rawhide the Cheyenne had used on him, so he reached into his moccasin and pulled out the boot knife working it into a position to cut the strap away.

Many thoughts were going through his mind. He had to get Ol' Red and his belongings back, but there were seven warriors against just him and Jimbo. He knew Three Eagles was hurt for he thought he felt the ribs cave in when he kicked him, but he couldn't be sure and he had no idea if or how badly any of the others were hurt when their horses fell. From the blood on Jimbo's face, he thought that last one that had been chasing him was either dead or severely injured, but he couldn't be sure of any of it. What he did know for sure was he didn't have his weapons or his beloved mule, and he wasn't leaving here without them.

This pinto mare was a very sturdy horse. She had stayed ahead of the three that were in pursuit, and she was also a beautiful dark bay with irregular pure white patches over nearly half of her body. He was glad he had ridden away on her for he feared if she had been in pursuit they would have caught him. Now he had to track them back to where ever they were camped and stay out of sight, and that would not be easy out on this nearly flat prairie.

He climbed off the mare letting her rest a while longer for he knew it would take some time for the Cheyenne to get back together. He figured maybe he should go after them before that happened but he figured they would see him coming and there were just too many of them with him having no weapons.

When he dismounted, Jimbo came right up to him, and the horse started to back away pulling hard on the reins that Zach was holding. With a slight raise of his hand, Jimbo stopped and he calmly talked to the horse until she had calmed down. He signaled Jimbo to stay then slowly and gently coaxed the mare into walking forward. With Zach's soothing voice persuading her it only took a few minutes until she had walked up to Jimbo and the dog responded by reaching up and licking her nose. She stood face to face with Jimbo studying him and Zach wondered just what was going through each of their minds. They stayed like that for nearly ten minutes then both of them turned and looked at Zach. He smiled knowing now the two of them were friends.

Jimbo took the lead while Zach staying on foot led the pinto north back to the rim of the basin. He tied off the mare to a sage, and he and Jimbo again crawled to the rim. The buffalo were still in the basin, but they had moved off to the northwest corner and although Zach could see them they were so far away now they were only tiny black dots against the dry grass. The day had warmed enough that there wasn't nearly as much fog coming off the ponds and creek, and the cool breeze that had started up was blowing that away. He was only about a mile from where he had kicked Three Eagles and made his escape, but he could see no sign of the Cheyenne, Ol' Red, or his horses. Three wolves were eating the remains of the buffalo carcass that was plain to see lying in the thick grass not far from the edge of the pond. The other one Zach had shot, hoping to make friends with the approaching Indians, was still lying there untouched.

He decided he needed to wait even longer before tracking the Cheyenne back to where ever they were camped. There were just too many of them to fight out on the open prairie. Walking back to where he had left the pinto, Jimbo jumped a jackrabbit. Although it was quite a chase, he came back with the rabbit in his mouth. Zach didn't figure it would be very smart to start a fire out in the open during the day so he stripped the hide off the rabbit and gave the whole thing back to Jimbo. Jimbo had filled up on the buffalo leg earlier so he just turned and walked away leaving the rabbit for Zach. Zach needed the meat and energy it would provide so he cut thin strips off it and ate them raw, all the while wishing he had a fire.

Two hours passed before he mounted up and followed the basin's rim around to where the Cheyenne had climbed up out of it and headed east toward the Seeds-Kee-Dee. Jimbo being well out in front found the trail long before Zach had reached it. With a silent hand signal, he then sent his big dog out ahead as he followed the path, keeping a wary eye for as far as he could see ahead.

Chapter 3

The Cheyenne's Camp

THE SUN WAS NEARLY down as Zach approached the first of the breaks on this west side of the Seeds-Kee-Dee. Suddenly Jimbo appeared out of the brush a little to his south where a small wash cut through the edge of the break leading down to the ancient floodplain of the river. As he eased back on the rein stopping the mare, Jimbo ran up to him with a low growl and Zach knew his dog had found the Cheyenne's camp.

Figuring he was about a mile from the river or maybe a little more he knew he would have to approach on foot. After riding the mare most of the day he was becoming more and more impressed with her. As he tied her to the largest clump of brush he could find he hoped with all his heart she wouldn't try to break free to get back to the Cheyenne camp and the horses she was used to being with.

From there he couldn't tell where the Cheyenne were camped, but he figured it was somewhere on the river. He moved across the top of the break to the north for nearly half a mile before he found another wash that would conceal him as he made his way down to the floodplain. Although it was now twilight, he was still relieved the wash went all the way to the river. The sides of the wash were slick with the melting snow making it quite muddy, and there was a trickle of water running down the bottom of it. He still had nearly three-fourths of a mile to go, and after only a couple of hundred yards, he climbed up out of the wash covered with mud figuring he would take his chances up on the flat ground. It was dark enough by now that he had a hard time making out the tree line of the Seeds-Kee-Dee, so he figured he was safe enough.

He moved slowly staying right along the edge of the wash, for he knew that movement of any kind could be seen a long way off. Jimbo, as always, was scouting ahead and when Zach was still a quarter mile from the river Jimbo and been there and back. With his dog as a scout, he knew the path ahead was clear, so he broke into a run and made it to the leafless trees in only a couple of more minutes.

Once in the protection of the trees, he stopped to access just what he had to do. Not having a weapon other than his small boot knife, he found a fist-sized rock on the river's edge and he started looking for a forked branch of the size to hold the rock. Once he had those items, he cut a strip of leather off the bottom of the buckskin shirt to tie the rock solidly between the forks of the branch. When finished, he swung the war club through the air satisfied it would hold up as a weapon but hoping he wouldn't have to use it. He then cut a straight willow and used another strip cut off his shirt to lash his boot knife on to it for a lance.

Jimbo didn't understand what the delay was and he could see no reason to wait. While Zach was building his weapons, he followed the river south until he came upon the Cheyenne. He circled their camp staying out far enough not to be detected. He could smell the familiar smell of Ol' Red when he got downwind of the horses and longed to see his lifelong companion. Jimbo didn't know, but the big mule could feel Jimbo's presence and was shaking his powerful neck trying to let Jimbo and Zach know he was ready for what was going to happen.

Zach was already moving toward the Cheyenne camp when Jimbo met him on the trail. Again, the deep soft growl told Zach the enemy wasn't far ahead. The big dog moved like a shadow through the brush and trees making no sound. It always amazed Zack how a dog that big could move so fast and make no noise at all. Zach, however, slowed down, carefully placing every step. The night was dark, and that was slowing him down even more, but he was a patient man and was not moving any faster than he could do so silently.

He could see the flickering light of their fire long before he was close enough to see any of the warriors. He slowed even more as he approached the small glade where they were camped. The breeze, still coming from the south was blowing the smell of roasting hump ribs right to him. His belly growled from hunger, and his mouth started to water from the smell, but he put the thought of food out of his mind as he counted five warriors up and moving around the fire. The other two were on their robes on the far side but right up next to the fire. The way they were laying he figured both of them were hurt.

He silently motioned for Jimbo to go to the other side of the camp and he took off like a gray ghost in the night. Zach knew his dog wouldn't make a move until he did and the odds were too high for them to attack now, so he waited. While he watched, so many different ideas tumbled through his mind, *"If he waited till they slept could he sneak in and take back all they had taken from him, no they would chase him later. He would have to take their horses or hurt them in other ways, so they could not follow."*

Although he had many times before, Zach Connors did not like to kill. He was raised in a God-fearing Christian home in Kentucky. He learned to read right out of the pages of the Bible, and he truly believed that killing was a sin unless it was to protect a person's life. Whether that person was himself, his loved ones or anyone else, he would kill without hesitation to protect his family or others. He watched these seven Cheyenne now eating his buffalo sitting around their fire. He smiled thinking how overly cocky they were, not one of them was on guard and they knew Grizzly Killer was still out there.

He sat there motionless for well over an hour studying each of the different warriors. He had decided that Three Eagles was one of them lying by the fire and the other appeared to have a broken leg. Zach figured the fractured leg happened when their horses went down during the chase. The other five all seemed to be in fine shape, and Zach knew he didn't want to have to take them all on at least not until he retrieved his weapons. He couldn't see his trusted rifle, the Hawken he had won at the very first Rendezvous, or his pistol, knife, and tomahawk but he figured they would be right there where the Cheyenne had piled their supplies. Another hour passed and he watched as it appeared they were getting their bedrolls ready.

Just before they laid down for the night Ol' Red brayed so loud it rattled through the trees, then the horses all started to stomp and whinny. All five of the Cheyenne went to the picket line, and one shouted making the sign for a wolf. He ran behind the horses with his bow drawn back to get a shot at what he thought was a wolf and in doing so he stepped right behind Ol' Red. With both hind legs, Ol' Red kicked and even from where Zach was hiding clear on the other side of their camp he could hear the sickening sound of bones breaking as both hooves caved in the warrior's ribs. The others rushed to him, Zach couldn't see from where he was hidden, but he could hear the injured one gasping for breath.

There was no doubt in Zach's mind that it had been a planned attack by Jimbo and Ol' Red. He figured most people wouldn't ever believe that, but he did. That mule and Jimbo were his constant companions and had been ever since the first winter he had spent in the mountains after his pa had been killed. He knew how smart and loyal both animals were and he wondered what they had in store next. Ol' Red was a large red Kentucky mule, bigger than most of the wild mustangs the Indians rode. He could pack more than a horse and although not as fast he could run farther than any horse Zach had ever seen. Ever since he had found Jimbo in an abandoned Shoshone camp, Jimbo and he had never been apart, and Zach believed Ol' Red and his dog communicated with each other, probably in the same manner that he interacted with them. He didn't understand it himself, but he knew it was real, for they always were right where he needed them to do what needed to be done. The Indians called it big medicine and Zach had just accepted it as a special bond they shared.

He watched the four still healthy Cheyenne help their downed companion over to the fire. Zach could tell by the way he was struggling to breathe that his ribs had punctured a lung. It was only a minute later he started coughing up blood and Zach figured he would be dead by morning. After they had the injured warrior laying by the fire one of them with a furious look on his face picked up his war club and headed right toward Ol' Red. Zach was now worried for the big mule; he was determined not to let anything happen to him. He would charge in with nothing more than his war club if need be, but he hesitated. He could tell even looking clear across their camp in the dark, Ol' Red had a very dangerous look in his eyes.

As the warrior approached and raised the war club to strike, Ol' Red reared and squealed a blood-curdling scream that made chills run down Zach's back. He then bounded forward at the warrior and in doing so broke the picket-line causing the warrior to dive side-ways just barely out of the way of Ol' Red's rock-hard hooves. With all this commotion, the other horses bounded away, but Ol' Red was still going after the warrior who was rolling across the ground desperately trying to stay away from his hooves. One of the other warriors picked up a lance and went charging at Ol' Red. Zach, without hesitation, threw the heavy war club all the way across the camp hitting the warrior squarely and caving in the back of his head. He landed on the ground face first. The other two jumped and turned to look at Zach as he ran to where he figured his weapons were laying.

He had been correct and in one swift motion, he reached down, picked up his pistol and pointed it at the two remaining Cheyenne still by the fire. Zach whistled once, and Jimbo appeared instantly behind the two and Ol' Red stopped his attack. Zach then motioned with the pistol at the warrior on the ground in front of the big mule to come over by the fire with the others. As he did Zach could see both fear and a burning hatred in his eyes. His hands were tightened fists and Zach couldn't tell just what he might try. Jimbo growled a very threatening growl and one of the others said something to him, but he returned a look that Zach didn't like. Jimbo growled again this time crouching slightly ready to attack, and the warrior stopped dead still.

He then motioned for the three of them to sit and slowly they complied. The six of them were now around the fire all but one staring intently at Zach. The one Ol' Red had kicked was barely breathing now and appeared to be unconscious. Zach looked into the faces of them all and then stared right at Three Eagles. He started moving his hands in the universal sign language most of the tribes could understand. He said, "I am Grizzly Killer, and my medicine is strong, not to be laughed at by the Cheyenne. One of you has already gone to the land beyond and another will soon join him; two more have broken bones. I will leave you the meat you stole from me so you can make it back to your lands. Gather your horses and take your wounded home. If you try to come after me, I will kill you all.

Jimbo was still behind them as Zach walked over and rubbed Ol' Red's cheek and let him nuzzle into his hand. One of the Cheyenne turned his head to watch Grizzly Killer, but Jimbo's growl stopped him short. He saddled his mule and tied the pack saddle and panniers from his pack horses behind the saddle leaving all the meat behind then led him back over in front of the Cheyenne. He mounted up and signed one more time, "I am Grizzly Killer, and I will remember you all."

Jimbo stayed right behind the Cheyenne warriors as Zach rode away from the fire and out into the cold night. When he was nearly a quarter mile away, he whistled and Jimbo followed silently disappearing into the night, leaving the Cheyenne sitting by their fire. The warriors didn't move for a few minutes even after Jimbo had left. Even though they all had a deep fear of the powerful medicine that Grizzly Killer, his dog, and mule had, they also had a building hatred and now wanted revenge.

Zach rode hard trusting Ol' Red to be able to see in the night back to where he had left the pinto mare. She was looking straight at them as they approached and whinnied as she caught the scent of the mule. Zach dismounted, softly talking to her and rubbing the side of her neck. He then put the pack saddles and panniers on her, figuring he just traded his pack horses for her, then smiled knowing he got the better of that trade.

He didn't believe any of the Cheyenne would follow him especially on such a night, but he still wanted more distance between them. With Jimbo in the lead, they headed west back toward the basin and the buffalo that were still there. The wind, although not blowing hard had shifted now, it was coming from the northwest instead of the south. He wrapped his sleeping blanket around him for more protection from the cold wind hoping if it were bringing a storm it would hold off a little longer.

They traveled many miles through the night, into the cold wind and then a sound could be heard. It was the mournful howling of wolves still a long way off coming to them on the icy wind. He was cold, tired, and hungry and started looking for a place to shelter, but in the dark of night out on this flat prairie he didn't have much hope, so he rode on.

When he figured it was past midnight, with his hands and face both burning from the cold wind, he whistled for Jimbo to come back and he stopped. The sage there was only a couple of feet high, but it was thicker than what he had been traveling through so he stopped. First, he scraped out as deep a hole as he could in the frozen ground and started breaking off the small dry limbs that he could find on the sage. Getting his hands to work in the cold took all his concentration. When he had enough material to get a fire started, he reached into his possibles bag and got his fire starter kit. By now, his fingers were so cold he couldn't get them to maneuver well enough to hold the steel, let alone get the charred cloth into position. He slid both his hands up under the saddle that was still on Ol' Red and let the mule's warmth slowly bring his fingers back to life. Once he thought he could move them well enough, he hurried and got a spark to take in the blackened cloth. The clump of grass he had frayed took the small glowing ember and a minute later a flame slowly grew. He placed the burning grass under the small pile of dry sage limbs and soon he had a fire burning.

With nothing but sage to burn he was feeding the fire almost continuously, but at least that was keeping him warm. For the few minutes, he could sit down by the fire, he held the blanket and buffalo robe wrapped around him and wished for a hot cup of coffee. Their coffee, like the other supplies from last summer's Rendezvous, had been gone for nearly three months now.

Although daylight was only a few hours away, it felt like it took forever before the sky finally started to lighten. Not all the stars had disappeared into the coming dawn when he kicked the fire out and mounted up. He wasn't sure how far he had traveled during the night, but he didn't think it would be all that far to the basin and the downed buffalo. With what was left of the first one and the second one not touched he figured he could get all the meat the horse and Ol' Red could carry in a couple of hours then he could start the hundred-mile walk back home.

He urged Ol' Red into a gentle lope and within an hour he was approaching the eastern rim of the basin. Before he got to the rim, he could see dark clouds rolling in from the north and he wondered if this long cold winter was ever going to end. As he crested the rim and looked down to the ponds and the downed buffalo, a dozen wolves were feeding on the carcasses.

Chapter 4

A Hundred Miles From Home

RUNNING WOLF STOOD OUTSIDE the lodges looking north as the latest of these seemingly endless winter storms approached. The grass of the meadow was just starting to show through the snow enough that the horses could get to it and now another storm would cover it again. Luna, his white wolf, ran up to him. She had been up on the hill just south of the big meadow still looking for Grizzly Killer and Jimbo to return. She was nearly a year old now, just a couple of months older than Gray Wolf, his son and Morning Star, Grizzly Killer's blue-eyed daughter.

Sun Flower came out of Grizzly Killer's lodge and gave Running Wolf a small piece of pemmican then went into his lodge and gave Raven Wing, her sister, the last of it. When she came back out, she saw the worried look on Running Wolf's face and knew he felt the same concern as she and Shining Star. Grizzly Killer had been gone now for four days, and another storm was about to come down on them. They all wondered how far from home had he gone. Had he found the meat they so desperately needed? But in the back of all their minds was the burning question, *is he all right?*

Sun Flower looked at Running Wolf and said, "This was the last of it, my brother," Running Wolf just nodded, then headed out to the horses. He had prepared himself for what had to be done and had already made the decision which of the pack horses would have to be sacrificed to keep them all fed until Grizzly Killer's return. The horses were in poor condition after the long, hard winter so the meat wouldn't be right, but it was food, and it would keep Raven Wing and Shining Star healthy enough to be able to nurse the little ones.

Luna was by his side as he led the thin and weakened horse downstream a little way and tied her to a tree. As Running Wolf softly talked to the unsuspecting mare thanking her for giving her life that they might live, Luna ran to the top of the hill again. She stood there looking north and started to howl. It was an eerie sound that was entirely different than when she would howl into the night or answer other wolves howling off in the distance. This sounded to Running Wolf more like she was calling maybe to Jimbo and Grizzly Killer to return.

Zach wondered how he was going to chase off a dozen hungry wolves or if he was going to have to take the time to hunt again. He started off the hill toward the first pond where the downed buffalo and wolves were when Jimbo stopped and raised his head staring straight toward Black's Fork and home. Zach watched his dog closely looking for any sign from him of danger, but

Jimbo was tilting his head slightly back and forth like he was trying to figure something out. Zach studied the area to the south and west where Jimbo was looking but could see nothing at all. Then he caught movement out of the corner of his eye and watched as all the wolves were heading in that same direction, altogether abandoning the buffalo carcasses.

He wondered what was out there that would cause all the wolves to leave the easy meal they were enjoying. He had no answer, but he knew he had to get the meat he needed before they decided to return. With Jimbo leading the way they trotted out across the basin to the carcasses. Zach was pleased the wolves had only been at the soft belly portions of his second kill, but the first was almost gone.

He wasted no time in skinning this yearling bull and filling the panniers until he had a hundred pounds on each side of the mare. He then tied the panniers of his second pack horse over Ol' Reds saddle and filled them with two hundred and fifty pounds of the meat. He knew these were heavy loads, but he felt both Ol' Red and the mare were strong enough to make it.

It was early afternoon as he headed out on foot leading the mare he knew Ol' Red would follow along with him wherever he went. The cold north wind was carrying with it the first snowflakes of the storm that had been building all day. Zach pulled his wolverine skin hat down even farther over his ears as he climbed up out of the basin heading south by a little west back toward Black's Fork and home.

The snow had cut his visibility down to less than a half mile as he trekked across the short sage prairie hoping he could get back to the river and find some protection from the storm before dark. He wondered again about the wolves, why would they have left those kills like they did just as he was getting to them and what could Jimbo hear or sense that was out there? He had no answers as the snow covered the open ground.

He set a grueling pace for himself, but the pinto mare and Ol' Red didn't seem to mind. The wind had died into only a breeze and was hitting their rumps as they moved further south. Jimbo was out in the lead as usual and would return every half hour or so just to let Zach know all was clear. By late afternoon the snow was letting up some, but by now Zach's moccasins were soaked through, and his feet were dangerously cold. He knew he had to stop soon and get a fire going, but he didn't think he was far from Black's Fork, so he pushed on.

He started climbing up the slight grade of a hill, and when he reached the top, he was relieved to see the watercourse of Black's Fork less than a mile away. He pushed on but was worried; his feet felt like wooden stumps rather than living flesh. The pain from the cold was still there, so he hoped that meant that frostbite hadn't yet set in. Ten more minutes and he entered a stand of cottonwoods along the river.

The snow had nearly stopped, and the sun was peeking through the cloud bank just above the horizon as he picked up an armload of dry branches for a fire. The sun's rays were shooting their brilliant color under the dark clouds making a spectacular display, but he couldn't take time to enjoy it, he had to get a fire going and warm his half-frozen feet.

By now he was shaking almost uncontrollably, and he dropped his fire steel twice as he tried to get a tight grip on it. It was only by the force of will that he was able to get a spark to take in his last fragile piece of charred cloth. He was shaking so bad now that he was afraid he couldn't put the tinder bundle on the tiny ember without putting it out. Again, he willed his hands still. A few gentle breaths later and the tinder was in flames. Ten minutes later he had his feet nearly in the growing flames of the fire, rubbing one and then the other.

Jimbo was sitting by him watching every move. Zach wasn't talking to him like he usually did so the dog knew something was wrong but didn't know what it was. Ol' Red and the mare were standing there motionless with the heavy packs of meat still on their backs, but they too could sense something was wrong.

The warmth of the fire finally started to sink into his cold feet and hands and as it did pain started shooting through them. They hurt much worse now than they had with just the cold. He kept rubbing more vigorously than ever, knowing the life-giving warmth was saving him. The snow had stopped and the sun had set by the time he stood again and was able to walk over and take the heavy packs off Ol' Red and the pinto. His feet were tender and he stepped carefully, but his trusted mule and the new horse had to be taken care of. The grass was sparse, but they would have to make do, he needed to keep his feet by the fire. He told Ol' Red, "Boy, I'll strip some bark for ya in the morning."

He hadn't taken the time to set rocks in a fire ring at first, so he did so now wanting the heated stones to warm his bed. Then he put two large strips of buffalo meat on sticks over the fire. While he waited for the meat to cook, he pulled off his moccasins and set them by the fire to dry and continued rubbing his tender feet. He had been cold before during the first winter he had spent alone, without his pa and had to learn how to make warm clothing and moccasins to stay warm, but he had never had his feet this cold before. It hurt to touch his skin, and he worried about being able to walk the sixty or seventy miles he figured it was back home. He knew he could ride, but that would mean leaving buffalo meat behind and he didn't want to have to do that.

As the fat from the meat started to drip into the fire, the smell was more than he could take. It had been two days since he had eaten the goose and he was hungry. He pulled the strips of meat off the sticks and knowing Jimbo wouldn't care that it was nearly raw gave the first one to him, then he bit into the warm near bloody meat. He could feel the warm juices hit his empty stomach and for a minute wondered if they would stay down. He slowed his eating giving his empty stomach time to adjust to the warm meat and soon he could feel the warmth radiating through him from the inside as well as from the fire outside.

He turned his moccasins and watched as the moisture steamed out of them making sure he didn't get them to close to the hot flames. After doing this several times, he pulled them back on his tender feet. The warmth radiated through his feet and up the calves of his legs and he closed his eyes for a minute enjoying the feeling. He slowly stood up and was pleased the pain wasn't as bad as he had expected.

After checking on Ol' Red and the mare one more time, he gathered enough firewood to last through the night, stacking it within easy reach of his bedroll. The sky was clearing, the storm of the day was over, but with the clearing sky, the temperature was dropping. He could hear wolves howling way off to the north as he rolled the heated rocks from around the fire into his bedroll. As he wrapped the blanket and buffalo robe over him, Jimbo curled up on the bottom of his bedroll not too far from the warmth of the fire.

Zach was dead tired. It had been a long hard day, so sleep was almost immediate. It was along toward morning before he woke up to add more wood to the nearly cold coals. He had to stir the coals and blow life back into them before the new wood finally caught fire. He heard the wolves again way off to the north and wondered if they were the same ones that had been in the basin. He thought about them leaving again and still wondered why they had left those two buffalo carcasses the way they had. He thought about the warm, inviting bodies of his wives, Sun Flower and Shining Star and his baby girl, Star, with her bright blue eyes and infectious smile as he dozed off into a sound sleep again.

The stars were gone but the sun wasn't yet up when he opened his eyes next and again, the fire had gone out. He listened before he moved just like his Pa and taught him. A man should always make sure he hears all the natural sounds before he moves after he had been asleep in case danger was near. Jimbo was gone on his usual early morning hunt, and he could hear Ol' Red and the pinto mare munching on the bushes growing along the river.

He stirred the coals just like he had during the night then once again blew life back into them and soon had a warm fire burning again. He moved his feet rubbing them together and although they were still tender, they were much better than they had been the night before. The large heated rock he had put in the foot of his bedroll was still slightly warm, and it had kept his feet warm through the night.

A cold shiver ran down his back as he threw the heavy robe off and stood in the brisk morning air. He stepped a little closer to the fire and held his hands over the warm flames for a minute then warmed his moccasins until he could feel the heat penetrating the layers all the way to his toes.

After cutting two more large strips of buffalo and setting them on sticks over the fire, he went out and started cutting strips of green bark off the cottonwoods. Once he had an armful, he went out and divided it evenly between Ol' Red and his new mare. She came right up to him and although he had lost two pack horses to the Cheyenne this beautiful pinto was probably worth more than both of them. She was actually in a little better shape than Ol' Red, but he would never say that out loud, not wanting to hurt the big mule's feelings.

Jimbo had just returned from his early morning hunt as Zach sat down by the fire to eat the now cooked strips of buffalo meat. He smiled at the sight of Jimbo and reached out to pull the feathers of a prairie chicken from the corner of the big dog's mouth and said, "Looks like ya already found your breakfast, big feller." Jimbo was always hungry and sat on his haunches wagging his tail knowing one of the pieces of meat was his and patiently waited for Zach to give it to him.

Zach found the more he moved, the better his feet felt so without further delay he kicked the fire out and loaded the heavy packs on Ol' Red and the pinto. As he headed upstream, he hoped he could make it back to the warm embrace of his beautiful wives in just two more days of hard travel.

As the sun moved higher in the sky, its warming rays made Zach, as well as the animals, feel better. If he were riding instead of on foot and the animals were in better shape, he figured he could make the fifty or sixty miles by dark, but that wasn't the case. He stopped every couple of hours for a little while to rest Ol' Red and the mare then at close to noon he came upon some open grass and took the heavy packs off them. He let them graze for a couple of hours since he figured this might be the best grass they find. While the livestock grazed, he built a small fire and roasted a couple more strips of buffalo. After loading up again, they continued upstream until the sun was nearly down.

This had been the best day since he had left home looking to make meat five days ago. The storm of the day before had passed entirely. The sun shined bright in the brilliant blue sky all day long, and the slight breeze carried just the first hints of spring. The Uintah Mountains were still buried in deep snow only twenty miles to the south, and the stark white of that snow made the blue of the sky even darker. Zach found a thick stand of cottonwoods on a wide bend in the river. The buds that were starting to swell on the willows along the river so they would provide some forage for Ol' Red and the pinto and there was plenty of firewood.

As he started a fire and set up camp for the night, his mind was on his family at home. He had been separated from them for more extended periods of time, but this had been the hardest. Knowing they were nearly out of food when he left, and he'd been gone almost a week. He knew Running Wolf would have butchered one of their pack horses by now, but he knew that wouldn't be good meat. He couldn't get them off his mind, and after he and Jimbo had eaten their buffalo strip dinner, he crawled into his bed robes earlier than usual, hoping sleep would ease the longing he felt to be home.

The sky along the eastern horizon had barely started to lighten as he stirred the coals and blew the fire back to life. He didn't even take the time to eat this morning, he just packed up and started up the trail before the sun was up. He shivered in the cold morning air, but that just made him push even harder to stay warm.

By midday, he was only ten miles from home, and he wanted to push ahead and get there, but with Ol' Red and the mare loaded as heavy as they were he had to stop and unload them to rest for an hour or two. Now he had the time he started a small hand sized fire and cooked Jimbo and himself a good-sized strip of the buffalo. He had barely finished eating his piece of meat when Ol' Red came over and nudged him in the shoulder telling Zach that he was ready to go.

By late afternoon Zach could see the hill at the north end of the big meadow and he could smell just a hint of wood smoke on the breeze that was blowing gently downstream.

He had made it back home, and Jimbo had already run ahead to let them know they were coming in. Zach sighed with the knowledge he had less than a mile to go.

Chapter 5

Good to be Home

LUNA MET JIMBO WHEN he was barely out of Zach's sight. She jumped with excitement as they met. The white wolf laid down in front of the Jimbo letting him sniff her all over. It had been Jimbo that had found Luna when she was a small puppy after a bear had killed her mother. Even now with Luna nearly full grown she still looked at Jimbo as her protector.

Jimbo stopped only briefly to greet her then ran on to the dugout and buffalo hide lodges that was their home. Sun Flower was by the outside fire boiling a roast from the horse Running Wolf had butchered. Boiling was the only way they could make it tender enough to eat. She was setting down the bladder water pouch from adding some to the pot when she saw a big dog come running up the trail.

She yelled for Jimbo, and as he ran up to her, she dropped to her knees to hug him. Shining Star came running out of their teepee, and Running Wolf and Raven Wing theirs, and Jimbo ran to each in turn. When he got to Running Wolf, he stood up on his back legs putting his front paws on his shoulders, his head now higher the Running Wolf's and give him big lick right across the face. Running Wolf held him by the fur on the sides of his head and asked, "How far behind is Grizzly Killer?"

Jimbo jumped down and ran to the edge of camp, stopped and waited for Running Wolf to catch up. Running Wolf jogged down the trail right behind Jimbo and Luna. When they met Grizzly Killer, Running Wolf knew he'd had trouble. He wasn't riding Ol' Red, and the pack horses he had left with weren't with him. He was leading a horse that he had never seen before, and for a moment he just stared. The pinto mare Grizzly Killer was leading was one of the most beautiful horses he had ever seen.

Zach held up his hand when he saw the questioning look on his brother in law's face and said, "I will tell of my hunt around the fire, these animals are loaded mighty heavy so we must not wait. Running Wolf reached out and Zach handed him the lead rope for the mare, and he smiled as she followed along without him pulling the rope at all. Just before they reached camp, Ol' Red let out an extremely loud bray, letting the other horses and the rest of world know he was back home.

Shining Star with their baby in her arms and Sun Flower both ran to their husband and he wrapped his arms around them both. He was relieved to be back in the embrace of his two loving wives, but he lingered there for only a moment. He needed to get the heavy packs off the backs of Ol' Red and the pinto. He kissed his wives and Star then turned away to unload the faithful animals. Running Wolf was struggling with the heavy packs on the pinto as Zach walked up to help. Zach was a big man standing a bit over six feet tall and was several inches taller than Running Wolf. It was easier, by far, for him to lift the panniers high enough to get them off the sawbuck pack frame.

With the packs off and both animals rubbed down Running Wolf led them across the creek and out in the big meadow with the rest of the horses, stopping at the stream long enough for them to drink. Zach's feet were mighty sore. He had walked for three days in snow and mud and cold. They didn't hurt as bad as they had when they had almost frozen, but they were mighty tender, and he was glad his walking was over.

The three women went right to work caring for the meat. While Sun Flower and Raven Wing hung most of it in the smokehouse, Shining Star cut two roasts off and put them on the spit over the fire to cook. She took the boiling horse meat off and set it aside to cool and said, "Jimbo and Luna will enjoy that much more than us." She then turned and smiled at Zach saying, "We are glad you are back, my husband, we did not think you would be gone so long."

"I didn't want to be, but the buffalo were a long way away, and I found no other game closer," he replied.

Once the chores were all done, Running Wolf built up the side of the fire away from the cooking roasts. They all sat on their robes to listen to Zach tell them of his trip. There were looks of concern on their faces as he told them of the Cheyenne and how he had to go into their camp to get Ol' Red.

He told them of the morning after, of going back to the basin only to find wolves at the downed buffalo and of the wolves leaving, telling them that it was midmorning and the wolves all left just like they were being called away. Running Wolf asked, "What day was that?" Zach replied, "Three days ago." Running Wolf was silent for a minute, and so was Zach, he could tell his partner was pondering something. Then Running Wolf said, "Three days ago midmorning is when I butchered the horse. While I was doing that, Luna ran to the top of the hill where Sees Far is buried and howled for the longest time. It was not the same sound as when she howls at night; I even told Raven Wing it sounded like she was calling out to something, I believed she was calling for you and Jimbo to return, but maybe she called the wolves away from your buffalo."

Zach stared at the white wolf laying right beside Running Wolf. He didn't know what to make of this. Could Luna have known and indeed called the wolves away from his kills from nearly a hundred miles away? His wives and partner believed she had great powers, much more than an ordinary wolf. Running Wolf believed she was his spirit helper and Zach knew the two of them had an extremely tight bond, but then so did he and Jimbo but what Running Wolf was talking about here was much more than just a close bond. Luna would have had to know about the wolves and that he needed them to leave the kills. She then would have to be able to make them hear her from a hundred miles away.

Most Indians are very superstitious and found it much easier to believe in such things than Zach did. However, he had seen a lot in the years he had been living in this wilderness that he couldn't explain, and it seemed wolves were at the center of most of it. Running Wolf believed wolves had great power and that they could think and reason as well as a man, but he also thought they could control the minds of other animals as well. Many times in the past, Zach had seen things he couldn't quite explain, and he couldn't quite believe this was possible, but he couldn't disbelieve either.

After the buffalo meat was roasted they all enjoyed the first good fresh meat they'd had in months, then afterward they sat around the fire with Zach holding his baby girl until the chill of the night sent them to their lodges. Star had fallen asleep in his arms, and Shining Star took her daughter from his large, strong hands and put her to bed. Sun Flower added some wood to the small fire there in the center of their teepee.

Zach's feet were tender, and he winced as he sat down to pull the moccasins from his feet. Sun Flower told him to lay back and she would help him. As she slowly pulled the shoe off, he jumped slightly and then she saw the reddened skin with patches of the skin peeling from his foot. Shining Star knelt as well and asked, "Grizzly Killer, what has happened to your feet?"

As she started very carefully to remove the other moccasin, he sat up and saw both feet were red and looked raw. He then smiled at the two beautiful faces with worried looks staring at him and said, "I guess they got a little colder than I figured."

Shining Star got some bear grease, and the two women gently rubbed the oil into his sore feet. When they had finished, they helped him out of his warm winter buckskins, and he crawled into the soft robes of their bed. It felt so good to be at home. He smiled as he watched both his beautiful wives slip out of the soft doeskin dresses and slide their naked bodies up against his. He was back home and safe in the arms of his wives. His tired body was so relaxed he fell asleep at once.

When he opened his eyes the next morning and listened for the sounds of morning, there was light coming in from the smoke hole of their lodge. Sun Flower was still snuggled up next to him, but Shining Star and their baby were not there. He could hear the outside fire crackling and felt the warmth of the small fire she had started in the fire ring in the center of their teepee.

Sun Flower had felt him move slightly and smiled looking up into his blue eyes. He started to roll toward her for a kiss, but she stopped him and slid up onto him. While looking into each other's eyes, they kissed passionately and then made love. They laid there together for the longest time enjoying the warmth of their bodies and the love they shared, then with a slight smile she said, "I need to go help Shining Star and Raven Wing fix our morning meal." She started to push away, but he held her tight against him until she relented and they kissed again. He watched with pleasure as she stood in the dim morning light of their teepee and slipped her soft doeskin dress on, wrapped a blanket around her shoulders and stepped out.

Zach lay there alone listening to the sounds of his family outside as they started cooking more of the buffalo meat for their breakfast. His feet were sore enough that he wasn't in a hurry to stand upon them, but staying in the robes for very long was not something he was used to doing. He sat up and looked carefully at his feet, relieved to find the skin was peeling like a sunburn and nothing any more severe than that.

He was getting dressed when Shining Star brought him in a cup of pine needle tea. Since they had run out of coffee and now pemmican, their diet had been only meat. The Indians used the pine tea for something different in their diet. It also provided some of the nutrients they were missing from their meat-only diet. He sipped the hot tea from his tin cup and Shining Star smiled as he made a face, then said, "I know you do not like it my husband but drink it, it will make you feel better.

Shining Star knelt by him and looked at his peeling feet then rubbed a little more of the bear grease on them as he laid back again enjoying the attention. When she had the grease rubbed in she brought out a new pair of moccasins that she had made for him and said, "I made these for you for the coming spring. They are not as warm, but they will be better for your feet." He smiled, leaned forward and pulled her up against him. With his big rough hands on each side of her beautiful face, he stared into her dark eyes then kissed her waiting lips.

Zach remembered back when he had first met Shining Star and how he had thought about leaving her in her Ute village for he was already married to Sun Flower. He remembered the conflict within himself about being with two women at the same time. Because she was Running Wolf's sister and he had saved her from Black Hand, the Ute War Chief who had taken her, everyone expected him to take her for his second wife, even Sun Flower. He finally relented and made peace with himself. Now he couldn't imagine his life without her. He loved them both, and now he figured he was living his life just as he was meant to live it here in the vast, rugged wilderness of the Rocky Mountains.

How his life had changed. The thoughts kept coming as he held her close to him. He had expected to be a farmer and hunter in the woods of Kentucky, married to his childhood sweetheart, Emma Potter. He hoped Emma was as happy as he was.

He kissed Shining Star once more then released her. She stood and reached down to help him stand. He winced just slightly as he put his weight on his feet, but after he took a couple of steps, he smiled at her again, and said, "You are right, my love. These moccasins are so soft and fit so well they ain't rubbin' on my feet at all."

She beamed with pride that he was pleased and held open the door flap for him to go outside.

It was now what the Shoshone people call *yu'a-mea,* the warming moon, which he figured to be about the middle of March. The long, bitterly cold winter was nearly gone. He knew there would still be storms, he had even seen a foot of snowfall in June but the long dark bitter cold days of winter were gone for another year. For now, they had meat, and he hoped it would last until the game started to return to the meadows and hills near their home here on Black's Fork.

As he stepped out into the morning light Running Wolf was coming back from checking on the horses. He smiled when he saw that Zach was up and said, "Grizzly Killer, my brother, that beautiful mare you brought with you has fit right in with the herd and that big mule of yours acts like he's protectin' her."

Zach smiled already knowing those two animals had become friends on their journey home. He stood there and stared out at the meadow and herd knowing a few more days of sun and the snow would be gone from the meadow grass. The snow that fell from the storm four days ago was now gone, and there were only patches here and there in the meadow.

Zach walked over and picked up Star from her cradleboard and bounced her on his knee while the buffalo was heating up over the coals. She smiled at him with her sparkling blue eyes, and he lifted her above his head in the fashion she enjoyed so much. She had just finished nursing, and her full belly didn't like the quick movement. She spat up, which ran all down the side of his face and buckskins. Running Wolf started laughing as Shining Star and Sun Flower came running over to him. Once Star was safely in her mother's arms, Sun Flower and Zach walked over to the creek, and she helped him clean up in the icy water. When they walked back over to the fire Running Wolf was still chuckling, and the three women all had smiles on their faces.

Jimbo and Luna were out hunting together, and Zach was amazed that he hadn't heard them leave this morning. Just about the time the roasts from last night were good and warm, Zach saw Jimbo with Luna only a few yards behind him running for all she was worth trying to keep up with the big, long-legged dog. They were coming across the meadow from the west, Zach knew at once Jimbo had found someone or something he wanted to tell him about. As the Dog and white wolf came into camp, Jimbo ran right to Zach and growled his soft low growl from way down in his throat. That told not only Zach but Running Wolf and the women there was danger and immediately Shining Star and Raven Wing picked up the babies and took them into Grizzly Killer's lodge.

Sun Flower picked up the .36 caliber squirrel gun Zach had given her while he grabbed his Hawken and horse pistol. Running Wolf was ready with his Kentucky long rifle, and they crossed the stream following Jimbo and Luna out across the meadow at a fast jog. Zach's feet were mighty tender, but the new moccasins fit his feet well and were so soft they weren't rubbing on his sore, peeling feet.

They slowed down and crawled the last little ways to the top of the ridge that made up the west side of the meadow. Jimbo wanted them to hurry so with just a quick look and seeing nothing they continued jogging down through the quakies and patchy snow following the dog and wolf.

Zach figured they were between two and three miles from the dugout when Jimbo and Luna abruptly stopped in the small clearing just ahead of them. Both Zach and Running Wolf instinctively checked the powder in their pans and quietly snapped the frizzens in place then continued forward at a slow walk studying the area all around them carefully. As they approached where Jimbo and Luna were in the clearing, they could see the tracks of several horses moving in single file. Before another thought had time to form a gunshot echoed through the forest coming from the direction of their home.

Chapter 6

Cheyenne Captives

WITH ONLY A QUICK glance at one another Zach and Running Wolf, both started out in a hard run. Within seconds, Jimbo and Luna were nearly out of sight heading back to their lodges. Zach ignored the pain in his feet as he ran, but after a mile of hard running, they both had to slow their pace. Zach pushed himself until it felt like his lungs were going to burst, but they were still a couple of miles from home.

He silently cursed himself for leaving the women unprotected with both him and Running Wolf away. Although he knew they had done that countless times while hunting in this area that most of the Indians were now calling the land of Grizzly Killer. They were both nearly gasping for air as they crested the ridge on the west side of the big meadow. The first thing he saw when he crested the ridge was that their horses were gone. Ol' Red was still standing in the meadow, but the horses were all gone.

Without stopping, they continued, and Zach could see Jimbo was already at the lodges. Ol' Red was standing alone in the meadow with his head down, and he could see, at a glance, something was wrong with his trusted mule. When they were closer, he could see two arrows sticking out of the big mule's shoulder.

Near panic set in as he ran toward the lodges. He wanted to stop and care for Ol' Red, but their wives and babies were his main concern. Ol' Red barely raised his head as Zach ran by. They were only a couple of hundred yards from the lodges and still they could not see Sun Flower, Shining Star, or Raven Wing. With all the strength either of them had they ran on. Jimbo and Luna were by the fire and Zach could tell something on the ground held their attention.

It was Shining Star on the ground. Luna was laying right up against her while Jimbo gently licked her face. Grizzly Killer's heart nearly stopped as he jumped through the icy water of the stream and dropped to his knees beside his wife. Tears filled his eyes as he saw she was still breathing then he started looking for her wounds. Her hair was bloody, and he could see where the blood had trickled down her face, but Jimbo had licked that off. He gently felt around the wound, and as he did, she opened her eyes and moved. When her eyes focused and she saw Grizzly Killer's face above her, tears filled her dark brown eyes, but as she started to speak Running Wolf ran up in total panic and yelled, "They must have took the babies and the girls too! I can't find any of them. Shining Star tried to shake her head but the pain she felt stopped her. She then said in a weak but sure voice, "No, my brother, Gray Wolf, and Star are in their cradleboards under a buffalo robe under the big spruce just out of sight.

Running Wolf turned and bolted away as Zach picked up Shining Star and carried her into their lodge. Although she was taller and a little heavier than Sun Flower she still almost looked small against Zach's large frame. He had just got her laid on their bed robes when Running Wolf came through the door carrying a cradleboard in each hand. The babies were both sleeping soundly, and neither had been touched.

Shining Star smiled and said, "We heard them coming and hurried to hide the little ones." Her eyes then filled with tears as she said, "They took my sisters. I tried to stop them. Sun Flower shot one of them, but then another picked her up by the hair and threw her over his horse in front of him. I jumped at her and tried to pull her off, but they must have hit me, for I don't remember anything else.

Running Wolf looked like his whole world had just ended, as he stared at his sister and asked, "You didn't see what happened to Raven Wing?"

Again, tears rolled down her cheeks as she gently shook her head.

The cut in Shining Star's head was small, but the bump left by the warrior's club was large. Zach cleaned the cut, and by the time he was finished, Shining Star looked at him and with a strong and determined voice she said, "My husband, my brother; go and bring my sisters' home and kill every one of those that would attack our home."

At that moment, but for only an instant, she saw something in the eyes of her husband that almost scared her and in that instant, she knew he would not return without Sun Flower and Raven Wing.

Running Wolf looked into the eyes of his sister and asked, "How can I leave you, hurt and with the little ones?"

She just smiled up at him and said, "I will be fine. I have enough milk for both of them. I do not know how many there were that attacked us but there were too many for Grizzly Killer alone, and you have to get Sun Flower and Raven Wing."

He nodded, then looked at Zach saying, "I will get everything we need, you go and care for Ol' Red."

Zach looked into the eyes of Shining Star and then she could see nothing but love in his sky-blue eyes. He bent down and gently kissed her then stood and stepped outside.

To his surprise, Ol' Red was standing right outside their lodge with Jimbo on one side and Luna on the other. The arrows were buried deep into his shoulder, but there didn't seem to be a lot of blood. Zach walked up and looked at the arrows, confirming what he already figured. They were Cheyenne. He was sure it was the same ones he had fought just days ago, and now he wished he would have killed them all. The thought had his eyes glaze over, almost like in death, and he vowed he would not make that mistake again.

Ol' Red jumped a little from the pain as Zach pulled one, then the other Cheyenne arrow from his shoulder. The blood flowed freely from both wounds and Zach let it do so for a moment to help clean the inside. He then applied direct pressure until the bleeding stopped. Both babies were still sleeping, and Shining Star carefully stepped outside and walked over to see how bad Ol' Red was hurt. Zach looked at her with worried eyes, and she just smiled and said, "You go and bring my sister's home. I will take care of these wounds on Ol' Red."

Zach looked at her saying, "That is a nasty bump on your head, you shouldn't be up and moving." The look she had on her pretty face told Zach talking would do no good, they all would do what they must.

Although the big mule wanted to go, he knew he couldn't travel, and Zach patted him on his neck and said, "Not this time ol' friend, you stay and get better." With just a single blanket tied over their shoulders along with their possibles bag and weapons, Running Wolf and Zach were both ready to head out. Zach hesitated one more time turning back to Shining Star, but with a very determined look she said, "Go now, you must hurry and bring my sisters back."

As he looked over at Running Wolf with his bow and quiver over his back and Long Rifle in hand, he was on his knees with his white wolf. He told Luna to stay and watch over Shining Star and the babies. Luna whined for just a moment then licked his face and ran over and stood right beside Shining Star. With a look of determination Running Wolf looked up and said, "Grizzly Killer, we go now and do what must be done." Zach nodded and they headed out at a fast-paced jog on the trail that led down Black's Fork, the very path Zach had just come home on.

The Tracks of the Cheyenne's horses were plain and easy to follow. Jimbo ran out in the lead a couple of hundred yards scouting ahead, as he usually did. Zach was in the lead and set a pace that he thought both of them could stay with most of the day. He knew they would have to stop and rest in order the catch up with their wives and the Cheyenne. They would have to run hard and for longer each day than the Cheyenne could ride.

Many thoughts raced through his mind as he jogged along only occasionally glancing down at the tracks. Was Sun Flower and her sister hurt? Would the Cheyenne torture them, kill them, make them slaves, or take them for their own women? Zach had never seen two more beautiful sisters than Sun Flower and Raven Wing, and he knew the Cheyenne warriors would take advantage of them. With all these thoughts, his anger grew even stronger, and he vowed over and over again he would make them pay. As he jogged along, he realized that his rage would only hurt him, so he shook those thoughts from his mind. His mind needed to be clear and calculating to not only catch the fleeing Cheyenne and rescue their wives but to exact punishment for attacking their home and taking the women.

After covering about five miles, he stopped, and Running Wolf knelt and examined the tracks. He couldn't determine how many horses they were following; the tracks were all bunched together over the top of one another. He could see they weren't getting any older which meant so far, they were keeping up. He found a drop of blood just off to the side of the trail, and they both worried hoping it wasn't from their wives. Jimbo came running back to see why they had stopped and Zach could tell Jimbo was telling them to hurry.

Their rest stop lasted only a couple of minutes and when Zach said, "Let's go!"

Jimbo took off so fast he was a couple of hundred yards in the lead within seconds. Zach could feel his sore feet as he started out again and he knew they needed time to heal, but he couldn't stand the thought of Sun Flower or Raven Wing in the hands of those warriors that were out looking for revenge for what he had done to them.

Eight miles ahead of Zach and Running Wolf, nine Cheyenne hunters trotted their horses following Black's Fork as it flows to the northeast. The sixteen horses that made up Zach and Running Wolf's entire herd were being herded along in front of them. Raven Wing with her hands bound and a lead rope tied to the bindings was sitting behind a Cheyenne called Silent One. The lead rope was tied around his waist so she could not get more than a couple of feet from him. Sun Flower, however, was still thrown over a horse on her belly right in front of Black Otter. He was forcefully holding her there by her hair.

They had stopped only once for just a few minutes since they had taken the women and she had scratched and bitten him hard fighting to get away until he had beaten her into submission. Now she was forced to ride like this as punishment. Even though she was nearly unconscious, she could feel every bounce of the horse's gait, and she was in pain. The trotting gait of the horse had her stomach and ribs hurting terribly, and Black Otter would viciously jerk her head up and then back down every little while to make sure she knew he was in total control. Her lip was swollen and bleeding, and her left eye was going black and blue. She wanted to cry, but she knew she must show no fear. If they thought she was weak and afraid the beatings or torture would get much worse.

Sun Flower thought of Grizzly Killer and Running Wolf and knew they would be following. She longed to be in his strong and protective arms once again. Knowing Grizzly Killer and Running Wolf would be on foot she wondered how long it would take them to catch up. She did not believe these Cheyenne knew that they had raided the home of Grizzly Killer. She figured if they did they would be in a much bigger hurry than there were now. She couldn't understand their language, but by their actions, she felt the raid was not preplanned.

In fact, this was just a hunting party looking for game, although they were from the same Cheyenne village as the ones that had attacked Zach it was a different hunting party. This long hard winter had been hard on everyone living in this vast wilderness, and most people were traveling great distances looking for game. They had come into the land of Grizzly Killer and finding no game they came across these three beautiful women alone and had taken the opportunity to capture them. They would have taken all three of them, but Black Otter had used his war club on Shining Star as she was fighting to save Sun Flower, so they had thought she was dead.

Although the Cheyenne were not traveling fast, they kept the pace steady. Zach and Running Wolf were not able to gain any ground on them throughout the day. The only real advantage they had was the Cheyenne didn't know they were as close behind as they were.

They kept the pace steady until early evening then stopped for the night in a thick stand of cottonwoods. Silent One took the lead rope that was tied to Raven Wing's bound hands and tied it to a cottonwood branch and pulled it up tight so she would have to stand. Black Otter, however, just threw Sun Flower off the horse by the hair, she landed flat on her back knocking the breath from her lungs. Barely conscious she laid there gasping and tried to suck in the air she so desperately needed.

Raven Wing had never felt so helpless in all her life as she did now, seeing her younger sister suffer this way. Before she even got a breath back, Black Otter reached down and grabbed her hair, dragging her over to a tree by Raven Wing and tied her securely to it.

Raven Wing could do nothing but stand there with arms and hands firmly tied above her head. She wanted desperately to go to her sister and wished Sun Flower would not have fought so hard against the Cheyenne warrior.

One of the Cheyenne left on horseback riding along their back trail making sure no one was following. He rode back a little over five miles and finding no trace of anyone following went back and joined the rest.

The weather had warmed considerably since Zach had been through here just a couple of days ago but it was still freezing at night. Neither Sun Flower nor Raven Wing were given a robe of any kind. Raven Wing could dance around a little to stay warm, but Sun Flower was tied laying down and couldn't get off the frigid ground. By the time the Cheyenne had all the horses cared for, and on a picket line Sun Flower was fully conscious and shivering from the cold.

The Cheyenne built just a small fire, making sure it couldn't be seen unless someone was right there close. Then they sat around eating some dry jerky. After eating they rolled out their sleeping robes and got ready for the night. It wasn't long after that that Silent One walked over to Raven Wing and untied the rope that was holding her hands above her head and started to lead her to his robe. She stopped abruptly and without saying a word or without a warning of any kind he swung the end of the rawhide rope hitting her across the face. The sudden pain and shock caused her to react without thinking, and she kicked with every bit of strength she had connecting solidly with the center of his groin.

The pain he felt was so severe it took his breath away. He fell forward onto his knees with both hands now trying to protect his manhood. Raven Wing could think of nothing now but to fight and she kicked again this time connecting with the middle of his unprotected face. She felt his nose break, and he went over backward then she kicked one more time hitting him again in the groin.

He was in so much pain he couldn't breathe. He could see nothing but shooting lights behind his tightly closed eyes. The pain was so intense he started to retch and then gag. With her hands still bound she turned and ran out into the dark just as fast as she could run Moments later, two of the other Cheyenne were running after her.

Chapter 7

The Escape

ZACH AND RUNNING WOLF could not go on any longer. Neither of them wanted to stop, but after running most of the day their bodies could go no further, and they had to stop and rest. They found a protected grove of cottonwoods right along the river and stopped. Having not eaten anything at all during the day, their bodies needed food and rest. They left in such a hurry they hadn't brought anything at all with them. Even though the buffalo was warm and still on the spit over the fire, neither of them had thought to bring it.

They dared not build a fire for if the Cheyenne were diligently checking their back trail they didn't want to be seen. It was near dark as they rolled out their blankets to get a few hours rest. Although they were physically exhausted from their day-long run, their minds were on their wives. Zach's mind couldn't slow the thought of what a group of enemy warriors could be doing to his beloved Sun Flower Woman. She was his first wife and ever since the day he had rescued her, Raven Wing, and their friend Butterfly, he had loved and protected her. He blamed himself for not being there, but deep down he knew, living in this wilderness there was no way to protect everyone all the time. But this was different, for he knew the warriors that had taken them were Cheyenne and he thought he must have led them right back to their home.

Exhaustion finally overtook his troubled mind, and he dozed off to sleep. Jimbo silently left his master and moving like a shadow through the night, followed the Cheyenne's trail nearly to where they were camped.

Jimbo was about a mile from the Cheyenne camp when he stopped dead still and lifted his head scenting the air. His keen nose had caught the slight scent of a familiar smell. As his nose worked through the hundreds of aromas on the breeze drifting upstream, his hearing caught the soft footsteps of someone running his way. He knew the footsteps were still some ways away, so he ran on, not as fast as before but with all his finely tuned senses focused on the trail ahead.

After running another quarter mile, the smell was much stronger now and the footsteps much louder, but there were stranger smells as well and the steps were of more than one person. He knew the smell was Raven Wing and he instinctively knew she was in trouble.

The two Cheyenne warriors that started out after Raven Wing at first thought this was a fun game. They had not realized how strong and athletic Raven Wing was. She had grown up competing with her brother Spotted Elk who was now the War Chief in the Shoshone village of

Charging Bull. She competed in races against not only her brother but with most of the young men in their village, and she was always one of the fastest.

It had now been nearly two hours since she had kicked Silent One and had run away from her captors and the two Cheyenne chasing her were now getting tired and angry. She fought with the bindings on her hand as she moved and thought about Sun Flower still back with the Cheyenne, beaten and laying there and tied to the tree. She felt terrible about leaving her there alone but knew she had to get back to the little ones.

Her legs were tiring, and her chest hurt from gulping in the vast quantities of air she needed to run that far that fast. Knowing she had to rest soon and not able to hear the Cheyenne behind her at that moment she jumped off the trail and ran a quarter mile into the short sage and laid down flat. She knew she was well hidden, but she was also damp from sweat from the run. The breeze was only slight, but against her damp skin, was mighty cold. She started to shiver.

Jimbo still running silent as a ghost was forming a picture of what was ahead in his mind. The only information he had was the scent coming to him on the slight breeze and the sounds from his keen hearing, but he knew from those scents and the faint sounds of footsteps that strangers were chasing Raven Wing. The hair on the back of his neck started to stand up as he ran along and a nearly silent growl began to rumble softly.

He was concentrating on the smell of the strangers and ran past where Raven Wing had jumped from the trail. The scent of the strangers on the breeze was coming to him much stronger now. He slowed and then stopped, dropping to his belly.

Silent One had managed to slowly crawl over to their fire and laid there in the dirt barely within the warmth of the fire. Black Otter had tried to help him, but Silent One refused the help, he was embarrassed that he had let this happen. He was furious at Raven Wing and himself that he had allowed a squaw to do that to him and he wanted revenge. The sharp sickening pain had subsided unless he tried to move, so he laid there motionless thinking of the ways he was going to make the squaw pay but that would come later, after Wounded Elk and Long Shadow brought her back.

He could now feel the swelling between his legs and when he moved even slightly the pain shooting up through his lower body was unbearable. He laid on his back with his legs apart waiting for the swelling and pain to stop. Several hours passed and yet Long Shadow and Wounded Elk did not return. He could now move a little but still had to be careful, for the swelling was still there.

Sun Flower had seen her sister kick Silent One and make her escape, and her heart was glad Raven Wing had gotten away. She still feared for her sister for she knew if the warriors that went after her caught her it would surely mean a slow and painful death. She knew, too, how fast of a runner Raven Wing was and in the dark, she didn't think they would catch her. The side of her face was bruised and sore. Her eye now black and blue was nearly swollen shut. She knew Grizzly Killer and Running Wolf would be on the trail behind them but how far back? They had come so far today, and she knew her husband and brother-in-law were on foot. She was shivering from the cold, her belly and ribs were bruised and tender. Her scalp hurt from Black Otter pulling her around by her hair all day. She closed her eyes and tried to call to Grizzly Killer with her thoughts and waited for him to come. She knew he would come. She just didn't know how long it might take.

Jimbo stayed down on his belly waiting as the footsteps got closer. The strangers weren't running now they were looking through the brush. He couldn't smell the familiar smell of Raven Wing on the air anymore and didn't know why, but the scent of the strangers was getting stronger.

Raven Wing had rested for several minutes now and she was cold and shivering, so she got up and started out again into the cold night. She knew the Cheyenne would still be following her, so she headed out farther away from the trail and river. Soon she was over a half mile from the river. Just like her sister, she knew her husband and Grizzly Killer would be following, and she longed to find them. She jogged on into the early hours of the morning but staying well off the trail.

Wounded Elk was approaching where Jimbo lay crouched into the brush. He was frustrated they had not found this fighting Shoshone squaw, and he could not find her trail in the darkness. He and Long Shadow had been looking now for most of the night. He could not believe a squaw could have run away from them. He thought she had to be hiding somewhere behind them, so he stopped to turn back. He heard only a slight scraping of the brush as Jimbo leaped. Then, almost instantly, he felt the mighty jaws on his neck. Jimbo's weight carried him to the ground. He tried to yell for Long Shadow, but no air came from his lungs as Jimbo's powerful jaws clamped down on his throat. He felt a bad tearing and immense pain then a wave of warmth as his warm blood flowed freely over his chest. He was looking up and wondered why the stars were slowly fading out of sight.

Jimbo stopped for only a moment as the strong scent of the fresh blood filled his senses. He knew he was a long way from his master and he couldn't smell the scent of Raven Wing any longer. Without any hesitation, and just as silently as he had come, Jimbo headed back to Grizzly Killer and Running Wolf.

Long Shadow heard Jimbo's attack but he was over a hundred yards away and in the darkness, could not see a thing. It took several minutes for him to find Wounded Elk. He nearly stumbled over him when he did. With only the light from the stars and a waning moon, it took another moment for him to realize Wounded Elk's throat had been completely ripped out, his sightless eyes still staring at the stars. With his knife in hand, Long Shadow carefully looked all around, but he couldn't see or hear anything out in the night. He headed back to their camp to get the others to help.

Raven Wing continued to put distance between herself and the Cheyenne. How she wished she knew where Running Wolf was. She longed to be in his strong arms, but she was more concerned with Gray Wolf and Star for they had hidden the babies just before the Cheyenne had attacked. She had seen the warrior hit Shining Star with his war club and had seen her go down. If she was dead Grizzly Killer and Running Wolf would think the Cheyenne had taken the babies too. She feared the two helpless little ones were still under the low branches of the pine they had hidden them under. She couldn't put that thought out of her mind, and she pushed through the darkness heading back to their home knowing that Running Wolf and Grizzly Killer would be somewhere on the trail in pursuit.

As the darkness started to fade into the gray light of early dawn, Raven Wing was still twenty-five miles from home. She was cold and exhausted, but the thought of the little ones kept her moving on. She hadn't had anything to eat since the Cheyenne had taken her and she worried that the babies hadn't either. She could feel the pressure in her full breasts as they bounced while she jogged along and knew her son and Star needed the nourishing milk. Tears filled her eyes as she thought of Sun Flower left there tied to that tree, beaten and bruised. She hoped the Cheyenne didn't take out their anger with her on her sister. As bad as she felt for leaving Sun Flower behind, getting back to the little one was more important. Then there was Shining Star—her Ute Sister the Cheyenne had left for dead. The more she thought about what had happened, the more determined she became to continue until she was home.

The lump on Shining Star's head throbbed with every heartbeat. She was having spells of extreme weakness and dizziness and at one point had passed out for a little while, but she had nursed both babies, changed the soiled packing of their cradleboards and had them sleeping safely. She knew she needed to eat, but she was nauseous, and so light headed she didn't feel like going out to the fire and getting the buffalo off the spit. She just sat there in the teepee on the buffalo robe with the little ones and waited for her strength or Grizzly Killer and Sun Flower to return.

Deep in her heart was fear, would Grizzly Killer catch the Cheyenne in time. She knew Grizzly Killer would not return without his first wife because of how he loved her. She could feel the love he had for them both, and it made her feel good knowing he had done the same for her. She knew however that their enemies were mounted and he and Running Wolf were on foot.

Shining Star had been taken once herself by Black Hand the War Chief of the Sahpeech band of Utes. It was Grizzly Killer and her brother Running Wolf that had tracked them down then Grizzly Killer had killed Black Hand in a knife fight. That was the first time she had ever seen Grizzly Killer, he had saved her that day from a man she did not want anything to do with, and she knew he would do the same for Sun Flower.

Her mind was clear, but her vision was blurry then it would clear and once again become blurred. She feared for all of them. Black Hand had been alone, but Sun Flower and Raven were taken by a full Cheyenne war party, and that was a lot even for men with as powerful of medicine as Grizzly Killer and Running Wolf.

She needed to lay down and sleep, but she had to care for the babies. She was afraid if she went to sleep she may not wake if the little ones needed her. Gray Wolf started crying, and that woke up Star as well. They wanted out of the cradleboards so they could crawl around the teepee. It took all her strength, but she freed them from their boards and smiled as they played with one another.

After she nursed the babies one more time and laid them down to sleep, she went out to care for the wounds in Ol' Red. She was still fighting the spells of dizziness, but they seemed to be less as time went by. She found Raven Wings medicine kit and picked the healing plants as Raven Wing had taught her and mixed a poultice. Ol' Red shook slightly as she packed the thick green paste into the deep arrow wounds. As she turned to go back inside with the little ones she got dizzy and collapsed right there at the entrance to their lodge.

It was still a couple of hours before dawn when Long Shadow jogged into the Cheyenne camp and told everyone that Wounded Elk was dead, that it appeared a wolf had attacked him. Long Shadow and Black Otter got Wounded Elk's horse then mounted their horses and went out to retrieve the body. Sun Flower was still shaking from the cold, and she hurt all over, but she would not give them the satisfaction of knowing how bad she was hurting.

When Long Shadow and Black Otter returned with Wounded Elk's body draped over his horse the others were ready to ride. Silent One was still by the fire, and two of the others helped him mount his horse, he straddled the mustang very slowly and moved around until he found a position that he thought would allow him to ride. Oh, how he wanted to get his hands on that Shoshone squaw, he thought. When he had finished with her, she would never again be able to kick another man.

Black Otter led one of the other horses over to Sun Flower and untied her tether from around the tree and motioned for her to climb up on the horse. Although the pain nearly took her breath away, she wouldn't let it show on her bruised and battered face. She just grabbed hold of the horse's mane and jumped up on him. She bit her lip against the pain in her ribs, belly, and head as she did so but she never let it show. He then untied the lead from her hands, tied a loop in it and placed it around her neck tying the other end around his wrist.

They moved out still following Black's Fork towards the Seeds-Kee-Dee. They were well out onto the flatlands by the time the sky started to lighten along the eastern horizon.

Zach and Running Wolf were up when Jimbo came running back to camp. The big dog came right up to Zach and started with his low deep growl letting Zach know he had found the Cheyenne. Zach looked up at the night sky and prayed that they were not all that far ahead.

The sun was up when they reached the spot where Jimbo at attacked and killed Wounded Elk. Running Wolf tried to make out what had happened, but the horses had nearly destroyed the tracks from Black Otter and Long Shadow loading up the body. If Running Wolf had looked just seventy-five yards north of the trail, he would have found Raven Wing's footprints running away from them all.

When they got to the Cheyenne's camp, the sun was now well above the horizon. They studied the campsite thoroughly finding where Silent One had fallen and then crawled to the fire. They saw the trees where the women were tied. Zach's heart nearly broke when he found blood where Sun Flower was tied. He knew it was her because she had drawn a small medicine wheel in the dirt by the tree to let him know she was alive. They could even see where she had jumped up on the horse, but they could find no sign of Raven Wing. The horses had destroyed the tracks where she had run out into the night.

Running Wolf was worried as he looked to the east. Where was his wife, the mother of his son? He had to believe she was still with them for they had seen no sign anything had happened to her on the trail. He figured the Cheyenne were now five or six hours ahead of them and moving faster the than he and Grizzly Killer could run.

Chapter 8

The Trail East

THE CHEYENNE HEADED due east leaving Black's Fork as it flowed its way northeast and headed across the dry baron flatlands. They would hit the river again as it turned back to the south before it joined the waters of the Seeds-Kee-Dee, but they thought this would save them time heading back to their village.

Their village was located on what the Cheyenne call *Minnii'yohe', Moon Shell River,* known to the trappers as the North Platte, south of where the Sweetwater joins it. Black Otter's hunting party had been a failure. They had not found the buffalo, elk, antelope, or deer their village so desperately needed. They had found a small camp with women and were taking them back so their trip of over two hundred miles to the west would not be a total loss. Even that had been a near failure, they'd had to kill one woman, and another had escaped. Wounded Elk was dead, and Silent One could barely ride because of his bruised and swollen manhood.

Black Otter's mood was dark and that mood spread through the other Cheyenne as well. Sun Flower for the first time was now fearful for her life. She thought the anger they all felt at some point would be taken out on her. She had noticed Silent One staring at her several times throughout the morning, but she couldn't tell if it was hatred or desire that was in his eyes.

Black Otter had not let go of the rope around her neck as they had traveled east, but to her relief, he hadn't been cruel with it either. Sun Flower was glad they were only moving at a walk. She thought that was because Silent One would not be able to take the bouncing of a faster gait. She smiled thinking that Raven Wing kicking him the way she had would help Grizzly Killer catch up to them.

They stopped at midday, and Black Otter sent two of them to check their back trail. He then walked up to Sun Flower and in sign asked her name. Knowing not to make him angry again she made the sign for Sun and then Flower. He stared at her for a moment then gave her a piece of jerky and walked away dropping the rope as he did so.

She watched Silent One, through her one open eye, very slowly slid off his horse and then walk away keeping his legs apart which brought a smile to her inside. She hoped Grizzly Killer would catch up before he healed for that would mean one less he would have to fight.

Raven Wing ran toward home setting a grueling pace, but by midmorning, she had to stop to rest, but even as she rested, she walked knowing each step was one step closer to her child and home. She started to jog again, then walked, she found she could cover more ground by changing back and forth between walking and jogging than by running until she had to stop completely to rest. By midday, she was still eight or ten miles from home, but she pushed on.

By late afternoon her legs were too weak to continue, she knew she must stop and rest. She got down on her belly and drank long and slow from the icy waters of Black's Fork and tried to guess how much farther to get home. In her mind was the little ones hidden under that big pine back behind their lodges and the buffalo robe they had thrown over them. Then the vision of Shining Star laying there by the fire after the Cheyenne warrior had brought his war club down upon her.

With these thoughts in her mind, she felt a strength she had never felt before, a force that must have been given her by the great-spirit for she got back to her feet and continued. Only a few minutes later the hill at the end of the big meadow came into view, and she knew she was less than a mile from home.

Zach and Running Wolf started out on the trail, and as always, Jimbo was well out in the lead. It wasn't long until they could tell the Cheyenne horses had slowed to just a walk. They both knew they could go no faster than they were or they would never last out the day. They continued their even paced jog, hour after hour, across the barren landscape after their wives.

When they came to where the Cheyenne had stopped, by checking the horse dropping they both thought they might have gained a little on them, but there was no doubt their wives were still miles ahead. They both were getting weak—this was the second day with no food. The snow was gone in this area, and they had seen where some antelope had crossed heading north. Neither of them wanted to take the time to hunt, but they knew they would never catch the Cheyenne and get their wives if they became too weak to keep up with them, but they continued.

This country was dry, they were now far enough from the mountains the snow was gone, and they carried no water with them. From where they were they both knew it was another twelve to fifteen mile-run to get to the river. They needed food, water and rest, and the thought of what the enemy warriors were doing to their wives was nearly more than either of them could stand.

Zach hoped the Cheyenne would spend some time by either Black's Fork or the Seeds-Kee-Dee giving him and Running Wolf time to catch up. He now knew this was going to be a much harder chase than he had hoped for and they could not keep up this pace without food or water.

Jimbo once again returned to them, but this time he had a rabbit in his mouth. They stopped once they got to a shallow wash and built a small hand sized fire in the bottom of it. The rabbit was still half raw when they ate it, then pushed on.

Late afternoon found them on the western breaks of Black's Fork on their bellies looking down at the river. The vegetation along the river was sparse here, and they could see no sign the Cheyenne had stopped. They were getting to their feet when Jimbo growled. They froze, and a moment later a small herd of antelope came into view. They were slowly moving toward them, grazing on the sage and dry grass as they moved along. Zach checked the wind, but the air was barely moving. Another five minutes and they would be in range of his trusted Hawken.

Would firing the gun warn the Cheyenne they were being followed? Running Wolf very slowly started to raise his rifle, but Zach reached out and stopped him. He then whispered the Cheyenne might hear the shot. Running Wolf still moving very slowly lowered the gun and started to slide his bow from off his back, but the wary, sharp-eyed little prairie goats saw the movement and bolted away back from where they came. Not a word was spoken as they watched the dozen or so antelope run out of sight. It would be another day with no substantial food.

There wasn't much daylight left as they approached the river. Now Running Wolf had his bow in hand with his rifle slung over his back. They approached slowly hoping there would be game of some kind by the water. A flock of ducks took to the air but nothing they could get a shot at. It was plain for them to see where the Cheyenne pushing Zach and Running Wolf's horses had crossed the river, but they could see no tracks made by the small feet of Sun Flower or Raven Wing.

Black Otter still held the lead rope that was around Sun Flower's neck as they pushed on east. They had stopped barely long enough to let the horses drink as they crossed Black's Fork, he wanted to make it to the Seeds-Kee-Dee before dark. Sun Flower's eye was still swollen shut and was still very painful, as was that whole side of her face. Silent One had not spoken a word all day, and although he was still cautious how he sat on the horse, Sun Flower could tell it was getting easier for him to ride.

She wondered about Raven Wing, had she found Grizzly Killer and Running Wolf, had she made it back to their home. She wanted to cry but knew she could show no weakness to her captors. There was no doubt in her mind her husband was behind them, but how far. How far would they travel before he would catch them and what might happen to her before he did? Black Otter had treated her better today, but the bruises from yesterday were still painful. She did not know any of the Cheyenne tongue and had no idea where they were going or anything else that was being said.

It was nearly dark when they come down off the breaks west of the Seeds-Kee-Dee. Black Otter stopped in a stand of cottonwoods on a big bend of the river. Sun Flower didn't move until he motioned her to get off the horse then came over and untied the rawhide from her wrists. She rubbed her hands getting the blood flowing through them again, then walked over to the river and washed her face and drank of the cold, clear water.

The lead rope was still tied around her neck, but Sun Flower did not try to remove it, she did not want to bring on the anger of Black Otter again. Silent One was watching her as she made her way back to where they were building a fire. She still could not tell what he was thinking, he scared her more than the others, but she wasn't sure why. After the horses were cared for the warriors, all come to the fire. They were talking more tonight than at any time since they had taken her and she wondered why. She noticed all of them except Silent One had something to say.

Black Otter wanted to build a burial scaffold for Wounded Elk in the trees here along the Seeds-Kee-Dee, but some of the others thought they should take him back to Cheyenne lands to be buried. Sun Flower did not know what they were discussing, but she could tell by their tone it was important. After their discussion was over, they chewed on dry buffalo jerky but none of them offered her a piece.

Raven Wing's legs felt like they would no longer support her as she entered the clearing of their home and stopped. The first thing she saw was Ol' Red standing over the unmoving body of Shining Star with Luna lying alongside as she lay on the ground in front of her teepee. She then heard a baby whimpering and tried to rush forward, but her legs didn't react as fast as her body had and she fell forward, hitting the ground hard.

Shining Star heard her fall and opened her eyes. She wasn't sure why she was laying on the ground, and she didn't know what had awakened her. She lifted her head off the ground and moaned softly from the throbbing pain that started in her head but seemed too radiant down through her neck and shoulders. Then she could hear the little ones inside beginning to cry, and she tried to overcome the dizziness to go to them. Another sound came to her. It was Raven Wing's voice coming to her from behind.

Raven Wing's legs were so weak she was having a hard time standing, so she crawled from where had fallen to Shining Star. Her heart rejoiced when she saw Shining Star move for she thought she was dead. She called her name and when Shining Star slowly turned her head toward her tears of joy filled her eyes. Shining Star smiled a slight smile then said in a weak voice, "The little ones are inside."

Raven Wing put her hand on Shining Star's cheek, the lump on the side of her head had grown so much her face was swollen, and the whites of her eyes were bloodshot. Seeing Shining Star like this brought back the sight of

Sun Flower's swollen and battered face. She hoped that after Grizzly Killer rescued her, he and Running Wolf would exact a terrible revenge on the Cheyenne warriors that had done this to her family.

Zach and Running Wolf both knew they could not run as they had for another day without the energy a good meal would provide. They had to make meat and along this river was a good place to look for it. They could tell by the tracks drying in the mud that they were now a full half day behind the Cheyenne, too far now to hear a gunshot. They split up with Zach and Jimbo going upstream and Running Wolf going downstream. A soft whistle told Jimbo to stay close, and the big dog stayed right by his side.

Zach figured he had gone a little over a mile when a doe and yearling fawn broke from the trees along the river and ran out through the brush. With the liquid like motion that came from a lifetime of practice, he brought up his Hawken and with a smooth follow through dropped the yearling before either deer reached the bottom of the break.

Running Wolf was watching five antelope on a hillside still a few hundred yards away when he heard the faint report of Grizzly Killer's rifle. He had taken the three eagle feathers from his hair getting ready to try and flag the antelope to him, but after hearing Grizzly Killer shoot, he turned and headed back. There was no doubt in his mind if Zach shot he had hit his target for he knew how good Grizzly Killer was with a rifle.

As he walked back toward the river crossing, he thought back to when Zach had taught him to shoot a gun and how bad he had been at first. Zach had been patient and persistent enough that now Running Wolf himself was deadly accurate with his own Kentucky long rifle, but the past was past and the memories of that time would have to wait. His loving Raven Wing and her sister Grizzly Killer's first love were with a war party of Cheyenne and what they must be going through was foremost in his mind.

He started a small fire when he got back to the crossing and waited for Zach to get back. It wasn't long before Jimbo came running up to the fire with Zach carrying the back straps off the deer and one hind quarter only a couple of hundred yards behind. Within minutes they had the meat roasting. For over two days now they had only shared a small, tough rabbit and as the meat cooked the smell made both of their bellies start to growl.

After eating their fill, they cooked the remaining meat for morning and what they couldn't eat they would carry with them

The two of them were exhausted, it had been two full days of running, and in doing so, they had covered over sixty miles. Now, with their hunger sated, they laid down by the warm fire and were asleep within minutes. Jimbo had eaten most of the liver when Zach had gutted the deer, and he too curled up by the fire and slept. The last thing Zach heard were the coyotes yipping somewhere downstream from them.

Zach felt Jimbo lick his face and he heard the familiar low growl that comes from way down in the big dog's chest. He was alert at once and had his hand on his Hawken. Once Zach was awake Jimbo took off out into the darkness heading upstream. He woke Running Wolf and then fixed his blanket best he could to look like he was still under it and had Running Wolf do the same. He then put a couple more logs on the fire and he and

Running went out into the brush away from the light of the fire to wait. Neither of them knew what Jimbo was concerned about, but they both had faith in the big medicine dog.

Only minutes later Zach heard the ever so soft sound of buckskins scraping against a branch. A moment later two shadows were moving toward the fire and then he heard the soft twang of a bowstring. Just as the sound of arrows striking their blankets came to his ears, he heard Jimbo's vicious attack a couple of hundred yards upstream.

Chapter 9

Attack in the Night

THE BRIGHT FLASH of powder igniting in the pan of his Hawken momentarily blinded Zach as he squeezed off his shot, but even before he could see, again he dove off into the darkness just as an arrow split the air where he had been standing. He hit the ground and rolled as another blinding flash of light broke through the night—a shot from Running Wolf's rifle.

Zach laid there in the darkness without moving. He didn't know if either his or Running Wolf's shot had hit their mark. He needed to reload but knew the movement would bring attention to his current position. His pistol was tucked into his waistband, he had put it there when he fixed his bed, but now he was lying right on top of it. He didn't want to move for it might give away his position, so he stayed still, waiting for his eyes to adjust once again to the darkness.

As his eyes slowly adjusted, he could see a body lying on the other side of the fire, but there was no other movement or sound. He wondered if these were the Cheyenne that had taken Sun Flower and Raven Wing, was his wife close? Had they doubled back in the night to catch them unaware? Was Sun Flower alright? What was Jimbo doing? He knew he had to shake these questions from his troubled mind to better face the danger right before him.

Several minutes passed, and he hadn't heard a sound. Ever so slowly he rolled enough to pull the pistol from his belt. Still, he heard no sounds. Jimbo had not returned, and he wondered again about his dog. More time passed with no sounds coming to him except the soft sounds of the water as it flowed on toward the Seeds-Kee-Dee. He had always had patience. When hunting, he could sit motionless for hours on end. But this was different. If Sun Flower was near, he must find her before these Cheyenne rode off with her again. In his mind, he figured this had to be the same warriors that had taken her. Very slowly and with as much care as possible he got to his feet. After slowly stepping behind a tree he slipped the pistol back under his belt and reloaded his Hawken. Knowing Running Wolf was off to his left he started moving to his right toward the river.

Long Arrow the Crow warrior that had shot the arrows into Zach's sleeping robe couldn't believe he and the other warriors he rode with had been fooled. They were on their first horse stealing raid of the year, and as they were setting their camp for the night, he had caught just a whiff of smoke from Zach and Running Wolf's fire, so the five of them came to investigate. He saw there were only two of them and they were asleep by the fire so he knew it would be easy to kill them and steal their horses and supplies. He hadn't even taken the time to find they had no horses before he and Buffalo Calf snuck in and shot arrows into their empty blankets. Now Buffalo Calf was dead, and he heard a wolf or dog attack behind him. All he could think about now was getting back to where Fire Maker was holding the horses.

Zach paused as he got to the river's edge but only for a moment as his eyes strained to see into the darkness ahead. He started forward again skillfully moving around the brush making no sound at all. A sound came to him from the far side of the fire, and he paused again, then another sound but this time he could tell it was a man falling to the ground.

He wondered if Running Wolf was hurt but knew his Ute brother could take care of himself. He continued upstream still not seeing or hearing anything at all in front of him. He had expected Jimbo to be coming to him so now he wondered about him as well. He then heard the faintest sound—footsteps just ahead and off to his left. He listened. It was one man creeping through the brush. Now he hurried. If there was a chance he could catch this enemy he could find where Sun Flower was being held. He was moving faster now, speed giving way to silence. His left foot came down on a stick, and it snapped before he could stop. It wasn't a loud sound, but to Zach, it sounded as if it echoed through the night.

Long Arrow's sharp ears picked up the snapping twig and broke into a full run to get away from whoever it was following him. When Zach heard him run he did the same. In places, the underbrush was thick and running full out in the dark of night through the brush and trees was hazardous.

Zach's feet were powering through most of the undergrowth, but he tripped on a downed branch, and that sent him sliding to a stop on the side of his face. Long Arrow heard Zach fall and was surprised how close it sounded. He thought he was getting close to Fire Maker and the horses, so he ran on into the dark.

Zach didn't bother with the scratches on his face as he bounced back to his feet, but he knew whoever it was he was chasing would have heard his fall. Long Arrow was now nearly a hundred yards in front of Zach, but in the dark, he couldn't tell for sure how much farther it was to reach his friend and the horses.

Long Arrow started slowing and straining his eyes to tell just where he was. He knew he was now much farther ahead of whoever was chasing him and he figured he had to be close to Fire Maker. He whistled like a bird letting Fire Maker know it was him coming to him when he tripped and fell over Fire Maker's lifeless body.

Zach heard something ahead then the sound of running stopped, he slowed to a walk not wanting to run headlong into an ambush. Still moving but now very slowly he continued toward where he had heard the sound. He was aware of the danger ahead, in the darkness and this thick brush under the cottonwoods that bordered the river the enemy could be anywhere waiting for him. The thought of Sun Flower was still with him even though he knew it was clouding his judgment; he couldn't shake the image of her from his troubled mind.

Long Arrow seen Fire Maker was dead, he was lying in a large pool of his own blood. He shook off the shock, and then he wondered, how did this enemy get in front of him to be able to kill Fire Maker? He never did see any horses, and no one would be camped this far from a village without horses. Was it really men they had attacked? Or had the spirits tricked them in the darkness of this night.

For the first time since he was a child, Long Arrow was afraid. He had faced an enemy many times in battle without fear, but this was different. This enemy must be able to see into the darkness. How could they have killed Fire Maker and yet still be behind them? He then remembered hearing a wolf attack, and he knew then what had happened to his friend. He became even more afraid wondering if those they attacked were spirits that could change into the body of a wolf for he knew a wolf would not attack a man for no reason. He glanced around him wondering if the spirit wolf was nearby. He listened but could no longer hear the man that had been pursuing him. The longer he waited, the more the darkness seemed to close in around him. It felt like a heavy blanket holding him down that he couldn't see through. He wished they would have never made this journey so far from the safety of their Absaroka home.

Zach was aware the warrior he had been chasing had stopped so he didn't pursue any further. Moving like a ghost in the night, he turned toward the river and continued upstream until he was sure he was behind where the enemy must be waiting for him. Circling behind the warrior he hoped to come up behind him instead of walking into the ambush he was sure was there.

There were many thoughts now going through Long Arrow's mind. Where were his other two friends that had gone to the camp with him to steal horses? Where were their horses that Fire Maker had been holding? Could spirits use the white man's guns? He knew spirits could change into animals but could a white man's spirit do the same or did this spirit turn into a white man just like he had turned into a wolf. The spirit out there in this darkness must be from a white man to kill Buffalo Calf with a white man's gun. Where had this spirit gone, why could he no longer hear the man chasing him, had he changed from a white man back into a wolf?

With his courage waning Long Arrow wanted to run. He had never been afraid in battle, and death did not scare him. But he couldn't fight evil spirits that tried to keep him from traveling the warrior's path to the land beyond. What had they done for *Akbaatatdia,* Maker of All Things Above to let this evil spirit come among them? These were the thoughts and questions running through him as he felt a presence behind him. He hadn't heard a thing, but when he turned to look, he saw a large white man pointing his deadly gun right at him.

Zach had used all the skill that a lifetime of living in the wilderness could teach him as he snuck up behind Long Arrow. He moved ever so slowly making no sound at all. Long Arrow believed the big white man was an evil spirit that had just appeared because no man could come in that close without making a sound.

Long Arrow very slowly laid his bow on the ground then Zach motioned for him to do the same. Zach stepped back a step and then motioned him to get to his feet. As he stood Zach could tell even as dark as it was this warrior was not a Cheyenne, this was a Crow he did not doubt that. Disappointment flooded through him as he realized Sun Flower was not close by.

Zach had fought the Crow before, that first winter coming to the mountains with Gen. Ashley a large party of Crows had attacked them and stolen 17 of the horses. That fight was the first time Zach had ever killed a man.

He wondered if these warriors were from a much larger party, like the one he had fought against those years ago with General Ashley and his Pa and if so where they might be.

Long Arrow wasn't nearly as tall and Zach but was wide across the shoulders and even in the darkness Zach could tell he was powerfully built and was glad he hadn't had to fight him. He could tell by the way he was looking at Zach it would be a fight to the death and it still may be. A sound came to them both out of the darkness from the south, and both men glanced that way. Then came a familiar whistle from Running Wolf and Zach answered. A few moments later, even though they could not be seen, the footsteps of two men yet were plain to hear as they approached.

Zach knew one of them was Running Wolf from the whistle and had assumed the other was going to be another Crow. A moment later they could see shadows moving in the darkness and then Running Wolf appeared pushing another Crow in front of him. This Crow had one of Running Wolf's arrows sticking from his right shoulder. As of yet, no one had said a word. Zach could see well enough that this wounded warrior was in a lot of pain. Although his face was expressionless, the pain showed in his eyes.

Zach asked as they walked up, "Are there any others, brother?"

Running Wolf shook his head no. He then looked around and saw the dead warrior laying in the brush and simply asked, "Jimbo?" Zach nodded then Running Wolf continued, "Where is he?"

Zach replied, "Haven't seen him since we came upon this here dead one."

Running Wolf's response was with a definite tone of caution, "Then there may be more of 'em."

Zach just nodded and said, "Let's find out."

They moved through a small clearing in the brush and came upon Long Arrow and the body of Fire Maker. By pointing with his rifle, he led their two prisoners back a few yards into the clearing and made then sit down. The wounded one was light-headed from loss of blood and required help to keep from falling.

Running Wolf said, "Grizzly Killer, this one I shot is still bleeding. He will not live long if it don't stop."

Both Crow warriors recognized the name Grizzly Killer when Running Wolf said it. They looked at one another wondering how they could have attacked the camp of the great Grizzly Killer. Both had heard all the stories of the great white warrior and knew his medicine was powerful. Long Arrow knew then that Fire Maker was killed by the great Medicine Dog not a wolf. These weren't spirits after all. Now he had seen firsthand the medicine of Grizzly Killer was more powerful than any other warrior he had heard of.

Long Arrow expected to die. He had made a fatal mistake, and in his mind, he was preparing to die. Then the tall white man knelt by Kicking Dog and started helping him with the arrow that was buried deep in his shoulder. Some of the stories he had heard about Grizzly Killer said he was fair and did not like killing. Could these stories be true? Would he not kill them and take their scalps?

Running Wolf was behind Kicking Dog who was now very weak. Grizzly Killer had him support Kicking Dog while he cut off the shaft of the arrow. He then carefully removed the blood-soaked buckskin shirt. This wasn't a chipped stone arrowhead, for the last couple of years, Running Wolf had been making his arrow points from the iron hoops from broken barrels. These metal points seemed to penetrate deeper into the game he shot with an than the old chipped stone heads.

Zach could tell he didn't have a choice. He would have to push the point on through the shoulder and pull it out his back. This would be mighty painful for this Crow warrior but trying to pull it out the way it went in would do much more damage to his shoulder. Zach motioned for Long Arrow to come and help hold his friend. Long Arrow could not believe that this white man and Ute warrior that they had tried to kill were now helping his severely wounded friend. Right now, he didn't have the time to figure this out. He knew he must help Kicking Dog.

With Long Arrow holding onto Kicking Dog's left shoulder and Running Wolf supporting his head and back, Zach then laid the flat of his knife on the cut off arrow shaft and using the butt of his pistol hit the knife blade hard. Kicking Dog jumped and gasped from the pain, but now the iron point was entirely out the back side of his shoulder. With one more swift motion Zach pulled the rounded shaft on through the gaping wound.

Blood was flowing freely now from the wound in his back, and Zach used Kicking Dog's shirt as a bandage to put pressure on both front and back to stop the bleeding. Long Arrow watched in amazement. Why would these enemies try so hard to save Kicking Dog? He didn't understand the reason but was grateful all the same. Zach cut the shirt in half with half of it on the back wound and the other half on the front. He motioned for Long Arrow to push down onto the injury, putting pressure on both sides until the bleeding completely stopped.

Using the universal sign language of the Indians, Zach asked, "How many more Crow are with you?"

Long Arrow said, to the surprise of both Zach and Running Wolf, in accented and broken but understandable English, "One hundred warriors four-day ride north. Follow Blackfoot, Strong Bow. Lose trail, steal horses instead make war on Blackfeet."

Remembering Strong Bow from last year's Rendezvous, Zach asked, "Is Strong Bow raiding down here to the south?"

Long Arrow replied, "Cold Maker come, much snow, lose tracks, not find where go."

The sky was starting to lighten when horses could be heard coming right towards them. Kicking Dog's shoulder had now stopped bleeding so Long Arrow was sitting there surprised they had not bound his hands. Zach and Running Wolf both had their rifles up and ready.

Zach was wondering now if more Crow were coming but a quick glance at Long Arrow told him that was not the case. Zach reached over and picked up Long Arrow's bow and quiver and handed it to him. Long Arrow smiled and nodded at Grizzly Killer, and in that briefest of exchanges, Zach knew he could trust this Crow warrior that only moments ago was trying to kill him.

Chapter 10

The Chase

RUNNING WOLF WENT left while Zach went to the right. Long Arrow stayed right there to protect Kicking Dog. It was just a couple of minutes later when Zach could see through the dim light of now early dawn five horses trotting towards them. It was odd, he thought, for none of these horses had riders. His mind raced. Did the riders of these horses slip off and were now sneaking in on them? He studied the brush and undergrowth all around very closely looking for any movement, but in the shadows of this predawn light, he couldn't see any movement at all. Then, to his right, Long Arrow stood up. Zach immediately pointed his Hawken at him, wondering if he had been tricked.

Long Arrow called out softly in his Crow tongue and one the horses turned slightly and headed right to him. Then Zach saw Jimbo behind the other horses herding them back from where they had spooked and ran when he had attacked Fire Maker. A soft whistle and Jimbo came running right up to him.

Running Wolf came in behind the horses taking Jimbo's place, and within the next minute, they had all five horses. Long Arrow had set his bow back down getting control of the horses when Zach came over with Jimbo by his side. He jumped at the sight of the enormous dog and reached for his knife and war club. With a simple wave of his hand, Zach told Jimbo to sit, and he stopped and sat without taking another step. Long Arrow stared at him for the longest time; he had never seen a dog that big. He was more significant than the big gray wolves of his homeland many day's ride to the north.

Zach then waved his hand in the circle over his head and the big dog took off without hesitation and was out of sight seconds later. Long Arrow watched Jimbo disappear into the shadows and brush then turned back to Zach with a look of surprise and asked, "Big medicine dog?" Zach nodded then said as he signed, "I have sent him to make sure no one else is in this area. With a look of disbelief, he turned and looked out into the brush at the direction Jimbo had gone.

Running Wolf had started a fire next to where Kicking Dog was lying naked from the waist up. It was a cold morning, and the slight breeze made it very uncomfortable. Long Arrow and Zach had all five horses tied to trees and had come over to the fire when Jimbo came back in. Long Arrow jumped back again when the huge, fierce-looking dog trotted up to his master. That brought a smile on Running Wolf's face as he said, "You are not the first man the big medicine dog has startled." The Crow warrior stepped back up to the fire, but it was easy to see he was nervous standing there with the men and dog that had just killed many of his friends.

Long Arrow didn't understand why they had spared his life and was trying to save Kicking Dog's. They had even given him his weapons back. He had made several mistakes this night, and against any other people, he would now be traveling the warrior's trail to the land beyond. Instead, he was standing with the very men he had tried to kill.

He looked across the fire at the famous grizzly claw necklace around Zach's neck, then up into the big white man's eyes. He could see in those eyes the heart of a great warrior and the compassion he was now showing, but there was sadness there as well that he didn't understand.

Zach looked back at Long Arrow and signed again as he said, "Three days ago, a Cheyenne war party attacked our village and took our women and all of our horses. We are following them to take back what they took and to make them pay for taking our women. We are taking three of your horses now so that we can catch up to the Cheyenne and our women. We leave you two of them so you can go back to your own land."

Long Arrow again was surprised. He had expected them to take them all. He had been defeated this night and didn't understand the generosity that Grizzly Killer and his Ute partner were showing him. The Cheyenne were hated enemies of the Crow people as well. He would have loved to ride alongside these great warriors after the Cheyenne just as he had his Crow brothers against the Blackfeet ten suns ago. However, he knew his duty was to Kicking Dog. He must get him back to their people safely and care for the bodies of their fallen friends.

Zach left Long Arrow and Kicking Dog's horses then mounted up and rode back to their camp. They rolled out their blankets and got what little they had brought with them. As they crossed the river, Jimbo again was in the lead with Zach with Running Wolf bringing up the rear leading their spare mount. They were following the well-defined trail of the Cheyenne as they pushed the stolen horses in front of them.

A strong gusty south wind started blowing as the sun came up, warming the air along with the rising sun. Zach thought only about catching up to Sun Flower. He smiled slightly. He was now mounted and knew he could ride faster than the Cheyenne could push their horses in front of them.

Sun Flower had spent another long cold night tied to a tree without a blanket, and it had been almost freezing near the bank of the Seeds-Kee-Dee. She was shivering uncontrollably when she finally felt the warming rays of the morning sun. She knew what these Cheyenne were doing; making her life so miserable she would be a willing slave to them when they finally gave her food and a blanket. She had seen slaves treated this way before by her people.

However, she knew her husband, and she knew, without question, Grizzly Killer was coming for her; all she must do is survive. She told herself repeatedly she could survive anything to be back in the powerful arms of Grizzly Killer once again.

She was surprised that the Cheyenne didn't seem to be in a hurry this morning like they had up until now. It was apparent they didn't feel like anyone behind them could catch up or they had nothing to worry about if they did. She watched as they built a burial scaffold for the dead warrior. With his body wrapped in his sleeping robe, she had not been able to tell what had happened to him. She had hoped it was Grizzly Killer, but she knew it wasn't, for if he were that close, she would be with him now instead of still a captive of these Cheyenne.

After Black Otter and the others were satisfied that Wounded Elk was properly laid to rest, they crossed the river and headed east once more. Again, Black Otter had tied the rope that was still around Sun Flower neck to his wrist before they headed out.

Raven Wing opened her eyes just as the first light of dawn was coming through the smoke hole of Shining Star's lodge. She reached out and gently touched Shining Star's arm, relieved it was warm and that she was still breathing. Gray Wolf and Star were both sleeping soundly. She breathed deeply of the smoke-scented air of the lodge then slowly moved her sore legs.

She carefully got up wondering about Sun Flower and hoping Running Wolf and Grizzly Killer had caught up with her by now. She added wood and blew life back into the coals of the small fire in the center of the lodge then went out and filled their heavy black cooking pot with water and set it by the side of the fire to heat.

Ol' Red was still just outside the lodge, and he watched her as she had gotten the pot full of water. Once it was heating, she went back out and checked on his wounds. Whispering to the big mule, he nuzzled against her as she gently scraped the dried poultice from the wounds exposing the nasty jagged holes the Cheyenne arrows had left in his shoulder.

Star started to cry, and as she went back inside, she breathed a deep sigh of relief when she saw Shining Star had picked up the baby and was starting to nurse her. The concern was still there for even in the dim light of the teepee she could see Shining Star's eyes were bloodshot and had dark circles under them. The whole side of his face was still swollen and discolored from the bruising.

Raven Wing mixed several plants from her medicine kit and made a tea with it after Star had finished nursing she took the baby from her mother and gave the hot tea to Shining Star to drink. By then Gray Wolf was awake and hungry, so she nursed him before mixing another poultice and taking it out to pack into the wounds on Ol' Red.

Standing there beside Ol' Red she stared up at the snow-covered peaks towering above them letting the warm south wind hit her face. There was another storm blowing in she could feel it and the worry for her sister, husband, and brother-in-law was plain to see in her tired eyes.

Although the sky was clear Zach could feel that the hard, south wind was blowing in another storm. He knew if the ground was covered with snow, they could lose the trail the Cheyenne were leaving.

It was nearly midday when they came upon where the Cheyenne had camped and saw the burial Scaffold. Running Wolf figured they were just four or five hours behind now, so they crossed the Seeds-Kee-Dee and headed out across the barren hills still following the Cheyenne's trail toward Bitter Creek some fifty more miles to the east.

This was new country for Zach and Running Wolf. They were familiar with the land a hundred miles to the north, but neither of them had been through this area before. The land is barren but not the flat plains like further north. This area is marked with steep-sided buttes and deep cut canyons with a lot of rolling hills in between.

By midafternoon they thought they were gaining on them some, but now it was clouding up, and the warm south wind had shifted. It was now coming at them from the northwest, and the temperature was dropping fast. Zach could feel the moisture in the air now and pulled his wolverine cap down tighter on his head.

Another hour and the snow had started, and by late afternoon they were trudging through three inches of fresh snow, and it showed no signs of letting up anytime soon.

They had lost all signs of the trail the Cheyenne were leaving and were now just following wherever Jimbo was leading them. Neither Zach nor Running Wolf doubted the big dog's ability to follow the trail. By early evening though, it was apparent to both of them Jimbo had lost any scent in the deepening snow and strong wind.

They pushed on, following the lay of the land until it was too dark to see. Then stopped under the protection of a cliff on the southeast side of a butte they had been skirting. The snow was now over six inches deep. It had let up a little, but the cold north wind kept blowing.

After hollowing out a spot up next to the cliff where there was a little protection from the wind they got a fire started and huddled around it wrapped in their blankets and chewing on the cooked meat from the deer they had from the night before.

Not many words were spoken by either of them as they fed dry sage and greasewood into the flames. Zach's mind was on what Sun Flower and Raven Wing must be going through as captives of the Cheyenne. He worried too about Shining Star and their babies back home alone. Knowing she was hurt when they left and not knowing for sure if she was alright was a constant thorn of fear in his heart.

Black Otter and the Cheyenne pushed hard until nearly dark and then made their way down into a steeply sided wash. Sun Flower had been shivering almost uncontrollably for the last hour, and in her mind, she didn't believe she would still be alive in the morning. She longed to see Grizzly Killer one more time before she left this world for the land beyond, but she feared that would not happen.

The Cheyenne built two fires in a brush-filled wash, and to her surprise, Black Otter led her over to one of them and had her sit down where she could feel the heat of the flames against her dangerously cold skin. She sat there nearly numb both physically and mentally from her ordeal. The cold had helped the swelling in her battered and bruised face, but her ribs and stomach still were extremely tender from the pounding of the horses ride that first day. Her wrists were now bloody from the rawhide they were tied with, and she worked her finger back and forth trying to keep the circulation going in her hands.

Black Otter stood above her staring down then he grabbed her by the hair and pulled her to her feet. She looked defiantly at him, and he smiled at the fierce strength this small Shoshone woman had. He then pulled out his knife and cut her hands free. She knew it didn't matter that she was free. If she ran from them now, she would never live through this cold, snowy night. In her heart, she knew she had to endure whatever she must until Grizzly Killer found her.

It was a cold and sleepless night for Sun Flower and the Cheyenne as well as Zach and Running Wolf. Snow tapered off about midnight, but the cold north wind continued to howl through the sage. Just before dawn, the wind direction changed slightly where Zach and Running Wolf were huddled, creating an eerie moan as it blew through the rock formation at the top of the cliff.

Jimbo was the first to stand, stretch and yawn even before the first gray appeared along the eastern horizon. Zach added more wood to the fire and was relieved stars were filling the dark heavens above. He knew when the sun finally rises this time of year it would bring warming rays to this cold and barren land.

Running Wolf stood too, but he just stared east into the darkness and thought of Raven Wing and Sun Flower, their beautiful wives being with the Cheyenne this long cold night. As the thoughts raced through his mind, he made a silent vow to himself that those Cheyenne warriors would pay for what they had done and for what he imagined they were doing.

No words were spoken as Zach walked over to where the horses were tied, none were needed. Both men knew the longer this chase lasted, the more danger their women were in. Without waiting for light, they mounted up and headed east again.

As the first dim light of dawn washed over the land, Zach could see a high ridge several miles east of them. One question flooded his mind; where did the Cheyenne go? Was there a visible trail over the ridge or did they go around it? And, if so, did they go north or south? He was watching the ground closely for any sign of the trail the band had to be leaving, but a half foot of snow had covered all traces. Up until now, he figured he could see where they would have gone because the land had dictated the most accessible route, but with this high steep ridge that was about to change.

The sun was up and shining brightly on their faces as they approached the high, steep ridge. They stopped to study the ground closely looking for any indication which way the Cheyenne had gone. Running Wolf was down on the ground walking in circles looking for a sign of any kind; a branch on sagebrush broken or out of place. He was studying the ground ever so carefully to the south while Zach was doing the same thing off to the north a little way.

Ten minutes passed with Zach's ordinarily gentle manner about to break when Jimbo barked to get their attention. He was over a quarter mile north of Zach and Running Wolf and had just come up out of the steep-sided wash where Sun Flower and the Cheyenne had spent the night. He could smell the familiar smell of Sun Flower in several areas in the wash, and there was now a large, plain trail to follow.

Zach and Running Wolf wasted no time at all riding their Crow mounts hard to get to where Jimbo was standing. By the time they reached the wash, Jimbo was already down in the bottom again and heading out the far end of the trail following the familiar scent of Sun Flower. He felt he had to protect her and all his family just as much as Zach. The big dog knew it was up to him to find her and now that her scent was lingering in the air he was determined to find her. Running Wolf took only a moment to feel the coals of their fires then rode on after Zach and Jimbo knowing they were still four or five hours behind.

Chapter 11

Black Butte

BLACK OTTER WAS STILL holding the rope tied around Sun Flower's neck, but since last night he had not bound her hands. At first, she had refused his offer to share his blanket, but before morning she was so cold she had laid down with him. She tried to stay warm by the fire, but with the wind swirling in this wash, it just wasn't working. She told herself repeatedly she could endure anything until Grizzly Killer found her, and if laying with this brutal enemy turned out to be one of those things, well, she would have to endure that as well.

As she laid down into the warmth of his robes, her mind wandered to memories of Zach, her great white warrior. How he had rescued her, Raven Wing, and Butter Fly from those Frenchmen. She remembered the first time they had made love together in the warm sun on the south beach of Sweet Lake. How she had fallen in love with him before she even knew him and how much she loved him now. These memories were her salvation as she endured having to lay with this Cheyenne just to stay alive.

They were up and on the trail again before light and to her relief, Black Otter gave her one of his robes to protect her from the cold. She wondered how long she would have to be with this Cheyenne before Grizzly Killer found them. She knew deep within her heart that he would find her. She just didn't know how long it might take.

The sun was now up, and the cold north wind had stopped as they rode across a large basin and up onto its rim to the east. Here the land fell away into a series of canyons and arroyos with flat-topped buttes for as far she could see.

She looked back behind them hoping to see some sign that he was back there, even though she knew if he were he would not let himself be seen. Black Otter watched her and saw the look on her face. It was apparent she expected someone to be back there. Before they continued, he had Brave Bull, and Eyes Like the Antelope stay behind to watch for someone following them. He told them to stay all day and meet them on Bitter Creek, due east of the Black Butte. Brave Bull was silent as he looked west along their back trail, Eyes Like the Antelope nodded to Black Otter letting him know he understood.

The two of them watched Black Otter with his Shoshone Squaw and the others until they were out of sight, heading east before they started looking for a comfortable place to spend the day while watching their back trail. Neither of these men thought anyone would have followed them this far just for one woman and even if they did, their trail was well-covered with snow. Black

Otter was just being cautious and both of them understood, but still, neither believed they would see anything at all.

Raven Wing had not slept much at all between caring for the restless babies and her Ute sister. Shining Star seemed to have had violent dreams much of the night. Raven Wing's body had not had a chance to recover from the long run getting home, and she felt weak and listless as she heated water for more of the healing and pain-killing tea she had been brewing for Shining Star.

Luna was inside the teepee with them this morning still lying by Shining Star's side. Once the water was hot, Raven Wing poured it into a cup she had already filled with a variety of dried petals, leaves, ground roots, and bark. She mixed them just the way Blue Fox had taught her. She wasn't much more than a child when Blue Fox, the great Shoshone Medicine Man from Charging Bull's village; the village where Raven Wing and Sun Flower were raised, taught her to be a healer. Now, many considered her to be a powerful medicine woman herself. Their parents and brother still lived in Charging Bull's village in the valley of the Popo Agie just east of the towering Wind River Mountains.

Shining Star smiled crookedly at Raven Wing, letting her know that she felt a little better and truly appreciated Raven Wing's care for her. Raven Wing said, "It looks like you feel better this morning."

Shining Star slowly nodded her head, saying, "I do, now I can only see two of you instead of the four of you that were here last night."

They both smiled but the movement of the muscles in her face made Shining Star wince slightly. While the bruising and swelling were both down and her vision improving, Raven Wing knew it would take many days of care for her to heal. Most would not survive being hit by a stone war club that way.

After she cared for the babies, Raven Wing carefully handed Star to her mother and she picked up little Gray Wolf. They sat there in the warm, dim light of the teepee and suckled their babies then softly sang them back to sleep.

Ol' Red had not crossed the creek to go out into the meadow to graze since Raven Wing had returned so after she repacked his wounded shoulder with a fresh, moist poultice, she led him slowly across the stream out in the bare areas of the meadow to graze. He was limping as they moved, but she knew he needed to eat to heal just like people do and the movement might be painful, but it would help him not be so stiff later.

Eyes Like the Antelope and Brave Bull found a good place where they could see out across the basin they had just crossed and sat down to watch the barren land behind them. The first couple of hours they were both diligently waiting for any sign of movement, but as the sun rose higher into this early spring sky it warmed the chilly air, and both men started to doze. Neither of them had slept much because of the cold, snow, and wind all night. Now, with the suns warming rays against their skin and hours of staring out across a plain devoid of any movement except an occasional hawk, conversion waned and eventually, their eyes closed.

By midmorning, the snow was melting rapidly, and the sun's glare was making it hard to see as Zach and Running Wolf rode east. Zach stopped on the west side of the basin and looked at the plain trail the Cheyenne were leaving in the snow and the thought of an ambush flooded his mind. He turned to Running Wolf and said, "If we stay on this trail they could be leading us into a trap."

Running Wolf stared east across this broad, barren basin filled with nothing but grass and short sage then replied, "They have not yet checked their back trail... why do you think they know we are following?"

Zach shook his head and said, "Don't know, just don't feel right to stay right on their tracks."

Running Wolf nodded and said, "I go north, you go south, and we meet up again on the other side."

Zach nodded and turned to the south off the trail the Cheyenne were leaving.

He whistled once for Jimbo then turned and rode for nearly a mile south of the trail then turned east again. His eyes were scanning the land ahead as he loped through the melting snow. Movement caught his eye off to his left and he brought his Crow mount to a halt and watched. Only a moment later he saw it was just a coyote sneaking through the sage away from him. He started up again seeing a herd of antelope off to the south several hundred yards away.

Half an hour later he was nearing the eastern rim and ready to turn back to the north to find the Cheyenne's trail and meet Running Wolf. Just as he was making his turn, Jimbo came running back to him. Zach could tell instantly Jimbo had found something simply by the way he was running. When he got close, the big dog growled the soft rumbling growl from deep in his chest telling Zach that trouble was ahead.

He stopped and tied the horse to a sage, checked the powder in the pan of his Hawken and followed Jimbo through the sage on foot. Ten minutes later Jimbo dropped to his belly and Zach did the same, he couldn't see anything ahead, but he knew his dog, there was no doubt in his mind there was danger close at hand.

A quarter mile further north he could see Running Wolf approaching, leading the spare mount and with a silent hand signal told Jimbo to go and warn him. Jimbo took off, and it still amazed Zach how a dog that big could run through the brush without making a sound. He waited and watched until Running Wolf tied off the horses and was sneaking through the brush behind Jimbo.

Zach still could not see anything, but he started crawling forward being careful where he placed his weight. He hadn't gone far before the cold, melting snow had soaked through his buckskins and had his hands stinging. Suddenly there was movement only twenty-five yards in front of him.

Eyes Like the Antelope sat up out of the sage, yawned and rubbed his eyes. Zach was utterly motionless, and he knew if this Cheyenne looked his way he would be seen. He couldn't see Running Wolf or Jimbo and didn't know how far away they were, but he knew he couldn't lay in this snow in plain sight for long before the warrior in front of him looked his way. He waited only another moment then, in one swift motion, jumped to his feet. Eyes Like the Antelope turned toward him and was so surprised at seeing this sizeable white man so close to him he stepped backward and tripped over the still sleeping Brave Bull and fell flat on his back.

Zach stepped forward, but Eyes Like the Antelope was back on his feet instantly with his knife in his hand. Brave Bull was startled but instantly alert, and just as he was getting to his feet, Jimbo attacked. Nearly two hundred pounds with jaws powerful enough to crush bone hit Brave Bull before he had his feet securely under him. Jimbo's teeth clamped down on the back of Brave Bull's head nearly ripping his scalp off.

The suddenness of Jimbo's attack made Eyes Like the Antelope jump out of his way, and that gave Zach time to rush forward, hitting him on the side of his head with the barrel of his Hawken and knocking him to the ground. Then, with a swift kick, Zach sent the knife flying from his hand. He started to get up again but another kick, this time to the ribs, rolled him over onto his back gasping for air.

Brave Bull was laying on his side with both hands holding his now bleeding scalp in place and moaning slightly from the pain. As Running Wolf came running up, he marveled at the speed in which this fight was over. It had only taken seconds but then he had seen Grizzly Killer and Jimbo in battle before, and he knew how effective the two of them were together.

Brave Bull opened his eyes only to see the curled lips and long sharp teeth of Jimbo just a foot in front of his face. He could feel the blood still flowing between his fingers as he tried putting even more pressure on his head to stop the bleeding.

As Eyes Like the Antelope got his breath back, he looked up and saw Zach's necklace. His eyes got wide as he saw the dozen four and five-inch grizzly claws. He had heard the stories of Grizzly Killer, the great white warrior, and his big medicine dog. Most of the Cheyenne did not believe anyone could have as powerful of medicine as the stories said Grizzly Killer had, but now he believed. Where had he come from? It was like they had just appeared out of the brush. What did Grizzly Killer, a white man, want with him and Brave Bull?

Grizzly Killer spoke and signed as he did, "Where are the two women you stole?"

Eyes Like the Antelope just stared up at him making no effort to answer. Running Wolf stepped up with his knife drawn and now the look on his face became one of concern. Zach asked again, "Where are the women?"

Now the look on Eyes Like the Antelope became defiant as he looked at Running Wolf standing there with his knife in his hand. Zach struggled to control his anger. These were the men that had taken his beloved Sun Flower and Raven Wing and had nearly killed Shining Star. Zach was out of patience and was feeling no mercy at this moment. Not waiting for Running Wolf and his knife he pointed his Hawken at Eyes Like the Antelope's right foot and pulled the trigger.

Eyes Like the Antelope jerked from the shock and pain of what had just happened. The heavy lead ball had ripped through the top of his foot taking blood and bone into the soft ground below. His breath was coming in gasps as he tried to deal with the pain and his eyes were closed tightly. When he opened them again, he saw Grizzly Killer reloading his deadly rifle with a look in his eyes that told of both anger and resolve. Eyes Like the Antelope knew in that instant Grizzly Killer would do anything and everything to get his questions answered.

Zach signed again, "Where are the women?" He then pointed the rifle at Eyes Like the Antelope's knee. Eyes Like the Antelope tensed, his breathing was now coming in short shallow gasped as he braced for the impact of another shot.

Brave Bull shouted something, and Zach hesitated. Although neither Zach nor Running Wolf could understand him, they waited for him to continue. With his hands still on his ripped and torn scalp, he told Eyes Like the Antelope to tell these men what they wanted to know. For it was easy enough for them to follow the trail anyway and there are only two of them against the six Cheyenne.

Eyes Like the Antelope could see the wisdom in what Brave Bull had said and he could also see the rifle pointed at his knee which helped with his decision. Still reeling from the shock of his ruined foot he slowly signed, "Bitter Creek east of Black Mountain." Then he added, "One woman not two."

Zach didn't understand all the sign and was not familiar with this country. He understood Black Mountain and bad water creek, but he didn't know where either of these was. He looked at Running Wolf, but he just shook his head for he had never been here before either.

They both understood the one woman and Zach signed back, "Two women!"

Eyes Like the Antelope signed, "One run away," That took both Zach and Running Wolf by surprise, which one had gotten away and where was she? Then Eyes Like the Antelope signed again, "When you catch Black Otter you will die."

Zach grinned as he signed back, "I will catch Black Otter, and I will make him pay for taking our women, then he will die." A shudder ran through Eyes Like the Antelope for the look in the eyes of Grizzly Killer made him believe Black Otter would surely die.

They left the two wounded Cheyenne where they were and went back and got their horses. As they started out on the trail again, Running Wolf found the two Cheyenne's mounts tied just over the rise from where they were sitting and took them along leaving the two wounded Cheyenne on foot.

The trail turned slightly north of east and now having extra mounts they pushed the horses into a lope and kept them there until they could feel them tiring then stopped and changed mounts. By midafternoon they could see the towering dark butte and neither of them had any doubt that was the Black Mountain the Cheyenne had mentioned, but how far east is Bad Water Creek? Neither of them knew.

Zach wondered which of their women had gotten away. In his mind, it would have been Sun Flower; she was always the bold and defiant one. Both were strong and agile, but it was Sun Flower who was fearless and never shy or intimidated, but he had to admit it could have been either one of the sisters.

They came to a place where the Cheyenne had stopped to rest their horses and Running Wolf jumped down to check the horse droppings. They were still warm, not more than an hour ahead. They pushed on until sunset then slowed to a walk as the light faded into evening. The evening star was shining brightly when Jimbo came back letting them know the Cheyenne were just ahead.

Chapter 12

Bitter Creek

WITH THEIR HORSES SECURELY tied to the sage, Zach and Running Wolf proceeded on foot until the flickering yellow flames of the campfire could be seen. With the tracks of all their horses, the Cheyenne had stolen they hadn't known how many they were up against. Both wanted to get in close enough to see whether it was Sun Flower or Raven Wing that was still with these enemy warriors.

They slowly and carefully moved around the camp staying out far enough they wouldn't be seen or heard until they located the horse herd. More of these horses were their own than were the Cheyenne's and Running Wolf's familiar smell didn't bother them at all as he moved in whispering ever so gently to them. He found his beloved Chestnut and stroked his neck. With their horses being calm in recognizing the smell of Running Wolf none of the Cheyenne's horses made any fuss either. Zach, however, had sent Jimbo to the far side of the camp so his presence would not spook the Cheyenne horses.

Running Wolf stayed there with the horses as Zach continued around the camp. They were still far enough away from the fire they hadn't been able to count the enemy or tell which of the women they still held captive. When Zach was about a third of the way to the other side he stopped and got down on his belly.

There were no trees or even much brush along Bitter Creek, in fact, there was very little water trickling down this little depression as it cut a swallow path across the dry and barren landscape. From the edges of the water to the edges of this shallow wash the ground was crusted white with alkali making it clear to Zach why they called this Bitter Creek. There were short, stunted sage and rabbit brush, but where Zach was—even being on his stomach— his head and back reached the top of the brush.

He slowly crawled forward keeping his head down until he could hear the Cheyenne speaking plainly, then he slowly raised his head just enough he could see ahead. His heart rejoiced as he saw Sun Flower sitting by the fire, but that joy turned to instant fury as she turned her head and he could see in the light of the fire her bruised and swollen face. The rope was still around her neck but the look on her face was still proud. It was easy to see these Cheyenne had not dampened her spirit. It hurt him all the way to the core that she had to endure this, that he had not protected her. He was her husband, it was his duty to protect her, and he had failed.

He knew he must shake the anger from his mind as he counted five Cheyenne around the fire. He needed clear thoughts to plan how to take on this many of enemies without putting Sun Flower in more danger. He watched not only the camp but all around trying to determine if there were others outstanding guard. He figured there were for it would be foolish for anyone not to have a guard posted.

Raven Wing sat in the dark, warm teepee suckling both babies as she watched Shining Star struggle in her sleep. The side of her head was still swollen, and her pretty face partially distorted from the swelling. Her eye was black and blue, she appeared to be having a bad dream, and Raven Wing wondered if it was a dream or if her sister was in pain from the wound to her head. Star had gone to sleep in her arms, but little Gray Wolf was wide awake. He was making baby sounds as he tried to talk to her and she couldn't help but smile as he looked up into her face.

She worried about her sister and her man wondering if they were alright and she worried about Shining Star as well. She had never seen a head injury this bad and didn't know if she would be all right. Looking into her eyes, she could tell it was severe—for the centers of her dark brown eyes were not the same size. She was still getting dizzy and could not walk or even stand for long, and she had given her nearly all the healing plants she carried in her medicine kit. She wouldn't be able to get more until the plants all bloomed again in the summer. She was using now mostly a tea of white aspen bark to help with the pain in Shining Star's head.

Shining Star jumped, and her eyes opened, she then slowly sat up. Luna had been laying there beside her and licked her face as she sat upright. She stared at the small fire burning in the center of the teepee for a moment then she looked at Raven Wing and said, "They have found

Sun Flower, I seen it in my dreams. I don't know what happened because I woke up."

Everyone considered Raven Wing a powerful Medicine Women, but she had never considered herself that. She thought if she had the power to be a great Medicine Woman she would know just what Shining Star's dream meant. She would know what was happening with her husband, and his partner and closest friend, Grizzly Killer, but all she knew for sure was she worried about them all.

Zach was in easy rifle range now, but he wanted to get a little closer for his second shot with the horse pistol that he carried in his waistband. He moved ever so slowly toward the fire. It was up to him to fire the first shot, that had already been decided before Running Wolf and he had split up and he knew Jimbo wouldn't attack before he told him to.

He was close enough now that he knew if one of them looked they would see him. He didn't want to shoot until he knew where the guard was. Moving ever so slowly, he pulled the pistol from his waistband, laid it on the ground beside him and waited.

Jimbo was on his belly on the far side of the fire waiting for Zach's command to attack. He had already picked up the familiar scent of Sun Flower, and he had spotted her by the fire. The soft low growl was sitting there deep in his chest, every muscle in his vast body was tense as he watched. She was a big part of his family, and he knew with every primal instinct that he must protect her.

Running Wolf was now in the short rabbit brush between where the horses were tied and the fire waiting for Grizzly Killer to fire the first shot. His bow was lying right alongside him as he looked down the barrel of his Kentucky Long Rifle. He heard a sound behind him; it was a footstep, then the gentle tone of a voice softly talking to the horses. He didn't understand the words, but the meaning was plain. The Cheyenne was keeping the horses calm as he approached them while making his way around the camp.

He knew any movement might be seen, so he stayed motionless. This enemy was behind him, but he didn't dare turn to look, so he just waited. Soon he heard the footsteps again as the Cheyenne guard continued in the direction of Grizzly Killer.

Zach was close enough he could hear them speaking around the fire and wished he could understand their words. He knew they would be expecting their friends that were watching their back trail and he figured it was them they were talking about. Silent One had not spoken, just sat and listened as he usually did as Black Otter and the others wondered why Eyes Like the Antelope and Brave Bull weren't there yet. Then Silent One slowly got to his feet. Zach could tell by the way he was moving he was hurting and wondered what had happened to him.

Silent One spoke with a voice of authority as he told them it was this woman's fault that Wounded Elk was dead and now Eyes Like the Antelope and Brave Bull were probably dead as well. He was slowly walking around the fire toward Sun Flower as he spoke, but Zach could not understand any of what he was saying. When he got behind her, he reached down and picked up the rope around her neck and viciously jerked her to her feet. That swift, violent movement had pulled her right into Zach's line of fire as Silent One told the other Cheyenne she must die right here and now.

Running Wolf couldn't shoot either as Silent One now had her pulled up next to him. Then he pulled out his knife. Sun Flower swung her hand down and behind her hitting him squarely between the legs again. Just as he doubled over in pain so bad his vision was blurred, he was hit from behind by two hundred pounds of growling fury. Jimbo hadn't waited for Zach's command; he had seen Sun Flower was being hurt and attacked. All the other Cheyenne jumped to their feet and both Zach and Running Wolf fired.

Two of the Cheyenne were now on the ground, one dead and not moving the other jerking from the mortal wound. Jimbo had Silent One's right hand, the one that had held the knife in his powerful jaws. Bones were crushed as the massive dog bit down then shook his head back and forth trying to rip it from his arm. Black Otter dove for cover as Zach fired his pistol hitting him in the leg. Then, an arrow stuck into the chest of Standing Horse bringing him fully upright. As he stared in disbelief at the arrow sticking out of his chest another one hit him in the neck sending him over backward into the fire.

Zach heard the twang of a bowstring behind him and dived to the right. He felt a tug on the leg of his buckskin leggings, but the arrow only put a scratch across his skin as it passed through the soft leather legging. He knew the unseen guard out in the dark would have more arrows, so he hit the ground and rolled back onto his feet then ran into the darkness away from the light of the fire.

Sun Flower had dropped to the ground with the sound of the shots, but now it seemed to be over. As she looked up the first thing she saw was Silent One's knife laying right where he dropped it when Jimbo attacked. Then, the pungent smell of burning hair hit her and she looked at

Standing Horse with arrows sticking in his chest and throat and his head in the fire. Silent One was on the ground in more pain than he thought a man could endure. Jimbo still had his hand in his mouth and was pulling him across the ground.

Sun Flower reached out and picked up Silent One's dropped knife. She could see Black Otter was holding his leg, but he was out in the shadows of the night, far enough she had no idea how badly he was hurt. She removed the rope from around her neck and stood. Being aware that another Cheyenne was out in the dark guarding camp she looked around and smiled as she saw Running Wolf walking from the shadows into the flickering light of the fire.

She looked at Jimbo and said, "Jimbo, come." She smiled as the vast dog released Silent One's hand and came to her wagging his tail. Silent One looked at her with a burning hatred in his eyes as he cradled his ruined right hand. It was a look that told her he would be a dangerous enemy even with only one hand.

She didn't think about doing it; she just reacted to his glaring eyes when she raised his knife and threw it just as hard as she could. She watched the shock on his face as the knife buried in his belly just below his ribs, until his life slowly faded and his eyes glazed over in death.

Running Wolf saw what had just happened as he walked up to her. The questioning look on his face was plain to see, but the questions would have to wait. He raised his rifle at Black Otter and without hesitation, he fired his Kentucky long rifle. The lead ball caught Black Otter in the shoulder throwing him backward and flat to the ground. Bleeding uncontrollably, Black Otter didn't have the strength to move.

As Running Wolf started to reload, Sun Flower pulled his knife from the highly decorated sheath on his waistband, and he watched as she walked over to Black Otter. She bent over and slapped him across the face making him open his eyes. He stared at her as she signed to him, "You will go to the land beyond not as a warrior... not even as a man." Then, before he passed out again, she reached down and cut his manhood from his body. He jerked and moaned then she watched as his eyes glazed over in death.

Grizzly Killer hadn't run far when he spun and laid down flat once again. He strained to see into the darkness behind him, but there was nothing there but the blackness of the night. He wanted to run to Sun Flower, he needed to make sure she was alright, but he knew at least one more enemy was waiting there in the darkness. He avoided even looking toward the fire. He lay there motionless waiting and listening, but no sounds were coming to him, and he thought the Cheyenne was doing the same thing he was. This was a game of patience; who was going to make the first and maybe fatal mistake.

Running Wolf was aware there was another Cheyenne out there in the dark and not hearing a sound he figured Grizzly Killer was hunting him. He stepped away from the light of the fire and waited, knowing Grizzly Killer would not want him to leave Sun Flower unprotected again.

Sun Flower had been raised in this wilderness. She had seen and taken part in its brutal way of life before. She discarded her gruesome trophy then making sure these Cheyenne were thoroughly disgraced as well as defeated she went to each one taking their scalps. She knew Grizzly Killer did not usually take scalps and although she did not want the trophies, she wanted them to enter the land beyond knowing they were defeated in battle. Running Wolf had pulled the body of Standing Horse out of the fire, and when Sun Flower came to it, there was nothing left to cut off. She threw the scalps into the fire then walked away out of its light, knelt down and hugged Jimbo while she stared out into the darkness wondering about her man.

They all waited for the longest time with only the of sound the soft crackling of the fire and coyotes yipping at the night way off to the north. Zach waited until his patience was nearly gone. He almost didn't hear the ever so slight sound of buckskin rubbing against buckskin behind him. He spun, bringing his pistol up but the Cheyenne, Kicking Dog, with war club and knife raised was already diving at him. The massive stone club swinging caught the barrel of Zach's pistol knocking it from his hand then the full weight of the warrior came crashing down on him. The knife in Kicking Dog's other hand caught Zach's shoulder putting a nasty slice nearly to the bone. Zach pushed with all strength ignoring the pain in his shoulder and throwing Kicking Dog off to the side. He rolled away from him and onto his feet pulling his Cherokee tomahawk and knife from his waistband.

Zach had run far enough away from the fire that Running Wolf and Sun Flower could not hear the fight that had started, but Jimbo's keen ears picked it up. He ran from Sun Flower and disappeared into the night.

Kicking Dog came at Zach with his war club raised forcing him to dive to the left. He rolled over his wounded shoulder bringing a shooting pain through his whole body. It was going to be a fight to the death, and both men knew it. Zach, by the force of his will, had to ignore the screaming pain in his wounded shoulder as he rolled back up to his feet.

Kicking Dog could not see the blood that was soaking through Zach's buckskins in the dark, but he knew this enemy before him was wounded. He moved forward, not letting Zach get ready for his next charge. Something caught his eye to the left and he heard a vicious growl as nearly two hundred pounds of growling fury hit him from the side.

He felt the bone in his arm break as Jimbo's powerful jaws bit down on it as he was falling to the ground. He lost his grip on the deadly war club but was bringing his knife toward Jimbo then he felt a numbing pain as Zach brought his tomahawk down burying it deep into the top of Kicking Dog's head. Kicking Dog saw a light flash behind his eyes, and suddenly the pain was gone. He could see his enemy standing over him, but the fight was over. At first, he didn't understand what was happening to him, but then the light was gone, and the world around just seemed to drift away.

Chapter 13

Spring Camp

THE EARLY SPRING SUN had just hit the small makeshift cabin as Ely stepped out to take care of his morning duties. He looked over at their horses in the log corral and saw they were all watching him. They wanted to be let out for they were hungry. This had been a long hard winter all through the Rockies, and here in Jackson's Hole, it was no exception.

Grub was getting the fire started to drive the cold from their small cabin as Benny was pulling on his fur-lined moccasins. Benny stepped closer to the growing flames as he put on a heavy buffalo hide coat to go out and take the horses into the grassy meadow where the snow had melted off.

Ely stepped back into the now warm cabin and watched Grub getting dressed to go somewhere and said, "Where's ya goin'?"

Grub looked up and answered, "I gonna see if'n any of the others has any coffee they'd sell us. I's need some coffee, we's been out fer too damn long."

Ely looked at his long-time partner and asked, "If'n you had some would you sell it?"

The look on Grub's face turned to disappointment as he said, "Hell no, but I ain't as greedy as some."

Ely answered back, "It ain't gonna matter no-how, nobody got enough to last 'em through winter at Ronnyvoo last year."

"What can it hurt to ask?"

Ely shook his head and said, "Grub, you just go right on over ask 'em. I's gonna go out an help the kid make sure the horses is gittin' 'nough ta eat."

There were over forty trappers that had spent the winter together in Jackson's Hole this year. Grub and Ely spent the last several winters here, and this was Benny's second year. They arrived in late November and had built this small log cabin. It was only large enough for them to have a stone fireplace in one corner and the three of them to sleep but the fire kept it warm and that was what was important. The smoke vented through a hole in the roof right above the fire.

They had trapped last fall down along Grey's River and its tributaries. It hadn't been as good as they had done in years past, but they still figured they had taken enough beaver to get the supplies for another year.

Benny had learned fast from the two older trappers, he had turned just eighteen years old in the fall, but he had taken nearly as many beaver as either Grub or Ely. They usually cached their furs but since Rendezvous was going to be either east or west of them, they had carried them all with them here for the winter.

The trappers wintering here in Jackson's Hole were mostly Rocky Mountain Fur's men, but there were a few free trappers like Grub, Ely, and Benny. The trappers liked being together during the winter for protection and to help each other hunt, but mostly the trapping in the Rockies was a lonely business. Sometimes you could go nearly all year without seeing another soul, so the winters were a time of togetherness.

The men that Benny had come west with a little over a year ago were here; their camp was only a half mile from the small cabin. None of them had been experienced trappers, and they had pitifully few plews to show for the fall season. On top of that, they were a lazy sort either hoping or expecting someone else to do the hard work. That was one reason Benny had left them. Since he was the youngest, they treated him pretty much like a slave, but when he met Grub and Ely, they treated him like their equal and had taught him the ways of game. Benny was becoming a skilled mountain man that the two older men trusted and were proud of.

As the long cold winter dragged on, the short burley Melvin Tillman became more and more withdrawn from the other trappers and he, along with three of his friends, had started a couple of fights, mostly over meat missing from other trappers. Everyone seemed to know it was Mel and his friends taking it and after one incident Ely said, "Ya know, if those feller's is hungry any of us would share what we got, ain't no need fer 'em to sneak around stealin' it."

To that Benny had replied, "He's too proud to ask but too lazy to go hunt for himself."

Grub shook his head saying, "Now ain't that somthin', too proud to ask, but not too proud ta steal. Just one more reason why I like it alone out here away from everybody."

With the melting snow, the streams were starting to open, and the three of them were getting ready for the spring trapping season. The Rendezvous this year was going to be split. The first over on the other side of the great divide on the Popo Agie, the second was much closer, just over Teton Pass and down into Pierre's Hole. They had decided they would trap their way to Rendezvous on the Popo Agie. After not having enough supplies to go around at last year's Rendezvous down on Sweet Lake, Grub didn't want to take any chances, so he wanted to be at the first Rendezvous. He said, "Ain't worth takin' no chance of Sublette not bringin' 'nough this year, I wanna be first in line fer them coffee beans and maybe just a taste of some John Barleycorn."

"A taste is 'bout all you could handle; ya ain't as young as ya used ta be," Ely replied.

To that Grub answered, "Maybe not, but I ain't never gonna be as old as you."

Benny just kept his head down grinning as he listened to his two friends kidding back and forth at each other.

It always amazed Benny how these two could go at each other all day long. They never got angry, they had grown up not far from each other on farms just outside Pittsburgh, and when Grub was only sixteen and Ely seventeen, they'd left home together working on a river barge taking supplies down the Ohio to the settlements along the way. When they reached the Mississippi, they stayed for a time in St. Louis, but the tale of the riches to be made in the fur trade had them following an old French trader west.

Benny loved listening to the two of them tell stories from their youth. He, too, had worked on the river for a while and he felt a kinship with them about that. They both had developed the skill to be extraordinary trappers, and they both loved the life and solitude these shining mountains provided. Benny was cut from that same cloth; he loved the wilderness and wanted to learn everything about it. Grub and Ely had been out here nearly ten years now, much longer than most and they were happy to teach Benny everything they had learned.

Danger was a way of life; hostile Indians, river crossings, avalanches, wild animals, severe storms, freezing temperature, wildfires, flash floods, and countless other dangers were all here to take a man's life. One had to learn to be watchful and weary every minute of every day. Not many men were suited to this life but those that were seemed to love it. Most of the trappers would only spend a few seasons trapping then go back to the relative safety of life back east. Some like Grub Taylor, Ely Tucker, Zach Connors, Jim Bridger, and now young Benton Lambert along with a few others would spend their lives in the wilderness of the Rocky Mountains, braving all the dangers with a love of life and inner strength that not many men possessed.

With the snow now melting, the streams were starting to run high, breaking up what ice remained. Against some of the beaver dams the ice would build up until the force of the water behind it broke through, nearly draining the ponds and the beavers would be hard at work rebuilding them. It was time to set out the trap lines. The three of them packed the horses and headed out following a creek that ran down into the Snake River from the east. Although their small cabin had kept them warm through the coldest months of winter, none of them were sorry about leaving. The three of them were enjoying the warming weather and were anxious to be on the move again.

Their horses were packed heavy with last fall's plews all tied into bundles as they followed game trails up and out of Jackson's Hole. What none of them knew or even suspected was Mel Tillman, and his three friends were following them. They were staying several miles behind, and when the time was right, they were hoping to cash in on the experienced trappers' success.

Ely was leading the way, watching not only the creek for any sign of beaver but the hills and forest all around them for signs of danger, but this creek showed very little beaver sign, so they pushed on making their way east.

It was new country for them. They were following the lay of the land, but these hills east of Jackson's Hole were turning into the towering peaks of the Gros Ventre Mountains mighty fast. They weren't making very good time for the trail was narrow and winding. By evening Ely figured they had only covered about ten miles. The next day was much the same, and when they stopped to noon, they hadn't covered more than two or three miles.

It was apparent to them all that this stream they were following had been trapped out. Most of the beaver sign they were seeing was from years past. It was clear to Ely that this close to where so many trappers spent their winters they had taken all the beaver from this area. They had to keep moving until they came upon a stream where trappers had not already been.

As they sat around their fire that evening, Ely, staring up and at high granite peak that was pushing its way for the sky just above them said, "Ya knows, one day and maybe sooner than any of us want they ain't gonna be no beaver left ta trap."

Grub slowly looked at his long-time partner and answered, "Maybe your right pard, I sure hope you ain't, but maybe you are."

Ely continued, "We come mighty close ta twenty miles up this here creek over the last two days and I ain't seen a single beaver lodge or newly built damn, not one. It sure ain't like it used to be."

With that said the three of them sat around the fire and watched as the flames licked at the fresh night air and the three trappers were each lost in their thoughts. The moon was rising over the peaks still east of them, and several wolves started howling to their north. Eerie howls joined in from the south.

Mel Tillman might be lazy and not much of a trapper, but he was still a smart and cunning man. Nothing about trapping was what he had expected, though. It was hard and miserable work. The cold water was numbing and painful, the oily castor taken from the beaver glands and used as an attractant had a horrible smell, and the work never stopped. Mel and his companions had taken some beaver over the last year, but even most of what they took had spoiled because they hadn't taken the time to scrape the flesh and fat from them thoroughly. He had seen the bundles of plews these two old trappers and the kid he had brought out from St. Louis had, and he wanted them. In his mind, the kid owed him, for he would never have made it out here if not for him.

Mel hadn't been happy when Benny deserted him to go with Grub and Ely for it was Benny that was doing most of their work. The more he thought about it, the more he believed the kid's plews belonged to him. He decided he was going to take them, so when he and his partners saw the three packing up to leave, they did the same.

Staying well back, they figured they would keep out of sight while they watched the experienced trappers. When the opportunity presented itself, they would move in and take the plews. If the old trappers and kid gave them any trouble, well nobody would ever find their bodies out in this vast wilderness.

Another couple of days passed as Ely led them further into the mountains. The next morning found them back up in the snow as they crossed a pass and looked southeast down a huge drainage. It started from the high granite peak that was now just north of them. They could see several pure white mountain goats standing at the base of the peak. There was an almost vertical rock wall where the snow couldn't stick as they crossed over the pass and headed down into the Granite Peak drainage.

A couple of miles from the creek they could now see a series of beaver ponds for as far as they could look down this canyon. In the first pond, they came to there was a family of beaver's actively repairing their dam from damage done by the fast-moving high waters from the rapidly melting snow.

Along the edge of the pond and up the hill from them they could see several large quakies that were nearly chewed through. The beavers leave them like that waiting for a good storm to blow them over, so they can get to the softer smaller branches at the top. They moved on for another couple of miles passing more than a dozen ponds, each one with the fresh sign until Ely came upon an almost flat meadow between two of the ponds. There were thick willows along the stream and quakies on the slope on their side of the creek and tall, dark pines on the opposite side of the rushing water.

They went right to work building a lean-to for them to sleep under and another to store their supplies. There was plenty of grass for the horses and wood for their fire. Grub stood after throwing a buffalo hide over the lean-to and breathed deeply the pine scented and said, "Ely, I think ya done good this time, looks like they is enough beaver here to keep us hoppin' all spring. Yes sir, ya found us a right fine spring camp."

Ely smiled as he nodded in agreement, then said, "Why don't ya send Benny out to make meat, I's tired of this hard jerky."

Grub didn't say a word, just turned and looked up to where Benny was dragging firewood down for fire and yelled up at him, "Benny, ya figure ya could go find us some fresh meat, we's tired of nothin' but jerky." Less than an hour later they heard the boom of Benny's rifle as it echoed up the canyon.

The trail the three of them were leaving was easy enough for Mel and his companions to follow. In this soft ground and patches of snow, it would have been impossible to cover their tracks anyway. It made it mighty easy for the men following to stay on the trail without ever getting close enough for them to be discovered.

Nels Mitchel rode up alongside Mel and asked, "Mel, how much further ya plan on goin' today. I got this here boil comin' up on my butt an I needs to get outta this here saddle."

Mel looked at him with disgust, but said, "Not much further. Those three ahead of us ain't in no hurry; we'll stop at the next level spot I find." Nels nodded his appreciation and went back to his place in line along with

Patch McCord and Phil Hurley. Phil was bringing up the rear, leading their three pack horses.

Benny came riding back into camp with enough meat off the yearling cow elk he had shot for their supper and breakfast and told Ely he would take a pack horse down in the morning and get the rest of it. Grub asked, "Ya see any Injun sign or anythin' we need ta watch fer?"

Benny got a real serious look and said, "Only a small huntin' party of Crow's, if that's whatcha mean."

Ely was grinning as Grub turned back to Benny and said, "Don't be a smart-ass kid, that ain't somethin' ta joke 'bout."

Benny looked at him dead serious and asked, "Who's jokin'?" but Ely and Grub both knew Benny would have never fired his rifle if there had been any Indian sign in the area.

After a few minutes, Benny grinned then said, "I did come across a pretty big set of bear tracks. We best tie these horses on a good strong picket line tonight, or we might be chasin' them tomorrow instead of trappin'."

Ely nodded, but Grub asked, "How big, is it a Grizz?"

Benny answered, "Naw, but I bet it's a big boar."

Grub replied, "Maybe we outa take turns watchin' tonight. You know how hungry and cantankerous they can be when they first come outta their dens in the spring." Ely thought for a minute then said, "Ya, you're right, no sense takin' a chance, missin' a couple of hours sleep ain't worth the trouble an ol' bruin could cause."

Mel and his partners were camped in the pines just before the pass that led down into the canyon south of Granite Peak. It was cold, and the howling wolves came in, so close none of the four of them got any sleep.

Benny had the last watch, so he'd already had five or six hours of sleep. He sat there by the fire and listened to his two older partners snore while he added just enough wood to the fire to keep it going. He could hear the wolves howling way up the canyon above them and right before morning the horses got nervous enough to stomp the ground a couple of times, but nothing more than that happened.

Chapter 14

Along Black's Fork

RAVEN WING OPENED her eyes just as the last of the stars were fading and the first light of dawn washed over the sky. Shining Star was sleeping quietly as were both babies and she thought of Running Wolf, her sister, and Grizzly Killer. She wondered about all three of them, and wondered, had Running Wolf and Grizzly Killer caught up with Sun Flower and the Cheyenne?

As more light came through the smoke flap bringing with it the promise of a new day a calm feeling came over her. Luna still lying next to Shining Star got up, came over and put her head on Raven Wing's lap, staring into her eyes. At that moment, she knew that her family was safe.

Shining Star stirred and opened her eyes, the swelling was down enough that both eyes opened wide. For the first time since the war club had hit her, the pounding pain in her head was gone. She smiled at Raven Wing and realized it didn't hurt when she did so. She sat up and looked over at the two babies still sleeping soundly, then at the white wolf with her head on Raven Wing's lap. Raven Wing sat up and said, "Our husbands and sister are on their way home. I know they are all safe." Shining Star smiled never doubting for a minute that Raven Wing was right.

Morning Star started to fuss, and she picked her daughter up. The dizziness was gone as she moved and settled back down of the buffalo robes to nurse her baby girl. Raven Wing reached out and gently put her hand on the side of her head then smiled again saying, "It is a good morning, the swelling is not so bad today."

Running Wolf moved the bodies of the Cheyenne away from the fire while Sun Flower treated the wound on Zach's shoulder. The cut was deep, and she used sinew from Zach's possibles bag and a needle to carefully sew the cut closed. Zach tried to keep his mind on other things to fight off the pain of what was happening. But it brought back memories of Shining Star sewing a cut closed on this same shoulder the first time he had met her after fighting the Ute war.

He watched Sun Flower's beautiful face now battered and bruised and thought just how harsh and violent this land he'd grown to love can be. He wondered as he had many times what his life would have been like if he would never have come to the mountains. Would he have been as happy on the farm in Kentucky as he is in these shining mountains with these two beautiful but very different women? He thought back to the Ute village on Rock Creek and how he struggled within himself about taking Shining Star as his second wife as everyone including Sun

Flower expected him to do. Now he couldn't imagine his life any other way. As Sun Flower finished wiping the blood from his arm and hand, he held her tight and looked into the heavens and thanked God for his life and keeping his loved ones' safe.

All three of them were exhausted after three days and nights on the trail with very little sleep. The threat from the Cheyenne was gone, so they stayed right there for the rest of the night. Running Wolf went out and checked on the horse herd then jumped up on his Chestnut and rode out and brought in the Crow and Cheyenne horses they had left a mile away before stalking in on the Cheyenne.

Zach looked at Sun Flower's black eye and bruised check in the light of the fire and felt terrible all over again that he had not protected her. When Running Wolf returned, Sun Flower told them of Raven Wing's escape—how she had kicked Silent One so hard he needed help the next day to mount his horse. How she had run out into the darkness so fast the others could not catch her and how one of them had been attacked and killed by a wolf while out looking for her.

Zach patted Jimbo on the head and said, "So that's where you went that first night, boy."

Sun Flower smiled and said, "I should have known it was Jimbo, not a wolf."

Running Wolf went through the Cheyenne's supplies and found jerky; then they rolled out their blankets close to the fire to sleep for the rest of the night. Zach looked Jimbo in the eyes and said, "Boy, you have guard duty tonight." Then he smiled knowing the big dog had guard duty every night. Sun Flower snuggled into Zach's strong arms feeling safe and content. It didn't matter they were nearly a hundred and fifty miles from home, as long as she was with Grizzly Killer she felt like she was home. Just before dawn a couple of wolves started to howl, and Sun Flower pushed even closer into Zach's warm embrace as they both enjoyed the wild, mournful sound.

Running Wolf was up and had the fire burning before the stars were all faded by the coming dawn. He needed to get back and find out if Raven Wing was alright. Jimbo had left on his morning hunt, and that alone told them all the area was safe this morning. He returned with a rabbit in his mouth but instead of taking time to cook it they loaded it with the other supplies they felt they needed from the Cheyenne and started pushing the two dozen horses west toward the Seeds-Kee-Dee, Blacks Fork, and home.

As the sun came up behind them, it cast its warming rays across the high desert landscape of flat top buttes and broad, barren basins, rolling sage and grass-covered hills with an endless sky overhead. Now that Sun Flower was safe, Zach could take the time to appreciate the beauty of this dry, treeless land. The size of the western frontier still amazed him even after all the years he'd lived here. He could see the snow-covered Uintah Mountains to the south-west and smiled knowing they were heading home.

Running Wolf left Zach and Sun Flower to manage the herd of horses while he rode north looking to make meat. It wasn't long until he topped a rise and in the broad, shallow valley below and next to a small winding stream, there were antelope scattered all along the sage-covered slope. He backtracked until he was well out of sight then tied his Chestnut to a sage and crawled back to the top of the ridge. He tied the two feathers he wore in his long black hair onto a stick and slowly raised them up above the sage he was lying in. The slight warm breeze that was blowing just made the feathers flutter and twist. It wasn't long before two of the small prairie goats were watching the feathers and started walking toward them. He knew how exceptional the antelope's eyesight was and even the slightest movement would be seen.

Laying there in the brush with his rifle to his shoulder motionless, he felt like it was days before one of the antelope got into range. He fired. One antelope fell, a second bolted out through the sage, running like only an antelope can. He had watched these graceful little animals many times but still marveled at their running speed and unbelievable eyesight.

After gutting his downed prize, he walked back and got the chestnut then loaded the antelope over the back of his saddle and rode back to where he figured Grizzly Killer would be. They were southwest of the Black Butte when Running Wolf finally found them again. Both Zach and Running Wolf were staying off the top of any rises trying to keep from being seen in case more enemies might be watching.

Once they met up again, they pushed northeast around another mountain that was pushing up from this broken country. They could see this one had both pine and quakies on its slopes and once north of it they pushed on to the Seeds-Kee-Dee.

They had covered nearly fifty miles this day stopping only once to rest the stock and cook the rabbit Jimbo had caught. The stock, as well as themselves, were ready for a rest. As Zach and Running Wolf watered the horses and let them graze, Sun Flower skinned the antelope, built a fire and then got several strips of the fresh meat roasting.

As the sun set, the whole western sky turned flame red with streaks of sunlight coming through the broken and scattered clouds. Just at dusk coyotes started their chorus all around them and if not for their worry about Raven Wing, Shining Star and the babies this would have been a mighty enjoyable evening. It was still cold at night, but the day had been warm, and Zach could tell with the melting snow the river was a little higher than when they had crossed just a couple of days ago. Another week or two and the crossing would be down-right treacherous.

Zach heard Jimbo get up for his morning hunt just as the sky was starting to turn gray along the eastern horizon. The fire had completely died out, and he held Sun Flower tightly in his arms enjoying her warmth. Again, this morning Running Wolf didn't wait for light, he was up right after Jimbo left and stirred life back into the fire. Sun Flower reheated some of the antelope she had cooked last night for their breakfast while Zach and Running Wolf got the horses ready to go.

They left before Jimbo returned knowing he would catch up to them in no time at all. From here Zach figured they were nearly a hundred miles from home by following Black's Fork and Black's Fork was still approximately fifteen miles to the west.

They had traveled only a couple of miles when Jimbo came running up alongside Zach, and with a simple hand signal he sent him on ahead as their scout as he always did. These horses were all used to the trail, and except for wanting to stop and graze whenever they came to a grassy area, they were easy to push along. Zach knew this country well, and he knew they would make good time again today. Still being out on the flatlands he hoped to cover as much country as they had the day before but the next day would be much slower going once they got into the foothills of the Uintah's.

It was midmorning when they got to Black's Fork, and Zach then told Running Wolf to take an extra mount and ride like the wind to get back home. He said to him that he and Sun Flower would bring the horses along following the river and he needed to make sure the women and babies were safe. Zach figured Running Wolf could make it by midnight by switching mounts but driving this horse herd would take over two more days. Running Wolf hesitated but only for a minute, he knew Zach was right, and he appreciated the fact Zach was willing to take the whole herd on his own. He needed to know if Raven Wing, Shining Star, and the babies were safe.

Running Wolf picked the beautiful pinto Zach had taken from his encounter with the group of Cheyenne hunters from the week before and headed straight west across the waterless badlands. There was grass along the river although it was last year's growth, it was all that was available to the hungry horses, and Zach let them graze for a couple of hours before he moved on. He was relieved Running Wolf would get back home tonight even if it would be very late tonight. He believed Raven Wing would have made it back home, but so many things could happen in this rugged country you could never be sure.

The sky had remained clear and the warm afternoon sun felt mighty good to them as they pushed the horses along the banks of Black's Fork. The cold winds from just days ago had given way to the first truly warm spring days. Although still weeks away from the buds opening on the willows and cottonwoods along the river, Zach could see they were swelling getting ready for the spring debut of green as the world comes to life after the long cold winter.

Sun Flower was content riding beside her man in the warm sun. Her bruised face was healing but still tender to touch. Her neck was chafed from the rope being around it for a couple of days, but she was happy now being with Grizzly Killer. She knew the one above had led him to her that day four summers ago and that they were meant to be together. She felt the scar from the Arapaho arrow just above her breast and now this ordeal with the Cheyenne, she knew she had been spared both times to continue her life with Grizzly Killer. She hadn't given him a child yet, and she didn't understand why but she was sure she was supposed to be with him, why else was she spared both times.

They let the horses travel at a comfortable pace not hurrying as they had before. Now that Running Wolf was going to be home, they didn't feel the need to push themselves or the horses nearly as hard as they had. They started seeing antelope out in the sage, and even a few deer ran from the willows along the river. There were ducks and geese in high numbers that would fly up ahead of them on the numerous bends in the river as it ribboned its way across this flatland before losing its waters to the larger Seeds-Kee-Dee.

As the warm days came more often, the water in Black's Fork kept rising. Zach could see a big difference just since they had left home. He had hoped to make it as far as where Ham's Forks runs into Black's Fork, but he could tell he had let the horses graze for too long, they weren't going to make it before dark. As he started looking for a good place to hold the horses and camp he thought about

Running Wolf wondering how far up the trail he would be by the time darkness fell.

Just ahead the river made a large oxbow bend. He could turn the horses loose in there to graze. Along the banks of the river was grass and if he and Sun Flower camped right at its mouth, he wouldn't need to hobble them or set up a picket line. There was one lone cottonwood growing near the bank and an old one that had been struck by lightning laying on its side that would provide good firewood. It was a perfect spot to camp, even though there was still a little daylight left they turned the horses into the oxbow and stopped for the night. With his hand making a circle overhead he sent Jimbo to scout the area around them for any unseen trouble.

After unloading what few items they had with them, Zach stood looking at the still, snow-covered peaks of the Uintah's. They were fifty or sixty miles southwest of them, but those mountains had become his home, and he longed to be back. He thought again about Running Wolf hoping he hadn't had any trouble and again about how he had left Shining Star there with the babies. He knew there was no other choice; they had to leave her there while they went after Sun Flower and Raven Wing but still, he worried. He knew head injuries could be trouble even days after they happened. He was sure Running Wolf would be there before morning, and he knew that Running Wolf was as worried about his sister as he was about his wife.

Sun Flower walked up to his side bringing him back to the present. He put his arm around her and pulled her close as she too stared at the towering peaks just above the area that had become their home. She had been quiet most of the day as her mind pondered on what had happened, and on the love she felt for Grizzly Killer. She knew he loved her just as deeply and she had never doubted, not even for a minute that he would rescue her from her captors. She could smell the musky smoke from many campfires on his buckskins as she looked up at him and said, "I worry for my sisters too, but my heart is glad, and I do not believe it would be if they were not alright." He smiled as he looked down into her dark brown eyes and nodded but she could see through his smile to the grave concern that lied beneath.

They started a fire and got some of the antelope roasting. Running Wolf hadn't taken any of it with him; he had wanted to travel lite. There was plenty of it, and Zach knew he wouldn't have to make meat until after they got back home.

Just before the sun went down, Sun Flower pulled off her dress, and as he had watched her do many times before, she walked over to the icy waters of the river and bathed. Her skin was covered with goosebumps as she walked back, and her teeth were chattering by the time she reached the warmth of the fire. He picked up his blanket, wrapped it around her and held her close until the shivering had stopped. She felt completely safe being in his arms once again. They made love by the fire, and the light faded with the setting of the sun.

Jimbo returned with a fat rabbit for his supper and after they ate they laid back down and watched as the stars slowly filled the rapidly darkening sky. With the horses grazing peacefully and Jimbo curled up by their feet and with Sun Flower safely in his arms once again, Zach dozed off into the first sound sleep he'd had in days.

Chapter 15

Spring Trappin'

MEL AND THE OTHERS were tired and ornery as the light finally drifted through the pines the next morning. They had kept the fire raging throughout the night thinking that was the only thing keeping the wolves at bay. None of them felt like packing up and leaving. The boil on Nels butt was coming to a head and he was trying to get one of the others to lance it. Finally, Patch said, "Come over here, if'n this is the only thing to get ya ta shut up 'bout it." Patch pulled out his skinning knife and stuck the end of it in the fire as Nels walked over and pulled his filthy greasy buckskins down past the boil on his rump.

Patch winced has he se the large red boil that looked as if it wanted to erupt then said, "Ya best lay down, ya might jerk and then have a whole slice taken out yer butt." Nels cursed, then mumbled, "Doubt it'd hurt any worse."

He laid down next to the fire and Patch took the tip of his very hot knife and in one motion pushed down into the center of the boil. The skin sizzled for a quick moment then the puss oozed out cooling the hot tip of the knife. Nels moaned as Patch wiped off his knife and said, "Ya need a poultice to draw out that puss, but since we ain't got nothing ya can just use some hot water."

Mel and Phil had been watching as Patch lanced the boil and both of them winced when the tip of the knife went in. Patch walked over to the other two and said, "One of us outta go see where Benny and them other two is goin'. Nels ain't gonna be ridin fer a day or two." Mel looked thoroughly disgusted and said loud enough for Nels to hear, "Okay, you and Phil go find 'em, but don't let 'em see ya, an don't leave no tracks they can find neither. If'n we need ta ride, Nels will either have ta ride or walk and try ta keep up 'cause we ain't gonna lose 'em."

Nels heard what was said alright and he knew well Mel meant it. Mel and Phil wouldn't hesitate to leave him out here alone for a minute. Patch, he wasn't sure about. He and Patch had been buddies for a long time. They had met up with Mel and Phil back in Missouri and had done some serious drinking a few times at the saloons along the waterfront in St. Louis. They had all been together now for well over a year and had always gotten along. Even Benny had been one of them when they came west, but it hadn't surprised Nels any when Benny left with those other trappers. Mel treated him like a slave, and none of them knew much about trapping, so none of them were making any money.

Nels didn't feel right about robbing the three they were following, he knew right from wrong, but he'd never been strong enough willed to stand up to someone like Mel Tillman. He knew if he didn't go along the others would just leave him, and he knew he could never survive out here alone. He didn't realize some brigades had lost men that would be glad to take in an honest, hard-working man and show him how to trap and survive. Nels felt he was caught, stuck with these men he didn't care for and doing things he knew was wrong and he hated himself for it.

While Patch and Phil were checking on Benny and the two old trappers, Nels boiled water in the coffee pot then took an old ragged shirt he still carried with his other truck and ripped an arm from it. He soaked it in the scalding water and when it was still nearly too hot to touch he held it on the extremely tender oozing boil.

The next morning Benny took a pack horse and headed down to where he had hung the elk up high enough off the ground he felt it was safe from any critters. Grub and Ely set out with their traps to get their lines set. Ely went upstream while Grub went down. Neither of them had to go very far before placing the first of the traps.

Grub found the first slide less than a quarter mile from their camp and stepped out into the icy water to pound in the stake to hold the trap. The slide where the beaver had been dragging aspen branches down the hill and into the water entered the top end of the pond where the water was quite shallow. Grub knew he had to be in water deep enough so when the beaver was caught, he couldn't get his head above the water so he would quickly drown and that required he wade out into the freezing water several feet. After getting the trap set, he put the oily castor on the top of the stake as an attractant then walked up out of the water and on to find the next slide.

His feet ached from the cold before he even had half of his traps set. He stopped to build a fire to warm up his aching legs and feet. Benny found him just as he was pulling off his moccasins to rub his feet. Benny smiled as he walked up to Grub's little fire and asked, "That icy water gettin' too much fer ya ol' man."

"By damn boy, I's been in cold water before, but that there is so cold it oughta still be solid ice," Grub replied then continued, "Ya have any trouble getting' that there elk back ta camp?"

Benny shook his head and said, "Naw, I had pulled her way up in a tree yesterday, so I just had to lower her down onto the horses. I cut her in half and put half on each horse. I hung her up in that stand of Pines down below camp."

Grub nodded his approval and continued rubbing his aching feet.

When Ely left camp, he had hiked right past all the closer ponds and slides and went all the way upstream to the very first pond they had passed coming down into this canyon. He figured to save the closer ones for later. Then he too started the slow and painfully cold process of setting his traps.

Patch and Phil were following the trail the three of them had left as they came down from the snow-covered pass. Phil was in the lead when he saw where the tracks they were following had stopped. It was in a bend in the trail, and it was the place where Ely had first seen the beaver ponds still a couple of miles below.

They stopped and tied their horses continuing foot until they were less than a quarter mile from the first pond when they saw Ely standing in the water well up past his knees driving a stake into the mud. Phil smiled and whispered to Patch, "Ya gotta give it ta ol' Mel, lettin' them their trappers freeze their asses off in that ice water and us gettin' all the plews is sure 'nough better 'an us freezin' tryin' ta trap them there miserable critters."

The thought of what they were going to do didn't bother Patch as much as it did Nels but he didn't feel good about it either like it appeared Phil and Mel did. They were downright excited about taking all the plews Benny, and the two older trappers had taken over the last year.

They watched from their hidden spot in the trees as Ely finished this set and moved on downstream to the next. Patch whispered, "Wonder how fer down-stream they's camped."

Phil looked at him and said, "Don't matter, they gonna be here a while 'til they's get all the beaver from this here stream. Then we's is gonna step right in and relieve 'em of their load. We's is goin' ta do 'em a favor. They won't have ta carry all them heavy plews to Ronnyvoo." He was grinning, almost chuckling at the joke he had just made. For Patch the money those plews would bring sounded mighty good, but he still didn't like the idea of what they were going to do to get them.

The two of them rode back up over the pass and back into their camp; it was early afternoon when they got there. Nels had just put the hot wet rag on his boil another time, and Mel was adding more wood to the fire. They dismounted, and Phil handed his reins to Patch to take the horses then looked at Mel and said, "They's settin' their traps down t'other side maybe six or seven miles. We didn't get any too close, but they's is gonna be there a while. There's beaver ponds goin' down that there creek fer as far as yer could see. I bet they's trap right there where they's at fer the next couple of weeks or maybe more."

Mel smiled at that news and said, "Well we just gonna wait 'til they's got their trappin' done and then we's will go on down and relieve 'em of their heavy load."

Benny picked up the traps Grub had left and said, "You sit there by the fire ol' timer and get yer feet warm, I'll go get the rest of these set."

Grub answered, "Ya best watch who you callin' ol' timer, ya damn kid, er I'll shows ya I ain't as old as you figure."

Benny just smiled thinking he had got under Grub's skin a little but it was all in fun and Grub was glad Benny was there to help.

Benny hadn't gone far when he found the next slide, and as he waded out into the freezing water he figured Grub was right, this water was so cold it still should be ice. By the time Benny got the rest of the traps set, his feet and legs ached from the cold so bad he could hardly walk. When he got back up to the fire Grub had made, Grub had left, but he added some more sticks and blew life back into it. Then he removed his moccasins and rubbed his aching feet.

He thought about home and how he had hated farming. He knew he was meant to hunt and trap, but farming was never as painful or dangerous as trapping. The cold got right down into a man's bones and caused this ache that just wouldn't leave. The work never seemed to stop; you were either wading in this freezing water setting traps, or wading in the freezing water checking the sets, then skinning the beaver and scrapping the hides and stretching them on the willow frames. If you weren't doing any of that, you were making the willows frames or hunting for food. Then there were the horses that had to be watched and cared for. You had to tan the hides of the game you took, out of those hides you had to make your clothing, moccasins, ropes, and packs. You had to keep all the tack for the horses in good shape and while doing all of this you had to keep a real close watch for Indians, bears, mountain lions, a cantankerous moose, and even the tiniest of mice could get into your truck and ruin everything that you have. You had to make sure your guns were always in good working order. If the flash hole got dirty your rifle wouldn't fire, and your life surely depended on your guns, both your rifle and pistol and you had to keep your traps in good working order.

It seemed the only time there wasn't work stacked up waiting for you to do was the dead of winter. There was still work of course the horses had to be fed and watered and firewood was a continuous job, but there was a lot of down time in winter. It could get so bitter cold you just stayed inside all the time and that would start to wear on a man more than any work did. Even braving the below zero temperatures to go out and make meat was a well-needed break from setting in the tiny cabin feeding wood to the fire and staring at the walls and each other. Then there were the dangers, crossing the raging rivers in the spring, avalanches in winter, rock slides in summer, blizzards, and lightning strikes, winds blowing over trees, a broken bone or an infected cut or animal bite. Hydrophobia from an infected bat, wolf, or coyote, and the ever-present danger of the Indians

. Some of the Indian tribes seemed to accept the white man trapping in their lands like the Shoshone, Crow, and

Utes but others; tribes like the Blackfoot, Bloods, Gros Ventre, Cheyenne, and Sioux and many more just seemed to want to kill anyone that trespassed on what they considered their lands. At times, even the friendly tribes could turn hostile mighty quick if they felt like they had been wronged in some way, then there were the ever-present dangers of hunger and thirst. Sometimes it took days and days to find a water hole or anything at all to eat, any of these things could cost a man his life, and only he and his god above would ever know if he went under.

Benny looked up at the towering Granite Peak just a few miles north of him, with the blue sky and billowing white clouds behind it. He watched a pair of golden eagles soaring the heights above the pines covering the ridge tops and listened to the blue jays in the forest behind him. He could smell the scent of the fresh pine as it mixed with the sweet smell of the burning pine from his small fire. He watched a weasel still with its white winter coat chase a squirrel up a tree then heard the last desperate chatter of the squirrel as the weasel made its kill then carried the lifeless squirrel back to her little ones. He watched a bright mountain bluebird sitting on a willow branch waiting for any unsuspecting insect that might move within his view.

Benny loved being in the Rockies; he knew this was the life he was meant to live. Even with its dangers, pain, and hard work. He loved being here alone, right now by this little fire all by himself as he watched and listened to the wonder of nature all around him. It filled him with a sense of awe and wonder. He loved these two older men as well, and he had learned it was alright to go out and be by yourself, but a man needed the help of others as well, he needed their friendship, company, and protection. Yes, he loved being alone working his trap line, but it was comforting to know Grub and Ely would be in camp when he returned.

While Benny's feet warmed by the flames, he held his soaking wet moccasins over them until they were almost too hot to hold and then pulled them onto his still cold feet. The heat felt good on his feet and lower legs as he put out the fire and headed back to camp.

When he walked in Grub had cut a roast off the elk Benny had hung in the tree that morning and was getting it set up on a spit over the fire. Ely had his wet moccasins set on stakes drying in the warmth of the fire and he was sitting there rubbing his cold, aching feet. The two older trappers looked up as Benny walked in and Grub asked, "Ya get 'em all set?"

Benny answered, "Well if'n I didn't I'd still be carrying 'em now wouldn't I?"

"Didn't nobody ever teach ya any respect fer yer elders?" Grub replied.

Benny didn't answer he just smiled at Grub, then Ely said, "Come on over here and finish dryin' out, Benny, an' leave that cantankerous ol' fool alone."

The rest of that day was spent doing camp chores. Benny cut several small logs and lashed them together onto the tree, so they had a table to prep their meals from. He then stretched out the elk hide and started scraping it making sure all the flesh, fat, and such was removed making the rawhide ready for the brain and water mixture that was used to tan the hides into a softer usable leather. This hide still needed the hair scraped off, but they didn't have enough ashes in their fire pit for that just yet. Benny would leave the hide staked to the ground for the next couple of days until there were enough ashes to cover the hair side of the hide. After the ashes set on the hair for a couple of days and kept it moist, the hair would scape right off the hide then he would be able to start rubbing in the brain and water mixture.

Ely watched Benny working that hide, and he was amazed and pleased with just how fast Benny was learning. When Benny had finished scraping it, Ely walked over and smiled. He didn't think he or Grub could have done any better.

The next morning, after eating a bit of leftover elk roast the three split up to go and check their trap lines. Ely went upstream to where he had started, and Benny went downstream to where the very last trap was set while Grub started right by camp working downstream. They had thirty-two traps between them. Grub and Ely each had ten while Benny had an even dozen. With the traps being set for less than twenty-four hours they didn't figure they would have much of a catch today but if they had caught a few they wanted the traps cleared and reset.

Ely got to the set, and he could see right off something was amiss. The ground was all tore up right where the slide entered the water. He couldn't see his stake at all. There had been a couple of times in the past he had lost a trap because his stake had come loose and the beaver had been able to swim away with it, but this looked different. He cautiously looked all around before he stepped out of the cover of the trees and started down the slide. When he got into the first muddy area, he could see, plain as day, the track of a giant bear. He looked behind him and all around again then went on to the water's edge.

He turned around again and studied the area all around him but still couldn't see a thing. Every time he turned his back to the mountain his skin crawled with the feeling he was being watched. In the mud, there at the edge of the water, Ely found his trap with its ring still around the stake that had been pulled from where he had pounded it in. The remains of a beaver's foot were still stuck in the jaws of the trap. A bear had definitely robbed this trap, but that isn't what had Ely upset right now. He indeed hated losing a good plew; that was money in the bank, but he couldn't shake the feeling he was being watched. What he didn't know, was the bear up the hill somewhere watching him or was it something much more dangerous. After all, they were in the Gros Ventre Mountains.

Chapter 16

Being Watched

MEL AND PHIL WERE setting on the bend in the trail still a long way above that first pond. They could see Ely standing there by the edge of the pound, but they were too far away to tell anything at all about what he was doing. Phil said, "What'd I tell ya; they's there alright, an' there's 'nough beaver ponds ta keep 'em there awhile too."

Mel didn't say anything for a few more minutes. He watched, thinking he didn't want to wait long before the three moved on, but he didn't want to move too quickly either and miss out on a lot of plews those fellows were going to trap.

Ely had lived in these mountains for nearly ten years now; he knew to trust his instincts, but he couldn't tell for sure what his instincts were telling him. He stopped and studied every little opening up on the hill behind him. He knew a bear had robbed his trap of the beaver and it could very well be that same bear now satisfied having just eaten a sizeable beaver was sitting up in the trees watching him, but what if it was more than that, Indians wouldn't let you see them unless they wanted you to. He decided to go on downstream checking the rest of his sets and see just what happens, keeping a mighty cautious eye all around while he did so.

Mel and Phil waited right there until Ely had moved on down out of site and then mounted up and rode back up over the pass and to their camp. Nels had most all the infection drawn out of the boil now, and it was feeling much better. When Mel and Phil rode in, they were surprised to find Patch and Nels saddling their horses. Mel asked, "What's goin' on boys?"

Patch looked up and said, "Goin' ta make meat, we's tired a livin' off jerky. They were a few elk grazin' in that little flat you can see below us from over by the creek an' we gonna see if'n we can get us one of 'em."

Mel just nodded and waved. Fresh meat sounded mighty good to him as well.

Ely had taken his time checking the rest of his traps; the bear had taken his only catch. He had watched above and behind him all day long but had not seen hide nor hair of anything they needed to be concerned about. It was apparent there was a large bear actively working this area, and they may need to get serious about killing him if he kept stealing their beaver but for right now Ely figured losing one beaver was the cost of trespassing on this bear's home ground.

When he walked into camp, neither Grub nor Benny were back yet, so he got the fire going to warm up his frozen feet and legs. As he pulled the wet moccasins off his aching feet, he wondered how many more years his body was going to hold up to the rigors of this life he so loved.

It wasn't long until Grub came walking up the trail carrying one large beaver. He set it off to the side and smiled saying, "Damn pard, this here ol' coon is sure glad ta see that fire. I figure that stream has the coldest water I ever stepped my foot in."

Ely smiled as he said, "Well Grub, I don't reckon that waters any colder. I just reckon you is gettin' too old to take it anymore."

At hearing that Grub bristled up then said, "Maybe's your right, we is getting' a might long in the tooth fer livin' like this, but what else we gonna do that we's any good at."

Ely looked seriously now at Grub shaking his head and answered, "I don't reckon we can do nothin' but this, anyhow nothin' that we'd like. I figure we is just gonna trap and hunt and live in these shinin' mountains 'til the good Lord calls us home."

Grub nodded saying, "I's know your right, Pard, that's just what we'll do, and we'll be a complainin' 'bout it all the way back home."

Ely chuckled at that then nodded his agreement and threw a couple more pieces of wood on the fire.

It wasn't long after that Benny came into camp carrying another beaver. He went right to work skinning the two beavers while Grub and Ely put together the willow frames to stretch them on from the pile of willow branches they had cut the day before.

While the three of them all worked together, Ely told them of the bear robbing his trap and the feeling he had of being watched all the time he was up there. That concerned both Grub and Benny and Benny said, "Don't ya figure we best go hunt us a bear? We could use the fat anyhow."

Grub added, "Ya know, Ely, Benny's right. If that old bruin gets into another trap, it could get downright costly sayin' nothin' 'bout what he might do ta the horses."

Ely nodded his agreement and said, "I know you two is right, but I just don't figure it was that bear that was watchin' me. I can't put my finger on it, but in the morning I's is gonna ride back up the trail aways and sees if'n I can see anything."

Grub knew Ely well, and he knew his longtime partner could be overly cautious but that cautious nature of his had saved their bacon more than once over the years, and he had learned never to question Ely's judgment.

Benny asked, "What can I do to help?"

Ely shook his head and said, "You two just work the trap line just like everything is okay. I'll just slip up in the trees before light and follow our back trail 'til I gets above that first pond. I'll be movin' slow and quiet so it might take me 'bout all day."

Grub and Benny both nodded, knowing if Ely didn't want to be seen no one was going to see him.

The next morning after eating more of the elk and listening to Grub complain about not having any coffee, Ely headed out just like he had each morning as if he was just checking the trap line. Grub and Benny headed down to check their trap lines.

It was another lovely spring day; the weather had been good now for nearly two weeks, and Grub knew it wouldn't go on like this much longer without a storm. He mentioned that to Benny and as Benny looked up at the warm sun just peeking over the eastern ridge. He knew

Grub was right and said, "You figure when we get hit it'll be rain or snow?"

Grub shook his head and said, "No tellin', but when we's get back I figure we best prepare for either." They had just arrived at Grub's first set and as Grub started out into the bitterly cold water, Benny nodded at him and continued down to the other end of the line.

Ely started out staying right on the trail just like he had the previous two mornings as the trail went in and out of the quakies. He hadn't gone far when he saw the track of the bear, but it didn't appear to be all that fresh. Long before he got to where the first beaver pond was catching the ice-cold water as the still heavy snow in the high country melted, he left the trail and started climbing up the hill. He was heading for a big high rock outcropping that he figured would give him a mighty good look both up and down this canyon—if he could figure out a way to get up on top of it.

The climb was steep and strenuous and much farther than it had looked but by early afternoon Ely had made his way above the rock outcropping and he now just had a short downhill slide, and he would be on top. This outcropping stood out from the trees and brush of the hillside and he knew if he stood his silhouette could be seen for a considerable distance, so he got down on his belly and crawled out onto the largest rock. It was the size of a cabin, and it made him wonder how long it had been standing guard over this canyon.

The view of the canyon was breathtaking; from the sheer granite cliffs of the peak at its top to the lush green of the pines down lower. He could see the cascading stream tumbling its way down only to be slowed by the numerous ponds that were made by the industrious beavers. The beavers that he and just a few hundred other brave men risk their lives every day trying to trap.

Even with all the dangers he loved the Rockies, he and Grub had lived out here long enough it had become their home. He knew there were others that had made these mountains home. Grizzly Killer is who came first to mind. Although he had never been as far south as where Grizzly Killer lived with his Ute partner and their beautiful wives, he had listened to Grizzly Killer describe the Uintah Mountains enough times to know he would like to see them. They were the dividing line between the Utes and Shoshone who had been enemies until Grizzly Killer had helped make peace between the two tribes.

Ely sat there enjoying this view. He could see the trail going up the canyon when movement caught his eye. That movement turned out to be over a dozen mountain sheep heading down the very path they had come down just three days ago.

He studied every inch of the canyon, but nothing seemed out of place. The air was crystal clear with no sign of smoke in any direction. He saw three wolves trotting down the trail where the sheep had been with their noses to the ground, undoubtedly following the scent of the sheep. He could see a pair of golden eagles along with several smaller hawks riding the air currents high above the canyon floor. The screech of one of the hawks almost echoed as the sound hit the huge rocks where he was laying.

It was late afternoon before he decided they were the only ones in the canyon. It must have been that bear that was watching him. Still being cautious he slid back off the big rocks and started making his way back to camp. The hill was steep enough he'd used his hands and feet to climb up it, but he was on his butt sliding most of the way back down.

Grub and Benny were both in camp and had two more beaver skinned and scraped when they heard the familiar sound of a chattering squirrel. They both knew instantly it was Ely coming back. Grub put his hands to his mouth and screeched like that of a screech owl telling Ely all was safe.

Benny was lacing one of the beaver into one of the willow frames as Ely walked in and set another beaver on the ground by him. Benny smiled as he looked up and said, "This here stream is better trappin' than any of 'em we hit last fall."

Ely smiled back and said, "You just might be right. Ya see that there big ol' rock way up on the side of canyon there? Well, that there is where I's been. Spent better part of the afternoon up there an' I could see a powerful long way. These ponds go on down this here stream fer as far as I could see from way up there."

Grub looked at the rock and said, "That looks to be quite a climb pard."

Ely nodded and replied, "Slidin' back down on my butt I reckon was worse. Feels like I got me some good bruises back there."

At that Benny started laughing and soon Grub did too. Ely shook his head saying, "It weren't that funny."

That got them laughing even harder, and soon Ely was laughing along with them. With all the hard work and danger this way of life afforded there weren't all that many things to laugh about. Laughing at themselves for even the slightest of things uplifted their spirits and made them all feel better.

During the night, heavy storm clouds had moved in, and it was slow to get light. Benny was up first and had the fire going strong when Grub and Ely crawled out of the lean-to. The fire felt good to both of them, and as Ely stood there by the warmth of the flames he looked up toward the granite-faced peak way up at the head of this canyon but all he could see were clouds, and they were lowering mighty fast. He looked at Grub and said, "I figure were gonna be in fer it boys, we best secure everthing and if'n we don't want wet beds tonight we best make sure that lean-to is watertight."

Grub looked at Benny and smiled, then Benny said, "Ya Ely, Grub said yesterday this weather we's been havin' couldn't last."

"Well, it appears the ol' fool was right, now let's get ta work," Ely replied then Grub made some remark neither of them could hear as he turned and started working on securing their bedrolls.

Benny grabbed an ax and headed down to the pines where the elk was hanging. He was going to cut pine boughs to cover the sides and front of the lean-to, but as he entered the stand of pines, a giant black bear stood up only a few feet in front of him. His rifle was over a hundred feet away back at the lean-to and the thought that was the last mistake he was ever going to make ran through his mind. He raised the ax over his head, and the bear ached his neck and charged. Benny brought the ax down with all his strength hitting the large black bear just above the ear. The bear's forward momentum hit Benny in the legs, and he cried out as he went over backward to the ground.

When Benny hit the ground, it knocked the wind out of him, and as he gasped for air with no success he expected to be bitten and clawed by the bear, but the bear was motionless, laying there on top of Benny's feet. A moment later, Grub and Ely both came running into the pines, and the first thing Grub saw was the ax sticking in the bear head. He stood and stared for a minute then burst out laughing, and said, "Damn boy, when did ya start huntin' bear with an ax?"

Ely dropped down to his knee's asking Benny if he was alright. Benny had started to breathe again but was still a bit shaken. A couple of minutes later he nodded his head at Ely that he was alright then looked up a Grub and said, "Didn't figure I needed ta waste powder on this here feller." Grub laughed but then got real serious and said, "Boy we done taught ya better than to leave your gun behind."

"Ya, I know, I figured for a moment there, that just might be the mistake that put me under," Benny replied.

Then Ely told him, "This here wilderness don't give a man many chances, I figure you just used up one of them chances, so you best be mighty careful from here on out."

They left the bear right where it lay, for now, figuring it could wait until they had the camp better prepared for the storm. Benny pulled the ax from the bear's skull and went right to work cutting a couple of armloads of pine boughs. Once he had them back to camp, they weaved them around the edges and front of both lean-tos. Benny had to get a couple more armloads before they had the lean-to with their supplies and plews weather protected. The first snowflakes were falling when they hung the bear from a tree. By the time they had it skinned, the snow was sticking to the ground.

Mel and the other three had been watching the storm come in since first light. None of them wanted to be caught up as high as they were in this storm, so they decided the plews Benny and the two old trappers had was enough. They would make their move on them today and get out these mountains. They had heard other trappers say Taos paid a lot better than at Rendezvous. They would get out of the wilderness and take their plews down there. If they didn't like Taos or Santa Fe, they could follow the Santa Fe Trail back to St. Louis.

The four of them were nearly to the first beaver pond by the time the first snowflakes started falling. They hadn't seen where Benny and the trapper's camp was, but they didn't think it would be all that much farther so they tied their horses back in the trees by that first pond and went on down of foot.

Benny had decided after they had the bear skinned he was going down to check his trap line before the snow got any worse and Grub, although not as excited about doing it as Benny, seemed to figure it was a good idea since there was no telling how severe or how long the storm might last, so Benny and Grub headed downstream while Ely stayed to scrape the bearskin and get it tied over the lean-to for that much more protection.

Mel saw the smoke from their fire and stepped back into the trees to watch. He was smiling when he realized how easy this was going to be since only one of the old trappers was there. He didn't know where the boy or other trapper was, but he didn't care, they could take what they wanted and be gone in just a few minutes.

Mel shouted, "Hello, the camp!" just as they came out of the trees into the clearing where Ely had picked to camp. Ely jumped and stopped tying the bearskin on the lean-to and instinctively reached for his rifle but he never got his hand on it when Phil shot his gun. The heavy lead ball hit Ely about halfway between his shoulder and breast. The force of the impact sent him over backward. He twitched a few times and lay then lay there motionless.

Nels pushed Phil from behind saying, "You murdering bastard, there wasn't no reason to do that!"

Phil just looked at Nels and laughed saying, "You ever touch me again an' you'll get the same."

Then Mel spoke up, "Knock it off you two. Them other two probably heard that shot. Nels, you and Patch go get the horses and bring three or four of theirs ta load up these plews on and hurry up, them there others might be back anytime."

Chapter 17

Into the Badlands

RUNNING WOLF STOPPED only long enough to change mounts as he crossed the dry, barren badlands well south of the river. It was just over 40 miles till he could see the river again, where it had made its bend, and he could now follow it all the way home. He slowed the thirsty horses to a walk for the last mile, cooling their heated bodies so he could let them drink as soon as they got to the water. After they drank, he changed mounts again and continued at a steady lope mile after mile until the light was gone and he had to slow to a walk. He figured it would take another four or five hours to get there keeping the horses at just a fast walk, but there were places where he was able to push them into a lope for a short period of time.

Shining Star was asleep, but Raven Wing could tell she was dreaming again. She was restless and at one point said something but Raven Wing couldn't make out what it was. Raven Wing laid there in the dark teepee. She had let the fire burn down to just coals as she wondered about her sister and husband.

She had known since this morning they were safe, she wasn't sure how she knew, but she did. Even knowing that, she still wondered where they were and how long it would take them to get home. She wondered what her younger sister had to endure and she hoped the Cheyenne hadn't taken their anger out on Sun Flower for what she had done.

Luna jumped up from where she had been laying alongside Shining Star and staring straight north through the teepee walls tilted her head back and forth whining softly. A moment later she went to the door flap and pushed her way out disappearing into the night. Raven Wing smiled inside knowing Running Wolf was coming home; his white wolf knew where he was and where he was going all the time. The Wolf had always been his spirit helper but since Grizzly Killer had saved Luna and brought her home there had been no doubt in any of their minds that Luna was indeed the wolf that was Running Wolf's spirit helper.

Running Wolf was now only five miles from home. It was nearing midnight when suddenly the Pinto he was now riding reared and tried to turn and run. Suddenly out of the pitch dark a wolf appeared directly in front of them. Running Wolf told Luna to stay while he calmed the spooked horse. His Chestnut was behind, but he was used to Jimbo and Luna both and knew the white wolf by sight and smell. Once he had control again, he slid off the pinto and had Luna slowly approach until the wolf and horse touched noses. Luna licked the pinto's nose and that calmed the horse right down.

A little over an hour later Running Wolf could see the flickering light of the fire Raven Wing had gone out and started knowing the rest of her family would be riding in at any time. He saw her standing there in the light of the fire and slid off the pinto running to her waiting arms. She breathed a deep sigh of relief as she held her man again but then noticed Sun Flower and Grizzly Killer were not right behind him and Jimbo always ran in ahead to let everyone know Grizzly Killer was coming.

She pushed away from Running Wolf just far enough to look into his eyes and asked, "Where is my sister, and Grizzly Killer? Are they alright?"

He smiled as he nodded then told her, "Yes, they are alright, I came ahead to make sure you and my sister are okay. Are you?"

"Yes, we are fine, your sister sleeps. She was hurt badly on her head. Her head hurts her and she doesn't sleep well, but she is getting better each day." She then asked, "How is Sun Flower? Did they beat her too?"

Running Wolf said, "She is healing. The swelling is going down around her eye, but the bruise is still there."

Just then Shining Star stepped out through the teepee opening and Running Wolf left Raven Wing and walked over to give his sister a hug. He gently held her as she asked, "Where are my husband and Sun Flower, brother?"

He smiled and said, "They are fine, and are bringing in all of the horses that was taken from us and all of the ones that the Cheyenne had since they do not need them any longer. I came ahead to make sure you two, and the little ones are alright."

She smiled at hearing that, but as she did, he could see the lump that was still there on the right side of her head. His look changed to worry as he looked at Raven Wing with a questioning look. Shining Star stepped away and said, "It is healing my brother, but Raven Wing thinks it still might take a while. I don't see three or four of you now like when Raven Wing got here. I didn't know which one of her was the real one.

He continued looking at his wife still worried for his sister. He could see the black in the middle of Shining Stars eyes were not the same size. The longer he looked at Shining Stars pretty face the more pronounced the lump became to him.

Raven Wing walked over to them and said, "Running Wolf, I have done all I can for her, now it will just take time for her to heal. She is much better than she was just a couple of days ago and I think she will be that much better again in a couple of more."

Shining Star could see the worry on her brother's face, and with a crooked little smile, she said, "I will be fine, my brother. I have a daughter to raise and a husband to care for. If it were my time to go, I would already be gone."

He heard his son start to cry and as Raven Wing started for the lodge opening, they all followed her. When Shining Star stood upright after ducking through the opening, she paused just a moment to steady herself, and the move was not lost on Running Wolf. He reached out to support her and helped her sit down on the buffalo robes while Raven Wing picked up little Gray Wolf. When Gray Wolf saw his father, he smiled and held out his arms for Running Wolf to take him. Running Wolf's heart swelled with joy as he took his son from Raven

Wing's arms. Gray Wolf laid his head on his father's shoulder and went right back to sleep.

After they had him laid back down, Shining Star asked, "Brother, when will Grizzly Killer and Sun Flower be home?"

He thought briefly before answering, "At least two, possibly three sunrises."

She smiled thinking it was good she would have more time to heal before Grizzly Killer would see her again.

Running Wolf went out and took care of the two horses by rubbing them down with dry grass and turning them loose in the big meadow. Although it was a dark night, the white patches of snow stood out. He was amazed how much of it had melted in the few days he had been gone. After checking on Ol' Red wounds and softly talking to the big mule, he stood there and gazed all around; he had truly come to think of this place as home. Most of the meadow was clear of snow now, it would still be a few weeks before the grass turned green with the new growth, but the horses still had plenty to eat now the snow was nearly gone.

Grizzly Killer opened his eyes listening to the natural sounds around him. The stars were still sparkling bright against the dark heavens. He listened to the soft melody of the water as it made its way down the channel that it had cut across these flatlands in a time long forgotten. A wolf was howling way off to the west somewhere, and then he caught the sound of a flock of geese lifting off the water somewhere downstream. He could hear the faint snoring of Jimbo still curled up at his feet and he could feel the soft warmth of Sun Flower's naked body pushed up against his. He looked at the big dipper and saw how far it had made it around the north-star and knew it was still two or three hours before dawn. With Sun Flower held tightly in his arms he closed his eyes and went right back into a restful sleep.

The next time he opened his eyes Jimbo was no longer lying at his feet, but Sun Flower's soft, warm body was still in his arms. The stars were now mostly faded with the coming of dawn. He felt refreshed. This was the first full night's rest he'd had in days. He moved a lock of Sun Flower's jet-black hair and kissed her, and at that, she rolled up on top of him and they made love again in the cold morning air.

Zach wanted to get back and make sure Shining Star, Raven Wing, and the babies were alright, but he felt so good this morning with Sun Flower next to him that he didn't want to leave. He watched the horses lazily grazing on the dry grass. This piece of land between the gently flowing river of this oxbow bend had been the perfect spot to hold them for the night. He looked out over these sage-covered hills to the north and smiled as he could see three herds of antelope. The game was returning; the long terrible winter was finally over.

Sun Flower had stirred life back into the fire and was roasting some thin strips of antelope as Zach brought the horses up one at a time to saddle them. He wished he had his saddle and Ol' Red to put it on. He then wondered about his big red mule, was he okay? How bad was his wounded shoulder? Once he had the horses all saddled and ready to go Sun Flower brought him a strip of hot antelope and they sat on the dead cottonwood and ate. Jimbo came back just as they were getting ready to go, but instead of carrying a rabbit as Zach expected he ran right up to them and growled the deep soft growl from way down in his throat.

Zach looked the hills over carefully for he was worried now, had the smoke from the small fire been seen this morning? Could the Blackfeet that the Crow had been following come this far south? He wanted to follow Jimbo and find out, but he would not leave Sun Flower and put her in danger again. They put out the fire then pushed the horses across the river and headed south out into the badlands.

He pushed hard keeping the horses at a fast gallop for nearly five miles until he was far enough from the river they couldn't be seen. He then slowed letting them walk for another two or three miles. He was thankful the snow had not been gone for long; the ground wasn't dry enough to be leaving a dust trail in the air behind them.

They started a slow turn now toward the south-west. He figured they were about fifteen miles south of where Ham's Fork dumps into Black's Fork and in his mind, that could be the place where Jimbo had found the danger, whatever that danger was he didn't know, but he did know his dog. When Jimbo told him there was danger, Zach knew it was near.

Instead of following Black's Fork back home, he was now headed for Smith's Fork. It wasn't a direct route, and it would mean pushing the horse herd through the much rougher country. But it was safer. Zach figured it would add another day maybe more to their travel but whatever the danger Jimbo had found he wasn't going to lead them directly back to their home.

These badlands were dry, rough barren hills mostly a slate gray color with no growth at all on most of it. There were places between the hills and on the flats that sparse grass and sage grew but mostly it was a vast area devoid of life. He knew the route he was taking would mean no water for the horses today and possibly much of tomorrow, but after having all they wanted to eat and drink through the night, he figured they would be alright.

He kept a steady pace skirting the hills staying as much as possible to the flats. Although they were moving right along it was far from a straight route as they tried to stay out of the steep, narrow hills. By late afternoon he really had no idea how far they had come. The winding, twisted route had kept them moving hard all day, but he really didn't know how far they still had to go to reach the cold, clear water of Smith's Fork.

An hour later found them at a wash coming out of the hills with a stream of water flowing in the bottom and they worked their way down to it. When horses wouldn't drink, Zach tasted the water and found a bitter mineral and alkali taste. They crosse and moved on.

They stopped for the night in a flat with a bit of dry, sparse grass between two hills. There was no wood here for fire and with a quick look around all they could find to burn was small stunted sage. It was nearly dark by the time they had enough sage gathered to cook more antelope strips.

Zach just left the horses loose again tonight he didn't figure they would wander off the little grass that was here. Sun Flower had finished cooking the antelope and as Zach sat down next to her, he longed for a cup of coffee and a biscuit. As he chewed on the antelope strip, he thought back to last year's Rendezvous and the lack of supplies that had made it impossible to get enough to last out the year. The flour and cornmeal had lasted only until the start of winter and the coffee was gone not long after that. Rendezvous this year was going to be east of the great divide up on the Popo Agie. Bill Sublette had promised he would bring all he could carry out for this summer's big meet.

It had been decided they would hold two Rendezvous this year one on the Popo Agie in July and another clear over west of the Teton's in Pierre's Hole in late August. The Popo Agie is where Sun Flower and Raven Wing were raised. Their mother and father Bear Heart and White Feather still lived there in the village of Chief Charging Bull, and their brother Spotted Elk was their war chief. They looked forward to Rendezvous every year but this year was special, the women were going home.

Zach was up just as the first hint of grey started along the eastern horizon and without taking the time to eat or build a fire they were on their way. By midmorning, the country was changing, and he figured another two or three hours and they would be at Smith's Fork.

They crested a slight rise and looked at the majesty of the snow-covered Uintah's rising into the bright blue sky overhead. In front of them no more than five miles away was Smith's Fork with the green of the pines mixed in among the leafless cottonwoods and quakies leading south into the canyon as it descends from the snowbound heights of the towering peaks rising to the heavens not all that many miles to the south.

They continued a little more westerly now, Zach knew the horses all needed water, so he headed in a straight line toward it. When they were only about a mile from the river, he noticed a large bunch of buzzards circling just this side of the river. He slowed, but the horses in front could smell the water and started to gallop. Zach and Sun Flower with Jimbo now right by them moved ahead with caution. The horses now nearly a quarter mile in front of them suddenly scattered running in every direction. Zach came to a stop and saw a Grizzly Bear that had been feeding on a half-rotten elk carcass stand up looking all around, not knowing whether to chase the horses or not. Thirst soon overcome the horse's fear of the bear and they were all headed for the river again.

All the hair down Jimbo back was standing on end, he wasn't growling yet, but Zach knew he would be if the bear got any closer. They turned giving the bear a wide berth but keeping a close eye on the area the bear was in. Zach watched the buzzards overhead very closely. He knew if they flew down to the carcass the grizzly was no longer there. Less than an hour later they were all drinking the icy clear waters of Smith's Fork.

Sun Flower built a fire in a thick stand of pine not far from the river and started more of the antelope roasting while Zach rounded up the horses that were scattered for over a mile up and down the creek. By the time he had them all back in a group, it was late enough in the day they stayed right there protected by the pines.

Zach let the horses graze on the grass along and river, and as he watched over them, Sun Flower came upon a flock of pine hens. With skill learned as a child, she picked up two large stones and within the next few minutes she had taken two of the large birds. When Zach walked over to the fire, he smiled as he saw the two hens on a willow branch spit over the flames.

They laid there within the warmth of the fire together as the flames slowly died away. Sleep came easily to them as the last of the fire disappeared, leaving behind the bright glowing coals that would give off warmth for hours to come.

Zach couldn't see through the tops of the pines to look at the stars to know what time it was when Jimbo's soft low growl awakened him. He was listening carefully into the night when one of the horses stomped the ground then a couple more whinnied and stomped as well. Zach sat up and pulled on his moccasins, then with his trusted Hawken in hand stood staring out into the darkness. Sun Flower added more logs to the still glowing coals, and as the flames flared up, Zach was staring into the glowing red eyes of a giant grizzly.

Chapter 18

The Trail South

GRUB AND BENNY HAD BEEN on the trail right close to the stream where it cascaded down a steep rocky drop off and the noise of the rushing water was so loud that neither of them had heard the shot from back at their camp. The snow was starting to fall much heavier as they approached the end of their trap line. Even though they wanted to check all the traps three hours later it was nearly a blizzard. They took the single beaver they had and headed back to camp. They were wet and freezing when they got back, Grub wondered where Ely was since there was no fire. He had an uneasy feeling as they got close and his sharp trained eyes was scanning every inch of the terrain all around camp. Grub brought his rifle up and in seeing that, Benny never said a word he just dropped the beaver he was carrying cocked his rifle and stepped off to the side so Grub was not in front of him.

The snow was sticking and covering the ground and as they walked into camp the first thing they both saw was the lean-to where their plews were stored was torn apart and all their plews were gone. Then Grub saw Ely lying in the brush right where he had fallen. He froze right there and told Benny not to move. Grub's experienced eyes studied the ground all around. He could see the tracks that the four men had left but the snow was covering them fast. He wanted to run to his lifelong friend and partner but he was afraid of what he was going to find.

Benny was looking at the torn-up ground as well; he could see where the horses had been led into camp and where the loaded horses had been ridden out. Even though the trail was plain to see they both knew if this snow kept up it wouldn't be long before it was completely covered up.

Benny said, "They're gone Grub, and he headed straight for Ely. Grub hesitated not wanting to find what he was afraid he was going to find. Benny knelt by Ely's side looking at the gaping hole in his upper chest when Ely gasped in a ragged breath. Benny turned to Grub and yelled, "He's alive, Grub!"

Grub ran to his side and said, "Benny, get the fire goin' an put a pot of water to heatin', then fix him a bed in this empty lean-to so's we can get 'em out a this here storm."

Benny didn't hesitate at all and while he was getting that done Grub took his knife and cut the buckskin jacket and shirt away from the ragged wound. He then carefully rolled Ely up on his side and checked to see if the lead ball had gone all the way through, but it had not so he knew the ball would have to be cut out.

Ely's breathing was so faint Grub was afraid it would stop at any time. He had lost so much blood he was nearly as white as the still falling snow. Benny got Ely's bed roll spread out under the lean-to and then went to help Grub. They carefully lifted him into the lean-to and then stripped him down to his waist. He never woke during this time but when they moved his arm enough to get the shirt and jacket off he moaned and Grub said, "Sorry ol' friend, we's tryin' to be careful."

Benny looked up at Grub and saw there were tears running down his beard-covered checks.

They were about to lay him back down when Grub placed his hand on Ely's back to support him and he felt a lump under the skin. He looked and it was the lead ball pushing up against his skin from the inside. So, while he was still unconscious, Grub took his knife and cut right across that lump, then working the ball between his fingers. The .50 caliber lead ball squeezed out through the cut. Benny got an old broadcloth shirt he carried from the pack and cut a piece of it big enough to put over the small cut and then they gently laid him down.

While Grub was cleaning the wound where the ball had entered, Benny worked on making the lean-to water-tight and as warm as he could. He ran to the stream several times bringing up rocks and built a fire pit with a high back wall that would reflect heat into the lean-to. He then moved some of the coals from their main fire over and built up the fire right in front of Ely's lean-to. When he was finished he asked Grub, "Anything else ya can think of I need ta do?"

Grub just shook his head, then said, "As much blood as leaked out of him he needs water or broth or somethin' but 'til he wakes up they ain't much we can do 'bout that."

While Grub was concentrating on getting the wound just as clean as he could Benny started studying the tracks. The snow was letting up now and most of the tracks were gone but there were enough under the trees that had been protected that Benny was pretty sure there had been four men. He followed the trail losing it a time or two out in the open but he picked it up again when they had entered the trees.

Grub had used the rest of Benny's shirt bandaging the wound in Ely's chest when Benny returned and had him covered up. The heat reflecting off the rocks Benny had got had the lean-to right warm. Grub was sitting there by that fire wishing he could do more for Ely when Benny came back and asked, "How's he doin'?"

Grub looked up and shook his head saying, "'Bout the same, he's barely breathin'. I done what I can, just don't know if it's enough."

Benny said, "I figure there was four of 'em, and they must a passed us while we was down by the creek 'cause their track is leadin' right on down the canyon."

Grub looked at Benny and said, "Them bastards deserve ta be hanged, ever last one of 'em, but we got Ely ta care fer as long as he's breathin'."

Grub never left Ely's side the rest of the day. Benny kept a good pile of firewood there for the fire and the coffee pot full of hot water setting on coals just to the side of the fire. He cooked more of the elk but he couldn't get Grub to eat, he said he wasn't hungry.

Benny had never seen Grub turn down food before, in fact Ely said that's why they call him Grub 'cause he was always hungry. Benny had never seen Grub like this, his usual good-natured demeanor was gone.

Benny thought long and hard about what to do next. By afternoon Ely still had not woke up but Grub said he figured he was breathing a bit better. Since Benny couldn't find anything more to do around camp he went up stream looking for where Ely had set all his traps. The beaver slides were plain enough to find and by late afternoon Benny had retrieved all of Ely's traps and had a beaver to skin as well.

As Benny walked back into camp he saw that Grub was on his knees looking up, then he heard him start to pray, "Dear Lord, I knows I ain't been the best person most all of my life but me and Ely has always tried to do what's right. Lord, I done everthing I know ta do fer Ely, but now he needs your help. Please help him ta heal and for those that done this, bring down the justice they deserve to 'em. Amen."

Benny was just standing there with his hat in hand. Grub hadn't heard him walk in and jumped a little when he noticed Benny. He walked over and put his hand on Grub's shoulder to show his support and Grub just nodded and went right back to Ely's side. Benny built up the fire and while drying his wet, cold buckskins and moccasins he skinned and scraped the beaver hide and stretched it on a willow frame. Again, Benny tried to get Grub to eat but he just wasn't hungry.

Ely was still pale, in fact Grub thought to himself, he had seen men already dead that looked better than Ely did, but Ely was still breathing. Grub even thought he saw his eyes try to open once but then figured it might have been just the flickering light from the fire.

Benny made sure there was plenty of firewood to last them through the night. Then he too looked up at the cold night sky and asked God to please help Ely. The sky was clearing, there were a few stars trying to shine through. It was going to be a cold night with the clearing clouds but the fire reflecting the heat was keeping inside the lean-to comfortable. Benny was keeping both fires going and was sitting between them where it was so warm every now and then he would get up and walk around to cool off.

As the sky cleared wolves started howling above them and the eerie sound echoed down through the canyon. Soon other wolves were answering from way down below them. After they quieted down they heard the slap of a beaver's tail and Benny figured one of the wolves must have gotten too close. It always amazed Benny how far away you could hear a beaver slapping its tail on the water. It was the beaver's universal signal warning all others of danger. Benny had seen not only beaver but deer and elk alike run for cover when the sound of the beaver's tail slap was heard.

Just as the sky was first starting to lighten with the coming dawn Benny had dozed off as he sat there between the two fires. In the few minutes he slept, he dreamed. He was alone and he was tracking the men that had shot Ely and robbed them of their year's work. The tracks were plain to see but the country around him was unfamiliar. The sun was in his face and he knew he was going south. Just then he heard a voice, it was Grub and he jumped, awakened by Grub's words, "Welcome back Pard, ya had us a might worried." Benny looked over and Ely's eyes were open and he was moving his lips, almost no sound was forth coming but they could tell he was asking for water. Grub raised his head while Benny held a tin cup up to his lips while he sipped in the refreshing water. His eyes were sunken back into his head and he was so pale he looked like a ghost, but his eyes sparkled bright with the love of life they had always had.

Benny boiled some elk with plenty of fat and made a good broth. Ely couldn't drink much of it but he did get some down. Grub finally took a few bites of the boiled meat after Ely closed his eyes to rest. The effort of swallowing the broth took what little energy he had away.

Benny was standing by the fire looking south down the canyon and Grub could see the faraway look in his eyes and said, "Whatcha thinkin' on, Benny?"

Benny slowly turned to Grub and said, "I had a dream, just as Ely woke up this mornin'. I had a dream; I think I'm supposed to go after those men that done this."

Grub looked at him with a very concerned look and said, "I jus' 'bout lost one partner, I's sure as hell don't need to lose you too."

Grub could see the seriousness of Benny's face as he stood there staring south. Finally, Benny said, "Grub, I knows this might sound loco but I really believe I am supposed to go after 'em. I don't mean I want ta go after 'em, I mean I'm supposed ta go after 'em."

Grub didn't say anything, he just watched Benny's eyes as he studied the country to their south. He didn't know just what Benny had dreamed but he could see plain enough that Benny had taken the dream as a sign from a higher power. Finally, Benny turned to Grub and said, "This is somethin' I got ta do. You take care of Ely an I'll meet the both of ya at the Popo Agie for the Rendezvous."

Grub could see there would be no talking him out of this but he still said, "Ya know this is crazy boy, goin' after at least four men by yerself, but if this is somethin' ya gotta do I ain't gonna try ta stop ya."

Benny went right to work gathering his truck then went and got his horse. When he led the tall buckskin into camp he asked, "Why do figure they left us horses? They would have had to know we would come after 'em…"

"Ya don't have ta be smart ta be a murderin' thief. I figure the only thing they was figurin' on was gettin' gone 'fore me and you got back." Grub replied but then continued, "Listen Benny, I knows you a man capable of doing this, but you mind everything we has teached ya. Don't take no chances. Them plews ain't worth dyin' fer."

Benny again looked south down the canyon then turned back to Grub and said, "It ain't fer the plews Grub, it is because we can't let men that would do this to our friend go free. It's 'bout doin' what's right, an I believe I am supposed ta make it so."

Grub just nodded as Benny climbed in the saddle then said, "They's more danger out there than just what's in front of ya, ya keep that in mind, ya hear?"

Benny nodded, then looked Grub in the eyes and added, "You don't let him die, ya hear?" Then turned and headed down the canyon.

Grub watched him ride away until he was out of sight then turned to look at the pale sleeping body of Ely and for the first time in his life he felt alone. He was worried about Ely; he had never treated a wound this bad and now Benny was gone.

He knew Benny was capable but still alone in this wilderness was dangerous for anyone. Grizzly Killer was the only man he knew that had actually spent a winter all alone and he had made out alright but then Grizzly Killer wasn't just an ordinary man.

He thought back over the past year to everything Benny had learned and hoped he and Ely had taught him enough. He truly cared for the kid, these three trappers had become as close as any brothers. The thought of Benny being all alone chasing at least four murdering thieves across these rugged mountains caused him to shudder. He then looked up at the clearing sky, removed his wolf-skin hat exposing his long greasy unruly hair and asked God to watch over his friends.

This was the first time in Benny's life he had been on his own. As he rode down the canyon following the hit and miss tracks of the men in front of him he thought about everything he must do.

The men had nearly a full day's lead on him and he could tell by where he could see the tracks that they were traveling fast. In the trees where the ground had been protected from the worst of the storm he could see the tracks quite clear but out the open meadows and clearings the tracks had been nearly washed away.

By nightfall he figured he had covered over twenty-five miles and he could feel his horse tiring under him. He stayed on the trail until it was too dark to see the tracks then stopped and made himself a bed in the soft needles of the pine thicket where he was mostly protected from the weather.

He ate a piece dry elk jerky and watched the quarter moon pass across the tree tops. The cold night air sent a chill through him as he pulled the heavy buffalo robe up around his neck. The mournful howl of a lone wolf carried on the breeze from somewhere way off to the west. As he had done several times throughout the day, he asked God to help Ely heal and to help himself find those that had done this and give him the strength to do what must be done.

The moon was down when he next opened his eyes and the forest was dark all around him. His belly growled from hunger, the single piece of jerky he had eaten at bedtime had long since gone. He sat up and picked up his pouch to get another piece of the three or so day supply he carried, but the pouch was empty. Rodents had carried it all off in the night. He cursed himself for being so careless then drank his fill of the cold water from his water pouch and rolled his truck in his bedroll and walked down to where he had his horse hobbled on the grass by the creek.

When he started out the stars had faded but the forest floor was still dark so he stayed on foot leading his horse until it was light enough to see. The tracks of the men and heavily laden horses he was following were plain enough on the soft floor of the forest but became much more difficult to follow in the open where the storm had washed most of them away.

Ely hadn't slept much during the night, the pain in his chest and shoulder had become nearly unbearable and so, for the second night in a row, Grub hadn't slept either. They didn't carry any medicines and Grub didn't know a lot about healing plants. He did know that aspen and willow were used by the Indians for pain so he stripped some willow and aspen of their bark and boiled it in the coffee pot. He then had Ely drink a little of the hot, bitter tea. He also kept elk broth hot by the fire just in case he got hungry.

By late afternoon, Grub couldn't see any change at all in Ely. He was still pale and his eyes looked like sunken dark holes in his face. Benny had dragged in enough fire wood that he hadn't needed to worry about that and he had been able to keep the fire built up and Ely warm enough up until now. As Grub watched his friend fade in and out of consciousness he noticed he was starting to chill and beads of sweat was forming on his brow. As he gently wiped off his face he could tell a fever was starting to set in and now he truly feared for his best friend's life.

Chapter 19

The Long Way Home

RUNNING WOLF STEPPED through the opening to Grizzly Killers lodge to the smiles of both his sister and his wife. Ever since the attack by the Cheyenne, Raven Wing had stayed in this lodge with Shining Star and tonight would be no different. With both babies warm and asleep snuggled in their soft rabbit fur blankets, Shining Star rolled over under the buffalo robes giving her brother and Raven Wing as much privacy as she could. Running Wolf laid down next to Raven Wing closed his eyes and was sound asleep in less than a minute. Raven Wing gently put her head on his shoulder and thanked the one above for bringing him safely back to her.

She listened to his deep heavy breathing as his exhausted body was now totally relaxed and thought about how unlikely a couple they were. A proud Ute warrior and a Shoshone maiden. She remembered back to the first time she ever saw him at the warm springs over by Bear River as he backed up Grizzly Killer in his fight with the Frenchmen. Back then she never would have believed that she was meant to spend her life and raise her family with this man that should have been her enemy. She was happy and content, Grizzly Killer had made this happen and she would be forever grateful to him.

Daylight spread through the forest bringing the dim light to the inside of the lodge. Star started to fuss and then cry which woke Gray Wolf and he started crying as well. Shining Star sat upright and smiled when the movement had not caused the pain and dizziness that she had been experiencing. Running Wolf rolled over as Raven Wing got up as well. He watched as the two women nursed the babies, he was glad to be home but he wondered about Grizzly Killer. Where was he? He didn't expect him home for another day maybe two but he still wondered if they were alright. Even through Grizzly Killer was the greatest warrior Running Wolf had ever known, he was well aware even the greatest can be beaten, if not by his enemies, by this wild and dangerous land.

Running Wolf watched Luna, although he hadn't known it she had not been asleep all night. She had set there by his feet and looked as if she was staring through the buffalo hide covering of the lodge at what was happening on the other side. He wondered now, what could she see that he couldn't? She was his constant companion but she was still a great mystery to him. She seemed to see more and know more about what was out of their sight than even Jimbo the Big Medicine Dog. Did she know where Grizzly Killer was? Was he in some sort of trouble or is that why she was so intently staring at what to him seems like nothing at all, or was it just the mysterious nature of this beautiful white wolf that he could not yet figure out?

Raven Wing and Shining Star had gone outside now and had the fire going but Luna had stayed there with him. The smell of smoked buffalo roasting soon had him and Luna out by the fire. In the full daylight, he looked at his sister's head wound. He was concerned for the lump still plainly showed through her thick black hair. When Raven Wing told him it was only half the size it was two days ago he wondered how she had survived. He and Grizzly Killer had left in such a hurry they were not aware just how bad she had been injured.

Jimbo took a small step forward, but Zach softly whispered stay and the big dog stopped. His growl was still there but very low, Zach could see the glowing red eyes plainly but the rest of the bear was barely visible in the flicking light cast by the fire. The bear wasn't moving, just standing there on all fours. Zach figured he was only thirty yards from them and he knew if the bear charged the single shot from his Hawken would not stop a charging grizzly. They all were as still as the trees in the forest around them. Zach was afraid if any of them moved the bear may charge. Jimbo must have had the same thought for his tail wasn't even quivering.

They had been motionless now for several minutes but it had felt like a lifetime when a log in the fire popped. This wasn't just any pop it was loud enough they all jumped some. Sparks flew ten feet away from the fire and a cloud of smoke and tiny embers was launched into the air above them. It startled the bear as well for he jumped out into the night and was gone.

Zach stood there even longer waiting, listening trying to see into the darkness but there was nothing. The horses settled down and Jimbo stopped his growling. Zach finally turned to see the relieved look on Sun Flower's bruised face. He smiled at her and said, "Good thing he found that old elk carcass, if he would have been hungry we might've been in some trouble." She sighed in relief and asked, "Do you think he will come back?" "I don't reckon so, I figure he ate 'til he was full or he would have come after us. He will go sleep it off somewhere, you get back under the blanket and get some rest, I'll stay alert and keep an eye on the horses for whatever is left of the night."

She laid back down but sleep wouldn't come, she watched Zach and Jimbo as they patrolled around the horses and camp. It was chilly and then when the faint light of early dawn started to creep across the forest it got down right cold. She was just about to get up and add more wood to the fire when Zach brought an arm full over and built the fire back up. He stood there warming himself by the fire as she watched.

A grizzly that close is always a fearful thing, but she had always felt safe when Grizzly Killer was with her. Ever since that first time she met him with Raven Wing and Butterfly at the warm springs. He didn't know her then, had never seen her before, but he had fought to keep her safe. She watched him standing by the fire and felt a need to be next to him. She stood and with the blanket wrapped around her shoulders she went to him and leaned against his tall solid body. He smiled as he put his arms around her and she pressed against his chest enjoying the feeling of his strong arms around her.

Zach thought back to when he had turned south away from Black's Fork. What was there that had had Jimbo warning him? The confluence of Ham's Fork with Black's Fork was a popular camping stop for many of the tribes as they pass through this country. He figured it was probably Shoshone for this was mainly their land but with no villages making this area their home he wasn't sure. This area was mainly used for people traveling through or hunters looking for meat this time of year. He knew whoever was there may well be friendly, but he hadn't wanted to take the chance they weren't. Now he had to push the horses through thick forest and up over the steep ridge higher into the mountains to get back over to Black's Fork and home.

Once Zach and Sun Flower had eaten and packed up ready for the trail again they headed south following Smith's Fork to a place he had been over many times while trapping. It was a pass in the ridge he figured would be the easiest place to cross with this herd of horses. Moving this herd through the forest they were now in was much slower than it had been out on the flats and they couldn't travel any faster than a slow walk.

Clouds were starting to build up over the mountains this morning and he hoped they didn't get caught in another early spring storm. He had been in these mountains long enough to know these storms could easily dump two or three feet of snow. The snow usually didn't stay on the ground long but it could be like it was the middle of winter while the storms lasted.

If he could have stayed on Black's Fork he figured he could have been home by tonight but being where he was it would take at least another full day maybe more depending on the weather and if the trails were clear of snow. He really didn't have any farther to go it was just he had to push his herd of horses on the narrow steep trail over the ridge that separated the two Forks that runs into the Seeds-Kee-Dee.

They hadn't gone more than a mile when Jimbo came back to them. The hair down the middle of his back was standing up. Zach was leading the long string of horses with Sun Flower pushing them from behind. He stopped, then after letting Sun Flower know to hold them there he rode ahead following Jimbo. Only a quarter mile ahead he could see the tracks of several horses heading up stream.

He stepped out of the saddle and studied the tracks, but the main thing he could tell is there were quite a few of them. The way the tracks were stepping over the top on one another on the narrow trail made it impossible for him to tell just how many horse there were. If this was hostile Indians like the Cheyenne had been he didn't want to tangle with them again, especially while he had Sun Flower with him. Jimbo wanted to follow the tracks, he wanted to know who was that close to them, but with a simple hand signal that they had practiced for years the big dog came right to Zach's side and just sniffed at the air that was coming down the trail. Zach carefully turned making sure any tracks they had left were well covered or hidden and they made their way back to Sun Flower and the horses.

At this point Zach didn't want to go any further upstream for he didn't know how many warriors were up there. He didn't know whether they were friendly or not and now in his mind he was thinking they were probably a hunting party looking for game here on Smith's Fork. He figured their main camp was below them, probably at the confluence where Ham's Fork empties into Black's Fork.

Many questions were running through his mind. Could these be the Blackfeet that the Crow, Long Arrow had told him about? If it is, are they here hunting for game after this long cold winter or are they already raiding this early in the year? Or worst yet are they looking for him? He knew the Blackfeet wanted revenge against him for his killing their War Chief Thunder Cloud a couple of years ago at Rendezvous. Even last year north of Sweet Lake he had led a charge against the Blackfeet to protect Robert Campbell's brigade of trappers coming to Rendezvous from the north-country. Their new War Chief Strong Bow had seemed to know who he was and had made a threatening gesture. He stopped himself, these thoughts were nothing more than his mind working on the unknown. He didn't know who these people are and with Sun Flower and all the horses with him he wasn't going to find out either.

He decided then they would make their way up over the ridge just by following the game trails. He would take care to cover their tracks where they entered the forest and started up the ridge. He knew it would be difficult and would take longer to get home but it would be the safest way to go, after all Sun Flower had been through enough danger. If these tracks were made by some enemy, they were not going to find Sun Flower or their horses anywhere along Smith's Fork.

Jimbo took the lead with Sun Flower leading the horse herd as Zach stayed behind them all. When the last of the horses were a quarter mile above the trail Zach went back on foot and carefully covered their tracks. Since they were in a thick pine forest by carefully picking up the dry needles and sprinkling them over the tracks it looked just like the needles had fell naturally from the trees. Zach spent over an hour making sure even the best of trackers would have to look mighty hard to see the tracks that were there under the bed of dry pine needles.

Sun Flower pushed hard following Jimbo who had stayed on the well-used game trails as they twisted and turned their way toward the top of the ridge. The trail wise horses dutifully followed along in single file. Zach was now a little over an hour behind them still on foot making sure the trail would not be easy for anyone to follow. In places that turned into a lot of work, covering the tracks of two dozen horses where the trail turned steep and muddy, but he worked at each spot until he was satisfied.

By early afternoon Sun Flower came upon a large clearing and stopped back in the forest aways and told Jimbo to go get Grizzly Killer. The big dog responded without hesitation and thirty minutes later, Zach rode up. Sun Flower's smiling face greeted him, even though the bruises still showed a little she was still a mighty beautiful woman and he thought to himself like he had countless times before, *"I must be the luckiest man in the mountains."*

He looked at her smiling face then the grass and sage covered clearing in front of them and nodded to her and she kicked her horse and led them all out into the clearing. The horses started munching on the grass at once but Zach stayed on his horse studying the area above them carefully. With a looping circle over his head he sent Jimbo to scout a big circle around them. When he was satisfied they were safe and he had a plan to proceed in his mind he stepped down off the horse and into the loving arms of Sun Flower.

This ridge separating the two forks was high and rugged. Right above them there were cliffs and rock outcropping coming straight up out of the forest. They would have to stay below these bare rock faces working their way back toward the north to get around them. Zach wanted to be on the other side of the ridge top before dark otherwise he wouldn't dare light a fire. They still had plenty of the antelope so making meat wasn't a concern at all.

He didn't let the horses rest and graze for long, he didn't know how long it would take to make their way around the cliffs. This time when they started out he took the lead right behind Jimbo while Sun Flower brought up the rear.

When they left the clearing toward the higher rock face there were no established game trails so Zach was just picking his way through the forest. As they got closer to the rocks he had to maneuver around deadfall, large boulders, and several narrow steep little ravines. Two hours later he didn't think they had even covered a mile.

The sun was getting low in the western sky when he finally crossed the spine of the ridge and started the long decent toward Black's Fork. Zach got onto a well-used trail heavy with elk tracks and was following it when he came upon a seep that the elk had been using as a wallow. Below the little seep only a couple of hundred yards was a crystal-clear spring bubbling up out of the ground. Even though the grass was from last year, this was the best feed these horses had for quite a while and they all went right to grazing.

They would camp right here for the night. They were far enough from the ridge top he would dare make a small fire and the water was sweet and cold. He looked over the country to the west, this had become his home. The sky was partly cloudy and even before the sun set the clouds were reflecting the brilliant colors of the suns light. Thirty minutes later the red orange glow filled the whole western half of the sky with the fiery colors even reflecting off the snow-covered peaks that were towering above them to the south.

This was the first time Zach had been on this part of the ridge and he wasn't sure how long it would take them to get down to the trail along Black's Fork that was now just a few miles below them. Once he hit that trail he knew he was less than a day from home. Less than a day from seeing Shining Star and their sweet baby girl Star.

Sun Flower had brought in an armload of good dry wood for a small fire and Zach dug out a small fire pit up under the thick branches of a very large old pine so its thick branches would break up what little smoke the dry wood would produce.

A few minutes later Jimbo came into camp carrying a pine hen for his supper. They watched the brilliant colors of the sunset slowly fade as they ate roasted antelope and listened to Jimbo crunch the pine hen bones as he ate his catch.

As much as Zach enjoyed the feel of Sun Flowers naked body pushed up against his, he couldn't get his mind off the tracks down on Smith's Fork. Who is it? What are they doing? Are they friendly? Sun Flower could tell his mind was troubled and she knew it was because of her they had taken this long difficult trail today. Finally, Zach pulled her tight up against him and said, "Maybe we'll have ta move ta someplace less crowded."

She laughed out loud and said, "My husband, I will live wherever you are, my home is with you, but we are the only people that live on the whole north side of our Uintah Mountains. Where are you going to find a place less crowded than right here where we are?"

A tree fell in the forest down below them with the sound echoing off the cliffs above and a moment later a pack of coyotes started their high pitch yips down along the rivers with the sounds carried up to them on the breeze. Then another, even more intense thought came to him, *"This is my home and no one is going to drive me away."*

Chapter 20

The Old Crow

MIDMORNING FOUND BENNY riding hard, he wondered how Ely was doing and wished he was here with him right now. Ely was the best tracker Benny had ever seen, Grub was mighty good but Ely was the best. The tracks Benny was following appeared to him to be about the same age as they were when he started out and if that was the case it meant he wasn't gaining on them. Ely would know that for sure and Benny cursed himself for only being able to guess. He had learned a lot about tracking, hunting, and trapping over the last year but you could only get as good as Ely or Grub with experience and right now he wished he had more.

The tracks were heading nearly straight south except where the terrain made them vary. It was obvious that they were traveling mighty fast, pushing the heavily loaded horses just as hard as they could.

By night fall when Benny stopped, his horse was nearly spent. He felt bad for having to push the tired animal so hard. He knelt by the tracks and smiled as it appeared to him he had gained some on these ruthless thieves he was chasing. He then stripped the saddle and with clumps of dry grass brushed the crusted white later from the tired horse.

The grass here, as everywhere else on the range was dry and matted down from the weight of the heavy snow all winter. As the tired horse reached down and started pulling the dry clumps up and eating them, Benny wished he had a bag of corn or oats for the tired animal like his father used to feed the mules back home after they had been pulling a plow all day. That thought brought back memories of his home and he wondered how his Ma and Pa were doing, how his younger brothers and sisters were. He had never been homesick, even when he had first left home to work on the river barges. Farming had never appealed to him, but he still missed his family and wondered about them from time to time.

His belly growled, he hadn't had anything to eat since his single piece of jerky the night before. As he drank his fill of water he realized this chase may take much longer than he had realized and he was going to have to make meat. The thought of taking the time to hunt didn't settle well in his mind, for he felt an urgency to catch up and make the men he was following pay for what they had done to Ely.

Grub and Ely had taught him well over the last year. They had taught him the most important thing for survival in this harsh wilderness is you must take care of yourself first. Without food, you die! Without water, you die! Without shelter, you die! Without paying attention all around, all the time, you die! He thought about Ely telling him that repeatedly and Grub just smiling and nodding his head and would then say, "Best listen to 'im boy, he knows what he's talkin' 'bout."

The moon was now just slightly less than a quarter and was casting an eerie light around the edges of the cloud it had just gone behind. Benny laid down and pulled his buffalo robe up over his shoulders. With nothing to cook he hadn't taken the time to build a fire this night.

He thought about the men he was following and wondered who they were. He wondered what kind of men it would take to just up and shoot someone like Ely just to be able to take what didn't belong to them. He had seen men on the river that were awful mean and he had seen his friend get killed with a knife but that was a drunken fight. It appeared to him Ely had been shot just so they could steal the plews. He was having trouble concentrating, his tired mind was jumping from one thought to another. A wolf howled off in the distance and a moment later was answered by one that wasn't too far away. Benny drifted off to sleep thinking about a deer or elk steak roasting over a crackling fire.

Ely had another restless night, so this made the third night in a row Grub had not slept. He dozed for a few minutes now and then but the worry he felt for Ely kept him awake and checking on him regularly. Ely's fever hadn't seemed to get any worse but it hadn't broken either. In the lucid moments when Ely was awake Grub would get him to swallow a little of the aspen and willow bark tea he kept warm by the side of the fire. Grub wasn't sure it was helping but he didn't seem to be getting worse so he kept the tea brewed and kept Ely drinking as much as he could.

Grub wiped the beads of sweat from Ely's brow again then stared into the dark looking down the canyon. His tired mind wondered about Benny, he felt concern for his young partner as well as Ely. He hoped Benny had the skill to take on the task he had set out to do. He watched a small cloud drift past the small crescent moon and listened to the wolves howling in the canyon above him.

The next thing he realized it was light, the morning sun was just cresting over the eastern ridge and there was an old Crow Indian couple standing only twenty feet from him. He jumped up reaching for his rifle but as he did he saw a teenage boy with a bow at full draw with the arrow pointing right at his chest. Grub froze right where he was not moving at all and the old warrior's wrinkled face smiled and he walked over and picked up Grub's rifle then nodded at Grub and signed friend. Grub was still trying to understand what was happening and didn't respond. The old Crow warrior signed friend again and Grub returned the sign friend and with sparkling eye's that belied his age the old Crow handed Grub's rifle to him.

Grub breathed a sigh of relief as the boy lowered his bow and arrow and Grub took his rifle and set it right back where it had been. Just then Ely moved and as he did he let out a loud moan. All their eyes were now on Ely and the gray haired old woman walked right past Grub and knelt beside Ely. She put her hand on his forehead then took the bed roll she had tied over her shoulder off and unrolled it exposing another rolled up piece of leather, as she unrolled it Grub could see there were a variety of plants in it. She said something Grub didn't understand and the teenage boy came right up and handed her his buffalo bladder water pouch.

She looked at Grub and asked something that he didn't understand. When she saw the confused look on his face she motioned for him to get out of her way and when he moved back she saw the tin cup and tea setting by the fire. The fire had died out after Grub had drifted off to sleep so the tea was cold but she started talking again and Grub smiled to himself as both the old man and boy immediately started to build the fire back up.

She looked at Grub again and pointed at the cup of tea and he handed it to her at once. She looked in it and smelled it, then looked back at Grub and nodded her approval. She then crushed up some of the dried plants from her medicine kit into the tea and motioned for him to heat it by the fire that the old man and boy had just got going again. As he did that she carefully unwrapped the crude bandage Grub had placed over the bullet hole in Ely's chest and examined the now oozing wound. She bent over then smelled it, once she seemed satisfied the wound was clean, she took small pinches of two different plants from her kit and ground them into a fine powder in the palm of hand then sprinkled them in and around the wound. She then carefully put the bandage back in place.

Ely was unconscious but was moaning with each movement, but when the tea was hot once again she lifted his head and forced the tin cup between his lips and poured the warm liquid into his mouth until he started to swallow. His eye's opened then for the first time and the shock was evident in his sunken and dark eyes. He tried to jump back but was too weak to do so, all he could do was stare into the wrinkled face that was right in front of him. He tried to say something but she just kept pouring the tea into his mouth and he had no choice but to swallow it.

When she seemed satisfied that she had forced Ely to drink enough of the hot, bitter tea she gently set his head back down. Grub hadn't said a word but was very grateful this old Crow Indian woman had come along and helped. Ely's sunken eyes were watching every move they were making but he couldn't find the strength to move or even speak. The old woman stared into Grub's dirty face that was mostly covered with a long greasy beard but she could see the gratitude in his eyes. She then took some of the plants she had ground up in the tea and talking just as fast as her old hands were moving made Grub know to make more tea with them when the sun was setting and give to Ely.

Grub and Ely had lived in the Rockies now for nearly ten years and they knew much of the Indian sign language. Through the hand signs the different tribes could communicate with one another even though their languages could be very different. Grub couldn't understand a word of what these people were saying but through sign language they could make each other understand. He asked them through a series of hand gestures if they were hungry and before any of them could answer the look on the boy's face told him they were. Grub motioned for him to follow him and they went to the stand of pines and cut enough off the elk to feed them all.

They roasted the elk over the fire and it was obvious to Grub they hadn't eaten for quite a while. Although a complex conversation using only sign was difficult Grub wanted to know what they were doing here and where they were going.

He found the boy was by far the easiest to communicate with, so using careful sign he asked why they were here alone and asked their names. Grub didn't understand all the sign the boy was using as each tribe does have their differences, but he was getting most of what the boy was trying to tell him.

The old man was Standing Bear and his wife Sky, they were the boy's grandparents. The boy is called Horse. Grub was guessing on what some of the hand sign meant but Horse could see he was having trouble and slowed down and repeated the gestures until Grub nodded he understood. Horse told him their village was a small one and had traveled many days to the south looking for game as they were all hungry, but they had been attacked by Blackfeet four days ago. He had helped his Grandparents escape and they have been on foot making their way back to Absaroka ever since. They didn't know the fate of the rest of their village.

Grub asked them to stay and they would dry meat for them to take on their journey back to their home. At first, Horse did not understand but after he realized what Grub had said he smiled and talked to his Grandparents and a minute later the old man nodded and Grub breathed a deep sigh of relief that this old woman would be here to care for Ely.

Grub started right in lashing together a drying rack and told Horse to bring up the rest of the elk and bear and start cutting it in strips to dry. By the time Grub was satisfied with the rack Horse, Standing Bear, and Sky were all cutting the meat into strips. Grub smiled at Sky as she was not satisfied with the way Standing Bear or Horse was cutting the meat and she told them to stop and get wood for the fire. Grub watched with amazement at her skilled hands as she cut the meat in strips thin enough to smoke and dry quickly. He wondered how many animals she had cut up in her long life.

It appeared to Grub that Ely was resting easier than he had been, and when he started to wake up old Sky made more of her tea. She again gently lifted his head but this time Ely was able to drink the warm liquid without her forcefully pouring it into his mouth. Grub silently watched and he wasn't sure but he thought there was a little more color in Ely's cheeks even though his eyes were still sunken and dark all around them.

By the next morning Ely's fever was gone and Grub would forever be grateful to this old Crow woman and her medicine kit. Horse had kept the fire under the drying rack going ever since they started it and Grub figured by the end of the day the meat would be dry enough it should last them until they got back to their Absaroka home.

Grub watched carefully each time Sky made the tea, he wanted to remember just how to make it himself. He hoped he could convince them to stay for another day or even two but right now he didn't know if that would be possible. He wished the language wasn't the barrier that it was. Finally, he decided he was just going to ask them to stay, it may not work, he wasn't sure he could make them understand what he wanted but he had to try.

Grub got Horse to understand he wanted them to stay for a few more days, he told him they could hunt more meat as there were many elk in this canyon. When he was finished Horse nodded and turned to his Grandfather and spoke softly to him. Grub really wished he understood the Crow tongue. Standing Bear listened but slowly shook his head no saying something that again Grub could not understand. Horse turned back to Grub and signed part of what his grandfather had said. They must get back to

Absaroka and find out what has happened to the rest of their village. Grub looked over at old Sky knowing she was Ely's best chance to survive. He then signed to Horse he would give them a horse and all the meat they could carry if they would stay and Sky would care for his friend for just two more days. Horse smiled, for he wanted to stay. In the short time, he had been there he had grown to like this dirty hairy faced white man and he would like to hunt with him. He turned and again spoke softly and with respect to Standing Bear. Standing Bear listened and Grub could tell he was in deep thought, then he turned and looked at Sky. Sky didn't say anything but the look on her face made Grub think she was telling him it was alright with her to stay a couple of more days. Standing Bear was in deep thought but finally nodded his approval, they would stay for two more suns.

Grub started right in lashing together another lean-to without asking for any help, but Horse could see what needed to be done and started bringing in the poles and pine boughs that grub needed as he continued. Within a couple of hours Grub had a lean-to large enough for the three of them to sleep under and stay out of any weather that might come along.

Old Sky nodded her approval and started setting out what little they had. Sky had escaped with her bed roll and medicine kit and Standing Bear had a single blanket, but Horse had been concerned only with getting his grandparents away from the Blackfeet and had left everything but his bow and quiver of arrows behind.

With about three hours of daylight left Grub and Horse went hunting. A little less than a mile below camp was a meadow that Grub had seen elk in most evenings. He knew the elk would be bedded down in the trees not far from the meadow during the day. He also figured if he and Horse could get set on the edge of the meadow without spooking them they could take one when they came in to feed just before dark.

Grub led Horse right along the creek, skirting the opposite side of the beaver ponds until they were just below the meadow. Moving ever so slowly and being as quiet as they could, they moved up into position one on each side of the meadow and waited motionless for the elk to move into the open.

Time slowed to a crawl as Grub waited. He had always had patience while hunting, but today seemed different. He hated to be away from Ely, he wondered where Benny was and what he was doing. Was he okay? Had he caught up with them yet? Had he run into the Blackfeet like these Crow's had? He tried to shake these questions from his mind as he sat and waited, leaning up against a big pine.

An hour passed and it seemed like a week, he couldn't clear his troubled mind. When suddenly, a memory from the distant past came to him. A traveling preacher had come through their little farming community and his mother had made them all go and hear the sermon on a Sunday afternoon. He couldn't remember how old he had been but he could remember how he hated to take a bath and get in clean clothes to go.

He hadn't remembered that preacher in all the years since and wondered why he would think of him now, but he was thinking of him. He couldn't remember the preacher's name but the words were like he was hearing them right now. He was telling all listening about the power of prayer. About how God is always listening and if you pray with a sincere heart and believe in God he will answer your prayers. He remembered how the preacher had told them that God's answer might not be the one they wanted to hear and that we may not always understand why God does the things he does, but he would always answer if you were sincere and believed.

Grub sat there motionless and quiet leaning against the pine, his mind wondering why that memory, so long buried had surfaced now while he was waiting for the elk to come. He couldn't see Horse but he could see the thicket the young Indian was hiding in. He found he couldn't concentrate on hunting as his mind went back to the preacher that he had heard just the one time when he was a small boy.

Grub closed his eyes and remembered his mother later that night helping him say a prayer before she tucked him into bed. A powerful feeling came over him then, and he had a powerful urge to pray. Even though he couldn't remember the last time he had actually knelt down and said a real prayer. He moved slowly as he leaned his rifle against the tree and removed his fur hat. He then got on his knees and put his hands together like his mother had showed him when he was a child and in a humble voice, soft but plain he poured out his heart to God; "Heavenly Father, I knows I ain't ever been a religious man, and I knows you got no reason ta listen to me, but if you are listenin', my friends is needin' your help. Ely is a layin' up there with a hole through 'im and Benny is, well I don't know where Benny is, but I know he needs your help. If you would help Ely to heal up and watch over Benny so he don't make no mistakes like young men are apt to do, I will be forever in your debt. And if it ain't too much trouble please help Horse, Standing Bear, and Sky make it back to their home safely. I know they don't believe in you the way we do, but they is good people and they need your help too."

Grub opened his eyes and as he did a feeling of calm came over him. It was a feeling like he had never felt before, something he couldn't explain but he felt like everything was going to be okay. He looked back over to where Horse was hiding and just as he did a dozen elk came out of the trees in single file and walked right past the thicket where Horse was hidden.

Grub watched, anticipating what would happen next. A moment later, a yearling cow jumped in the air and the elk all scattered in every direction. The yearling ran out into the middle of the meadow and stood there. Although it was a long shot for him, Grub was slowly bringing up his rifle to finish the job when she took two steps sideways and fell over.

Grub could see the colorful arrow shaft sticking out of her side just behind her shoulder. He kept his rifle trained on her until he was sure she couldn't get back up. He stood up and motioned for Horse and the two of them slowly walked out into the meadow to her. Grub didn't really know this young Crow but he felt pride in the young man and knew that Horse would be a great Crow warrior in the not too distant future.

Chapter 21

Home at Last

ZACH WAS AWAKE like he normally was just as the stars were starting to fade. He laid there listening to the sounds of the forest around him. He could hear birds starting their morning chorus and the raspy cawing of a couple of crows flying over the tree tops. He could hear the horses munching on the dry grass and thought in just a few short weeks the new grass would be growing and the horses would be putting the weight they had all lost back on.

Sun Flower snuggled tight up against him and he hugged her enjoying her warm and willing body. He would have loved to take the time to make love to his beautiful wife but he felt an urgency to get home. Had Running Wolf made it okay? Did the tracks on Smith's Fork mean more trouble for them?

He threw the warm robe off them and the cold crisp air made them both gasp and get dressed mighty quick. They didn't take time to build a fire this morning they just saddled up and started down toward Black's Fork before the sun even peaked over the ridge top just east of them.

They hadn't gone far when they came across a well-used game trail and with Zach leading the way they made good time coming down off the ridge. Sun Flower was again bringing up the rear with the now two dozen horses between them. Less than two hours later he rode out onto the main trail along Black's Fork and smiled knowing they would be home today well before dark.

It was already daylight when Shining Star first opened her eyes. She could see the blue of the sky through the smoke hole in the teepee. She could hear the soft breathing of her brother and Raven Wing as they slept just across the small fire pit of the large teepee. Neither of the babies had awakened yet and then she realized her head was not hurting like it had nearly continuously since the Cheyenne warrior had tried to kill her with his war club. Luna came to her, licked her face and she smiled at this beautiful white wolf that had grown to be a loving pet more than the wild wolf that she was.

She reached up and gently rubbed her hand over the lump that was still on the side of her head but she thought it felt smaller again today. She hoped it would be gone before Grizzly Killer saw her again. Oh, how she longed for him to be home and Sun Flower too, she missed them both. Although Running Wolf and Raven Wing had said she was alright they also said she had been beaten and she hoped her pretty face was not scarred.

She slowly set up and smiled again as the movement had not caused any pain. She knew she was healing but wished the lump was gone. She looked over at Star and little Gray Wolf then noticed Running Wolf watching her. He hadn't moved but his eyes were open as he watched every move she was making. She smiled at him and he asked, "How is my sister feeling this morning?"

She smiled and answered, "It is going to be a good day, the pain in my head is gone and the lump I think is smaller today."

Neither of the babies had stirred yet so as quietly as possible she slipped on her soft doeskin dress and stepped out into the chill of the morning. There were just a few white fluffy clouds up over the peaks south of them but the rest of the sky was a clear blue. Most of the snow was now gone except on the higher slopes up above them. The river was running high, almost threatening to spill over its banks with the rapidly melting snow in the high country and she knew it would be like this for the next several weeks.

Running Wolf stepped out of the lodge with Luna. As Shining Star was starting the fire, he rushed over to help and she told him, "I am fine, my brother, and very capable of making the morning fire."

Luna had left them, she ran to the trail that runs down Black's Fork and sat and watched. Running Wolf watched her tilting her head back and forth as she stared down the trail and smiled thinking that she knew Grizzly Killer was coming home. He didn't know how she knew, but he expected Grizzly Killer, Sun Flower, Jimbo, and all their horses to show up sometime today, partly because it was time and partly because of the way Luna was acting.

Running Wolf said, "I think Grizzly Killer and Sun Flower will be here today, look at Luna… I believe she thinks so, too.

Shining Star smiled and said, "I have missed them so much, I hope you are right." Just then Raven Wing stepped out with both babies in her arms. Running Wolf went right over and took his son from her arms. Neither of them had cried yet and Shining Star come over and took Star to let her nurse. In just a few minutes, both women were sitting by the fire with the nearly year-old babies suckling at their breasts.

Crossing Black's Fork was now a difficult ordeal. The big meadow was on the other side and that is where Ol' Red was, so while the women were nursing their babies, Running Wolf went out to check on and change the poultice on the big mule's shoulder. As Running Wolf approached, Ol' Red came to him. He was surprised the mule wasn't limping more than he was. Ol' Red could be stubborn and when he looked at the wound he shook his head and told Ol' Red he wasn't fooling anybody and he wasn't going anywhere for many suns to come.

When Running Wolf had finished changing the poultice he turned to walk away Ol' Red followed and when he told the big mule to stay and then turned again Ol' Red pushed him in the back with his nose nearly knocking Running Wolf off his feet. Running Wolf knew how close the relationship was between Ol' Red and Grizzly Killer and he knew the big mule wanted him to take him to where ever Grizzly Killer was. Instead of being mad he just talked to Ol' Red telling him that Grizzly Killer would be here today rubbing his neck as he talked. As he walked away this time Ol' Red just stood there and Running Wolf truly wondered if the mule had understood what he had said. An hour later Luna was still staring down the trail and now Ol' Red was just on the opposite side of the river watching the trail just like Luna was.

Zach wasn't pushing hard, he knew he didn't have to in order to make it home by midafternoon. The horses were following along with no problems, all of them were well used to the trail by now. They had left early without taking time to eat so by late morning in a meadow he had been in many times before, he stopped. The horses all went right to grazing while Sun Flower started a small fire and cut several thin strips of antelope and put them on sticks to roast over the fire.

Jimbo knew they were close to home now and another three or four hours would see them there. Zach could tell he wanted to take off and let everyone in camp know they were coming. He and Sun Flower ate the hot strips of antelope and threw one to Jimbo, then with nothing more than pointing his finger up the trail he told Jimbo to go and let them know. Zach, Sun Flower, and the horses had been on the trail about another hour when Zach figured Jimbo was probably just making it there.

Running Wolf and the women had just finished their midday meal when Running Wolf saw Luna getting mighty excited and he figured the others were getting close. It was only five minutes later when she howled and as they all looked they heard Jimbo's familiar bark answering her back. She took off down the trail and within a couple of seconds was out of site. Another five minutes passed when they saw Jimbo's huge frame come around the last bush. Luna was acting like a puppy at his side jumping up on him wanting to play but Jimbo just ignored her and ran right to Running Wolf. He stayed in front of Running Wolf just long enough for the pat on the head then went to Shining Star and the baby then to Raven Wing and Gray Wolf. He stayed with each for only a second or two with Luna still by his side. He then looked across the river and saw Ol' Red, he barked a greeting to the big mule and bounded across the rocks that formed their makeshift bridge.

Ol' Red let out a bray that echoed up through the canyon, kicked his hind legs into the air then waited for Jimbo to reach him. When Jimbo got to him Ol' Red lowered his head and waited for Jimbo to give him a big lick across his nose.

Shining Star, Running Wolf, and Raven Wing were all watching and they had seen this greeting many times before but it always made them smile seeing the bond these two different animals shared. They were as close of friends as Grizzly Killer and Running Wolf were and they all knew it and accepted it as fact.

Once their nose touching ritual was over, Jimbo raised up carefully setting his front paws on Ol' Red's side and he sniffed the shoulder wound and poultice that was still there. He then dropped down on all fours and started to bark at the rest of them. Raven Wing smiled and shook her head and said, "I think Jimbo is telling us it is time to change the poultice again." She got right up and mixed what little she had left in her medicine kit. Jimbo waited right there until Running Wolf carried the new mixture on a fresh bandage across the river and changed the dressing on the big mule's shoulder. Jimbo and Ol' Red then touched noses again then Jimbo followed Running Wolf back across the river to camp.

Two more hours passed and Jimbo who had been laying by the fire jumped up and started down the trail again. This time Luna was running right alongside of the big dog. Just a few minutes later Zach saw movement a hundred yards in front of him and smiled knowing his dog had come back to greet him. With less than a mile to go Zach pushed the horses into a trot and just a few minutes later he could see smoke and less than a minute after that the tops of their lodges came into view.

They were all standing there waiting but Zach saw only Shining Star. She was happy her man was back, the swelling in her face was gone and the lump on her head was barely noticeable. Zach jumped off the horse and ran to her. She threw her arms around him and hugged him so tight she felt the familiar pain shoot through her head again so she let off some. Their lips met and they enjoyed a long passionate kiss as Running Wolf was directing the horses across the river. Old Red brayed his excitement with the return of his friends and only a couple of minutes later, Sun Flower pushed the last horse across the river. She smiled at her sister seeing Raven Wing was all right and then at Shining Star who was now pushing out of Grizzly Killer's arms to greet her.

Sun Flower slid off the small Cheyenne pony she had been riding and the two wives of Zach Connors just stood there for a minute staring at each other. When they spoke, it was at the same time and it was the same words, "Are you alright?" Then they nodded, smiled, and hugged one another. Sun Flower could see right off that the lump was still on the side of Shining Star's head and to Shining Star the slight discoloration around Sun Flower eye was plain to see but even with the still healing injuries it was a happy homecoming for everyone.

Sun Flower then picked up Star and played with her until Zach came over. The happy little girl wanted her daddy which delighted Zach immensely, so Sun Flower then picked up little Gray Wolf. Sun Flower still did not understand why she hadn't been able to give Grizzly Killer a child but she felt blessed that he loved her anyway. She knew most Indian men would have left her by now, but with Grizzly Killer she would never have to worry about that. She could feel his love deep in her soul and she knew he will never leave her.

That evening they talked around the fire until it was late catching up on everything that had happened. When Zach and Sun Flower learned how bad Shining Star had been hurt, Zach felt even worse for leaving her but she smiled and said, "What choice did you have, my husband? You couldn't leave Sun Flower with the Cheyenne and I am fine, I am healing and I cared for the little ones. I did what I had to do and so did you. We all do what we must when we must to care for our family, our village."

Zach put his right arm around Shining Star and his left around Sun Flower and hugged them both enjoying the feeling of their love and the closeness he felt to each of them.

When Zach told of the tracks he had seen over on Smith's Fork and how Jimbo had warned them off from following Black's Fork, there was concern by all of them. It was decided they would ride a large circle around their home each day for the next few days making sure they weren't surprised again like the Cheyenne had surprised them.

It was still cold as they moved away from the fire. Tonight, would be the first time Running Wolf and Raven Wing went to their own lodge since the attack by the Cheyenne more than a week ago. It had seemed like it had been much longer than it actually had. With this warming trend over the last several days and the snow now gone from the big meadow and around camp it seemed like spring was already here, but this is the Rocky Mountains and Zach knew more spring storms could make it feel like winter all over again.

Zach kissed little Star gently on her forehead and watched as Shining Star tucked the soft rabbit fur blanket around her. He breathed a deep sigh of relief that his family was all safe and back home again. Sun Flower brought in a burning ember from the outside fire and started the small fire in the center of the teepee. Zach watched with delight as his two wives slipped out of their soft leather dresses and got under the warm buffalo robe. As he laid down between the two and felt their warmth against his skin he drifted off to sleep a happy and contented man.

When Zach opened his eyes, the teepee was still dark but the sky was just starting to lighten as he looked up through the smoke hole. He could still feel the warmth of his wives against him and hear their deep breathing letting him know they were both still asleep. Not wanting to disturb either of them he just laid there enjoying the feeling. He heard Jimbo, who was curled up just outside the lodge opening make a slight sound then get up. A moment later Luna joined him and the two of them went out on their morning hunt.

A short hour later they were all up standing around the outside fire. It was time for the spring trapping season. Zach figured they should have had their trap lines out at least a week ago or maybe even sooner. The clear morning air waited for some smoked buffalo to cook. He smiled thinking he sure would rather have been trapping than how they had spent their last week.

He and Running Wolf talked about where to start trapping this spring. Since this was their home range they were careful not to take all the beaver from any one area. They always left enough that in two or three years they could trap that stream again with success. They decided to trap the streams to the west of Black's Fork at least for the next few weeks.

Running Wolf and Zach took turns setting and checking the trap lines. One of them was always in camp with the women and babies. It made for longer days and harder work but they felt safer that way. The water was not much warmer than the ice had been just a few weeks ago and it was running high and fast. Trapping in the spring was dangerous and extremely cold work. Getting in that icy water deep enough to drown the beavers they caught nearly took their breath away and the cold made their legs ache clear into their bones.

A couple of days later, Zach was riding a wide circle around them checking the area for any tracks or signs anyone else was in the area. Ol' Red was getting better but Zach thought another week was needed before the big mule would be ready to carry him so he was still riding the Crow horse. He had found this horse was a good trail horse. He was sure-footed and paid close attention to where he was going. He wasn't as sure-footed as Ol' Red but no horse Zach had ever ridden was. He had nearly completed his circle when he decided to climb to the ridge top where he could see down the other side into Smith's Fork. Jimbo was out in front like always when he stopped dead in his tracks. Zach saw this and stopped his horse as well. He got off, tied the horse to a tree and walked up to where Jimbo was standing.

He softly patted his dog and whispered, "What is it, boy?"

Then he saw the smoke. It wasn't much, just a campfire, he figured, but there was no doubt at all someone was down on Smith's Fork only a couple miles below him.

Chapter 22

Escaping the Blackfeet

IT WAS A COLD MORNING as Benny threw his sleeping robe off and stood up. The sun was not yet up but its light was painting the scattered clouds with brilliant shades of red and orange. Benny thought about an old saying he had heard along the Mississippi from the sailors, "Red sky at night- sailor's delight, red sky in morning sailor's take warning".

He watched the sky get brighter red as the sun got closer to showing its blinding light over the eastern horizon and wondered if he would be in for a storm before he caught up with the men he was following.

Benny's belly growled from hunger and he knew he couldn't go on much longer without taking time to hunt, but not this morning. He figured he might find a rabbit or maybe even a deer or elk on the trail and if he did, he would be ready to shoot. With that thought he checked his rifle and made sure there was fresh powder in the pan, then he carefully closed the frizen and saddled his horse.

When he set out he kicked his horse into an easy lope that covered the ground quickly and it was a pace the horse could maintain for miles at a time. He was nearly four miles from where he had slept when the sun finally came up and spread its very welcome warmth over the land he was riding through.

Movement caught his eye and he brought the horse to a walk then stopped and stepped out of the saddle into the sage and bitterbrush that was all around him. He wasn't sure what he had seen move in the brush in front of him. He hoped it was a rabbit, as they were mighty tasty, but he would take anything right now, even a snake if that's what it was.

Two steps forward and he could hear something start to hiss, another step and the hiss turned into sort of a growl, now he side-stepped, not being sure what he was walking into. He moved until he could see around the brush that was in front of him. It was hiding a badger. he now saw. He was backed into his hole with a big mound of fresh dirt pushed out in front of him.

Benny had never eaten a badger before but he was so hungry he didn't even hesitate to bring up his rifle and shoot. He started a small fire right there where he was and while the fire was getting going he skinned the badger and got it roasting over the flames. The meat was sizzling and hot but not cooked through when he sliced off a hind quarter and start to eat the juicy but tough meat. He thought as the half-raw juices dripped off the thin beard on his chin that it wasn't half bad. It wasn't hump ribs but it sure beat starving to death.

He stayed there only long enough to finish cooking the badger, then cut it up and put it into his jerky pouch, kicked out the fire and headed south once again. The tracks he was following looked to him like they weren't moving as fast now, and he believed he was catching up. It might still take several more days but unless something happened to him or his horse, in the next few days he would catch them.

Benny couldn't see them but five young Blackfeet warriors were just over the ridge to the east hunting for their main group when Benny had shot the badger and they had heard the shot.

This was the first raid these five had ever been on and they were excited to prove they were good warriors by taking many scalps. They rode hard to reach the ridge top then dismounted and crawled the last few feet. They watched Benny cook the badger, waiting for any other white men to join him, but when none did, they all knew this lone white man would be their first scalp.

They took only a moment to prepare themselves, after all, they were five against one. They wouldn't need to build their courage or ask for the Great Spirit's help to rid their land of one puny white man.

They mounted up and rode hard to catch Benny, staying on the back side of the ridge where they couldn't be seen until the last minute. When they burst over the ridge Benny was only a quarter mile from them. He heard the war cry before he saw them. Panic shot through him as he kicked his horse into an all-out run. Looking at the terrain in front of him and trying to find a route that would save him, he turned to the west away from the Blackfeet as they screamed and hollered their war cries. They screamed to instill fear and panic in their enemies and in Benny's case, it was working very well.

He had fought Blackfeet before, last year when they were attacked on their way to Rendezvous with Robert Campbell's brigade, only then he hadn't been alone. The Blackfeet hadn't seemed so scary while he was with Ely and Grub and all of Robert Campbell's men.

He knew they were Blackfeet or a close relative of the Blackfeet as soon as he had seen them. Grub and Ely and taught him how to identify the different tribes by the way they dressed, wore their hair, and decorated their horses. Another glance back and he knew these were Blackfeet for sure, but he also saw they were not gaining on him. He was standing in the stirrups, leaning out over the horse's neck talking to the buckskin and trying to urge more speed out of him. A mile of hard running and he could feel his mount was tiring. Another glance back and he knew the Indian's horses were tiring just as fast. Maybe faster, for he believed he was further ahead of them now. Not knowing how much farther his horse could run, he started looking for a place to fight them.

Benny could remember Grub and Ely both telling him about fighting Indians. He could hear Ely in his mind saying, "Injuns don't want ta die any more 'an you do. They ain't afraid of it, mind ya, but they don't wanna die, none of 'em do. So, if'n you gotta fight, ya make sure yer first shot takes one of 'em out. The rest will be mighty leery ta keep comin' atcha after they see one of their friends with his blood leaking out all over the ground or half his head missin'."

He knew he was going to have to fight. This country was broken hills with a lot of brush and dry grass, not a lot of trees or rocks to hide in. He could see a canyon heading off to the southwest that had timber in it, if his horse could only keep up this speed for another half mile.

A quarter mile to go and he could tell his horse was done in. If he forced him to keep up this speed, neither him nor his horse would survive. He glanced back again and the Blackfeet were nearly a half mile behind. So, he gently pulled back on the reins bringing the buckskin to a walk. He was still a couple of hundred yards from the trees but he figured he couldn't make it on foot before the Indians got to him. He also knew he wouldn't be steady enough to shoot straight if he was out of breath after a two-hundred-yard sprint.

His horse was just standing there with his head down, his sides heaving in and out trying to suck in enough air to recover. Benny had no time; no time to run, no time to think, he just reacted. He pulled his pistol and shot the exhausted horse in the head. As the horse fell, Benny dove behind it and using it as a rest for his rifle, he took careful aim on the lead warrior. They were running straight at him so no lead was necessary. He put the front sight right on the warrior's face and slowly squeezed off the shot.

The heavy lead ball hit the Blackfoot in the throat going out the back of his neck, taking part of his spine and nearly taking his head clear off. Blood sprayed all over the two warriors that were right behind him. He did a back flip off his horse hitting one horse behind him in the front legs and sending that horse and the warrior riding him to the ground, hard.

Benny hadn't seen what had happened. After he shot, he was concentrating on how fast he could reload. He was expecting to hear the thundering hoof beats of the others bearing down on him, but he didn't hear a thing. As he primed the pan and snapped the frizen in place, he rolled over again and brought his rifle up, but what he saw surprised him. There were two rider-less horses with two of the Blackfeet trying to help the one whose horse had fallen get up off the ground. While only one of the five was still on a horse, Benny figured if he was going to make it to the trees this may be his best chance.

He grabbed his bedroll- everything else he needed was in his possibles bag which was already over his shoulder. He jumped up and ran toward the trees. Never in his life had he run so fast but he was only half way to the trees when he heard the hoof beats of a running horse. He stopped and turned. Only the warrior that was still mounted was charging at him. He knelt bringing the deadly rifle up to his shoulder and just as the young warrior released an arrow Benny shot. He let the recoil of the rifle carry him over backwards just as the arrow went over the top of his falling body, missing by less than an inch.

Benny's shot hit the Blackfoot in the center of his chest knocking him off the back of the running horse. Just like the first one, he was dead before he ever hit the ground. Again, Benny was reloading with a speed he didn't know he was capable of. Fear can make a man move mighty fast he figured. This last warrior's horse was just standing there between him and the dead Indian. As he looked back at the other three they didn't appear to be in any hurry to come after him so he gently started talking to this Indian horse and was pleasantly surprised when he just stood there and let him approach. He mounted the horse but now instead of running he defiantly held his rifle in the air shouted, "You come after me, you Blackfoot bastards, and you'll get the same as your friends." He figured they couldn't understand any of what he had said, but he figured they would get the message just the same. Then he turned and stayed at a slow walk until he got to the edge of the trees.

Benny's heart was beating so fast it sounded like drums in his ears. He now took the time to reload his pistol but his hands were shaking so bad it seemed to take him forever to finish. He chided himself, talking out loud saying, "What the heck is the matter with you, Benny? You're a shakin' like our old dog used to when he was shittin' out a peach pit, now lots worse than durin' the fight."

He knew he needed to get as much distance as he could between him and the Blackfeet, but this horse was as done in as his own had been, and he wanted to make sure the other Blackfeet were going to leave and not come after him. He figured where ever their main camp was they would send a serious war party after him after killing the two that he had.

Benny watched from the trees as the two still healthy Blackfeet helped the injured one up on his horse. Even though he was now over a quarter mile away it was plain the injured one couldn't use his right arm at all and was favoring his right leg. He figured when he went down his horse must have rolled over him.

After the Blackfeet had their companion sitting on his horse they loaded the body of the first one Benny had shot over the back of his horse then slowly led the horse out to where Benny's buckskin and the other warrior was laying and loaded his body as well. It took them quite a while as they were watching the trees where Benny had gone, more than completing their gruesome task.

After they rode away, Benny rode back out to his horse and pulled the saddle off the dead animal and put it on this Indian pony. Benny was pleased that the horse was well behaved and didn't seem to mind the new saddle at all. The steel bit was another story… the horse didn't want any part of the bit in his mouth so he figured he would just use the rawhide bridle that the Indians used.

As he headed out again he knew he had to find the trail of the men he was following all over again. Not only that but he had to make his trail hard enough to follow that the Blackfeet that he was sure would come after him couldn't follow or at least wouldn't follow just for one lone man. He doubted that would be the case after he had just killed two of them. Even as young as he was, he knew that revenge was a powerful motivator, if it wasn't he wouldn't be here on this trail alone.

Benny figured he had ran his horse as much as three miles from where he had last seen the tracks of those he was following. He knew it would be easy to back track and get back on their trail, but that would put him that much closer to the Blackfeet so he figured he had better follow a course parallel to the way he was going for several miles then cut back to the east until he crossed the tracks again.

With Blackfeet in the area he knew it was possible they would find the tracks and follow these murdering thieves and deep down he almost wished they would. However, if that happened it would mean that him, Grub, and Ely would lose a whole year's worth of work.

This Indian horse was well mannered and easy to ride and after the exhausting run Benny was surprised how fast he had recovered. Heading south and trying to anticipate the lay of the land that was two or three miles to his east was no easy task. He also kept checking his back trail, for he felt sure the Blackfeet would come after him.

He came to a stream and got down in it, riding another mile to the west staying in the water then climbed out up onto a rocky ridge trying to cover his tracks. Staying off the skyline he studied the country behind him but, so far, there was no sign of pursuit. He then studied the country to the southeast trying to anticipate the route the men he was following would take.

Once he had a plan of travel in his mind he headed out again heading still south but now moving slightly back to the east as he went. Night fall found him crossing a deep and heavily timbered canyon. He stopped once he got to the bottom, there was a stream for water and at least some grass for the horse. He felt safe here, there was a rock face that nearly hung out over the stream and it was as pretty a place to camp as he had seen. He knew a fire could not be seen in these thick trees and it was too dark for the smoke to be a worry.

Benny sat there with just a small fire burning up against the rock face and ate more of the tough, stringy badger that he had cooked the night before and worried about finding the trail of the men he was after again. He wondered how Ely was doing. He knew he was hurt awful bad but he had never met any men tougher than Ely and Grub and he wouldn't let himself think anything but that he would recover.

The next morning, he was climbing out of this canyon just as soon as it was light enough to see. There was still no sign of pursuit and now the horse was fully rested he set a grueling pace.

Midmorning found him riding to the rim of a large broad canyon. Here the hills were covered with mainly brush, only pockets of timber here and there. He was still a half mile from the canyon's rim when he saw wisps of smoke floating in the air above the rim. He stopped and dismounted, wondering what was over that rim. Five hundred yards to his left was a stand of pines that went to the rim so he headed there.

Once under the cover of the trees he tied off the horse and worked his way to the canyon rim. A half mile below was a Shoshone village or at least it was a Shoshone hunting camp. There were six lodges and they were all on fire. He could see bodies lying all over the ground and there were nearly fifty Blackfeet warriors torturing the ones unlucky enough to have survived the initial attack.

Benny remembered last year when Ely, Grub and himself had come upon the Flathead village after Blackfeet had attacked and he remembered how it had made him sick and how no one had been spared. He shuddered at the thought of what those people were going through.

He watched, well-hidden in the stand of timber and saw movement just below him. He watched intently, then his eyes focused on an Indian girl not two hundred yards below him. She was trying to stay out of sight but was making her way out of the canyon. He wanted to help her but he knew any move he made may be seen, so he just watched as she climbed closer and closer to him. She was now only fifty-yards below him and from where she was to the top there was no cover.

He whistled softly like a bird to get her attention and she froze, her eyes scanning the rim and trees. He moved slightly so she would see him and when she did he could see the panic in her face.

There was one warrior off to the side of the village. He was way too far away to recognize the man but Benny remembered the horse. It was a horse he hoped he would never see again. It was the spotted horse of the Blackfoot War Chief, Strong Bow.

The girl hadn't moved and hadn't taken her eyes off him. Strong Bow was looking all around and Benny held up his hand motioning her to stay. A few minutes later, Strong Bow rode into the village and Benny motioned the girl to come forward. He could see the fear in her face but after a minute she knew she had no other choice. She slowly crawled up to the trees where he was waiting.

Chapter 23

Little Dove

BENNY REACHED OUT to the Indian girl and helped pull her up over the last steep rise into the trees where he was waiting. He could see the streaks of tears that had been running down her face, but right now her eyes were dry. With the fear showing on her face and her breath coming fast and shallow he figured the fear was keeping the tears at bay. He didn't believe she could understand his words but with as calm a voice as he could muster he said, "You is safe now miss, but we best get back in these trees a bit farther so we stay safe." She didn't hesitate but moved back away from the canyon rim.

He looked one more time at the carnage taking place on the canyon floor and shuddered at the thought of what was happening down there. Stepping back into the trees, he then turned and joined her. She watched him approach, fear still showing on her face. She was wearing a plain dress made of buckskin tied at the shoulders and covering her down to her knees. A leather belt around her waist with a skinning knife in a simple sheath tied to the belt. Her hair was coal black and hung nearly to her waist. Benny thought she wasn't the prettiest girl he had ever seen but she wasn't homely either. He judged her to be sixteen or seventeen, just a couple of years younger than him.

She hadn't said a word but she was watching every little move he made. He leaned his rifle against a tree and sat down on an old log to show her he meant no harm. That seemed to work but a minute later her lower lip started to quiver and once again tears were flowing down her cheeks.

Benny wanted to comfort her but he had no idea how to do so. He patted the log next to where he was sitting and a moment later she walked over to him and sat down. He noticed then her hands and knees were cut and scrapped from her crawling over the rocks and brush to come up the hill.

His horse was tied about fifty yards from where they were sitting and he motioned for her to stay there while he went and got his water pouch. When he got back he knelt in front of her and poured a little water in his hand showing her he intended to clean the scratches and cuts on her knees. When she saw the water, she held out her hands toward it and he handed the pouch to her.

He watched her take the pouch, put it her lips and drink several big swallows. When her thirst was satisfied she handed it back to him. He then reached out slowly to her leg, he watched her face as he did so and was relieved as she nodded an ever so slight nod. After washing the blood off both her knees he slowly poured a little water over her hands, he poured very slowly as she cleaned them up the best she could.

Motioning for her to stay, he walked back over to the rim of the canyon for one more look. It was a long way down to the village but he could plainly see there were now men staked to the ground and there was smoke from the fires burning on their feet. Shutters again ran down his back as the sight of the Flathead village from last year flashed through his mind. He knew they must leave this area before the Blackfeet left the village.

It was the morning of the second day and Grub knew Horse and his grandparents would be leaving today. He wished they would stay another day or two but he fully understood their need to return and find out the fate of the rest of their village. They had plenty of dried elk and bear to last them for many, many days to come. He fashioned packs out of the hide from the elk Horse had shot, then walked up and picked out their best pack horse and led her down into camp.

Ely's fever had broken, he was pale and very weak, his eyes were still sunken back in his face with dark circles around them, but he was lucid now and could speak a little but doing so tired him out. Grub was still mighty worried as he knew very well Ely may not make it, but he was going to do everything he could for him.

Grub and Horse got the packs tied on the horse leaving room for Sky to ride but when they were ready to go she told Horse and Standing Bear they could ride if they wanted but she was going to walk. Standing Bear then said something that she grumbled at and Horse smiled then looked Grub and signed, "Old people are like hard-headed horses."

Grub held out his hand to Standing Bear then walked over to Sky and hugged her. Her old wrinkled eye sparkled and she handed him her medicine kit. She said something and Grub looked at Horse who signed to him, "Friend."

He smiled at her and nodded then signed back, "Good Friend." She turned and started walking up the trail. Grub watched them walk until they were out of sight then turned and sat down by Ely.

His eyes were open and Grub looked as his partner and said, "Pard, you is mighty lucky them Crows came along when they did."

Ely answered, his voice weak and shallow as he said, "I dreamed they was comin. I seed the three of 'em comin' up the trail. I figure the good Lord sent 'em this way, can't figure why, but I figure he did."

Grub smiled and nodded, he too figured it wasn't just by chance those three Crow Indians were coming up this canyon right when they were needed the most.

Benny stood and held out his hand. The Indian girl looked up at him, took his hand and followed him through the trees to the Blackfoot's horse. She saw the horse still had some paint on his neck and rump from the warrior that had ridden it and she stopped dead still and pulled away from him recognizing the markings as Blackfoot. Her hand went to the knife in her belt and she looked at him with a hatred that scared him a little.

Then he realized what she had seen. He held up both hands and said, "I took this horse off a Blackfoot I killed." Figuring she would have no idea what he had just said he started to use sign language and hoped he was getting it right. When he finished she dropped her hand with the knife and said in broken but understandable English, "I talk white man words, better than you talk with hands." Then just a slight smile came to her lips and she stepped forward.

Benny breathed a sigh of relief and stepped up into his saddle. Holding his arm down for her he helped her swing up behind him. He walked to the edge of the trees and studied the open hills that lay ahead. He didn't want to ride across that open country but he didn't want to be this close to the Blackfeet even worse.

He knew that riding double he wouldn't be able to push the horse as hard as he would with two. He figured it was nearly two miles to the next cover and he was going to cross that two miles just as fast as he dared push the horse.

He started in a gentle lope and she had her hands on his sides holding on but he urged the horse into a run she slid her hands all the way around him and he could feel her pressed up against his back. Benny had never been this close to a girl except his sisters, and he didn't know how to feel. He knew she was just holding him to stay on the horse but being pressed up against him the way she was, was causing feelings in him he had never felt before. He could feel himself turning red and had to force the feeling of her pressed up against him from his mind.

It took just over five minutes to cross the open area and he slowed to a walk once he entered a forested draw. The draw was leading him to the southeast; the very way he needed to go to try and pick up the trail of the men he was following. In the timber, he couldn't travel any faster than a walk but she kept her arms tightly around him anyway.

The draw turned straight south and he stayed down in it to avoid being seen. They had been moving for over four hours when they came to a little meadow with a beaver pond in it. He stopped there to rest the horse and themselves and refill his water pouch.

He took the water pouch and walked up the little creek until he found some faster moving water and knelt and refilled the pouch then cupped his hands and drank his fill of the cold clear water. He noted there was beaver activity as he had seen plenty of fallen quakies. Even though the day was warm for being this early in the spring the breeze blowing down the draw had a chill to it.

He walked back toward where he had left her and the horse and realized he hadn't even asked her name. Then a bit of panic hit him as he realized she could take the horse and ride away leaving him there stranded with no horse. He hurried back down the creek cursing himself for being so foolish when he stepped around a large pine and the sight before him made him freeze in his tracks.

He suddenly found it very warm and he was having a hard time breathing. She was standing in the creek completely naked washing the scratches and cuts on her legs. The water was very cold and with the cool breeze, she had chills and goose bumps all over her smooth dark skin.

Benny had never even been close enough to touch a girl before and had never seen one naked at any distance. He felt like he should turn away but suddenly he realized he really liked what was he was seeing. He couldn't believe she wasn't trying to cover up. Then with her teeth chattering she stepped up out of the water, picked up her dress and walked straight toward him. She stopped just a few feet away and slipped the dress back over her head and he watched as it slowly slid down over the curves of her body.

She was cold and the scratches and cuts looked painful. She had nothing with her except that simple buckskin dress. He hurried over to the horse and grabbed his sleeping robe and offered it to her. She smiled and walked to him, turned her back and waited for him to wrap the robe around her. He could feel her shivering through the robe and figured this little meadow was safe enough for a fire.

He was having a hard time trying to get a fire going, for the sight of her standing in the creek was all he could concentrate on. She didn't know what was wrong but she could tell something was making him act strange. She had stopped shivering by the time he got the fire started, but the warmth it provided was very welcome to them both.

Benny finally built up his courage enough to talk to her again and asked her name. She realized then that she had never told him. She smiled and said, "I called Little Dove."

Without looking her in the eyes he replied, "That is a pretty name, Little Dove. I am called Benny."

She was watching his expression and asked, "Have I displease you, Benny?"

At that he looked up at her and shook his head. Now he was embarrassed for the way he was acting.

She smiled and asked, "White man have funny names, what do Benny mean?"

He smiled at that, he had no idea how to answer her, he could tell her it was short for Benton but he didn't know what Benton meant either. He finally said, "I don't know what it means, it is just a name my mother and father called me."

She looked intently at him then said again, "White man have funny names."

Benny had spent two winters in the mountains and both winters had been spent with other trappers in Jackson's Hole. He had heard many stories of how Indian women were free with their bodies. Just hearing some of the stories other trappers would tell made him turn red. He remembered many of the trappers would go long distances out of the way to visit villages where the women were very free with sex and some even said the men would share their wives with visitors to show their hospitality. Benny didn't really believe the stories, he figured it was just the trapper's way of entertaining themselves, but now he wasn't so sure.

Little Dove was watching him carefully. She liked this young white man. He had saved her and was kind to her. She didn't want to do anything that would displease him. The fact that him seeing her without her dress on would make him uncomfortable never entered her mind. All the women bathed in the open along whatever stream or lake they were camped by. It was their way of life and she did not know or understand any other.

It was the middle of the afternoon and Benny felt safe here. They were totally secluded; the water was good and he figured come evening there would be game of some kind coming down to this beaver pond to drink. Benny was wearing his buffalo robe coat and was quite comfortable while Little Dove had kept his buffalo sleeping robe wrapped around her to ward off the cool breeze.

He was hungry and knew she must be as well. He pulled out the cooked badger looked at it and said, "I have to make meat, and this tough, stringy badger wasn't good when it was fresh. She looked at it and nodded in agreement.

He walked around the pond to the opposite end of the meadow looking for tracks along the way. He smiled when he found a heavily used trail with deer and sheep tracks on it leading up to the edge of the pond. He set himself about fifty yards from the trail and figured it would be an hour or better before any animals would be moving.

He thought about what he was doing here with an Indian girl who had just lost everything she had ever had or had ever known while the men he was chasing, the ones that had shot Ely were getting further and further away. He couldn't figure anything else to do except what he was doing. He couldn't just leave Little Dove all alone in this wilderness with nothing. He thought about Ely and wondered how he was doing and then thought about Grub… what if Ely didn't make it, what would Grub do?

Just then a twig broke up in the trees and he slowly readied himself. A couple of minutes later he saw movement as a ewe and two yearling lambs came into view. Benny preferred to eat deer and elk but one of those yearling mountain sheep would taste mighty good after what he had been eating. He took careful aim and fired, dropping the closest lamb instantly.

He worried some about the sound of his shot but he really thought the heavy timber and being down in the bottom of this draw would muffle the sound enough it couldn't be heard too far away.

They enjoyed fresh lamb loin as the light faded early down in the bottom of the draw. They ate in silence for neither of them felt much like talking. It got cold quickly after the sun disappeared behind the western edge of the draw and he figured it was going to be a cold miserable night. He walked out into the forest and brought in enough wood to keep the fire going through the night. She had the buffalo robe, he would have to make do with just his coat.

When he returned with all the wood he could carry she had the robe laid out by the fire and was lying in it. He smiled at her then sat down by the fire where he could reach the wood and try to stay warm. When he did, she threw back the buffalo robe inviting him to lay with her.

Chapter 24

What Happens Next

ZACH WATCHED FROM the ridge top for several more minutes figuring what he should do. He considered this was his back yard, even the Indians called this whole area on the north slope of the Uintah's the land of Grizzly Killer and he had to find out who was down there. He patted Jimbo one more time and said, "Well, boy lets go see who come ta visit."

Jimbo started down a game trail that worked its way through the thick forest. He was staying within easy sight of Zach who was on foot leading his horse. Zach loved the forest, the smell of the pine, the chattering of the squirrels, and even the squawk of the blue jays. The world around them was coming to life after the long, cold winter.

A gust of wind came up the ridge and Jimbo stopped to test the air with his nose. A moment later, Zach caught just a slight hint of wood smoke from the fire down below. He tied his horse to a tree once again and went the rest of the way on foot. He moved forward slow and careful not making a sound as the soft soles of his moccasins touched the forest floor. Jimbo was now right by his side and excited in anticipation of Zach's next command. After all these years Zach still marveled how a dog as big as Jimbo could move through the trees and brush without ever making a sound.

Long before he was close enough to see them he heard laughter and voices and to Zach surprise the words he was hearing were in English. These had to be trappers that were working their way up Smith's Fork for the spring season.

He knew better than to just walk into another man's camp uninvited but he needed to know more about them before he let them know he was there. Staying in the thickest part of the trees he carefully moved closer. When he was about fifty yards out he sent Jimbo to the other side of their camp with nothing more than a silent hand signal the dog knew well. Jimbo would stay out of sight until Zach called him out or trouble started- whichever came first.

A few more feet and Zach could see four men. Two of them were off to the side skinning a beaver the other two were drinking what appeared to be coffee by the fire. Zach watched for several minutes, one of the men was a short burley fellow. Zach could hear only part of what he was saying but it sounded like they were talking about going over the mountains and on down to Taos.

Zach cocked his Hawken then stepped out from behind the pine and shouted, "Hello, the camp, is it okay ta come in?" The men that were skinning the beaver stopped and grabbed their rifles as well as the one that the shorty burley one was talking too. The burley guy just stood there with his coffee cup and shouted back, "Come on in if'n yer friendly."

Zach was holding his rifle with just one hand so they could see he wasn't a threat and walked on in. As he got closer to the fire he smiled and said, "Is that real coffee ya got there?" "Naw, it's just some plant we boil, don't know what it's called but some feller showed us this last fall when we run outta coffee.'

"Oh," Zach said, "I just call it Injun Tea."

As Zach walked into their camp he saw the bundles of plews these men had and then he saw what a miserable job of skinning they were doing on the beaver they were working on. He knew these same men had not put those bundles together. He saw their horses, ten in all, that were in a makeshift pole corral, but what troubled him the most were the three rifles that were still pointed at him. He had a bad feeling that something here was wrong. He was being friendly enough, so why were these men still holding their rifles on him?

He moved his rifle over to his left hand, then held out his right hand to the short burley fellow and said, "Name's Zach Connors, boys. I've been trappin' over west of here but it's all but trapped out. Figured I'd move over east an' try up Henry's Fork for a month or two before I head on up north for Rendezvous." He then pointed over to their bundles of plews and continued, "Looks like you feller's hit the jackpot last fall. That's some nice bundles of plews ya got there."

Then Phil spoke up, saying, "That ain't none of yer concern."

"Sorry, just tryin' ta be friendly, I ain't had nobody to talk to all winter" Zach replied.

The short burley one then held out his hand and said, "Name's Mel Tillman, that ornery one there is Phil Hurley." He then pointed to the other two and said, "That's Patch McCord and Nels Mitchell." He then asked, "Ya said ya ain't talked to nobody all winter, ya mean you spent the winter here all by yer self?"

Zach nodded and said, "Yep, ever since '24 when me an' my Pa first come out here, but a Grizz got Pa that first year. I do see Injuns on occasion but white men only at Rendezvous." Zach hated lying, by adding this last bit to his story but he figured it was mostly the truth.

Phil then asked, "You on foot all by yerself?"

Zach shook his head no and said, "Naw, I tied my horse up in the trees when I smelled your fire and come on down on foot. Wanted ta make sure you weren't hostile Injuns 'fore I let myself be seen."

Patch and Nels had lowered their rifles, but Phil was still holding his at the ready. Zach could tell by Phil's manner and look in his eyes he wasn't a man you could turn your back on. Zach tried to pull as much information out of them as he could by being friendly and acting like he wanted someone to talk to, but Mel was real careful with his words and the other three didn't really talk at all.

After a few minutes of mostly one-sided conversation, Zach said, "Well, it was sure good ta talk to you fellers for a while but I best be movin' on. I got some country ta cross 'fore nightfall."

At that, Phil raised his rifle pointing it at Zach and said, "Only place yer goin', Mister, is ta show us where yer plews is."

Mel grinned but Nels and Patch both looked surprised. Zach's tone now got serious and he said, "You best lower that rifle, Mister, or you ain't gonna like what happens next."

The wicked grin on Phil's face told Zach all he needed to know, there would be no reasoning with this man.

Zach moved his hand ever so slightly. The four of them were all staring at him as Jimbo attacked from behind. Jimbo jumped while still ten feet from Phil and all two hundred pounds of him hit Phil in the back. Phil fell forward with his rifle discharging into the ground in front of him. Jimbo jaws clamped down on Phil's throat ripping through the skin and flesh and tearing into the artery under his left ear.

Mel and the others jumped back as blood sprayed out from the gaping hole in Phil's neck with every beat of his heart. When Mel looked up, Zach's Hawken was pointed right at the center of his chest. None of the three even tried to help Phil and within a minute all movement had stopped. His heart had pumped the last of his life-giving blood out onto the ground next to their fire.

Nels and Patch were terrified, that was plain to see and even Mel had fear in his eyes. Zach calmly and very softly said, "I told him he wasn't gonna like what happened next." He continued without ever changing his tone, "Gentlemen, this here is my partner Jimbo and he don't like people pointing guns at me."

Zach let that sink in for a long minute then said, "I don't much like it either, so I'm gonna leave now and go back to my home on the other side of this ridge and if I ever see any one of you again, *ever*, it will be your last day on this earth."

Not one of the three of them said a word, they just stared in fear and disbelief at what had just happened. Zach backed his way back up the hill until he was out of sight with Jimbo right by his side.

It was several minutes before any of the three of them moved, then Nels said in a shaking voice still full of fear, "We's lucky that murderin' bastard didn't get us all killed."

Mel just stood there looking at the forest where Zach had gone then said, "Let's get loaded up and get the hell outta here."

Nels and Patch didn't say a word, they just headed to the horses and started to load. Within an hour they were headed back down-stream the way they had come. All three of them could see the mountain passes to the south were still snowed in. They would have to find another way to Taos. They left Phil's body right where he was laying, none of the three of them even had a thought of taking time to bury him. They didn't even take his rifle or pistol, they were in such a hurry to leave.

Grub kept the tea he was giving Ely brewed most all the time and every couple of hours he would have him drink as much as he could. Ely had lost enough blood it was going to take a long time for his body to replace it, but he did seem to be getting a little stronger each day. Ely would sleep most of the time and just the effort it took for him to speak a few words would tire him out. One time when he was awake and feeling a little stronger he asked Grub where Benny had gone and when Grub told him he said, "Ya shouldn't let 'im go, they's was four of 'em and it was his old pards." Hearing that took Grub by surprise. Then he looked at Ely and said, "They wasn't no stoppin' 'im pard, it was like he had to do this, but we sure didn't know it was his old pards."

Grub worried about Benny now he knew who had shot Ely and taken their plews he worried even more. Could Benny do what he would have to do to men he had rode with? The more he thought about that he believed he could. He had faith in Benny, he was bright and determined and had been taught right from wrong. It was plain enough to Grub that Benny had been raised by good people.

He thought about Horse and Standing Bear and especially Sky. The wrinkled old stubborn Crow women that had come along at just the right time. Grub really believed without her help Ely would not be alive right now. He hoped the best for them and the rest of their village.

As the stars faded away with the coming light of the next day Benny laid there with the buffalo robe wrapped around him and Little Dove. She had her head on his shoulder with her arm over his chest and the warmth of her body next to his felt mighty good. She was still asleep and her breathing was slow and deep. He thought about what she had been through just the day before and marveled at the inner strength she must have.

It was cold in the bottom of this draw this morning. The fire had long since burned itself out. Benny hadn't wanted to wake Little Dove to add more wood all night. He liked the feeling of her lying next to him, he even liked the feeling of her needing and depending on him. She was bringing out feeling he had never experienced before and he really liked what he felt.

He had not slept at all through the night as his mind was on this girl lying next to him and on what he had to do. She excited him, he had feelings he had never felt before but at the same time he felt a burden and responsibility for her. Although he had no intention of leaving Little Dove behind he also had no intention of abandoning his task of finding the men who had shot Ely.

She was pressed up against him so tight he could feel her heart beating and feel the slightest movements she made and all this excited him. She was the reason he had not slept all night even though he had his arm around her he wanted to touch her and kiss her but he did not dare.

She opened her eyes and smiled at him. He made her feel safe although she knew if the Blackfeet found them they would be just as dead as the rest of her family and friends. Her heart ached for the loss of her loved ones but being a child of this wilderness, she had seen this kind of loss before. It hadn't happened to her before but she knew life must go on and she was determined to put the death of her village behind her. This white man called Benny had saved her, in her mind she now belonged to him. She didn't understand why but that excited her, she liked him, this man with his strange name that didn't mean anything.

Benny smiled back at her then rolled out from under the robe into the cold morning air tucking the robe in around her. He added wood and blew life back into the fire, just a minute later she too got up keeping the robe around her. She went to the lamb they had hanging in a tree a couple of hundred feet from where they were sleeping and cut out the other loin and brought it back to the fire.

While the lamb cooked he told her of the men he was chasing and why and told her she will have to come with him at least for now.

She smiled at him and said, "You save me, I belong to you, I happy go with you."

Benny looked at her, surprised, and said, "Little Dove, you don't belong to me. You can do or go anywhere you like."

She smiled again even bigger and said, "I like go with you."

Benny didn't know what was going to happen when he caught up with the men he was following but right here and right now he was happy she wanted to go with him.

Not knowing where the Blackfeet would have gone when they left the Shoshone village, Benny was staying under cover as much as possible. He knew riding double was hard on the horse but Little Dove wasn't heavy and now that her touch wasn't making him nervous he really liked her arms around him.

The draw they were in was starting to turn more to the southwest and Benny knew he must go to the east to find the tracks he was looking for so he climbed up out of the draw heading toward the east. The ridge top was barren of trees and from up on this ridge he had a clear view of the land for as far as he could see. Just a few miles to the west was a large canyon and this little creek they had been following was flowing into the much larger stream in that canyon.

Little Dove pointed and said, "The white mans in village call that Ham's Fork."

Benny turned to her then and asked, "Was the white man in your village when the Blackfeet attacked?

She shook her head no and said, "He left three or four suns back to catch a'nii, what he call beaver."

"What is his name?" he asked.

"We call him Big Nose Tom and he stay in lodge of Blue Flower. No Shoshone man want live with her, she had three husband and all die. Big Nose Tom not afraid, he stay with her two winters and he is big and strong."

Benny nodded. He didn't know of Big Nose Tom but he had only been to the one Rendezvous and the trappers probably didn't call him Big Nose.

Benny studied the country south and east of him from this ridge top. It was dry land with no trees for as far as the eye could see. The only trees or bushes were down along Ham's Fork. Although he had never been there before he had paid close attention to other trappers and especially Grizzly Killer telling of this land. He knew that Ham's Fork ran into Black's Fork and he knew Grizzly Killer lived way up on Black's Fork. What he didn't know right now was where the men he was chasing were going or where the Blackfoot war party was going. He needed to find one and stay away from the other.

He could see for miles up and down Ham's Fork and there was no movement down there at all. There were several herds of antelope on the flats just south of him. Ham's Fork was flowing in a southeasterly direction so he figured he would stay just east of it down to Black's Fork. If he hadn't picked up the trail by then maybe he could find Grizzly Killer for some help.

Little Dove could tell he wasn't sure what to do and she spoke, pointing to the southeast, "The men you follow must have water, only water is river, it turn direction of rising sun maybe half day ride, then it turn again to south."

"Have been to the south?" he asked.

She nodded and said, "Many time we camp where this river runs into the other."

What other?" he asked again.

"The one that Grizzly Killer live on," she answered.

Now he was even happier she was with him- he had a guide going into country he had never before seen. He asked, "Have you been where Grizzly Killer lives?"

She shook her head no and said, "I have never been to Grizzly Killer village but I know it is on bank of river up where river enters high mountains."

He started down off the ridge working his way between the rocks and the short stiff sage. They hadn't gone far when he saw dust in the air along the river north of them. It was many riders moving much faster than he was following the river south. It had to be the Blackfeet.

Chapter 25

A Cozy Little Shelter

GRIZZLY KILLER STAYED up in the trees out of sight but close enough that he knew what the men he had just confronted were going to do. He believed they would leave; the look of fear on their faces had convinced him of that, but he wanted to be sure. That short burley one had a look about him he didn't trust. Two hours later, he walked back down to where they were camped still being careful to stay out of sight in case they were waiting for him. He was disgusted by the fact they hadn't buried their companion, so he took the time to cover the body with rocks to keep the animals and vultures away from it.

He followed their tracks down Smith's Fork until he was convinced they were leaving. He then turned and worked his way back up the ridge. It was just before dark when Jimbo ran ahead into their camp letting everyone know he was coming home.

Ol' Red let out a bray that Zach figured could be heard for miles when he rode into camp. It was obvious to all of them Ol' Red was tired of being left at home while Grizzly Killer and Jimbo left. Zach dismounted and Running Wolf was right there to take the reins, he gave a quick kiss to Shining Star and the baby, then to Sun Flower and stepped across the fast-moving runoff water of Black's Fork on the rocks that were now nearly covered. Ol' Red was on the other side waiting for him.

Zach softly talked to the big mule as he put his arms around his neck and hugged him and told him just another week or so and he would take him instead of a horse. Ol' Red nuzzled his hand letting Zach know he was ready to go now. Zach had seen the big mule take out his jealousy on a horse once before, it was a horse Zach had ridden when a grizzly had hurt Ol' Red and he was a little worried for this Crow pony he had been riding today, but Running Wolf led the horse across the wild river and right up to Ol' Red and Zach made sure there wasn't going to be any trouble before Running Wolf turned the horse loose.

Benny moved the horse slowly around the other side of the ridge they were riding down, until he was out of sight of the Blackfeet. He didn't want to stir up any dust. Little Dove had stiffened and was squeezing her arms around him tight at the first sign of the Blackfeet. Once they were out of sight on the eastern side of the ridge he could see there were several draws leading downward. They were filled with tall brush and a few quakies growing where the snow was slow to melt and the ground was staying moist late into the summer.

He knew they had plenty of water for a day- maybe two- if they were careful and it was cool enough the lamb quarter they brought would last a couple more days. He headed down the steep side hill into the bottom of the closest draw and was surprised to find a trickle of a stream running through the bottom of it.

He was nearly out of the trees toward the bottom of the draw before he found a spot level enough for them to camp. It was still early in the day but he didn't want to take any chances of them being seen by the marauding Blackfeet. He stopped right there and Little Dove slid off the side of the horse. Benny patted the horse's neck as he stepped out of the saddle. He was pleased this really was a well-trained and stout animal. He hadn't shown any signs at all of tiring carrying the two of them.

Little Dove hung the lamb quarter from an aspen branch, not as high as she would have liked it but these were just small quakies and they had very little rope.

A gusty south wind was starting to blow and they both figured that meant a storm sometime in the near future so Benny started to look for some way make them a shelter. Walking back up the steep draw he started bringing dead fall logs down to this level area and started to put together a lean-to. He wasn't sure what he was going to cover the top with but anything would be better than nothing. Little Dove was bringing down fire wood and had a fire pit scraped out with a nice stack of fire wood right in front of the lean-to.

Benny stood back and looked at this little camp they had set up and wished he had some of the hides and supplies that were with Grub and Ely, but he didn't. The thick bushes just above them were like everything else this time of the year; they didn't have leaves yet but he started cutting the branches and laying them across the logs that made up the top of the lean-to. When he was satisfied, he started to dig and pull clumps of grass that were growing in the draw and covered over the branches. It took most of the afternoon and he was exhausted but he had put together a fairly, weather-tight, little shelter just big enough for the two of them.

The sun went down early and about the time it did, the gusty wind started to shift from the south to the northwest. With that change, the temperature dropped quickly and he decided that, with the wind, smoke from a fire couldn't be seen. It took several tries to get a fire going and finally they both huddled around a small, fitful fire.

The fire was warm and comforting and Little Dove sliced off strips of lamb and they ate in the protection of their shelter. With the fire's reflected heat and out of the wind it wasn't at all unpleasant.

As the light faded Benny thought about the trail he still had to find and about Ely looking as pale as a ghost the last time he'd seen him. He thought about the Blackfeet and was more than a little concerned that they were heading in the same direction he was. Where were they going? Little Dove was moving around behind him laying out the buffalo robe for them to sleep under but right now his thoughts were what he must do tomorrow. Where must he go to find the trail of whoever he was following and at the same time avoid the Blackfeet?

He crawled out from under the lean-to and checked on the horse making sure he was secure and could reach plenty of the dry grass then came back and added more wood to the fire. With the clouds that had now moved in, the sky was dark and the only light at all was coming from their fire. He took the time to climb up out of the draw to where he could see for miles and miles to the south and east and in all the miles he could see there was no light at all. He was relieved the Blackfeet were not camped close enough to see their fire.

He could feel the first tiny snowflakes hitting his face when he returned and Little Dove was already under the buffalo robe. He removed his heavy coat and offered it to her. She took it and rolled it up for them both to use as a pillow. Just like the night before, she lifted the robe for him to get under it, only this time she had removed her dress and was completely naked waiting for him to lay with her.

He froze perfectly still staring at her beautiful body, not able to move or speak. His breath was coming in short shallow pants much like an overheated dog. She smiled at him and held her other hand out to pull him under the robe with her. He followed her lead- not knowing what he should do. He laid there and his whole body was as stiff as a board. He was afraid to move because if he did he would rub up against her.

She could tell he liked her a lot, but she couldn't figure out why he was laying here like his body was a log. She rolled up on her side with the front of her whole body pressed up against him. She then moved her hand up across his chest and around his throat, then up along his cheeks and she softly ran her finger over his lips. His breathing was coming even faster now and she pulled herself up on him and put her lips on his. The stiffness melted right out of most of his body as he relaxed and held her tight up against him.

Neither of them got much sleep that cold, snowy night and neither of them even realized it was as bitter cold as it was and that it had snowed nearly a foot by the time it started to get light the next morning. Benny was lying there with Little Dove wrapped tightly in his arms and he didn't want to let go for fear his feelings would vanish. He never wanted to lose it. Never in his life had he felt this way.

She opened her eyes and loved the feeling of Benny's arms tightly around her. His now naked body felt like it was part of her own. She was no virgin, Indian children often experiment with sex at an early age, but she had never felt like she did this morning. She didn't want to let go of this white man with the strange name. She was afraid she might lose him if she did.

Benny looked deep into her obsidian black eyes. They had just a hint of brown but the light from the snow made them sparkle with light and then he slowly kissed her again and said, "I have to get a fire started, the snow has put out all of the coals."

She smiled up at him and then with a mischievous look on her face she pulled the buffalo robe off them both and pushed his warm naked body out into icy snow.

The snow had been wide spread during the night, covering most of the intermountain west. Grub cursed the cold and snow even though in his camp with Ely on Granite Creek in the Gros Ventre Mountains they had only received a couple of inches of the cold wet snow.

Ely was getting stronger each day but this cold wet weather didn't help him any. Grub had a nice warm fire going with the heat reflecting off the top of the lean-to and Ely remarked, though his voice was still soft and weak, "Grub, you is like an ol' hen tendin' her chicks. I's is gonna be okay. If'n I was gonna die I would a done it by now."

Grub looked at his partner and said, "Okay, I's just gonna set back here an' watch ya check yer traps this afternoon." Grub could see the look in Ely's eye deflate and figured he had gone too far. They were both silent for a while then Grub said, "I'm sorry, pard. I know yer feeling a little better but we both know you got one hell of a ways ta go yet. That feller that shot ya damn near put you under."

Again, there was silence for a few minutes then Ely said, "Pard, don't ever be sorry fer tellin' it like it is. An' don't you never think I ain't appreciatin' ever thing yer doin'. I knowed I be feedin' the worms and pushin' up daisy's if'n it wasn't fer you."

Grub looked at him and said, "I figure it was that old Crow woman that saved ya Pard, her and the good lord."

Ely nodded at that but then said, "Don't sell yerself short, you been here when neither one of them have been."

"I don't figure the good Lord as ever left yer side either. I figure we both ought ta say our thanks ta him." Grub replied.

Ely didn't say another word but looked at Grub, nodded then closed his eyes and said a silent prayer giving thanks for his good fortune and good friends.

Zach stepped out of his lodge to just a skiff of new snow. It seemed the main storm moved across Sweet Lake and on east to where Benny and Little Dove were. Here in the Uintah's they had just received the tail end of it. Zach was troubled this morning as he watched the clouds moving rapidly overhead. The high peaks to his south was hidden with the still thick layer of clouds. He thought again as he had many times in the past, *Ya just never know what a Rocky Mountain Spring will bring.*

The trouble he felt he didn't believe was the weather. No, this felt like something else but he wasn't sure what that something else might be. Jimbo came up alongside of him and a minute later Luna come up alongside of Jimbo. Both the dog and the wolf were staring downstream. Neither of them were growling or making any aggressive moves at all, so after a couple of minutes Zach turned back and started on their morning fire.

He greeted Sun Flower and just a minute later Shining Star brought out Star tightly bundled in soft tanned rabbit fur. He took the baby and the women started working on their morning meal. Both the swelling and bruising on both of his wives were mostly gone now. You really had to look close to see any discoloration on either of them. The lump on Shining Star's head was no longer visible. You could still feel it slightly by gently moving your fingers over it but both women had healed up just fine.

Running Wolf and Raven Wing joined them and little Gray Wolf's eyes were wide with the bright snow, he wanted to get down and play in it until Running Wolf give him a handful of the cold white stuff.

Zach was troubled and he didn't know why. This was a peaceful, loving camp this morning, yet he couldn't relax, something was out there that was making him feel this way but he had no idea what that might be. He thought about the three men and wondered if they may be looking for him to get even for the death of their friend but he didn't believe that. They hadn't even made the effort to bury him. He thought about the Cheyenne; would they be coming back? That didn't make sense either, though, the only ones that knew where they lived were dead. The Crow had told them that a large Blackfoot war party was raiding to the south but would they come this far south?

The feeling he had just wouldn't let up. Maybe because Jimbo and Luna had spent all morning sitting at the head of the trail staring down stream. Zach had learned years ago not to ignore his feelings, whether he was alone or with his family and now he knew there was something he needed to do. Just figuring out what that something was sometimes was the biggest problem.

Running Wolf was getting ready to check their trap line when Zach stopped him and said, "Brother, I need you to stay with the women again. I must ride the trail downstream. I do not know why but something is calling me that way. Jimbo and Luna have sensed something as well, so I must go find out what it is. I can't say how far I will need to go or how long I will be gone but this is something I must do."

Running Wolf never questioned Grizzly Killer. He just nodded and asked, "Have you told the women?" Zach shook his head and then headed back to the fire.

He could see the sadness in the eyes of Shining Star. Even though she would never say anything, her heart ached to spend more time with him. It felt to her like he had been gone way too much since most of the snow had melted. She understood why, it was not by choice but she didn't like the feeling of being without him-no matter the reason.

She put on a brave face, smiled and kissed him goodbye then stepped back and watched Sun Flower do the same. They both knew Grizzly Killer wouldn't be leaving if he didn't feel this was important but all of them would have been more comfortable if they knew where he was going and what he was looking for.

Zach himself wished he had the answer to those questions as he headed back down the trail with Jimbo in the lead.

Chapter 26

Battle on Black's Fork

BENNY LANDED JUST outside of their lean-to in the eight inches of fresh snow. The freezing snow took his breath away as he rolled away from her. He jumped up, cold and wet, his naked body shivering in the cold air, then he jumped back in the lean-to next to Little Dove. She was giggling until his cold wet body touch her warm dry skin. She tried to push him away but he wrapped his arms around her and pulled her closer to him. She stiffened then relaxed into his arms and threw the robe up over them again and they made love one more time.

It was nearly midday before they left their little camp, riding out into a completely white landscape. The clouds were still overhead but far out to the west the sky was clearing. The air was crystal clear and it looked like he could see forever as they rode out of the little draw and onto the flatlands still heading south.

Benny was worried, he had no idea how he was ever going to find the trail of the men he was following now that snow had covered everything, but he knew he must try. He was scanning the horizons in every direction for any movement, still worried the Blackfeet may be close. It was several hours later, when they could see the waterway of Ham's Fork off to the west and that of Black's Fork to their south.

He stopped the horse and studied the country all around them one more time. He was worried about the trail he was leaving in the fresh snow. If any of the Blackfeet crossed their trail it would be simple task for them to follow and kill him and Little Dove. Both knew they would never have any chance if the Blackfeet found their trail.

He had just started moving again when Little Dove pointed to the southeast and in an excited voice, a little louder than she intended said, "Gwiipe! Gwiipe!" Benny did not understand what she was saying but he could see where she was pointing and there seemed to be a light smoke haze over the river to the south and east of them.

He turned in the saddle toward her and she realized then she had spoken Shoshone instead of English and smiled at him and then said, "Smoke."

Benny nodded and turned west, they rode to Ham's Fork and crossed to the west side stopping only long enough to fill his water pouch and let the horse drink his fill.

Benny wondered if that could be from the men he was chasing, but then he decided it could not be. The smoke from a single fire he didn't believe would spread out that much, he figured that is where the Blackfeet were camped. After crossing the river, he continued west for several more miles. He wanted to make sure there was no way the Blackfeet could see them, so he then turned south again. It hadn't snowed near as much down on these flats, the snow was only a couple of inches here on the sage and clumps of grass. On the barren ground, the snow was nearly melted off.

With no sun, it had been a cold day so Little Dove kept the buffalo robe wrapped around her. Benny figured they were now over ten miles west of where the Blackfeet were camped, if the smoke they had seen was indeed the Blackfeet. He stopped again to look over this flat barren land, He was trying to figure out which way to go having no idea at all where the men he was tracking were headed and he had never been in this part of the country before.

Zach rode down the familiar trail with renewed caution this time. He had no idea what was compelling him to ride. He was again mounted on the Crow horse. Ol' Red had just stood back with his head down when he threw the saddle on the horse this time. Right now, he was much more concerned about what was out here and how far away whatever it was might be than he was about the big mule's feelings.

He traveled only at a fast walk and Jimbo kept coming back wondering why he was going so slowly, but the dog had sensed trouble as well and was ranging out no more than a quarter mile in front. Although Zach was not traveling fast he kept a steady pace and by late afternoon he was nearly thirty miles from home. He was beginning to wonder if he was just imagining trouble for he hadn't seen any sign of anyone so far.

Early evening found him nearly thirty-five miles downstream and still no sign of any trouble. He sent Jimbo to scout the area for any trouble then set up a small camp under the cottonwoods on a bend in the river, He then scraped out a small fire pit under the cottonwoods where he hoped the branches would break the smoke from a small fire.

The light snow had slowly melted throughout the day but as the sun went down a chill filled the air until it got down right cold. He had brought a small amount of smoked buffalo and some jerky with him which would take care of his hunger but what he really longed for this cold night was a cup of hot coffee.

He had finished eating as the light was fading along the river, the clouds of the morning had moved on to the east and the sky was clear. Stars were just becoming visible when Jimbo's ears perked up. He was intently staring up the trail and a minute later, his low growl started from way down in his chest. Zach kicked out the fire and picked up his rifle and disappeared into the brush. Jimbo went to the opposite side of the trail and out of Zach's sight.

Several minutes passed and Zach hadn't heard a sound. Although he had always been patient, not knowing why he was here and not knowing what Jimbo had heard was trying that patience. He would have much rather been in the teepee bouncing Star on his knee and watching Shining Star and Sun Flower doing their nightly chores.

A twig snapped not far up the trail so he checked the powder in the pan of his Hawken and quietly closed the frizen. Another minute passed without a sound. He slowly pulled the hammer back on the rifle getting ready to fire when Jimbo came trotting out the shadows, tail wagging with Ol' Red right behind him. Zach breathed a sigh of relief then another of disbelief. His big red mule wasn't going to be left behind again and had followed them all day long.

Zach stood shaking his head not knowing how to feel. He loved the big mule as much as he did Jimbo and he didn't want him hurting his wounded shoulder, but Ol' Red, Jimbo and himself had been through a lot together and he trusted the mule much more than any horse he had ever ridden. As Zach walked toward him, Ol' Red threw his head up and down then nuzzled his hand as he patted the side of his neck. Zach smiled and asked, "Are ya sure your up ta this big feller?"

Ol' Red raised his head up and down again and Zach said, "Okay, feller we'll see how ya do carryin' me in the mornin'."

As Zach laid down on a soft bed of last fall's dropped cottonwood leaves, a pack of coyotes started in their high pitch yipping on the low hills just west of the river. The river had widened out some here and was flowing flat, it wasn't masking the sounds of the night that were all around him. Sometime in the night he heard a lone wolf howling somewhere downstream and again he wondered why he was here on the cold ground instead of home in the arms of his warm and loving wives.

It was barely light enough to see the trail when he headed out the next morning. This time the saddle was on Ol' Red. Zach tied up a makeshift halter for the Crow horse and being used to the trail she followed along behind Ol' Red without any trouble at all.

It had been a long and cold night and even though it was still cold Zach was glad to be moving again. They were another five miles or so downstream when the sun finally came up and he rode up on the east side of a small hill to let the warming rays of the sun warm him. Even Jimbo laid on the little hillside soaking up the heat.

They were out of the foothills with the trees and brush and were now starting out onto the flats. The country north of the river is now low rolling hills covered with sage. Zach stopped often to study the country around him and had decided he wasn't going any farther than the confluence of Black's Fork with Ham's Fork. He figured if there wasn't any trouble by then it was too far away to be a threat to his family and he was over half way there now.

Ol' Red seemed to be holding up just fine and didn't seem to be favoring that wounded leg at all. Zach still worried if he had to run for cover was his big mule strong and sound enough. Jimbo stopped on the trail ahead and Zach stopped Ol' Red just fifty feet behind his dog. Every sense was on high alert as Zach knew the big dog well. Jimbo had caught the scent of something ahead of them.

The river ahead made a series of oxbow bends and Zach crossed the swollen stream to the other side. The water was much deeper than he expected it to be and he had wet moccasins and feet when they climbed out. Jimbo had to swim across and the current pulled him downstream a couple of hundred yards in the process. Now Zach was on the north side but they were all wet and cold and he still didn't know what Jimbo had caught scent of ahead of them.

He moved north off the river and on to higher ground where he could study the land ahead, but still could see nothing at all. He moved over a quarter mile from the river, his eyes never the leaving the twisting curves of the muddy water. There what looked to be a shallow gulley ahead of them and again Jimbo stopped testing the air with his nose. Zach watched the dog now tense and leery, his eye caught movement, it was ever so slight but Zach yelled, "Come," and Jimbo jumped. He was just a blink of an eye too slow. An arrow caught him right through the lower part of his right hind leg. Zach heard the yelp and saw another arrow in flight but by now Jimbo was on a dead run and the second arrow hit a full foot behind him.

Jimbo yelped again and again as the arrow sticking out of his leg hit the brush as he ran back to where Zach, Ol' Red, and the horse was. Zach had his rifle up and ready to shoot but he couldn't see a target. Apparently, the Indians that were hiding in that gulley had been up against rifles before and wasn't giving him a chance to see any of them. Zach and the horses were now out of range of the deadly arrows. Zach jumped off Ol' Red when Jimbo got to him and in one quick motion he snapped the arrow shaft into two pieces and pulled it out of Jimbo's leg.

Zach knew from personal experience how painful an arrow through the lower leg could be. He still had the scar and deep muscle aches from time to time from the Arapaho arrow that went through his leg just last year. One glance at the pattern on this arrow told Zach this was Blackfeet he was up against this time.

He had been on the ground for only seconds when ten screaming Blackfeet came charging at him out of the gulley. Instinctively and in only a second, he raised his rifle and fired, hitting the leading warrior squarely in the face. He jumped on Ol' Red without using a stirrup and just hung on as the red mule bounded away from the screaming Indians.

Zach reloaded while on a dead run, not many men could do that as fast as Zach could. He had always been very good with a rifle, even when he was just ten years old hunting turkey's and white tails back home in Kentucky. He still had his pistol loaded so he had two more shots when he reached the top of the sage covered hill to the north.

He pulled Ol' Red into a sliding stop and jumped off before the mule had stopped moving when they reached the top. The Blackfeet were only seventy-five yards behind him and his next shot hit the closest warrior high in the left shoulder throwing him off his horse with a summersault over the horse's rump. He dropped his Hawken and pulled the pistol he had tucked under his belt and fired again, but this time he was just a little low. The heavy lead ball hit the horse right between her eyes sending the screaming warrior into the brush in front of him face first, knocking him out cold.

With three of the Blackfeet warriors down the others not wanting to ride into any more gun fire veered off giving Zach time to reload both guns. They didn't know all his guns were empty right then.

Benny and Little Dove were still riding south through the sage covered hills and flat lands toward Black's Fork when they heard the distant gun shots. Benny urged the horse into a lope heading south where the shots had come from. Two more shots rang out this time closer and Benny stood in his stirrups trying to see farther ahead. With shots that close together he figured there had to be trouble.

He stopped on the backside of the next rise and had Little Dove slide off the horse saying, "Stay down and out of sight while I see who is fighting ahead."

She simply nodded but her heart was breaking. She really liked Benny and she was afraid it was the Blackfeet up ahead and she was afraid Benny would not come back for her. She had been raised in a male dominate society and she knew it was not her place to question a man's decisions no matter how much that decision hurt her.

Benny stopped before the next rise and dismounted. He crawled to the top of the slight rise staying below the sage. From where he was it was only a quarter mile to the top of the next rise and he could plainly see a lone man on that rise. Benny could see the Indians were getting ready for another attack only this time three of them were sneaking around the hill to get on the other side of this lone man. In doing so they were going to come within easy range of Benny's rifle and maybe even his pistol.

Benny couldn't tell if the man across from him was a white man or Indian but to Benny it didn't matter—he was way out numbered. He watched as the three warriors were staying out of sight by crawling through the brush and the route they were crawling was even going to put them closer to him than he first thought they would.

He slowly removed his powder horn and possibles bag, then laid out six round balls each on a patch cloth that he had already cut to size. He laid his pistol right beside the possibles bag and made himself mentally ready to do what he had to do.

From where he was he hadn't been able to see the enemy well enough to tell they were Blackfeet but in his mind, he believed that is what they were. Benny could tell the four warriors still on horseback were getting ready to charge. He wondered just how close they were going to get before they charged again. Another hundred yards of them sneaking through the sage and they would be in easy range of his guns.

He glanced across the way and now couldn't believe what he saw. Standing next to the man was a saddled mule. Benny had seen many trappers use mules for their pack animals but he had only ever seen one man use a mule to ride, and that was the great Grizzly Killer himself. Now Benny got even more serious about helping with this fight. If that really was Grizzly Killer over there he couldn't miss even one of these Indians that were now nearly in range.

Benny had met Grizzly Killer last year when he led the charge to save Robert Campbell's brigade from the Blackfeet over on Sweet Lake as they were going to Rendezvous. Grub, Ely and Benny had been traveling with Robert Campbell's brigade when the Blackfeet attacked and if it hadn't been for Grizzly Killer and a couple hundred other trappers and friendly Indians he knew he wouldn't be here today.

Benny was moving very slowly so he wouldn't be seen as he brought his rifle up to his shoulder. He was trying to follow the lead warrior as he crawled through the brush but the sage in front of him kept obstructing the view from the rifles sights so he knew the timing would be critical for him not to miss.

He found a spot he could see plainly out in front of the lead warrior and aimed right at that spot and waited for the warrior to crawl into his line of fire. He knew it would be his shot that started this next battle, but then there would be one less of them to fight. Just two minutes later he squeezed the trigger until he felt the recoil slam back into his shoulder. He didn't bother trying to see through the powder smoke he knew the instant the gun went off his shot was true.

The other two Indians behind the first were confused. Had this enemy moved and they had not seen him do so? The smoke from the shot hung in the air over the sage so they knew where this unseen enemy was so they both jumped up charging up the hill at Benny.

Zach was surprised to hear the shot and as he looked to the north he too could see the gray blue powder smoke as it hung in the air over the sage. He then seen two warriors jump up from the sage right below where the smoke was lingering and charge up the hill toward whoever it was that had shot.

He watched as one of the charging warriors suddenly flipped over backward then he heard the report of another shot just as the warrior hit the ground. A blood cuddling war cry carried on the crisp air reaching him as the third warrior now seeing only blood lust charged on toward Benny.

The thunder of hooves brought Zach's attention back to the east. The four remaining Blackfeet had split their charge, two horses each in two groups charging at the same time but coming from two different angles. Zach knew he only had two shots so he figured he best try and take out the two coming from the right, he would still have to fight two of them but at least they would be together and he wouldn't worry about ones he couldn't see.

He fired his rifle while they were still a hundred yards out sending the first Blackfoot head over heels off the back of his horse. The second was only thirty yards when the ball from Zach's pistol tore a gaping hole through his stomach.

The instant Zach fired that second shot he jumped to the side as the other two were just as close coming from his left. As he did an arrow split the air right where he had been standing. Jimbo couldn't use his right rear leg and had it tucked up under him but these two charging horses couldn't tell this huge dog was anything but healthy as he jumped in front of them barking, snarling, and carrying on like he was the devil himself. Both Indian horses went berserk jumping and bucking and the more they bucked the louder Jimbo would snarl and growl. Soon one of the warriors was on the ground and had landed hard on his right shoulder. Zach ran over and kicked him just as hard as he could in the side of the head knocking him out for now.

This last warrior jumped off his horse landing on both feet. He had a knife in one hand and a war club in the other. The war club had a piece of rock the size of a man's fist lashed to a wooden handle with rawhide that was stained with the blood of many enemies.

The two men were sizing each other up when Zach signed, "I see your war club is well used, but only on women and children." Zach could see that had the intended effect, the Blackfoot in front of him was now furious and charged, screaming his outrage and swinging the deadly club. Zach was waiting and ducked under the swinging club but at the same time he was swinging his old Cherokee tomahawk hitting the warrior on his left knee.

The Blackfoot hit the ground but rolled right back onto his feet. His knee hurt and he could feel the blood running down his leg and filling his moccasin. Carefully he tried to put his weight on it but could only use it to balance himself, it wouldn't carry his weight.

Zach could see this warrior in front of him was in no condition to come at him again so this fight was mainly over. These men had shot Jimbo and tried to kill him. They were Blackfeet and no doubt part of the large war party the Crow had told him about.

Zach knew this Blackfoot could not live to tell all his friends that Grizzly Killer was in this area. He used the universal hand sign language to tell this warrior to drop his weapons and sit down but he just stood there defiantly still gripping his war club and knife. With a quick motion Zach threw his tomahawk. There was a look of surprise and shock on the face of this brave Blackfoot just as the sharp blade cut through the skin and breaking through the bone of the warrior's forehead just above his left eye.

Zach looked to the north wondering who was out there and if he was alright, but that would have to wait. Right now he had a wounded dog that he had to take care of. He walked over and pulled the tomahawk out of the Blackfoot's skull and wiped it off on the Indian's own breach cloth then walked over to where Jimbo was laying continuously licking the wound in his leg.

Benny had jumped to his feet when the two warriors jumped up and charged at him. With a hand as steady as it had ever been he fired the pistol hitting the one on the right and sending him over backwards. He was now standing there with an empty pistol and empty rifle on the ground at his feet. He could see the hatred in the face of this last warrior as he screamed his war cry while running at Benny. In his left hand was a stone headed war club and in his right a lance.

Benny bent his knees slightly ready to jump out of the way of the deadly lance. At twenty feet, the Blackfoot was ready to throw when suddenly out of nowhere a fist sized rock glanced off the side of his head. That threw him off balance and he dropped the lance as he hit the ground only a few feet in front of Benny. Benny took one step forward and kicked him in the face just as hard as he could then spun around to see where the rock had come from.

Little Dove was standing only ten feet behind him, he didn't know whether to be mad at her for disobeying him or grateful for her help. The adrenalin rush from the battle had not subsided and he picked up the lance and with a war cry of his own was ready to drive it through this warrior that was not yet dead.

Little Dove cried out, "No, no he must not die the death of a warrior. He will die the same death he gave to my people."

Benny stopped, he did not understand what she meant as she rushed forward to the dazed and barely moving Blackfoot. She looked all around but could see nothing to bind his hands with so she pulled off her dress and with her knife cut a leather strip from around the bottom then slid it back over her head. Benny stood in total disbelief at what he just witnessed, but watched as she bound his hands. With nothing else to use she cut a strip from all the way around their sleeping robe looking up once at Benny hoping he would not be angry at her.

Benny had no idea what she was doing until she tied the long buffalo strip around the leather binding of his hand and then around the saddle horn on Benny's saddle. She looked at Benny and said, "He must die the same way he make my people die." She then pulled her knife and cut off all his clothing and threw it all off to the side. The warrior was starting to regain consciousness by then but Benny could tell he was still dazed.

Little Dove, with her knife in hand, walked to the closest warrior Benny had shot, cut his leggings and breach cloth off as well and then said to Benny, "Make him look what I do."

Benny had no idea what she was going to do but he helped the hurting and dazed warrior to his feet and helped hold him up toward her as she reached down and cut off the dead warrior's manhood and threw it off to the side, she then took her knife and scalped him cutting deep enough the white bone was showing.

Benny was getting sick just like he had at the Flathead village a year ago when he had seen what these Blackfeet did to their victims. A cold sweat had broken out across his brow and he was swallowing fast try to keep it all down. He was having a very hard time watching as this girl younger than he, that had been so soft and loving all through the night, mutilated the warriors. Now he realized she intended to do the same thing to their prisoner.

It only took Little Dove a couple of minutes to do the same thing to the other dead Blackfoot. When she came back she spoke some venomous sounding words to the living warrior then spat upon him. She looked up at Benny and pointing over toward Grizzly Killer asked, "Benny know who is there?"

Benny looked over at the hill top again and could still see Ol' Red standing there with the saddle and said, "I ain't sure, but I bet that is Grizzly Killer."

Little Dove looked surprised then asked, "We go see?"

Benny nodded and said, while handing her the reins to the horse, "You go, I will get reloaded and be right behind you." He expected her to lead the horse but she jumped up on its back and kicked the horse into a trot pulling the Blackfoot Warrior off his feet and Benny just watched as she dragged his naked body through the sage and rocks. He reloaded as fast as possible then started out jogging after her.

Chapter 27

Hell Hath No Fury

JIMBO STARTED HIS DEEP down low growl. Zach patted him and said, "Easy feller... I figure they're friends."

When Little Dove was only about fifty yards out with Benny fifty yards behind her, she stopped and shouted, "Hakaniyun" meaning hello in Shoshone. When Zach heard the Shoshone greeting he stood and shouted back, again in Shoshone, "Haintseh" meaning, friend. He then raised his hand and waved them in.

Zach could see she was young, probably in her later teens and then he recognized Benny jogging along trying to catch up to them. Seeing Benny brought a smile to his face. Did this mean his old friends Grub and Ely were with him somewhere nearby? Zach had just put everything away he had used to wrap Jimbo's leg when she rode up. He looked at her now she was this close and knew he had seen her before. He then looked at the naked warrior that she had drug through the brush. He was bleeding from a hundred places now and didn't look like he hardly had any skin left. He looked back to Little Dove. By then, Benny had jogged up to him and said, "Grizzly Killer, I sure am glad ta find you."

Zach was smiling now. He held out his hand and Benny took it proudly and shook. Zach said, "Benny you're a sight for sore eyes. I must say, I'm mighty beholdin' to ya for helpin' out in this here little fracas. Who is your friend here?"

Little Dove spoke right up and said, "I Little Dove." Zach raised his hand to her and she smiled and said, "I see you at Sweet Lake… you marry cousin."

Zach smiled at her and nodded that he too remembered. He looked at Benny again and asked, "Is Grub and Ely with you?"

Benny shook his head and said, "Ely got shot, he was still alive when I left trackin' the one's that done it, but it were bad, Grizzly Killer. I don't know if he can pull through. Grub is there takin' care of 'im."

Zach was now concerned for his friends and asked, "Where are they, can we get to them to help?"

Benny just shook his head. "We was just a couple a days' east of Jackson's Hole trappin' up in the Gros Ventre Mountains, when four other trappers come inta camp. Me and Grub was out checkin' the trap line and they just up and shot Ely and took ever one of our plews. I ain't sure why, but the next morning I got this feeling come over me that I was s'posed to foller 'em and make things right. That was near on a week ago an' I been ridin' south ever since."

Zach nodded he understood then looked at Little Dove and asked, "Did ya pick her up for a guide?"

"It's a long story." He then pointed at the Blackfoot and continued, "We best do something with what's left of him. I ain't sure what she has in mind but I don't figure if we leave it to her, it's gonna be pleasant."

Zach turned to Little Dove and asked her something in Shoshone and for the next five minutes Benny had no idea what was being said. Zach's expression changed as Little Dove was talking and when she finished he nodded at her. She then took her knife and cut off the manhood and scalps of each of the warriors Zach had killed; two of them were not dead. One of them screamed so loud when she sliced through his scalp it sent chills all through Benny.

Benny asked, "Why do they do that?"

Zach answered, "They believe it is an honor to die in battle but if you lose your scalp it will shame you in the next life for you wasn't a great warrior. A man without his manhood is not a man at all, so she is sending them on their journey to the next life as shamed warriors with no scalps and they will wander forever without being men."

"Do you believe that?" Benny asked.

"It don't matter what I believe," Zach replied, "They believe it and I respect their beliefs."

Benny nodded that he understood then looked at the Blackfoot she hadn't got to yet who was still tied to the strap behind the horse and asked, "What is she gonna do ta him?"

Zach shook his head like he didn't know.

Then Benny asked, "Did she tell you why she is doin' this?" Zach nodded then said, "She said you done a mighty brave thing by savin' her and she owes you her life."

Just then, Little Dove walked back up the hill to them. She was carrying all the bloody scalps. Benny looked at the scalps, shuddered and said, "Hell hath no fury."

Zach looked at him as a chill ran down his back and nodded repeating softly what Benny had just said, "Hell hath no fury."

She talked to Grizzly Killer in Shoshone again and Benny could see disappointment in her eyes. She then nodded and went back to the warrior still tied to the horse. He was barely conscious as she reached down grabbed his manhood nearly lifting him off the ground then slowly cut it off and threw it out into the brush. Benny watched in disbelief, those were the same hands that had touched him with such loving care through the night. A pool of blood was forming under the Blackfoot and he had lost consciousness by the time she pulled the scalp from the skull. She then cut the buffalo strap at his hands and coiled it up and tied it on the saddle.

Benny was pale, very close to throwing up but he never said a word as Zach led the Crow horse up and handed the lead rope to Little Dove.

She smiled at him and took the lead, then grabbed a handful of mane and jumped up on the horses back.

Before Zach left, he went to the dead and mutilated Blackfoot and with his knife he cut a large grizzly foot print on the dead warrior's chest. When he looked up Little Dove was smiling at him but Benny just had a confused look. Zach didn't say anything for a few minutes then said, "We have to cut this on each one of them and then cover your tracks. The Blackfeet must believe I did this alone."

Little Dove jumped right off and looked at the way Grizzly Killer had made his cuts then she ran over to the far hill where her and Benny had fought and cut the bear paw pattern in each of the dead warriors then very carefully covered all their tracks from around the bodies before she came back. Zach was doing the same thing to all the dead Blackfeet that he had defeated.

Benny was confused as he could not see the reason to keep mutilating the dead.

Zach explained, "Benny, Injuns are a mighty superstitious people and they believe I have what they call big medicine or magic powers. If we make this look like I was by myself and killed these warriors by myself, then others may not be willing to come after me. If they think my medicine is strong enough, I cannot be defeated and they may leave and go back north."

Benny thought about that for a minute and nodded slightly as Zach continued, "Remember Benny, the best battle with any Indian is one you do not have to fight."

Benny nodded gaining more respect for the man they call Grizzly Killer all the time.

Jimbo hadn't moved and Zach asked him if he could walk or if he wanted to ride. Jimbo looked just like he understood the words as he got up still holding his leg up and started toward the river running on three legs nearly as fast as he always did.

As they rode back to the Black's Fork trail Benny asked Zach what Little Dove had said. He explained to him she wanted to take the time to stake out the Blackfoot and build fires on him like they did to her people, but I told her there wasn't time and the smoke might be seen. Benny wondered if that could have been any worse than what she did to him.

They hit the Black's Fork trail with still a few hours of day light and started upstream. Zach set an easy pace and would stop often so Jimbo could rest.

Benny got over being sick but he wasn't sure he would ever look at Little Dove the same way again. He couldn't believe a young girl could have so much violence in her. He told Zach that and Zach just smiled at him explaining, "Ya can't think like white people when you're with Injuns. They weren't raised like me and you was. They ain't Christians and they don't think like Christians. That don't make their ways wrong it just makes 'em different. This is a harsh land they live in and it takes a harsh people ta survive it. The different tribes has different beliefs but the fact is, the strong survive and the weak perish. Just like with white people there are good Injuns and bad Injuns. I come out here in '24 and my best friends and family is all Injuns. I don't question their ways. I don't look down on their beliefs, but I ain't lost my Christian beliefs, either. In a lot of ways those beliefs ain't all that different. They believe in a God and they believe he is the creator of all things. They believe in the afterlife and this life here on earth is just one journey on the trail of one's life.

Benny looked at him and said, "I never thought of it that way."

Zach answered, "Most people don't, I suspect as more an' more white people come west there'll be more an' more trouble with the Injuns. The Injuns just can't think like whites and most white people can't accept the Injun ways. I hope I'm gone by then. I so love these mountains and my Injun family it's a way of life I would hate ta see end.

Benny turned in the saddle and looked back at Little Dove. She smiled at him and that made a warm feeling run through his body and he said, "I love the mountains too."

It was near dark when they stopped for the night. They had traveled upstream far enough there was timber once again. Zach led them off the trail aways, out of caution in case there were other Blackfeet around he didn't want to be near the trail.

As they set up a small fire in a thick stand of pines. Little Dove set up a spit out of willow branches and put what was left of the lamb quarter on it. Benny took care of the horses but Ol' Red wouldn't let him near. Zach smiled and thought that mule was getting more stubborn all the time. He got up and went to the big mule and talked to him and had Benny come over and rub his neck. They both hoped the mule would be friendly after that. Zach told Ol' Red he was sorry for doubting him that he ran up that hill today just as fast as he ever could.

Benny sat by the fire staring into its flickering flames and said, "I guess I failed. I let Grub and Ely down. I ain't never gonna find them there polecats now."

But Zach replied, "I wouldn't be so sure of that. If it's the same fellers, I'm a figurin' it is we'll get 'em all right, 'cause I know where their goin', and there ain't but three of 'em left."

Chapter 28

Finding the Spotted Horse

IT WAS EARLY AFTERNOON the next day when Luna met them on the trail. Jimbo was still holding his leg up using just the other three. Zach had watched him all day amazed how he could run that way. He thought about the Arapaho arrow through his own leg last year and how he had such a hard time walking. Now, watching Jimbo he figured having an extra couple of legs would have been mighty helpful.

It was a happy reunion with Luna and Jimbo with the white wolf sniffing and licking Jimbo's wounded leg. Jimbo didn't run ahead to let everyone know they were coming in. Although he was doing just fine on the three legs it was tiring him out.

A half hour later, Zach could see the hill at the end of the big meadow and ten minutes after that the tops of the teepees. As they rode into camp the smell of roasting elk met them just as Sun Flower and Shining Star ran to greet him. Running Wolf was out with the horses and he came bounding across the fast running stream faster than was safe. When he saw Zach riding Ol' Red he was relieved to see the mule hadn't just run off.

Raven Wing recognized Little Dove first and went to welcome her. Little Dove saw Raven Wing and Sun Flower and started to cry. This was family, they lived in different villages but they were blood relatives and she knew now she wasn't all alone in this world. Luna wouldn't leave Jimbo's side as he curled up by the fire.

Running Wolf was the first to recognize Benny from the Rendezvous of the year before. His first thoughts were of Grub and Ely, just like Zach's had been. He greeted Benny and then all three women came over to welcome him into their camp.

Sun Flower saw the bandage on Jimbo's leg and she knew there had been trouble. They sat around the fire with the elk loin still roasting over the flames and told of everything that had happened. Raven Wing got her medicine kit and mixed a poultice using the dried herbs she carried and using the warm moist poultice she rebandaged Jimbo's leg.

They were all concerned about the Blackfeet being so close, but Zach figured these Uintah Mountains are mighty big and his little camp here on Black's Fork was small. The chance of the Blackfeet coming up this far and finding them were mighty slim, but he planned on keeping a very close eye on them just the same.

Running Wolf wanted revenge on the men that had shot Ely. Grub and Ely was who first taught Running Wolf English and to trap. He had known those two old mountain men longer than Zach had. He didn't want to believe Ely might have gone under.

Little Dove still had the buffalo sleeping robe wrapped around her for a coat and Shining Star went into their lodge and brought out a beautiful coat of soft elk hide and lined with rabbit fur and gave it to her. She held the coat and smiled then stood up and walked over to the stream, pulled her dress over her head and bathed in the frigid water. The water was two high and fast for her to get in so she just stood on the bank splashing and rubbing the cold water over her body. Zach smiled thinking that is something Sun Flower would do. Being naked in front of others didn't bother them a bit, it was just a normal thing to do. She slipped the dress back on and ran back to the fire barefoot carrying her moccasins.

Zach smiled as he remembered the first time Sun Flower and had done something like that and then laughed right out loud at the expression on Benny's face. Everyone looked at him wondering what was so funny. Little Dove put on the coat and stood there by the fire warming and drying her still wet legs. Benny still was staring at her in disbelief but even with all these other people around the sight of her naked excited him.

As they talked about what needed to be done, they decided Zach and Benny would leave the next morning. Their priority would be to watch the Blackfeet making sure they didn't come this way, if they did Zach and Benny would lead them away. Zach knew this area better than any man alive. He had trapped and explored every inch of these mountains and every stream running out of them from the Seeds-Kee-Dee all the way to Weber's River to the west. If needed he knew he could lose the

Blackfeet in these mountains far away from their home on Black's Fork.

Running Wolf wanted to go with them but he knew what a great honor it was for Grizzly Killer to trust him to protect his family and then there was Raven Wing and Gray Wolf. He wanted the thrill and honor of battle, he wanted revenge for what had been done to his friends, but right now the most important things in his life were right here in this camp and it was his job to keep them safe and he would do that to the death if need be. If it wasn't for Running Wolf, Zach would not leave again, for Running Wolf was the only man alive Zach trusted enough to leave his family with.

Sun Flower and Raven Wing were saddened, learning of the death of everyone in Little Dove's village. Little Dove's mother, Pine Flower was the sister of White Feather, their mother. Little Dove was about six years younger than the beautiful Sun Flower and she had always looked up to her. She was envious of Sun Flower for marrying such a great warrior as Grizzly Killer but now she had Benny or at least she thought she did.

Benny had proven to be brave and a good strong warrior but she didn't understand the way he looked at her after she had scalped and humiliated the Blackfeet warriors yesterday. She thought he would want to celebrate the great victory with her. Instead he and even the great Grizzly Killer were quiet and not boasting of the deaths of their enemies like the Shoshone warriors would do. She could see that white men were different and she would ask Sun Flower about that if she got the chance.

After she had warmed up Sun Flower took her into their lodge where there were many robes to sleep under and to make her a bed. Sun Flower asked, "Do we make one bed or two?" Little Dove smiled and held up just one finger and Sun Flower nodded and smiled back at her. They made up a soft warm bed big enough for the two of them, but before they went back out Sun Flower gave her a nearly white dress that was fully decorated with beads and quills. Sun Flower then took a couple of bright trade cloth ribbons and tied in her hair. She tied another around her waist that made the dress show off the curves of her body.

Little Dove had never been dressed up this pretty before, and she hugged Sun Flower then stepped out into the bright light. As she walked toward the fire everyone was watching her. Benny's jaw dropped open and the look on his face was total surprise. At that moment, he thought she was the prettiest girl he had ever seen.

The next morning even before all the stars had disappeared with the coming light, Zach and Benny rode out. Jimbo wanted to go with them but Zach told him to stay and protect their camp. The big dog was still using just three legs and as much as Zach would have liked to have him along he knew the dog needed rest to be able to heal quickly. Luna was still right by his side and the huge dog and white wolf just sat and watched as Zach and Benny rode out of sight.

Zach knew the trail down Black's Fork so well the dark forest wasn't a problem at all. A few small birds had started to sing in the willows along the creek and would stop as they rode by, only to resume when they were just a few feet past. The smell of the pine was strong this morning and filled the air with its always pleasant scent. There were the dark blue jays squawking at them as they rode past and they jumped a couple of snowshoe hares off the trail. Zach smiled as he thought they are a couple of lucky ones this close to camp for they were Jimbo and Luna's favorite meal.

As the sun got closer to peeking over the eastern horizon the sky turned a spectacular reddish orange. The few clouds that were in the eastern part of the sky reflected the color, making it even more brilliant. However, just a few minutes later as the bright yellow of the sun first peeked over the horizon the brilliantly colored sky faded and within only a minute the sky was back to normal.

Zach loved this land, he hadn't tried to change it, he lived with it not trying to force his will upon it. He had never tried to change the Indian people either, he tried to understand them. He accepted the fact many of the tribes seemed to relish war, although he didn't completely understand why he just accepted that was the way of life living here.

Since he had been in the mountains he had fought Crow, Cheyenne, Blackfeet, Arapaho, Shoshone, and a Ute, but he had also become good friends with most of the Shoshone and Ute people. He had been friendly with many other tribes at Rendezvous as well. The Crow, Flathead, Nez Pierce, and Bannock. These Blackfeet from the north, they seemed to be mortal enemies of everyone. It seemed to Zach they were intent on wiping out everyone that wasn't a Blackfoot. He had been told there were other tribes up north that were friendly to them most of the time. The Gros Ventre, Pigeon, and Blood were, at least that is what Grub and Ely had told him. Although he didn't understand why the Blackfeet were such a warlike people he didn't question it he just accepted that is the way of life and he had to deal with it just like they were doing right now.

Benny followed Zach closely, he was proud to be riding with the great Grizzly Killer. He had heard of him since before him and the men he was tracking had even got to the mountains. It seems stories of Grizzly Killer were told everywhere west of St. Louis. Benny had spent a little time with Zach at last year's Rendezvous and with Grub and Ely being goods friends of his he had heard many, many stories about him. Benny would never forget Grizzly Killer riding his big mule leading the charge against the Blackfeet at last year's Rendezvous with Jimbo running alongside.

As they rode downstream in silence at a steady trot, Benny remembered Grub talking many times about how Grizzly Killer had the two most beautiful women in the whole world for his wives and Benny figured Grub was right when he first met Sun Flower and Shining Star last year, but now he couldn't get the sight of Little Dove as she walked out of Grizzly Killer's lodge out of his mind. To him she was every bit as pretty as Sun Flower, Raven Wing, and Shining Star.

Zach wasn't overly concerned about the Blackfeet as they rode downstream. He figured more than likely they would be searching along the river down on the flats. When they got down to where the timber stopped he would take great care to cover their trail and hide any tracks they had left from the days before. From that point, north they would not be using the trails any longer.

They camped that night a full two miles from the river in a small stand of Chokecherry bushes. They were out of the timber except the cottonwoods along the river and after tonight Zach told Benny they would now be camping in just the sage.

So far, they had seen no sign of any Blackfeet or anyone else for that matter. Zach hoped deep in his mind they would give up looking to the west and concentrate their search to the east. Then he shook his head realizing he didn't even know if they were looking for him or not.

They rode back to the gruesome remains of their battle from two days before and Zach spent several hours hiding their trail that would lead an enemy up the Black's Fork trail, while Benny stood watch hidden in the sage from the top of the hill Zach had fought on. When Zach was satisfied they left a plain trail going back to the river and heading east.

They stayed three or four miles north of the river traveling slowly the rest of that day. Making sure to stay off the skyline by going around and not over the short hills. Every hour or so they would dismount and crawl to the top and look over the area all around them without ever exposing themselves. By nightfall they still had seen no sign of the Blackfeet. They had seen many small herds of antelope and a couple of coyotes and one family of foxes, with kits so little they barely had their eyes open, but no sign of the Blackfeet.

That night they stopped to camp between two small hills with no protection but the sage. They waited until dark to build a small fire so the smoke couldn't be seen and roasted pieces of smoked buffalo they had brought with them. Zach told Benny they were only a couple of hours from where Ham's Fork runs into Black' Fork and from what Benny had told him he figured the Blackfeet would be camped just east of there.

It was still cold every night, the little fire felt good as the stars filled the heavens above. A shooting star shot across the dark sky and Zach told Benny the Indians belief that a shooting star was the spirit of a warrior traveling the great white river in the sky to get to the other side.

They were an hour from their camping spot by the time it was light enough to see good the next morning. They crossed Ham's Fork about four miles north of where it empties into Black's Fork not all that far from where Benny and Little Dove had crossed a couple of days ago. They continued into the low hills about two miles north of a big bend in the river. They left Ol' Red and Benny's Blackfoot horse tied in the bottom of a nearly dry creek bed and climbed on foot to the top of the hill.

From there they could plainly see the horse herd between them and the river and the smoke from many fires at their camp along the river. Zach could plainly see two young braves watching the horses and a lot of activity in camp. He told Benny he figured they were going to send out search parties for their missing warriors.

Benny had told Zach about seeing Strong Bow on the spotted horse that first night on the trail not knowing the significance the spotted horse held for Zach. Now Zach remembered that dream about his Pa again. It was as plain as it had been when he had first dreamed it, if it really had been a dream. He had to kill the first man on a spotted horse and now he wondered if he and Strong Bow would have to meet to finally be done with his Pa's warning that was still in his mind, "Beware the man on the spotted horse."

They were too far away to see what was happening in their camp by the river but they could tell by the smoke and the horse herd most of the Blackfeet were still in camp. Not long after they could see them coming out to the horses and soon there were groups of ten or twelve riding out in all directions.

There were now only a dozen horses left in the herd and although Zach had been watching he had not seen the spotted one that Strong Bow rides. He figured the War Chief had his horse with him in camp. Zach just couldn't move on until he knew or at least figured he knew just what the Blackfeet were doing his far south.

Now most of the warriors were gone Zach wanted a closer look. They started toward the river on foot staying in the bottom of the little stream bed. When they got about even with the horses Zach peeked through the brush and seen the Blackfoot herd watcher was a boy of about twelve or thirteen. They moved on and was now only a quarter mile north of the main camp. Most of the fires were now out and Zach could now plainly see the spotted horse.

They started out again and Zach was very pleased with the way Benny was moving, silent and careful. He could tell Grub and Ely had taught him well. They hadn't gone but a few more feet when he saw movement to his right. He rolled bringing up his pistol as Jimbo came through the brush right to him. He was surprised and at first angry, this was the first time since Jimbo was a pup he had disobeyed him, but Jimbo was his friend and partner and just his presence made Zach feel better. He rubbed the big dog's ears and gave the hand signal that Jimbo understood so well. Go to the other side of them and wait.

Ten minutes later they were watching eight warriors still at their fires. Zach could see the coup stick lined with scalps that Strong Bow had shook at him last year but he didn't know which one of the warriors still in camp was the War Chief.

They watched and it was soon evident that most of the remaining Blackfeet were injured. One of them could barely walk, three or four more had bandages, and two were just lying by a fire. It was plain enough Zach figured to tell which of these warriors Strong Bow was after watching them for a short time. He had the presence of a leader, he was built strong and powerful. He stood a little taller than most of the others, one however was very tall and he was helping one of the wounded ones. Zach figured he was their healer or maybe even their Medicine Man.

Zach whispered right into Benny ear, "Cover me but do not let them see you." He then laid his rifle right by Benny and stood, walking right at Strong Bow.

Chapter 29

To Henry's Fork

MEL TILLMAN STOOD by their lean-to on the lower reaches of Henry's Fork looking up at the snow-covered peaks of the high Uintah's just south of him. He was tired of waiting for the snow to melt enough for them to make it over the mountains and on down to Taos. He was tired of this wilderness and the constant amount of work it was just to survive. Finding food alone for the three of them seemed to be a full-time job and then there was the constant job of bringing in fire wood.

He missed Phil, he knew he could never be trusted and could turn on anyone at any time but he would always do the killing, for killing had never bothered him a bit. Mel had killed but he really didn't like to. Phil, however, had seemed to relish it. Now all he had was Nels and Patch. Nels wasn't strong enough to even do what was needed. He hated killing and stealing, and Mel knew very well the only reason he was still with them was he wasn't strong enough to make it on his own. Then there was Patch; he didn't bully any and made Mel do his share of the work which he hated as well.

Mel was concerned about the big mountain man as well, Zach, was his name and his big dog, the one that had killed Phil. Were they far enough away from him that they were safe? Mel wondered. He had no doubt at all the big man would kill them if he saw them again and although he wouldn't admit it even to himself, the big man scared him. Oh, how he wished that snow would hurry and melt. Coming to the mountains to make their fortunes by trapping was nothing like he thought it would be. How he longed to be back in a city; St. Louis or New Orleans would even be better. If that snow would just melt they could get out of this God forsaken wilderness.

Daylight came slowly over the peaks of the Gros Ventre Mountains. The morning air had a crisp bite to it. Grub stirred the coals of their fire finding a still hot coal and carefully blew life back into it. Once the fire was going he could feel the heat reflecting into the lean-to where Ely was lying.

Days had passed, Ely seemed to be getting stronger but the progress was slow. Grub figured it was a miracle he was still alive. Grub got some of the smoked meat he still had from the elk Benny had shot roasting over the fire and thought about their young partner. He wondered where he was and if he was alright.

Although Ely slept most of the time he was strong enough now to talk and that had helped Grub's spirits. Grub still had the medicine kit the old Crow woman had left him and was mixing a poultice for his wound daily as well as making him drink the bitter tea.

When the tea was finished brewing Grub asked, "Hey Pard, is you awake?"

"Course I'm awake. How could a body sleep with ya making all this racket?" Ely replied.

Grub just ignored the remark and said, "I got yer tea ready," but to his surprise Ely said, "I ain't drinking any more of that devil's brew until ya get me outta this here bed. I need ta move a little. I need ta stand up and pee and then set up fer a while."

Grub was mighty concerned and said, "Ya sure ya outta be moving yet, Pard? Ya lost an awful lot a blood."

Ely looked at the concern of Grub's face and said, "I feel like if I don't move I is gonna die right here in this bed. I knows I gonna need help, Pard, but I feel like I gotta start movin' some."

Grub nodded and said, "I'll help ya all I can but I's feared it's a gonna hurt ya somethin' awful."

Ely nodded slightly to acknowledge he understood and Grub started removing the buffalo robe from over the top of him.

A chill ran through his body as the cold morning air hit him. He felt weak and helpless and he hated that feeling but he knew he had to start moving and rebuild his strength or he would die lying right there in this bed and that was not the way he wanted to go under.

It took extreme effort on both their parts but they succeeded, just like they had succeeded in every other task the two of them had ever tackled together. Ely was so light-headed when he finally got to his feet, Grub had to hold him up while he relieved himself and then helped him back down to sit by the fire.

Grub checked on the wound both front and back making sure it hadn't started to bleed again from the movement and was pleased neither side had pulled open. Ely drank the tea, the whole cup, and as Grub boiled the meat for a broth Ely said, "Leave a chunk of that elk in there. I need somethin' ta chew on."

Grub smiled as he handed Ely the cup and said, "Ya must be feelin' a lot better today."

Ely looked at his partner and replied, "Don't know that I is, but I can't just lay there no longer."

Strong Bow was looking away when Zach stood up and started walking toward him. Many of the others that were there saw him immediately and shouted, some rushing for their weapons. Zach held his hands out from his sides showing them all he was unarmed. He was trusting Benny and Jimbo with his life and he knew it but this is the only way he could think to end this fight with Strong Bow and keep his family safe.

He stopped and then made the sign for talk. All the others were now looking at Strong Bow as he stared, sizing up the white man before him. He studied every inch of Zach but his eyes stopped at his Grizzly claw neckless. Strong Bow froze for a moment as he realized the man he had wanted ever since the death of Thunder Cloud, their famed war chief, had just walked in to his camp alone.

Thunder Cloud had been his teacher and friend and Strong Bow had believed there was no man alive that could have beaten him, but this white man standing before him had. Word had spread all through the west that Grizzly Killer had beaten Thunder Cloud in a fair fight, but Strong Bow had never believed that. If anyone had beaten Thunder Cloud it was by ambush or from behind. Only now he wasn't so sure… Grizzly Killer had just walked in among several warriors alone without his deadly, long reaching gun. For a moment, that made

318

Strong Bow doubt his own beliefs, for this man was no coward.

Again, Zach made the sign for talk and Strong Bow this time stepped forward and signed, "You enemy, you die."

Zach just stood his ground and signed back to him, "You coward. Send your warriors to ambush me. Now all those warrior's dead! You not brave enough to come for me yourself."

Now Strong Bow was extremely angry. Zach could see in his face his taunting was working so one more time he signed, "All Blackfeet cowards. Your coup stick carries scalps of women and children."

At that, a young brave behind Zach, unhappy to be left behind to care for the wounded that morning raised his bow. He had it about half way drawn back when Jimbo's powerful jaws clamped down on his arm just above the elbow. The surprise attack from behind startled the young brave so much he cried out in fear and pain and then Zach signed, "Coward to attack me from behind."

With a simple movement of his hand he called Jimbo off but the damage done to the young brave's arm was serious.

Jimbo came to his side and waited. Strong Bow was now furious at his young brave, Grizzly Killer, and his dog. He yelled something Zach didn't understand and all four of the remaining healthy warriors started forward raising their weapons. The resounding boom of Benny's rifle sounded as one of the warriors was knocked off his feet and did not move at all. Both surprise and fear was now on their faces but one raised his war club and charged forward only to be doubled over with the second rifle shot. Benny wasn't used to the sights on Zach's Hawken and this shot was a little low hitting the warrior in the belly. Zach could see this Blackfoot would have a slow and painful death.

Benny was reloading just as fast as he could make his fingers move, but now all the others were taking cover from the deadly fire coming from the dry creek bed. Zach signed again to Strong Bow, "I am Grizzly Killer, this is my land. Leave now and you will live, stay and you will all die."

Zach turned and started walking back toward Benny. He hoped Benny had had enough time to get a least one rifle reloaded for he didn't know what Strong Bow would do. Strong Bow was beside himself with anger but he was their leader and he knew he couldn't let anger rule his actions. He, too, could see the fear in the faces of his warriors. Every one of them had heard the stories of Grizzly Killer and his big medicine dog. There was now no doubt in any of their minds even Strong Bow's that all the stories they have heard were true.

Strong Bow watched Zach walk away wondering if his medicine really was powerful enough to defeat them all. Right now, he wasn't sure and with two more dead and another hurt he wasn't sure what to do. How many men does Grizzly Killer have around him? How many more of his warriors was he willing to sacrifice to kill this hated enemy?

As soon as Zach was out of sight in the nearly dry creek bed he and Benny jogged north. They didn't stop for the two miles back to where they had left Ol' Red and the horse. Zach noticed now that Jimbo was using all four of his legs, he had a slight limp but the big dog was doing just fine. He thought after they figured out what the Blackfeet were going to do he would have a long talk with

Jimbo about obeying, but for right now he was mighty glad to have Jimbo along.

Zach hurried to the top of the hill from where they first observed the Blackfeet to see if they were being pursued. He watched for several minutes, he could still see the few horses that were left in the herd had not been moved and there was no movement in the creek. He knew his bluff of them not knowing how many men they were facing would be over as soon as they saw the tracks but at least now Strong Bow knew who he was up against.

They mounted up and rode hard back to the west. Zach had to know if any of the Blackfoot warrior bands were heading up Black's Fork toward his home and loved ones. They stayed a few miles north of the river well out of sight until the river made its turn back to the south and there they rode down to the trail to look for tracks. Without finding any they crossed over to the south side and headed east again. Staying far away from the river as they headed back so they wouldn't take a chance of meeting any of the Blackfeet along the river.

Jimbo was still limping but only slightly and had taken his usual place out in front as they headed back east at an easy lope. Zach noticed the wind picking up as the day progressed and it was becoming colder. He figured it had the feel of another spring storm.

He glanced over at Benny riding alongside of him and couldn't help but admire the young man. He had liked Benny when Grub and Ely first introduced him after the battle with what was probably many of these very same Blackfeet at last year's Rendezvous. For Benny to have taken out after the men that had shot Ely and stolen a whole years-worth of work by himself, Zach figured he knew everything he needed to know about him. Then to have risked his life to rescue Little Dove, a girl he had never seen before… yes, Zach liked Benny Lambert and would call him a friend for the rest of his life.

By midafternoon they stopped and put their heavy coats on and while stopped Jimbo came back running right up to Zach and started his low growl from deep in his chest. Benny looked at Zach and Zach replied, "Trouble close ahead."

This area had very little cover just short sage and rolling hills. Zach didn't know if the trouble was heading toward them or was just out in front. He dismounted and handed Ol' Red's reins to Benny and told him to go back over the last hill out of sight that he would go forward on foot and see just what was up ahead. Benny didn't say a word, just nodded as he took Ol' Red's reins and headed back.

Zach jogged forward with Jimbo staying right by his side until he approached the top of the small hill just in front of them. He then dropped to his belly in the sage and crawled until he could see over the top. Jimbo was right by his side and he too was on his belly alongside Zach.

There were nine Blackfoot warriors less than a quarter mile away. Three of them were off their horses looking at something on the ground. As Zach watched he could tell they were looking at and following tracks of someone or something. The Blackfeet on the ground were talking with the ones still mounted and pointing and he figured they were deciding whether to follow.

Zach didn't move, he just watched as the nine warriors headed south out across the badlands toward Henry's Fork. He watched them until they were out of sight then told Jimbo to go get Ol' Red. The big dog didn't hesitate as he took off and Zach watched in amazement; the big dog now was running without any limp at all.

Just a few minutes later, Jimbo was back with Benny and Ol' Red right behind him. They rode on down to where the Blackfeet had been studying the tracks and both Zach and Benny stepped to the ground and studied them as well.

After only a couple of minutes Benny said, "These here are the tracks of the men I've been a followin'. See this here track that's got a chip outa the front of its hoof? That's the very same one I followed outta our camp where I left Grub and Ely."

Zach nodded and said, "I figure it's the same feller's that I run into up Smith's Fork, the ones that was gonna rob me. As best I can figure with all these Injun tracks in the way, there is three of them with pack horses and it looks like they're headed to Henry's Fork, lookin' for a way to cross these mountains."

Benny looked at Zach and asked, "What do we do now?"

"We follow, if them Blackfeet catch up to 'em there ain't gonna be much left for us to do and all your plews will be gone as well."

Zach took a good look at Jimbo's leg. The wound didn't seem to be bothering him at all now but he wanted to make sure all this running hadn't opened it up again.

Zach just smiled and rubbed the dog's ears after he saw that both sides of his leg were still scabbed over. Zach simply pointed south and Jimbo took off following the trail of nine Blackfeet as well as Mel, Patch, and Nels.

Chapter 30

End of the Trail

THE TRAIL LED STRAIGHT south out into the badlands and Zach remembered the ancient medicine wheel and the fight with the Arapaho nearly a year ago. He figured if the trail they were on now stayed due south they would pass to the west of the medicine wheel by only a few miles.

Zach knew this country well, and he figured neither the three white men nor the Blackfeet had ever been here before. He knew Henry's Fork and the high country above Henry's Basin with its many lakes and streams but right now, that country was still covered with several feet of snow and the lakes were still frozen over.

It would be another two months before those white men would be able to fight their way through the passes and then they still had three hundred miles of unknown territory to cross to reach Taos.

The Blackfeet were traveling fast and by late afternoon, Zach knew the Blackfeet would catch the men they were following before he and Benny could catch up to them. Then there was the weather. That cold wind had continued and now there was a heavy bank of clouds coming in from the northwest. Zach knew they were in for another spring storm and he wanted to make it into the hills of the badlands and off these barren flat lands before they were caught in it.

They set a steady pace but didn't ride hard as they headed south. Jimbo never let up staying well out in front. Zach thought back to last year and the painfully slow recovery he went through with the Arapaho arrow going through his leg and was amazed at the speed in which Jimbo was recovering. They knew the Blackfeet were only a few miles in front of them and they didn't want to ride up on nine warriors ready for battle.

They rode into the barren gray hills of the badlands just as a cold sleet started to hit them from behind and Zach veered off the trail going further east. He knew the Blackfeet would be stopping as well and he didn't want to be near their trail.

They found nothing more than a rocky overhang between two gray hills in a tight little draw that Zach figured was the best they would find for protection this night and the three of them; Benny, Zach, and Jimbo huddled together under the overhang for what was a long, cold, miserable night. With nothing to make a fire out of and only a hard, cold piece of jerky to eat they were cold, tired, and hungry the next morning. Ol' Red and Benny's Blackfoot horses were the same. They had stood side by side with their rumps to the wind as the cold wind whipped the freezing sleet onto their backs and there was nothing at all for them to eat or drink.

They saddled up in the early morning light with both themselves and the horses having to force themselves to go. Jimbo was the only one that seemed anxious to be on the move. Zach rode slowly as he headed back toward the trail they had been following. The morning was dark and dreary although the storm was mostly gone, the clouds were hanging low and moving fast with the wind still gusting. It wasn't as bad as it had been during the night but it was still mighty cold. Benny never complained even one time throughout the miserable night or now riding through this cold wet land.

They reached the trail that was nearly washed away but to these men's trained eyes it was plain enough to see. Zach had figured all along they were headed for Henry's Fork and looking at the direction the trail was headed he was now more convinced of that. He decided they would leave the trail and ride hard across the badlands several miles to the east of the trail and try to make it to Henry's Fork at least as fast as the Blackfeet could.

The route Zach led them on was longer but he figured they would be traveling faster. They rode right past the ancient medicine wheel where just last year he had used the Indians strong belief in the spirits of their ancient ancestors and the power of this sacred place to drive a band of Arapaho back east to their own lands.

Zach knew Benny wanted revenge on the men who had shot Ely and stolen all their plews, but right now he figured these Blackfeet would do a mighty fine job of that. Although they wouldn't be hanged for the murdering thieves they were, both Zach and Benny figured the death the Blackfeet had in mind would be far worse than hanging.

It was the plews, a whole year of cold hard work, wading in water so cold your bones ached at night. Fighting the weather, the Indians, bears, wolves, cougars, and coyotes. Even the much smaller animals that could be such destructive pests, skunks, pack rats, weasels, otters, badgers, and even the little prairie dogs, the holes they dug could snap a horse's leg if you were not ever watchful. Yes, it was the plews they were after now. As far as Zach figured the Blackfeet could have the three men.

They reached the southern edge of the Badlands by early afternoon and Zach studied the two-mile-wide valley in front of them. He was looking for smoke or any other sign of where the three white men may be, but what he saw wasn't what he had hoped for. Maybe three miles to the west was a line of riders leaving the badlands heading toward Henry's Fork, the stream running down the center of this broad valley. They were too far away to tell but Zach knew they were the war party of Blackfeet but what concerned him most was there were now only seven of them.

Zach wonder where the other two were and were they scouting a different area or had they gone back to get Strong Bow? It was a full thirty miles back to their main camp. If Strong Bow was going to arrive how much time did he and Benny have before that happened? Zach knew very well just he and Benny alone could not take on Strong Bow and all his warriors. They may be able to handle the seven of them, though, if they planned well, with surprise and a lot of luck on their side. But, if Strong

Bow and another war party showed up he knew this chase was over and he told Benny that.

Benny looked at him and said, "Do ya figure we can make our move 'fore that happens?"

Zach shook his head and answered, "Just don't know, maybe, but it's gonna take a lot a luck."

Staying behind a low rise and some brush they made it down to Henry's Fork not far from where the first Rendezvous was held back in '25. Zach thought about that…being there with his pa. Although it had only been four years ago it seemed like a lifetime.

He was finding that he thought less and less of his life back in Kentucky, of his pa and ma. He still hoped the strange life he was living with two Indian women would meet their approval but even that thought came much less often than it once had. He was comfortable with his life and was happier than he had ever been. Living in this wilderness, even with all its dangers, like the one he and Benny were about to face, he knew he didn't want it any other way.

Zach crossed the stream leaving Benny on the north side and they slowly rode upstream looking for tracks or any sign of the three white men. Zach figured they would be headed up because he knew they were looking for a pass over the mountains. He smiled and shook his head knowing the pass at the top of Henry's Basin was one of the highest in all the Uintah's. It was a challenging climb for even the most knowledgeable of men and he didn't think these three were. Zach looked up at the towering peaks and knew it would still be another couple of months before even he would attempt it and, suddenly, he knew right where to go.

With seven Blackfeet in front of them, there was no doubt in either of their minds it would be the Blackfeet they must deal with, not the three white men. Neither Zach nor Benny were sure what they would find when they caught up with them but both knew it wasn't going to be a pretty sight.

Benny thought back to the Shoshone village and the men staked to the ground with fires built right on top of their bare feet and shuttered at the thought. He didn't feel a bit sorry for them either, they had shot Ely, one the best men Benny had ever known and he figured they deserved whatever the Blackfeet would do. He wanted their plews back and knew the Blackfeet would too. He thought back over the last year and all the work it had taken to get them and he was willing to do anything to get those plews back. The words of Grub then came back to him, "Take care boy, them there plews ain't worth yer life."

Benny trusted Grizzly Killer if not from the last few days and last year, he trusted him by reputation alone. It seems anywhere he traveled there was talk about the big mountain man and his huge dog. Most of the Indians believed he had magic powers and even his enemies like these Blackfeet wasn't sure whether they were looking for a man or a spirit warrior that could disappear at will and leave no tracks. They had heard stories of him turning into a giant Grizzly Bear and this was from some of their own warriors who had followed his tracks and seen for themselves as his tracks turned into those of a giant bear. Yes, these Blackfeet wanted revenge on Grizzly Killer but they were mighty nervous about it at the same time.

Benny was the first to come upon the tracks of both Mel, Patch, and Nels as well as the Blackfeet. The Blackfeet had slowed down now moving very deliberately. One had moved out ahead as their scout and Zach wondered why they were being so careful with seven against just three. The thought then came to him they think they are following Grizzly Killer not three nearly helpless trappers.

Zach slowed even more as they rode upstream, it made him nervous where the other two Blackfeet had gone. He decided to move off the trail, he knew this country well enough he didn't need to follow the stream to know where it was headed. He motioned for Benny to cross to the south side of the flooding stream and they headed through the dense timber toward the towering snow covered peaks above Henry's Fork.

They climbed for several miles following one game trail after another. They crossed signs of a bear with three tiny cubs that had recently emerged from her den and the forest seemed alive after the storm of the night before. The birds and squirrels were singing and chattering as they quietly rode through. Zach would have been thoroughly enjoying himself if it wasn't for this dangerous task they were heading into.

They continued riding higher into the mountains until the snow drifts stopped them then turned back to the west and Henry's Fork. Zach figured the three white men would be camped about as high up as they could, waiting for the pass to clear.

It had been a hard-slow climb through the forest. They rode through a small meadow and Zach looked up at the sun which was now peeking through a small opening in the slowly clearing clouds. He knew it would be after dark before they reached the place on Henry's Fork he figured they would find the men camped so they decided to spend the night right there. He knew the Blackfeet would be there long before he and Benny would and shuddered at the thought of what they would find.

They stopped and set up a small lean-to covered with pine boughs and set up a small fire pit right in front of it. After no sleep at all the night before Zach wanted to be well-rested before they faced the fight he was sure would come tomorrow. Jimbo brought in a large snowshoe hare and set it by the fire then left to go find another. Benny pulled dry branches off the pines that had been protected from the storm of the night before by the heavy branches above and built a nearly smokeless fire no bigger than his two hands while Zach skinned the rabbit and put it on a stick to roast over the small flames. The rabbit was nearly done when Jimbo came back with feathers stuck to his mouth. Zach smiled and said as he rubbed the big dog's ears, "Well feller, I hope it was one of them big blue pine chickens and not just a little ruffled one."

Mel Tillman was just walking back into their camp when an arrow hit him in the side of his knee. He cried out as he fell to the ground. Nels and Patch were both sitting by the fire waiting for a roast of the sheep Nels had shot two days ago to finish cooking. They both jumped up as the seven Blackfeet warriors rushed in. Nels froze in fear but Patch nearly had his rifle up when he was hit in the back with a heavy stone-headed, war club knocking him to the ground.

They were camped in an opening where Henry's Fork made a bend well up into the canyon, right where Zach figured they would be. It was a natural camping area but this time of the year with the river running so high from the melting snow the roar of the rushing water made it impossible to hear anyone approaching.

The arrow in Mel's knee had stuck hard into the bone and as the one who shot the arrow approached him he pulled the pistol that was tucked into his belt, but the Blackfoot was faster and kicked his painful knee breaking off the arrow and sending Mel's shot harmlessly into the sky. With the warrior kicking and poking him with another arrow, he made Mel crawl to the fire with the rest of the now jubilant warriors.

As darkness fell the three of them were staked to the ground. They had been stripped naked and were shivering uncontrollably from the cold. There was no doubt in any of their minds they would never get to see Taos; this was the end of the trail. The Blackfeet warriors were all around the fire eating the roasted sheep, laughing, and telling stories of the capture of the three trappers.

The pain in Mel's knee was nearly unbearable; the pain was coming from the stone arrowhead stuck deeply into the bone. Any movement sent excruciating pain all through his leg. When Mel thought the pain couldn't get any worse, one of the Blackfeet picked up a red glowing coal from the fire with two sticks and walked up and set it on Mel's belly. Mel screamed and the Blackfoot laughed. Then another warrior, not wanting to miss out on the fun, got a branch burning on its end and held it to the bottom of Nel's foot. He screamed from both the pain and fear and the Blackfeet all laughed even louder.

Patch was in pain from the severe bruise and knot in his back from where the war club had hit him but so far, they hadn't touched him with the fire. He was so cold he couldn't control the shaking of his body and the fear he felt was overpowering when one of the warriors knelt between his legs and with a chipped stone knife castrated him, sometime during this process he passed out.

Chapter 31

Die with the Devil

ZACH WOKE UP LONG before the first signs of light appeared on the eastern horizon. The clouds had mostly moved off to the east and there was a bite to the air that reminded him of the middle of the winter.

With a handful of small twigs broken off the underside of the pine trees the night before he blew life back into their small fire and as Benny crawled out from under the lean-to he said, "That there fire feels mighty good, Grizzly Killer."

Zach nodded and replied, "Well enjoy it for a few minutes. I figure were 'bout two hours from where I believe they'll be camped and I want ta be there by light."

Benny nodded as he held his hands over the flames rubbing them together.

The two missing Blackfeet had indeed ridden hard back to report to Strong Bow that they had picked up the trail of Grizzly Killer and two others heading to the mountains straight south of them. Strong Bow wondered if it was true. He had no doubt they had picked up a trail but Grizzly Killer had ridden west from here, he himself had followed the tracks for several miles but it was the best lead he had so with two dozen warriors they mounted up and rode south just as hard as they could push their horses.

The seven warriors had tortured and laughed at Mel, Nels, and Patch until well past midnight. By then none of them believed that they had captured the great Grizzly Killer. These three white men were weak, they cried and screamed like women, they were not great warriors. None of these men could have done what they knew Grizzly Killer had done, so they would torture and have their sport with these men until Strong Bow arrived and decided what to do next.

After the Blackfeet had stopped their torture of the three, Nels shook and cried throughout the night. It was so cold all three of them were shivering uncontrollably but it was Nels that cried nonstop. The bottoms of both of his feet had been severely burned and hot coals had been set all over his naked body. Nels was the easiest to make cry and scream out, so he had received the worst of it. Now, in the coldest part of the predawn his crying was all that was keeping him alive.

Mel too had been burned, the hot coals they had placed on him had burned well down into his flesh and he, like Nels, was barely alive. The breathing of both of them was fast and shallow. Nels crying had fallen into nothing more than weak whimpers were Mel had not made a sound since he had cried out when they placed the last glowing red coal from the fire in the center of his chest.

Patch had not been burned, in fact they hadn't touched him since that warrior had castrated him. He was in shock, his body fighting against the cold was all that had kept him alive. As soon as he had felt the pain of the first cut he knew the three of them were already dead and he could see no reason to fight to stay alive; he had completely lost his will to live. The human body however does not die so easy, and the Blackfeet knew that very well, they were very skilled at inflicting pain but keeping a man alive while doing so.

Zach and Benny had not spent much time at all around their little fire although its warmth felt mighty good. An hour after Zach had first blown life back into the few remaining coals from the night before they were only a few miles from Henry's Fork.

Zach figured the Blackfeet would already have caught up to them and in his mind, he was preparing to fight them to recover Grub and Ely's plews, he really expected the three trappers were already dead. He hoped the trappers may have taken out one or two of the warriors in a fight but as easy as he had walked in on them several days ago he doubted they would have put up much of a fight.

Jimbo ranged far ahead of them in the dark forest and an hour later as Zach rode Ol' Red into a small grassy meadow, the big dog came running up to them. His low growl told Zach he had found the enemy and it was time to proceed on foot.

Benny tied off the horse he was riding but Zach just dropped Ol' Reds reins. He knew the big mule would stay there until either he or Jimbo returned for him. He checked the prime of his Hawken and then his pistol. He made sure his old Cherokee tomahawk and knife were secure in his broad belt. He watched Benny prepare himself for the coming fight in much the same way and was pleased that the young man, still in his late teens, was so thorough. He smiled knowing Grub and Ely had taught him well. He looked up and seeing the big dipper had almost made its circle around the north-star, he knew that dawn was not far off. He then glanced at the eastern horizon and could see the first faint gray line of the coming dawn.

He looked back at Benny and the youth nodded. He then looked at Jimbo and said, "Show us the way, feller," and the big dog started out through the forest just fast enough Zach and Benny could easily keep up.

Thirty minutes later with the stars rapidly fading with the coming light, Zach and Benny with Jimbo right by Zach's side were in the forest just above where Mel, Nels, and Patch were staked to the ground. They could hear the whimpering cries of Nels but it was still too dark to see any details of what had happened to the three of them.

One Blackfoot who had been watching the horses walked over and added more wood to their fire. Once it was burning good again he picked up two burning logs and laid them across Nels lap. The blood curdling scream was Nels last grip on life and as the scream faded into the dim light of early dawn, so did his life.

The Blackfoot seemed disgusted that Nels had died so easily and he took out his knife and brutally scalped the already dead trapper. He then proceeded with his knife to totally mutilate the body.

The scream had not only brought Patch and Mel out of their stupor but had awakened the other six Blackfeet as well. Mel was so cold the shivering was completely uncontrollable. Even though the pain from the burns was nearly unbearable, it was the cold that he suffered from the most, he longed for the warmth of a fire.

Patch wondered why he was still alive for he had truly given up on life. He wanted to die, he could see no reason to go on living only to endure more pain. They had already taken his manhood and even though he knew Nels was weak that last scream had reached clear into his soul.

He had stopped shivering. His mind no longer had the will to live but his body wouldn't let go of life. His eyes were closed tight as he drifted off into a dream of a warm summer day of his youth. New Orleans was hot and muggy and he could see the big muddy river rolling by. In his mind, the warmth of the summer sun was warming his frigid body when Mel's voice, weak and without much force cried out, "You dirty, heathen bastards!"

Patch didn't open his eyes, he didn't want to know what they were doing to Mel.

Zach moved slowly and carefully getting into a position where he could see into the camp below. Benny was amazed at how a man as large as Zach could move with such ease and without making a sound. Although the coming dawn was bringing the light of a new day with it, in the forest it was still quite dark.

Finally, Zach could see all seven of the Blackfeet. He ignored the three trappers staked to the ground. His fight now was with the warriors—he figured the white trappers deserved their fate. With a simple, barely noticeable hand signal he sent Jimbo to the other side of the camp, knowing the big dog would wait there until he was needed. He whispered to Benny as he pointed to a large pine about halfway to the other side, "Do you figure ya can get to that tree stayin' out a sight?"

Benny nodded and Zach continued, "Have your rifle and pistol both ready. Our only chance is to take most of 'em out with the first shots, so make 'em count. When ya hear my first shot don't wait. If we take out two of 'em and Jimbo another that still leaves two that could get ta you."

Benny took a deep breath and nodded.

The Blackfeet was giving Mel his wish for the warmth of a fire. They had built up a pile of branches right up between his legs. Zach could hear their laughter as they set the branches a blaze. The fire wasn't actually touching the tender skin on the inside of Mel's leg and manhood but the heat got so intense the skin burned away and he could smell his own flesh cooking between his gasps and screams.

Then his head was jerked up and he felt the grinding cut of a chipped stone blade grinding against his skull and he was scalped. Mel lost consciousness before his head was dropped back to the ground. His breathing had now nearly stopped, he would never see the sun rise again as his life faded into the blackness of the unknown.

Benny was now in position but the Blackfeet were scattered. One of them was checking the horses, it looked to Zach like three others were planning something for Patch and only three were by the fire. He knew their best chance was to have them all by the fire so he waited.

The three approached Patch, his naked body still staked out to the cold ground. With a forked stick one of them picked up a hot coal while the one held his head and the other pried his right eye open. Patches body went stiff as he saw the red glowing coal drop into his open eye. He could hear the sizzling of the fluids even above his own screams as the Blackfeet laughed. These men were not warriors they screamed like women and children so they didn't deserve the death of a brave warrior.

Zach couldn't wait any longer, he knew these men deserved to die but not like this. He had been prepared to hang all three of them for what they had done to Ely but he couldn't watch any longer the cruel torture of men even if he felt they deserved it.

With his Hawken in one hand and his pistol in the other he fired and two of the Blackfeet standing over Patch were blown off their feet. Only a blink of an eye later, he heard two more-gun shots and he charged forward with his Cherokee tomahawk in one hand and knife in the other.

There was a look of complete surprise on the face of the last warrior standing over Patch as he seen Zach charging at him, but he pulled his knife and was ready as Zach approached. He heard the vicious attack of Jimbo then to his complete surprise an arrow stuck into the back of the warrior's leg right in front of him. The Blackfoot at the horses was shooting at Zach as Jimbo attacked and that had sent the arrow off its intended path. The Blackfoot's leg buckled under him and as he went down Zach brought his tomahawk up burying it deep in the warrior's chest.

Zach jerked the deadly weapon free and kept running toward their fire where the other three had been. He could see two of them on the ground and Benny was in a deadly knife fight with the last. Zach was still twenty feet away from being able to help Benny when Jimbo attacked.

Jimbo's attack was so swift Benny wasn't even sure what had happened but the warrior was lying on the ground in front of him with blood spurting out of the gaping hole in his neck where Jimbo's powerful jaws had ripped it open. This fight had lasted only seconds and seven Blackfeet lay dead or dying.

Zach asked, "Benny are you okay?" Benny was stunned and just nodded. It had happened so fast. He then remembered something Ely had told him, *"If'n ya gotta fight Injuns, surprise is yer best weapon and never think ta fight 'em fair. They will take yer hair any way they kin and you gotta do the same."*

Benny was shaking and he suddenly felt tired. He had fought Indians before and had killed some in the battle with these same Blackfeet at last year's Rendezvous and even several days ago. This was different, it was up close and personal. The fight had lasted no longer than it had taken to take a couple of deep breaths.

Zach's alert eyes scanned the area and he moved his hand in a circle over his head. Jimbo took off at once, blood still dripping from his jaws as he ran a full circle around them making sure no one else was near.

Benny's breathing was starting to return to normal, his racing heart starting to slow down. He looked up at Zach and the look on Zach's face told Benny that hadn't liked doing that any more than he had. Both men knew they had to do what needed to be done and both were strong enough to do it.

Zach walked over to the three white men and shuddered at the sight. Patch was still alive but both Nels and Mel were gone. Zach cut the rawhide straps holding Patch to the stakes in the ground then turned and told Benny, "I figure Strong Bow and the rest of them devil Blackfeet is on their way here, we best not dally. Get all your plews loaded on as many horses as ya need and I guess we best take this feller with us for now."

Benny nodded and headed for the horses.

This was the first time Benny had seen the faces of the men staked to the ground. He stood in stunned silence when he saw these men that were once his friends, men that he had rode with. He knew them well enough that he figured it was either Mel or Phil that had shot Ely. He didn't think Nels or Patch could have done it. He looked at the tortured and mutilated body of Nels and a shudder ran down his spine.

By now the fire had burned most of Mel's inner thighs and manhood away. Patch was still alive; a clear liquid was running down his cheek from his ruined eye and there was dried blood between his legs. He hadn't moved since Zach had cut the rawhide straps holding him.

In a voice, a little coarser than he intended Zach said, "I know your hurtin', Mister, but we gotta go. There's more of these devils on their way."

Patch finally summoned the strength to speak and said, "Just shoot me, Mister, please shoot me and get it over with."

"I ain't a gonna shoot ya, so if ya don't want more of these Blackfeet finishin' ya off ya better find the strength ta move." Zach replied.

Zach then went to each of the dead Blackfeet and quickly cut the outline of a bear track in their chests just like he had done with the ones a few days ago. He then scalped each one of them as a sign to the others they wouldn't go to the land beyond as honored warriors.

Patch finally got to his feet and stumbled down to the stream and tried to sooth the painful burned out eye with the cold water. He hadn't looked at Nels or Mel until he came back from the stream when he saw them he got sick, but he had nothing in his stomach to throw up but bile.

Benny had the horses loaded by the time Zach was ready to go and without saying a word he handed the reins of one horse to Patch.

Patch said, "Benny, I didn't shoot yer friend, it were Phil."

Benny turned and looked at him and said, "You ride with the devil, you die with the devil."

Patch stood there still completely naked and said, "I can't ride like this, you saw what theys did ta me."

At hearing that Benny said, "Either ride or don't it don't. Makes no difference ta me, but the rest of them Blackfeet ain't even a half day from here and there's more of 'em than we can handle."

Zach didn't know what Strong Bow would do when he found more of his warrior's dead. He hoped he would figure the loss of life was too high to continue pursuit, but just in case Strong Bow followed he wasn't going to lead them anywhere close to his family on Black's Fork.

They started up Henry's Fork then he cut back to the east following a creek into a steep rocky canyon. They split up several times and would meet miles ahead staying on the hard-rocky ground. He knew the Blackfeet could follow but it would take them a long time to find and then sort out the trail. He figured it may take days but he would eventually lose them. He then would follow the snow line high up on the mountains back home.

Chapter 32

Honor My Father

THE TWO BLACKFEET had just left their group of nine to ride back and let Strong Bow know they had picked up the tracks of Grizzly Killer. He had just been informed that the first band of his warriors had all been found dead, each one had been scalped and had their manhood removed. It was the track of the bear cut into each of their chests that made him start to doubt whether they would ever catch Grizzly Killer and make him pay for the death of Thunder Cloud two years ago on the eastern shore of Sweet Lake.

Strong Bow's hope was rising, as they now had a trail to follow. He took all his warriors and headed south across the bad-lands. Grizzly Killer's medicine could not be stronger than over a hundred Blackfoot warriors.

They rode hard across the barren hills of the badlands then turned up stream following the now two-day old trail up Henry's Fork. He slowed them down and sent scouts ahead and it was only a few hours later when one of the scouts came back to report all their warriors were dead and the sign of Grizzly Killer was carved into each of their chests.

Most of his warriors were now spooked, they didn't believe Grizzly Killer and his big medicine dog were just man and beast. Many believed he was an evil spirit just using the body of a white man. Strong Bow himself had fears about this man that had killed Thunder Cloud but he wouldn't let anyone know that. He ordered them to continue their pursuit but most of the warriors had had enough, even Stands Like a Bear his friend and a natural leader said, that their medicine had turned bad, that it was time to go back north to their own land. So, with much regret, Strong Bow led his men back across the badlands heading north. He carried his coup stick in his right hand as he rode the spotted horse to the top of one the highest barren hills and held it high over his head. He shouted his threats to Grizzly Killer—that one day they would meet again.

Zach and Benny were nearly up to the snow line. Patch was still with them but only in person, in his mind he had given up. There was no reason to go on living or even try to survive. He rode along in pain only because he didn't know what else to do. That night in the frigid cold as they slept by a small fire in the thick forest, Patch's body followed his mind and gave up. His cold stiff body was still curled up by the fire the next morning.

They buried him right there in the forest and as much as Benny wanted to hate him he didn't. Patch and Nels both had been the ones that had treated him the best on their way to the mountains. Even though Benny believed they all deserved to die for what they had done he now felt bad, at least for Nels and Patch.

When they finished, Zach walked out to a point and looked to the north. He could see for what seemed like forever across the badlands and flat lands of the high desert nearly all the way to the pass at the south end of the towering Wind River Mountains. He'd had a dream that night, a dream where he had seen Strong Bow mounted on his spotted horse holding the coup stick high over his head and shouting a warning to him that they would meet again.

It was five days later that Zach led Benny with all the pack horses off the ridge between Smith's Fork and Black's Fork. They had stayed up near the snow line working their way back to the west. Although Zach felt the Blackfeet were no longer in pursuit he couldn't be sure, so they had taken a route Benny figured was fit only for the mountain goats they saw along the way.

As usual, Luna met them on the trail nearly five miles above the dugout. She and Jimbo ran ahead letting everyone know they were coming home.

Three weeks later, Ely was up and walking around. His recovery from such a severe wound had been remarkable but he still couldn't lift his rifle and they hadn't moved from the camp where they had been all along. Grub had hunted and kept them in meat and had even continued to trap some. He had a dozen more plews drying on their willow frames.

They talked often about Benny, wondering where their young partner was and if he was alright. They worried about the Blackfeet that the old Crow couple and their grandson had told them about. Had Benny rode into them?

Ely worked his arm hard for the next three weeks and when he figured he was strong enough to ride they moved on. Throughout the rest of the spring they slowly worked their way toward the Popo Agie and the site of the Rendezvous. By the time the beaver fur wasn't worth anything with the onset of warm weather, Grub had taken thirty more plews. They both knew that wasn't enough to outfit them for another year but they knew they would get by just like they always did.

Benny was constantly on their minds; he was their partner and friend. Yes, he was a lot younger than either of them but the three of them had become like family. They hoped they would find him at the Rendezvous but neither of them really believed they would.

Zach and Running Wolf took Benny with them for the spring trapping. They had traveled over and trapped the creeks feeding the Bear River for the spring. Little Dove with the help of Shining Star, Sun Flower, and Raven Wing had built her and Benny a wickiup and Benny had really started to look forward to returning to Black's Fork every week or two.

With the Rendezvous being split this year, Zach wondered if they might get the supplies to the Popo Agie a little sooner than usual so by the first of June they were on their way. This was a journey they had made several times. Across the Seeds-Kee-Dee to the buffalo grounds then across the Sweet Water and on up to the Popo Agie as that is where Sun Flower and Raven Wing were born and raised. If they were early they would stay in the village of Charging Bull with family until the Rendezvous got under way.

It took them nearly ten days with their large string of pack horses carrying the plews of their own as well as

Grub and Ely's, along with other horses that would be needed to carry a year's worth of supplies back home. As they approached the village of Charging Bull, two young riders approached them. When they saw it was Grizzly Killer they rode like the wind into the village to spread the word.

Zach could remember when it was Red Hawk and Buffalo Heart that were the young men watching the village and the horse herd, but now his two long-time friends were young warriors and their jobs were to protect the village and hunt for the meat required to keep everyone fed.

It was a happy reunion for everyone. Little Dove relived the horror of the Blackfoot attack on her village in telling of the events at a council fire that night. For Sun Flower and Raven Wing, it was a homecoming. Bear Heart and White Feather had aged noticeably over the last year but for them to see and play with their grandchildren made the hearts feel young again.

The stories were told of the Blackfeet and Cheyenne and White Feather was very alarmed learning that both of her daughters had been taken, but with Grizzly Killer and Running Wolf she knew her daughters were as safe as it was possible to be.

They danced and told stories well into the night and the next day Spotted Elk left with a small scouting party to make sure the Blackfeet were not anywhere in this area. No one believed they would be since it had been nearly three moons since they had left the land of Grizzly Killer. However, the Blackfeet had caused so much death for the Shoshone. Spotted Elk, the brother of Sun Flower and Raven Wing and now the War Chief of the Eastern Shoshone, wanted to make sure.

Two days later word came into the village that there were trappers arriving at a bend in the river only a half days ride down stream so Zach, Running Wolf, and Benny saddled up and made the journey. Benny was anxious to find out if there was word of Grub and Ely he was almost afraid to hear. What if Ely hadn't made it?

They stopped and visited with a few old friends but so far none of them had heard from Grub or Ely. It was well past midafternoon when they gave up and headed back following the river. Jimbo and Luna was out in front as usual and this time completely out of sight, when all of a sudden, they he came running at full speed back to Zach. He was excited jumping and his tail was wagging. Zach wasn't sure exactly what his dog was trying to tell him when a familiar voice boomed through the cottonwoods, "Is you still ridin' that big Ol' mule, Grizzly Killer?"

Benny beamed with excitement, there was no mistaking Grub's voice, then they came into sight. Ely was in the lead just as they usually traveled and Grub was leading their five pack horses.

Benny kicked his horse into a dead run and slid to a stop right in front of Ely. He had tears in his eyes as he watched Ely carefully dismount. The old trapper and young man embraced and Benny said, "I figured you had gone under."

Ely smiled at him and said, "It's gonna take more than a ball from some stinking polecat to put this child under, but if it weren't fer Grub here and an old Crow woman, I just might have.

The next month was spent with friends and family while the trappers waited for William Sublette to get there with the supplies from Saint Louis. They all needed the supplies to make it through another year.

For Zach Connors and his family, it was an enjoyable summer with time shared between the Shoshone village and the camps at Rendezvous. Ely was getting stronger each week and had started to complain about Grub and Benny treating him like he was a cripple, even though he knew it was because they cared.

By the end of summer Ely had even started to shoot his rifle again even though, at first, he was only loading it with light loads. Grub, Ely, Benny and Little Dove had decided to hunt Buffalo with Grizzly Killer and Running Wolf and help each other to put a supply of meat in for the winter.

Just after they left the Shoshone village heading to the buffalo grounds just south of the Sweetwater, Zach rode Ol' Red with Jimbo right along-side out into the vast prairie. He needed to be alone although he didn't know why. He dismounted and let Ol' Red crop the dry grass while he sat down with Jimbo right by his side. The Blackfoot War Chief, Strong Bow, had been on his mind a lot lately and he figured he just needed to be alone to clear his mind.

From out in the prairie he could see a man walking toward him but he couldn't tell who it was. The heat waves coming off the dry ground were distorting the image. Zach watched as the man got closer, there was something familiar about his walk. Zach could see his father walking up to their log house back home in Kentucky after a long day working the fields. This man had the same walk. Suddenly the image cleared, it was Zach's father walking up to him. They embraced then sat on the hot dry prairie and Zach listened to what his father had to say.

Captain Jack/John Connors had been a man of honor and had raised Zach to be the same. He told Zach how proud he was to be his father and that Zach was still making him proud. He told him that he knew Zach was learning about the treachery of men but not to let others treachery effect the way he lives his life. He told Zach to always beware of the man riding a spotted horse, but not to let that become an obsession. They spent time talking about Zach's family about his daughter Morning Star and how much he and Zach's mother wished they could meet her and Zach's beautiful wives.

It was time to go, Zach wanted more time but his father just shook his head and walked back out into the prairie until he was out of sight. Zach just sat there staring out into the distance, then Jimbo was licking his face and he woke up. It had been another dream, but how could a dream feel so real? He sat up and stared out into the distance just like he had in the dream, only this time he could see the footprints of a man walking away from him.

He rode back to the others slowly pondering on what had happened. His father had appeared to him in a dream only one other time since the Grizzly had taken his life and then too he was warned about a man riding a spotted horse. This warning was different, did it mean he had been too aggressive in eliminating the danger of the man on a spotted horse? He went out onto the prairie thinking he needed to clear his troubled mind but now he seemed more confused than ever.

He returned to the others knowing he would always be watchful of any man riding a spotted horse. He also knew he would love his wives and raise his family in this wild and beautiful wilderness living each day to its fullest. He would deal with the dangers as they arose but he would never be looking for it and he would live honoring the name of his father. Yes, he would live his life with honor and raise his family with the love in which he was raised.

As he reached the rest of his party, Running Wolf, Grub, Ely, and Benny were stopped watching a dust cloud to the southeast of them. The billowing dust was rising several hundred feet into the air and it was getting closer to them by the minute. Grub looked at the others with a very concerned look on his face and said, "Buffalo, thousands of 'em."

Zach looked back at their families, kicked Ol' Red into a run toward them just as Ely shouted, "We best try an' make back across the Sweet Water 'fore they get to us."

They hit the Sweet Water in a dead run and splashed through the shallow crossing hardly slowing down at all and headed for a steep-sided butte only a mile or so north of the river. Once they were on top and felt like they were safe they stopped and watched as the buffalo approached the river. The stampeding herd went on for miles to the south. The dust was so thick they couldn't see anything but the leading edge of the mighty stampede. Then the wind shifted and the strong smell of burning grass hit them. Ely staring down at tens of thousands of running buffalo yelled, "Holy Mother of God, it's a prairie fire"

Zach sat atop Ol' Red, watched and wondered just what else this wilderness could hit them with this year.

Zach watched the concerned look on the faces of his loved ones then said, "The fire will burn itself out and the buffalo will settle down, we will hunt them as we do each year, it will just take us a while longer this year.

A Look at the next book in the series, Grizzly Killer: Where The Buffalo Dance

The fifth book in the action-packed, best-selling Grizzly Killer series.

After five years of living in the wild and dangerous Rocky Mountains, Zach Connors is concerned his Indian family will not be prepared for the eventual settling of the west. They have lived isolated in the wilderness their whole lives and have no idea how many white men will eventually come into their lands. Zach has seen the Indian tribes pushed from their homes in Kentucky and Tennessee because they would not learn to live in the white man's world. He wants to ensure his family and friends will survive in a world he is sure will change.

Known as Grizzly Killer throughout the west, Zach takes his Indian family to St. Louis so they can see for themselves the numbers of white men that are pushing the settlements further west with the passing of each year. It is a long and dangerous trip as they pass through the lands of the Cheyenne, Arapaho, and Pawnee as well as the land Where the Buffalo Dance as they follow the Platte River east. They find the dangers of the civilized world although different can be just as deadly as the dangers of the mighty Rocky Mountains.

Available from Wolfpack Publishing and Lane R Warenski

About the Author

Lane R. Warenski lives in a log home in Duchesne County, Utah, where he has an unrestricted view of the highest peaks in the mighty Uinta Mountains. He was raised being proud of his pioneer heritage and with a deep love and respect of the outdoors. Ever since childhood, following his father, Warenski has hunted, fished, and camped the mountains of the West. Whether it was the daily journals of William Ashley and Jedediah Smith or the fictional stories written by the great storytellers like Louis L'Amour and Terry C. Johnston, throughout his life, Warenski loves reading the history of the first explorers that came west, most of whom never dreamed they were opening this wild and rugged land to the pioneers and settlers that followed.

Find more great titles by Lane R. Warenski and Wolfpack Publishing at http://wolfpackpublishing.com/lanerwarenski/

Made in the USA
Las Vegas, NV
06 June 2023